TRAINER

A ROAD KILL MC NOVEL

VOLUME 7

New York Times Bestselling author
MARATA EROS

http://marataeroseroticaauthor.blogspot.com/

Marata Eros FB Fan Page: https://www.facebook.com/
AuthorTamaraRoseBlodgett/

Cover art by **Willsin Rowe**
Editing suggestions provided by **Red Adept Editing**

ISBN-10: 1548795852
ISBN-13: 9781548795856

WORKS BY TAMARA ROSE BLODGETT

The **BLOOD** Series
The **DEATH** Series
Shifter **ALPHA CLAIM**
The **REFLECTION** Series
The **SAVAGE** Series
Vampire **ALPHA CLAIM**

&

Marata Eros
A Terrible Love (***New York Times*** Best Seller)
A Brutal Tenderness
The Darkest Joy
Club Alpha
The **DARA NICHOLS** Series
The **DEMON** Series
The **DRUID** Series
Road Kill MC Serial
Shifter **ALPHA CLAIM**
The **SIREN** Series
The **TOKEN** Serial
Vampire **ALPHA CLAIM**
The **ZOE SCOTT** Series

Music that inspired me during the writing of TRAINER:

Carry Me by Eurielle

Often by The Weeknd

Dangerous Woman by Ariana Grande

DEDICATION

For all the Trainers of this earth.

I *see* you—others will *never* define your potential.
Only you own that.

1

TRAINER
FIVE YEARS AGO

Mama stops his hairy wrist, but I know it's gonna happen anyway.

The beatings.

And it does. I feel the air pass over my head as I duck instinctively, but the blow strikes me anyway. I bow forward under only the partial impact.

"Don't, Arnie! He's just stickin' up for me!"

"You don't need nobody standin' up for ya—you got me!" he roars, pounding his fist on his chest like an ape.

His meaty palm, just like all the others I've seen from Mama's men my entire life, hits me again.

I fall to the floor, hands striking the dirty linoleum to break my fall.

I know I can survive. Been surviving.

I've taken the beatings, whippings, cigarette burns, and tool marks for years.

But this time, something deep inside me snaps. I'm not five years old anymore, pissing in my own Wheaties. Pathetic. Scrawny.

"Look at 'im." Arnie's upper lip lifts in a sneer of disdain.

He's just Right Now Arnie. There've been an asston of Arnies before him.

They're all my mama ever picks.

Arnies.

"He's as dumb as a box of rocks." He grunts.

Yeah. That's true. I can't read. Can't figure. Can't do shit. But I can fight.

Wiping the blood off my lip with my index finger, I fling it to the floor.

I give Mama a look, and she gives a tiny shake of her head, begging me not to do what she sees on my face. The thrum of violence, always underneath the surface of my skin like an itch I can't scratch, is a current of agony.

Just one more time, I think. Trying to put up with another beating. For mama.

Then Arnie decides for me, releasing me from the prison of my own emotions.

He advances on Mama with sure strides. Eyes widening with familiar alarm, she spins, trying to run. In slow motion, he charges at her. His brutal grip closes around her long hair like it's a rope.

He yanks backward.

This is where I always insert myself, taking the beating meant for her. I take it until I can't gather breath in my lungs, can't see through the swollen eyelids, and can't stand because the room spins and my vision blurs.

Mama usually gets beat some too.

Not tonight. My body acts on its own. My mind is a distant observer.

Standing from my crouched position on the floor, I calmly pick up the ashtray. A smoldering cigarette gives a dying sigh as the last spiral of smoke rises from the glass perch where it rests.

Dumping the contents, I stride toward Arnie, who's no small man at six feet two.

But I'm taller.

Bigger.

I lift the heavy glass, turning it sideways so the jagged teeth of the design will do the most damage, and bring it down on his thick skull.

The dull thunk is audible even over Mama's hysterical screams filling the space of our small apartment.

Someone pounds on the wall. "Shud up!"

Mama and I don't listen.

We're too busy looking at the pool of blood growing underneath Arnie.

"Whadya do, Brett?" she whispers, eyes riveted on the spreading scarlet oil slick.

I take in the streaming tears sliding in between the bruises, both fading and new, on her once-pretty face and speak for the first time since Arnie came home from "work."

As a pimp.

"What I needed to," I answer softly.

"Oh, Brett, they're gonna put you away," she says on a horrified moan.

I nod. *Maybe.*

Then her features take on hopeful lines. "Maybe you didn't kill him?"

My eyes return to Arnie.

I frown.

His chest rises and falls rhythmically, stretching the red-and-black flannel shirt he wears to bursting.

I know what I gotta do.

"Yeah…" I scoop the ashtray off the floor. The blood smears look like the fingerpainting I did in kindergarten.

I lift the heavy glass in the only dry spot left. Some of the serrated edges are filled with gory things thicker than blood.

"What—*Brett!*" Mama screams.

I always finish.

Arnie needs finishing.

I use my muscles this time, pounding his skull until the brains come out.

Cocking my head, I study the gray chunks mixed with blood and other junk I don't recognize. Doesn't look like much.

And *this* Arnie ain't gonna ever call me dumb again. Ever.

Mama's screams are just white noise. I don't feel the hands she must put on me.

I'm all for the work.

The work of finishing Arnie.

Mama's crying, but I don't really notice. Mama cries a lot.

"Don't take my boy," she says, half-standing. "He's just a kid." Her dark hair's uncombed, flying around her shoulders as she whirls to look at me, brown eyes swimming with endless tears that roll down her face.

Mama's fingers grip the rolled-wood edge of the courtroom bench.

"Sit down, Ms. Rife."

Mama sinks slowly onto the hard pew, and I face the judge. He's a big fat dude with jowls that jiggle as he talks.

It occurs to me how funny it is. I want to laugh, but I bite my lip. He can make bad things happen.

"My client has an IQ hovering at the level that makes competency in question, Your Honor," my lawyer states.

Shame fills me like liquid heat, rising from my feet to my head in a wave of sickening nausea. *Why do people always find so many different ways to call me dumb?*

I turn and glare at Hammerstein, my lawyer, and his eyebrows drop above eyes slitted in anger—a look meant to shut me up.

He told me, over and over, "You got to keep quiet and let me do all the talking."

Kinda tired of people talking for me.

They been doin' it all my life. Beating me. Pretending I don't have a voice.

Until I didn't have one no more.

"He's also technically a minor."

This was what Hammerstein called his "ace in the hole." *Whatever that means.*

The judge looks unsure, looking from me to Mama, then staring at a stack of photos in front of him.

Low murmurs fill the courtroom, until I want to cover my ears. All the voices at once sound like angry bees trying to dive into my head like it's a hive.

The judge pounds a wood hammer thing on the big desk in front of him, saying in a booming voice, "Silence!"

Nobody says nothin'.

Finally, he speaks to Hammerstein, "Your client"—he shakes his head slightly—"Brett Rife, has displayed a level of violence that, when given his almost-eighteen-year-old status, is disturbing."

A lady sitting in front of a typewriter thing quits clicking away, hands poised above it as the judge pauses.

"Actually, it's a disturbing event regardless of gender or age group." He sighs, his eyes shifting to me again.

I stand there. I got nothing to hide.

Been looked at plenty. None of it good. Except by Mama. She did the best she could. She just chose bad.

Real bad.

"Brett, do you understand you could go to prison?"

I nod. "Yes, sir."

"How do you feel about that?"

I guess I'd get fed. And maybe not beat by all the Arnies. But who would take care of Mama?

Pressing my palm against my cheek, I chew on the inside. Helps me think. It takes some time for me to work through what I want to say, though, and to get a good enough answer ready.

The judge waits.

"I worry about what would happen to Mama," I finally admit.

I hear her begin to cry again in the background. Softly. Like the rain sounds when it lashes my windows during the night.

Not going to turn around and look at her. I need to pay attention to the judge. Important stuff is going to be said.

"Judge Carrol," Hammerstein says before the judge can answer, spreading his hands wide, "you've seen the medical report on this boy." He taps a folder full of paperwork set between us and the twelve people who will decide if I go to jail.

They stare at me.

I put my head down. Don't like being noticed. Makes me feel squirmy.

Dumb.

Heat climbs my nape.

"Yes," the judge says, and I can feel his attention like a weight. "There's been a lot of pain in your life, Brett." His attention takes in the jury too. "The medical reports of what this young man has suffered is almost more than I can bear to peruse…or think about."

I don't say nothing because it's the truth. The part about the pain.

"Brett, did you plan to kill Arnold Sulk?"

My chin hikes in surprise. Arnie? *No.* Just happened. My thoughts are so loud, I'm pretty sure I said them. But when I check people out, everyone's still waiting for my answer.

I glance at Hammerstein, whose face is screwed up tight. Probably constipated.

"No, sir. He was beating my mama, and I had to stop that," I say simply.

Another attorney is sitting at a table just like ours a few feet away. "So you beat him in the head until his brains leaked out onto the floor?" he asks. His light-brown eyebrows rise, and he smooths his hands over a fancy suit jacket.

Shame over my poor clothes stabs me again. Jeans and an old t-shirt. Don't have no money to look good.

"Objection!" Hammerstein bellows into the quiet.

But I nod. The other guy understands, fancy clothes or not. "Ah-huh."

I turn back to the judge. "I did that." I jerk my thumb at the other attorney. "What he said."

"He admits he killed Arnold Sulk!" The other attorney slaps his paperwork down on the desk and glares at Hammerstein.

I don't understand why everyone's mad. Can't they see that Arnie was gonna hurt my mama?

Had to stop it.

If I hadn't finished it then, he would have done it to Mama again. Or some other lady.

All the Arnies are like that. Like they were put on this world to do one thing.

"Why did you kill Arnold Sulk, Brett?" Judge Carrol asks softly.

I don't have to think this through at all. It's at the front of my brain, but the question seems as obvious as my answer. "'Cause maybe he was going to finish Mama." I hastily add, "This time." All the other times, I stepped in and took the pain so Arnie couldn't finish.

Like with all the Arnies before him.

That's why I have bad skin. From all the Arnies and their hands, fists, tools, and cigarettes.

The only place free of the scars is my ass end.

"Finish?" Judge Carrol asks, and Hammerstein groans, putting his face in his hands.

"Ya know, Judge…" I scratch my head, and the chain that binds my wrists rattles, thwacking the solid wood table. "Carrol," I add, finally remembering his name.

I smile broadly. I love the shit outta when I can remember something. It's a warm feeling. Not like the heat of my constant shame. But a good feeling.

Like I'm okay.

The judge smiles back.

"Killing—Arnie was goin' after my mama. And he could kill her, Judge, because she's a lady, and he's a man. So I had to kill him first so he wouldn't hurt my mama no more. That's what good men do—they protect ladies."

It was a lot of talking for me. It's a relief when I can close my mouth. I don't like talking. But talking is easiest when it's something I really believe in a lot. I turn my head, and my eyes find Mama.

She's got that look on her face—the look she gets when she's proud of me.

I smile at her. The purity of the moment surfaces in the room, and for a second, it's just me and her. Nobody else.

"Yes, they do, son. Good men protect women." Judge Carrol turns to the twelve people. "You are a jury of Brett Rife's peers. Do right by him."

The wood thing hurts my ears when it hits the desk this time.

Probably because the courtroom is so quiet.

"I did good?" I ask Hammerstein when he says the verdict went in our favor.

He nods. "I was apprehensive that you might incriminate yourself in there." Hammerstein gives my shoulder a hard clap, then his face seems to say he wishes he hadn't.

"It's okay. You're not an Arnie. I know what the difference is."

Hammerstein stares at me, and his eyes become sad. Kinda like Mama's, but somehow different. I might be dumb, but I'm really good at seeing sad in faces. Actually, I'm really good at seeing a lot of different stuff in faces.

"You're not a stupid boy, Brett."

I look down at my sneakered feet.

"Hey, listen to me."

Lifting my chin, I can barely meet his eyes. I know he's on our side because Mama told me so. But he said the *stupid* word.

That usually means I got to fight when that happens. I don't like to. But I've been made to.

It's all I'm good at.

I don't want to fight Hammerstein. He made the judge listen. I don't have to go to jail and leave Mama unprotected. That knot in my chest isn't tied as tight now.

Hammerstein might be a friend.

"I told a small white lie in the courtroom."

My eyebrows hike. "You lied? I thought you had to tell the whole truth or—"

Hammerstein lifts his hand in a gesture that means *silence*, and I shut my mouth.

"About your IQ."

Heat suffuses my face. The blood rushes in my ears with a dull, thumping river-like roar.

IQ is a number that measures how smart someone is. I bet mine is low.

His eyes study my expression. "I didn't give the number of your actual IQ because it's higher than I wanted the jury to know. Your shortcomings stem from environment and are not grounded in intelligence."

My eyes bug a little. "Are you saying that I'm *not* dumb?"

My heart starts to beat faster. A warm feeling swells around that tight spot in my chest, and I rub at it, thinking maybe it'll go away.

"Definitely not. You might be illiterate and have suffered mightily in your young life, but you're not a dumb kid. You just need the right person to teach you."

I like what Hammerstein is saying. Not sure it's true, though.

But there is one thing I can be sure of. "And no more Arnies."

Hammerstein's return grin takes up his entire face. "Absolutely no more Arnies."

But my smile fades.

There are always more Arnies.

2

KRISTA
PRESENT DAY

I set the ruler directly beneath the sentence and wait.

Ian places his tiny finger on top of the ruler in line with the first word in the sentence.

"Let teacher keep your place with the ruler while you sound out the words, 'kay?" I brush a strand of my scattered hair behind my ear.

Ian nods and begins, bouncing around in his chair as he reads. "And the mow-se…findz his how-se in…" He pauses, giving me an inquisitive look I know well.

"Hard," I interject then smile. Ian continues, "T*he*," he looks for affirmation again.

I nod encouragement.

I'm so proud of him. Those hard and soft consonants are buggers.

"Wall!" he exclaims, brown eyes popping with excitement at nailing the end word perfectly.

"And?" I prompt.

He props his chin in his hand, nose scrunched.

Come on. You can do it.

"Maggie said."

He didn't say "say-d." It's a win!

I go against professional decorum and hug Ian.

He squeals in delight.

We break apart, and he says. "I did a good job, Miss Glass."

I sweep his hair off his face. "Yes, you did. You got a hard consonant and tackled a sight word."

Ian nods and announces, "I'm hungry now."

Laughing softly, I stand, pushing my chair away and pulling his. "Well that's good timing because your mom is picking you up in…" I glance down at my huge brilliant white wristwatch. "Five minutes, partner."

"Yes!" Ian says, his freckled face lighting with anticipation.

He runs toward the swinging glass doors of the school, and I holler after him, "Wait for me."

"Ahhh," he says, slowing to a trot and dragging his little feet behind him. Kids always act like it's a crime not to be able to do everything at sixty miles per hour.

"Miss Glass?"

I turn, and the headmistress at our exclusive private school is standing in the threshold to the door leading to the catacomb of offices that is the beating heart of the building.

"I'll need to speak with you once Ian's mother fetches him."

My stomach does a delayed flop. Typical reaction to being called to see the boss.

I assume a neutral expression. "Of course."

With a phony smile plastered on my face, I march to the front of the building. My high heels echo as I move quickly before Ian decides to escape outside alone.

As soon as he sees me coming, Ian bursts out of the doors, backpack slung on a narrow shoulder, and hops down each broad concrete step.

Ian turns with a wide smile. It wilts around the edges a little when he sees my expression.

"What's wrong, Teacher?"

Truth with children, no matter how raw. It's my motto. Keeps things real.

After all, they're just little people. Just like the rest of humanity, only smaller.

"My boss wants to talk to me, and it makes me a little nervous."

He cocks his head, carrot-colored hair like a bright halo of fire around his face. "Why?"

Seeing his mom pull up in a sleek silver van, I shrug. "She's in charge of my work, and I want everything to be okay."

Ian walks forward, and I sink to my haunches, tucking my skirt behind my knees.

He cups my face.

The gesture makes me want to cry. Comfort sometimes comes from the most unlikely places.

"You're in charge of *you*, Teacher," he says simply. Hearing a faint beep, I stand, blinking away tears. Ian's hand is warm in mine as I lead him to his mother's car.

This is why I teach people to read.

I watch the horizon long after their car has disappeared into it.

Smoothing my skirt over my knees, I try not to let my confusion show, but I'm losing that battle with my nervous hands.

Ms. Rowe is a matronly woman, the quintessential headmistress stereotype—complete with glasses, hair pulled up into a steel-colored bun, and sensible pumps. "You're an excellent special needs teacher, Ms. Glass. And in the year you've been with us, I've had no complaints and want to retain you."

*However...*The unspoken word is like a ginormous pink elephant ready to launch onto my chest.

Rowe does a strategic fiddle fest, her restless hand moving a pen about five times. Finally, she spits out the unspoken *but*. "The State of Washington requires that special needs teachers take a sabbatical every third term for a period of one month. In which time, they teach a completely divergent group of learners."

I nearly stand.

There's *no way* I want to leave Alisa, Ian, Gregory, Mabel, and my other kids out to dry for a month! *Is she insane?*

"I'm sorry," Rowe says, reading my expression with a precision that speaks of her years of experience. Giving her readers a tense shove, she pushes the glasses higher up the bridge of her nose.

"Sorry," I seethe through my teeth, "but those kids *need* me. I can't just toss them aside for some teacher's union political bent!" In an effort to fake a calm I don't feel, I add, "It's destabilizing."

Rowe frowns.

I try to rein it in and can't. Tears threaten. I'm not a crier, but I'm so frustrated, I could scream.

What the actual fuck?

"It's a new law, but it was implemented just before your hiring." She gives a little shrug, and I sort of collapse against the chair.

I try for reason. "It's the end of the school year."

Rowe nods. "I know, I fought for the timing so you'd be winding things down, instead of gearing them up. It could have been arranged for mid-term."

Good Lord. I cross my arms beneath my breasts, eyes flung toward the ceiling to veil my disgust for a system I have such terrible control of. We're *teachers.* We're the first line of defense and learning for the nation's future, and they jerk us around because of what? Some political ideal? Some person who's never been in the trenches doing the job thinks *they* have insight. *Pfft.* They don't have any. Doing is knowing. Everything else is educated guessing.

Or *un*educated guessing.

Finally, I look back at Ellen Rowe. She sits quietly, and I suddenly notice how tired she looks.

"Does it affect everyone?"

She shakes her head. "Just teachers who are considered high-risk for burnout, or what they call 'over-teaching.'"

What a crock. The committee of "they" who decide stuff like an armchair god should have their collective asses kicked. How dare they presume to know what it means to teach fragile minds? They can't possibly understand the reward of seeing those kids' gain a skill with myself as the vehicle in reaching their potential.

Shit.

None of them will know what it takes for a dyslexic child to work around that small flaw in her brain.

Or how a kid suffering from Aspergers feels when he can't learn the way the masses can because he doesn't fit into the square box that society has made for them. I've seen plenty of enormously intelligent round pegs running around, and I'm glad to be able to help them in their journey.

Taking a deep breath, I unclench my fists, feeling the crescents my nails leave behind. "So who do I teach, and where is it?"

Mrs. Rowe's five-second pause tells me it's definitely bad.

"Well, here's where it gets tricky." She leans forward, lacing her slender fingers together. Her eyes sweep up. Her lenses magnify the unusually vibrant slate color. "Troubled juveniles, now adults, who cannot read."

Oh, boy. So easy. "So they just decided to be lazy? I'm trained to help special needs people, not those who fooled around while others educated themselves."

I'm ranting. I know this.

Rowe gives me the stare down. I fight fidgeting in my seat like a caught schoolgirl.

Finally, she says, "I think that's vaguely elitist, Krista. I don't want to lose you for a month." Rowe leans back, giving me a critical eye, and curses wearily, "Hell, I don't want to lose you for even a day."

"Damn," I say softly.

"Yes." She waves a casual palm around. "All of that."

Ellen folds her hands on her desk. "It's a small class, only three students. One-on-one, not all taught together. And they're lucky to have you. If they show progress, and you so choose, you have the option to continue their lessons through the summer."

"How old are these kids, again?" I ask, suddenly interested, in spite of being torn out of my element. The familiar.

Away from kids I know—and love.

"Oh, they're not children. They were troubled juveniles who couldn't read because of various circumstances. They're all between the ages of eighteen to twenty-three."

I'm twenty-three. I've never taught anyone close to my own age. Though my degree allows me to teach an expanded age range for reading, I'm strictly early elementary by choice.

"Okay," I say slowly.

"Good. I was hoping you wouldn't quit me."

All I can manage is a sad smile. "No offense, but I'm not quitting them."

"None taken." Ellen puts up her hands, and we stand at the same moment.

"When?"

Her exhale is softly frustrated. "Monday."

I have the weekend.

"Who's covering for me?"

"Lynn Doyle."

I love Lynn. She'll do her best.

"I can't say goodbye," I say, sudden tears burning my eyes again.

"You don't have to, Krista. You'll be back next year. The kids will all be four months older. That's all."

It's never all.

I turn around and walk out the door. Somehow, my leaving feels final.

"I'll email you the particulars," Ellen says to my back.

I nod but don't turn around. I want my last memory to be Ian telling me to be who I am.

The words of an almost-six-year-old are some of the wisest I've heard.

3

TRAINER
EIGHTEEN MONTHS AGO

Gotta good buzz goin'.

Feeling *fine.*

Meeting with my bud, tossing some brew. Friday night, and my job as a mechanic is *finito.*

I don't think about how I haven't seen Mama in three weeks. 'Cause if I do, I'll have to kick the latest Arnie's ass.

My eyes scan the dim interior of the bar, seeking out the ladies. Gotta have me some of that.

They're all so beautiful, it's hard to choose just one. Then my eyes land on a small blonde.

None of these skinny chicks are for me. I like a little meat on the girls. Tits and ass, as the bros call it.

"Brett, toss me a five. Gotta get myself another brewsky."

I frown. Todd is always mooching.

He's funny, though. Wish I had real friends, instead of these guys that just sort of hang around and offer nothin'.

I think of Mama again. Worry creeps in, spilling into the edges of my mind like sludge. I remember Hammerstein telling me I'm not dumb.

I think about the three and a half years I spent working hard without being able to read a word, the hassle of trying to get work. The lack of confidence.

The only thing I feel good about is chicks and fighting.

I love fucking. Because girls like me fucking them. I got a big dick, and that's good, but secretly, I just love the smell and taste of them. Their skin is so soft; they're so small and fragile. Takes the edge off me to just have them, to protect them, even if it's just for a time or two in the sack.

They never call me dumb. A complete bonus.

"Hey, dumbshit! The five!" Todd hollers, being his normal turd self, when I don't hand him the cash fast enough.

I flip him off.

He snorts and whacks me on the back of my head, making my longish hair sort of explode at the crown of my head.

A lot of the Arnies did that.

Turning smoothly, I sucker punch Todd in the gut.

Gasping, he sorta slides gracelessly off the stool and falls to his knees then his ass.

I toss the five on the floor in front of him and walk over to the blonde I pegged with my eyes five minutes earlier.

Just as I'm making my way, three biker guys walk in.

How do I know they're bikers?

They wear those cool-ass leather vests with patches. One in particular catches my eyes. It's a red diamond with a small number one and a percent symbol.

I can't read what's on the back in brilliantly and precisely done lettering, but it looks tight.

They move like restless jaguars, wild and slightly unkempt, prowling through the bar, not having to push people away. The crowd instinctively parts for them, letting them flow through like a river of muscled and leathered flesh.

Eyes missing nothing, they catch sight of me.

I don't look away. Not afraid of nothin'. Death will find me when it will.

I survived the Arnies—lost count on how many—so I don't scare easy.

There are three of these biker dudes. One has blondish-white hair and ice chips for eyes. Tall. Built. The other has black eyes and dark hair. He's also really tall and built. The third has dirty-blond hair and eyes that are light enough to pierce the haze of smoke in the murky bar. Built a lot like the other two, he's tall like me, but maybe a hair shorter.

His light-pewter gaze scrapes over me like I'm dog shit.

I've seen that look a hundred times—a thousand. I know I'm dog shit. But I won't back down no matter what.

Never have.

Backin' down would've gotten me killed.

This last guy is a problem. Unlike the other two, he reeks of the potential to be a dangerous fucker.

"Hi!"

Startled, I look down.

It's the blond.

I get an insta-boner. *Shit.*

One second, I'm thinking about getting my ass kicked over staring. The next, my dream girl of the night is right in front of me.

"Wanna dance?" She flutters long eyelashes over pretty brown eyes.

Ah-huh. Pouting, she slides her hand up the front of my shirt. It has pearl buttons, and I'm wearing my cowboy boots. Like the look a lot. Nicest clothes I got.

"You're hot, cowboy." The corners of her ruby lips turn upward.

I capture her hand and begin towing her across the dance floor. Not much of a talker. Gets me nowhere. I don't miss a month without talking to Hammerstein.

He's retired now. He became a judge after he helped me with Arnold Sulk.

And he still tells me I'm smart.

Every month.

"Don't visit your mama too much, Brett. There'll be an Arnie," he says.

He's right. There always is. They're different men, but they're all the same.

"You won't be able to hold back, son."

He's right. I won't.

So now I see Mama when I can stand it. Her birthday. Some of the holidays she made special for me when I was a kid. Nothing more.

I can't.

Can't stand the bruises. The withering of her body—and her soul.

I look at the blond and flatten my hands on the small of her back.

"God *damn*, you know how to touch a girl," she purrs, laying her small face against my chest. I'm tall, so she's kinda between my pecs.

I cup the back of her skull, and we rock to the music.

Feels good. My mind can't stop the spinning of anxiety it always has goin' on.

After a few minutes, the song changes to another one. Hot. Slow.

She moves the space between the buttons of my shirt apart and kisses the skin revealed there.

I bite back a groan like a hiss.

Love the ladies. Love what they have even more.

"Hey," she says softly.

My mind is already in bed with her. I forgot the bikers. My asshole friend, Todd.

Even my abused mother.

Everything is the blond before me with her soft body and curves in all the right places as she molds against me.

She tips her head back. "I'm going to go powder my nose, and I'll be right back. Then we get, 'kay?" She winks.

"Get?" I say in slow, lust-filled response.

A look comes over her face. I don't like it—the "Are you stupid?" look.

I fake it and make a mock-gun with my finger, pulling the trigger. "Gotcha—*get*. I get it."

I don't, but she laughs before sauntering away with a sway to her hips that keeps my eyes glued to her behind.

Adjusting my cock, I stroll to the entrance, letting the cool air caress me, evening out my nerves. I take in the primitive parking lot. Asphalt that was once smooth and perfect is now pitted with random patches of erupted gravel. I see the bikers' rides and admire their beauty. Motorcycles don't talk. They probably just make a dude feel good.

I rotate my neck, popping out the kinks. Always on edge. Hate it. Keeps me sharp, I guess. Needed to be that way since I was a kid. Old habits die hard.

Five minutes goes by, and I straighten. Seems weird the blonde isn't here. She seemed eager.

I tamp down the small hairs at my nape and scan the bar again.

The bikers are there, looking just as alert as me. They take long pulls on brews as their eyes glitter over the crowd.

Todd limps over, a five-dollar bill crunched in his hand.

"Fucker," he whines, hand at his bread basket.

"Don't be hitting me. Ever," I say absently, but I'm already moving through the door, skating around to the side entrance that lets people out of the bar.

Close to the bathroom, I remember.

I stop short as I round the corner. I blink.

The fucking blonde is on her knees, mouth on some guy's dick.

What?

My eyes flick to the other two men. Something's not right. One, I wanted her. I chose her, and she was mine for tonight.

Two, she doesn't want what's being done to her.

One of the men has her arms jacked behind her back and is shoving her down to the root of the other guy's cock. Trailing wetness travels her face.

Tears mean fear.

Pain.

Anger seals over me like a wet, hot kiss. I stride forward, my fist already clenched. Sweet adrenaline sweeps though my veins, lighting my senses on fire, chasing away the remnants of beer fog and the bad memories that take up precious space in my mind.

I'm ready.

They're not.

The third guy is observing or supervising, chuckling and egging on the other two.

Tears continue steaming down the blonde's face as she gags on his prick.

I take the laughing fucker down in a kick-and-punch combo that always works. My knuckles strike his throat, and he crumples, gasping for air. He grabs at the knee I just dislocated with a well-placed kick of my boot.

The guy getting his tool sucked widens his eyes. He opens his mouth to shout, but I grab the one who's holding the girl, his palm at the back of her head.

The same head I gently cradled while we danced as foreplay.

I hit the side of his temple with a closed fist, as hard as I can.

The blow demolishes the side of his skull, leaving an indentation as he topples like a tree.

Without the pressure on the back of her head, the blonde falls backward on her butt and looks up at me with a surprised *O* forming on her mouth as I neatly step over her.

Gripping the rapist's shoulders, I knee him in the crotch and toss him backward in a two-second move as smooth as breathing.

Never feel dumb when I'm handing out the punishment.

With a gurgled shout of pain, he grabs his cock and balls, rolling over to puke on the asphalt.

Pivoting, I hold out my hand to the blonde, but her mouth is opening and closing.

Then the bikers show up, looking as dangerous as I thought they would be.

Deep down, I know I can't take all three.

But Brett Rife doesn't back down.

I grab the blonde's hand, hauling her up and behind me.

The biker who looked so bad ass in the bar surveys the downed attackers and looks up at me and says, "This your work?"

I nod, as tense as a snake.

His pale-gray eyes move to the girl.

"Don't touch her," I say and mean it. No one hurts ladies when I'm around.

"No," he answers in a short word. "Don't hurt chicks."

I relax—only slightly.

His smile is sudden and broad. "Been sizing you up."

What?

Now I'm just confused, but don't want to show it. I look more closely at them. They look a few years older than me but definitely twenties, maybe close to thirty.

"I think I'm going to be sick," the blonde says from behind me.

"Have at it," the guy with platinum shorn hair says.

"She's had a shock," the guy with dark hair adds, some humor in his voice. "She could do this willingly at the club, ya know."

"What club?" I ask, hearing the sounds of my once-future bedmate heaving. Looks like there won't be any fun tonight. Plus, my fists hurt like hell.

The guy with the smoky eyes says, "We're always looking for good men to join the ranks. You want to have the tightest family you ever knew?"

More than he knows. I don't say anything, though. I don't trust nothin' that sounds good.

"I'm going home," the blonde says, wiping her mouth.

She's not looking that sexy anymore. There's vomit on her shirt, and her clothes are ruined. Plus, her eyes are angry and sad.

Not hot.

"Thanks for saving me, but I'm…" She shuffles her high heels around, casts a glance at the moaning trio on the ground, and looks up. "Not in the mood anymore."

The bikers laugh, and she gives them dirty looks before stomping off.

The guy with light-blond hair whistles low. "Headed that one off at the pass, brother. She's one of those psycho bitch types." He taps knuckles with the one with dark eyes.

"You did a fine job of dispatching this merry band of fuckers," the guy with the pale-gray eyes says, kicking the toe of the pantless guy, who'd been shoving his cock down the girl's throat moments before.

I say nothing.

"Can you talk?" he asks, peering into my eyes.

"Yeah."

"Fuck, he speaks!" The guy with black eyes says. "I don't know…" he continues, giving me a critical look. "Might be work. Seems a little slow."

Code for stupid. "I'm not stupid." I bare my teeth.

"Holy fucking christ, he's a hothead, to boot." Black eyes roll.

"I like that in a man."

"You would, Noose." The blond guy chuffs.

One of the men on the ground groans. It's the one I pounded in the temple. Guess I should be relieved I didn't kill him.

I grunt with dissatisfaction, casually walking over to his position. I bend my leg at the knee, lifting my cowboy boot high, and bring the heel down on his crotch instead. The move's so natural, I don't give it any thought.

He bellows.

I grin, thinking about how he was hurting the girl.

"I really, *really* like him," Noose says. He walks over to me, and I back away warily.

Noose raises his hands. "Gotcha." He looks at the blond guy. "This is Wring"—his head swings to Black

Eyes—"and this is Lariat." He pops a cigarette out of a pack and lights it, instantaneously shooting smoke rings in the air.

One of the Arnies was good at that. He would do it before he put his cigarettes out on whatever patch of my flesh was nearest.

I fight glaring at Noose. He's definitely not an Arnie.

He doesn't understand the expression and narrows his eyes. "We're with Road Kill MC, looking for prospects."

"What are those?"

"They're dudes that have to take shit, shovel shit, and be shit until they patch in and become our brother. You game?"

I think it through. I could be a part of something.

I'm not part of nothin' right now.

Todd chooses that opportunity to walk out and come into the middle of the three lying on the ground and the three offering me something…I don't even know what.

"Come on, Brett! Let's go get plowed." Todd staggers over, tosses an arm around my shoulders, and tries to passively dig around for my wallet. "I need another five-spot," he slurs.

"Or you could stay put with your friend here," Lariat says, sarcasm dripping from the word *friend*, "and have a meaningful drunk fest."

Wring's blond eyebrows rise.

Unhooking Todd's arm, I grab my wallet out of his hand and stuff it back in my jeans pocket.

Without my support, Todd stumbles backward, tripping over the top of the lead rapist, and falls on the guy's dick.

The fucker gives a hoarse shout at the newest insult.

Sometimes shit just works out.

I leave with his muffled screams in my ears.

Todd can deal with it.

I follow three guys I don't know, with a proposition I don't understand. I'm either brave or stupid.

Hammerstein says I'm not dumb.

If only I believed him.

HAMMERSTEIN
PRESENT DAY

"I'm sorry, Brett. I asked you—begged you—to keep a low profile." I hike the satin pant leg of my lounge pants in an effort to make crossing my legs easier then puff on my pipe, not especially enjoying the cool breeze that's stubborn enough to remain in June.

My eyes caress the undulating waves lapping at my concrete bulkhead on Lake Tapps. The lake is full this time of year, due to the post-Memorial Day status, but unseasonably cool weather reigns supreme, and not a water toy can be heard anywhere on the lake. In autumn and winter, the lake is a graveyard of torn stumps that rise from the remnant puddles like worn-out sentinels.

The Pacific Northwest sun has decided that early June will be cold. And what rays do break through the usual cloud cover are weak and uncommitted.

Brett is wearing a leather vest full of colorful patches.

I peer at the latest one and realize he's now "patched in" to the gang—a motorcycle gang.

His luminescent green eyes are clear, resolute. Brett Rife has done a lot of growing up since his trial on the eve of his eighteenth birthday. He's a man now, though he looked like one the day I met him.

Except for the eyes. His eyes betrayed him.

In my line of work as lawyer, and later as a judge, I saw a thousand wounded children's eyes before his, and Brett's were no different.

More severe and more tortured—but no different. When his worthless prostitute mother came to me, I almost didn't take his case.

But her eyes held love, and my weak heart held hope. Bad combination.

Brett Rife needed a champion. What he really needed was a father, but I couldn't be one. Never having children is easily the biggest regret of my life.

Now I'm sixty-five and spent. Career behind me. Arthritis clawing at my joints like a rabid animal.

However, if I can save one child—this child—then my life will have been worth something. Something greater than me.

I sigh.

Brett's got himself into a scrape. A large one.

"You put two men in the hospital, Brett," I restate the facts.

"They were hurting a la—girl," he corrects self-consciously. Many of Brett's behaviors stem from his chronic childhood abuse. He's afraid to speak because he fears looking "dumb." He was told he was stupid by the first man who occupied his home when he was very young and all the others who followed.

Brett Rife is not dumb. He's been brainwashed and tortured. He's come a long way, and our monthly, sometimes bi-monthly, visits have helped.

My wife, Eleanor, likes to make him home-cooked meals whenever she knows Brett's coming for a visit.

She warmed up to him slowly, until she got a good look into those eyes.

They melted her. Like they did me.

Like hot wax, we loved Brett Rife. The kid we never had. We love him now.

"Judge?" Brett asks, breaking into my thought stream. I manage a slight smile in response.

"You were saying that I"—his Adam's apple plows up and down—"hurt those guys."

"I'm certain they deserved it," I offer. Brett's sense of justice points due north.

He nods.

"That was eighteen months ago." Brett's hands spread, and he shrugs.

"They're making trouble, talking about how you took them by surprise. That the girl was willing."

His brows drop over intense green eyes, his most arresting feature. "They made her, Judge—forced her—holding her."

Brett crosses his arms, glaring at the gray waves that whip against the concrete bulkhead. As he stares angrily at the water, the waves beat the concrete as though sharing in his rage of those memories.

"Son?" I lightly tap his knee, and Brett reluctantly turns to look at me. "I believe you. But the girl can't be located to bear witness, and now you're part of this motorcycle gang."

"They're not a gang. We're like a brotherhood. We defend each other, watch out for each other."

So much is left unsaid.

Killing.

Crime.

An assortment of nefarious deeds, while done with others, are still prosecutable.

I scrub my face, noticing the day-old stubble. I'm such a lazy old coot now. Shaving every other day.

I chuckle, and Brett frowns.

"Forgive me, just thinking of how I've let my hygiene habits slide."

I lean forward, resting my elbows on my knees, and the whisper of pain reminds me that the temptation to become a snowbird beckons. Not sure how much longer I'll accept cool Junes when I can have hot ones somewhere south.

MARATA EROS

However, I'm not through with Brett Rife. When he's on a solid path, maybe Eleanor and I can escape the damp chilly winters of the Pacific Northwest—or June—as it happens.

"I'm retired from practicing, but I can help with this mess."

"Club's got a lawyer, Judge." Brett leans back in the patio chair, crossing his arms.

I nod. *Of that I am certain.* "Yes, but does he know your history?"

Brett nods, but his eyes are troubled. "Too much, I think."

"Hmm."

An idea seeps into my brain, and I turn it over slowly in my mind.

Brett watches me. One of the many things I like about the boy—I mean *man*—is that he doesn't rush people. Brett lets them be.

Finally, I say, "In this instance, your past is your greatest strength."

A few seconds drill between us.

"I killed Arnold Sulk. How is that okay?"

A look of perfect understanding passes between us. After a full minute of studying my house slipper, I finally say, "You still don't read?"

"You know I don't. Don't need it. Don't want it. The guys in the club don't need smart men. They just need good ones."

40

I nod, still looking at the quilted pattern on my deep-scarlet house shoes.

I lift my gaze to meet Brett's.

"Sometimes, if it appears as though someone is trying to better themselves, and they go to court"—I wave a hand around—"say, in the future, like the next half-year…"

Brett goes to sullen silence, and I let the pause become a moment before continuing.

"Then those efforts toward betterment could work in your favor."

"You're saying I have to go to Sylvan Learning center or some crap like that and be academic?" He slaps his thigh, planting his elbows on his legs, clearly frustrated by the thought. "Judge, hear me: I cannot read. And I don't speak too good, neither."

"You've improved immensely, and you're highly capable." I lean back, resting against the uncomfortable wicker patio seat that Eleanor likes the looks of, even though my old ass protests using it. "There's a special program—"

"No."

In a low, commanding voice, I say his name. "Brett."

He looks at me. His dark hair is pulled back into a severe ponytail low on his skull. It leaves his face naked. Stark. He's a hard young man, but his eyes are still wounded.

What can heal that? "Just give it a try."

"Don't want to be in a class full of people calling me dumb. Thinking it."

I shoo that thought away with another wave of my palm. "It's one-on-one instruction."

He stills, however. Brett is listening.

"It's a special needs teacher a young woman by the name of—"

"Nope." He stands up suddenly. "Not being in a class for retards. That's the same as dumb."

I stand too, gripping his shoulders, though his six feet five to my stooped five feet ten means I have to hike my chin to meet those eyes.

Angry eyes.

"Krista Glass does not teach retarded people. Not that it would be a bad thing if she were to. She specializes in teaching people who have learning disabilities, no more. Regular-intelligence folks or more than regular intelligence." My eyebrow rises significantly.

I capture his gaze, and he reluctantly meets mine.

"You are not dumb."

Brett grits his teeth.

"You have never been, nor will you ever be dumb, Brett Rife."

He dips his head so I can't see his expression, especially the windows to his devastated soul. His answer is a whisper. "Okay."

I make some calls, then we sit down to Eleanor's delicious supper of roast, mashed potatoes, and peas.

Brett has extra gravy.

No one would ever know that I claimed a victory for him—or he one for himself.

TRAINER

"You're going to learn-how-to-read school," Storm snorts, barely containing his laughter.

I whirl, and he flinches. "Listen, fucktard, the Judge says I can't have a re-do, or I'll go to prison for sure this time."

Wring strolls past, sees the look on my face, and blasts the heel of his hand over Storm's head.

"Fuck!" he hollers. "I hate those."

Wring smirks. "So stop giving our boy Trainer grief, and I won't be inclined to impart brain dusters."

"He's going to learn how to read," Storm says with a smugness I want to wipe off his face with my fist.

Wring gives him a narrow glance. "Maybe people that wish to improve themselves are braver than those who want to make fun of them."

I blink at Wring.

And with that, he walks away, whistling tunelessly. He whips out a switchblade and cleans his nails as he walks.

Storm's neck grows ruddy, and he turns to me. "I guess I was an asshole."

I don't miss a beat. "Yup."

"Didn't mean nothin'. I know it took you a million years to patch in and you did all kinds of stupid, gross shit."

"Yup."

"Fuck." He rasps a palm over his kinky hair. "Sorry. A couple of weeks ago, we were both prospects with the shit detail. Now you're patched in. Trying to make the transition is all."

"I don't sleep on detail," I comment, reminding him of the time he was supposed to be protecting one of the old ladies and fell asleep on the job.

Storm winces. "Hell, I'm never gonna live that down."

"Nope."

"You know, for a quiet fucker, you sure say a lot."

My lips curl.

Storm huffs, walking away.

A sweet butt comes up to me, showing me what she's got. Crystal is her name. A month ago, she wouldn't give me a glance because I wasn't real. I was just a prospect.

Now I'm really fucking real. Earned this spot. Hardcore.

"Hey," she says.

Just looking at her makes my dick stiff. She's a perfect woman, but like Noose says, she's conniving as fuck. I don't really know what conniving means exactly, but think it means she might lie and hurt everybody to get what she wants. Hard to remember that when the acres of smooth skin and smoldering hiked tits are packed against my chest.

I swallow.

Then she says the perfect thing for me to walk away.

"The other girls say you have a huge dick. I want to be split." She winks.

I sorta cringe back. Every sweet butt I have sex with, I love. Just for that time, in those moments. I don't hold nothin' back. Not one thing.

To know they talk about me like I'm just a cock, with no man attached, breaks me down some.

Feels raw.

"Not interested," I say quietly and disentangle myself from her clinging.

"What the fuck?" she says, sounding genuinely puzzled. "Is it because I wouldn't bang you before you patched in?"

Kinda, but if she wouldn't talk and say that shit, it might've happened. Everything she says is like a small weapon of words. Why don't people understand words can cause wounds too. Like they're not plugged into life or somethin'. Hell, I'm a dude, and that shit bothers me.

Only from women, though. Men, I couldn't give a fuck about.

Except Judge. He means more to me than he should. My eyes tear around the club before landing on the church door. For a year and a half, I've listened and participated in all kinds of things.

A small seed of happiness burrows into my chest like a worm, seeking its target.

The heart.

Crystal rants behind me, but I ignore her. I got church. The brothers are waiting.

The only real family I got.

Viper sits quietly in his chair, looking us over, like a king over his subjects.

Storm's late and comes in like a dog with his tail tucked.

Wring gives him a slanted stare, and he looks away from those incinerating-blue eyes.

I love the way the brothers take an insult to me like an insult to them personally. Even though they were hard on me, I could feel the training, the concern, and the shaping of who they wanted me to be.

Probably why my road name is Trainer.

Over and over again, they said I needed extra training. When they patched me in, they said I was all done. That I could train others now.

Trainer.

Stuck to me like glue. Like it better than Brett anyway.

"So we've got the gun running out of the way, though there's Bloods trying to reclaim their leader's territory."

"Always," Noose says, flicking the hard-boxtop cigarette lid over and back, over and back.

Noose would rather be outside blowing smoke rings than sitting still in church. This, I know.

Viper's pool-water eyes move to me. And I'm reminded that his eyes are the lightest blue I've ever seen. Just like mine are the lightest green I've ever seen. Kinda weird twindom.

"You're going to a school so you present well for a possible trial?"

I nod.

Storm opens his mouth, and Wring raises the switchblade from the nails he's been cleaning restlessly. Without even looking up, he says, "Don't."

Storm's mouth snaps shut, but Lariat and Noose give him a speculative stare.

"Shit," he mutters, running a nervous palm over his head.

Viper ignores them all and continues to stare at me.

"Don't want to, but Judge said it'd be 'prudent.'" I almost slap my hand over my mouth. I don't know where that word came from.

Snare whistles, sending me a wink. "Love the four-dollar word, Trainer."

I don't look at them, but I feel heat on my face. Don't know whether I'm proud or embarrassed.

I look at Viper instead. He seems safe.

"Good. Whatever he says. We won't drag our mouthpiece into this until we must. Al has plenty of Road Kill shit to manage without a little bit of trouble over a bar thing."

"It's not a little bit," I confess, and all eyes shift to me.

Noose doesn't look interested. That's when I figure he knows, but I gotta be sure. "You know?"

He nods.

"What the fuck is going on?" Viper says. For a moment, I feel sorry for him. He's always putting out fires, as Lariat says.

"I bashed this guy's head in with my mom's ashtray when I was seventeen."

Silence can be loud.

Like now.

"Jesus, Mary, and Joseph," Viper says, running a palm over his face a couple of times, then he turns to Noose, palms flat on the table. "You're supposed to vet men, Noose."

He shrugs.

Viper states, "I will not go back on a brother, but hell, this is complicated."

Noose shrugs a second time. "Juvie thing. Mom was in danger. Trainer stepped up and waxed him." He gives a chin flick in my direction. "Dig his innovativeness," he adds, almost as an afterthought.

Don't know the word, but I'm too embarrassed to ask.

"What's that mean?" Storm asks for me.

I duck my chin, hiding the smile.

Lariat says, "Means he's a McGyver. When shit needs doing, he uses whatever's handy. Innovation."

Viper rests his chin in his hand. "Now that dictionary time is over with?"

"If I do this class, then it looks like I've made good on being better, trying to self…"

"Improve?" Wring supplies. "What a bunch of trumped-up shit." Then he nods slowly. "But the courts like that crap. It was smart on your Judge's part."

My Judge. Yup.

Tears clog my throat. I've never cried in my life. Not one tear. But thinking about Judge looking out for me to the finest detail is…The gesture moves me, even when I fight being moved.

Viper's a sharp man.

He pounds the gavel—yeah, I know the name for that now too.

"Church's over."

The guys throw their chairs back and head out. When it's just me and Viper, he squeezes my shoulder as he walks out.

Hard.

I know what the unspoken support means.

Maybe I'm not so dumb, after all.

5

KRISTA

I look over the tips of my fuzzy purple bunny slippers at my mom.

She stares back over the rim of her teacup. "This is utter bullshit, just so you know my thoughts."

Like I'd ever have a choice. "God, Mom, I *so* know how dumb it is. But I'm hogtied by bureaucracy. It's Washington state. Sanctuary haven, taxation up the wazoo, and you know how liberal I am, but it comes at a price. Now the government has its nose up the ass of education, and I have to deal with the choice I made to become a teacher."

Mom rolls her eyes. They're not far from my color, but mine are a dark gray, like pewter, and hers are more like a blue that wants to be gray. We're two halves of the same whole.

Unfortunately, we're totally alike, so that causes some clashing at times.

"Why are they coercing you, honey?" She sets her teacup down in the saucer with a clank and begins to dunk the bag. It has definitely steeped long enough. The liquid is as black as tar.

"It's not technically that. The whole thing just feels like it is, though. Ellen Rowe wants to keep me, but it's part of giving high-needs teachers a break from the demands of our kids, and this hiatus to teach different learners has been mandated."

"Bullshit," she murmurs a second time.

Agreed. I give a rough exhale, attempting to rub my eyes out of my head. This change has not been a recipe for a good night's sleep.

"You'll make them stay that way."

I pop my eyelids open and frown. "Mom, please."

She smiles. "Why don't you have a night at our place? I'll cook."

Mom and Dad are on some crazy health kick, eating fats and eschewing bread.

I shudder. Give me all the pizza in the flipping world, carbs be damned.

"Are you going to do that steak-and-salad-plus-butter thing? Because, I won't lie, I don't know if I can handle it."

Mom brays like a donkey. "Yes, for certain I will be fixing whole foods that are good for you. Unfortunately,

I'm close to my cycle, so there will be special compensation for that."

My ears perk up, and I boing like a piece of toast in my seat, feet dropping to the floor, and lean forward. "So there'll be crap food in the house for us?"

Mom nods then shoots a covert look around my tiny condo as though Dad might be lurking there. "Don't tell Daddy."

"Jesus, *no.*" I toss a pillow at Mom, and she catches it deftly.

"Brat." She arches a dark eyebrow.

I deflate against the couch again, secure in my immediate junk-food future. "I know."

A few moments pass in comfortable silence, then after sipping cold tea, Mom says, "How many students?"

"Just three." I play with the fringe of my pillow. A Pier One hippie-chic type. Love it. Has every color in the rainbow. Tiny beads decorate the tips, and I roll the smooth glass between my fingers, liking the tactile moment. "Supposed to be kids that had learning disabilities. Disadvantaged kids."

Mom's brows pull together in a delicate frown. "Sounds just like what you're already doing. How's this a 'reset'?"

I shake my head. "Different. My age group. Two guys, one girl."

"Bizarre." Mom raises the teacup to her lips again.

I sigh for the second time. "Yup. But I'm recharged and ready. I get paid the full-time salary, but I'm only working for a four-and-a-half-hour block total."

Mom shrugs. "Weird and lucrative."

I jerk my head off the back of the couch. "Mom, you don't teach for the money. The pay's a joke, and teachers work like slaves. At least those of us who want to make a difference."

"Do you?"

I let the time between answering swell. I think of Ian's face when he mastered the hard consonant of *the*.

"*Oh*, yeah," I answer softly. "I think so."

"Then that's all that matters. You know Daddy and I have always encouraged you pursuing what you love. After all, what's good about spending the majority of your waking time working in a job you hate? Forget money at that point." Mom gives a small sniff of disdain and stands, tapping my foot with a finger.

I groan and plop my feet on the floor again. "I'm not getting out of my pajamas to go pretend to eat healthy food with you and Dad then secretly scarf down hot tamales and popcorn while we watch chick flicks."

Mom turns so that only her profile is visible. "I'll be tossing on my jammies the instant we pop through the door."

Nice. "Fine, I'm convinced."

Mom's smile widens. "Ah-huh, broke your arm." She winks.

Setting the empty teacup in my sink, Mom scoops her purse from its perch looped around the back of the wooden chair at my tiny, two-seater kitchen table, then grabs her coat as she heads out the door. I shove my feet into my Crocs by the front door then grab my slippers and follow her out, still wearing my pajamas. I lock the door to my condo before leaving.

Love my family. Love my life.

The smell of pancakes wakes me like the best alarm clock ever. I stir, barely mustering enough energy to rise from my warm cocoon of bed linen.

What a night. My tummy growls because the load of junk food I had last night awakened my metabolism.

Now it's time to pork on low-carb pancakes.

Gross.

I stuff my feet back into my slippers. The violet bunny ears with white centers wag as I pad from my old room into the kitchen. "Please tell me there's coffee and real pancakes."

Mom laughs. "It must be nice to be *you*. Only child, every need met, get to have breakfast in bed."

"I'm out of bed, Mom," I comment with a grump. Not a flattering description. Princess, etc. Maybe I might be one.

I pretty much am.

Dad breezes in, looking much younger and buffer than a fifty-year-old guy should. "Hello, Pumpkin." He kisses my temple then frowns, his eyes sweeping my form.

"Are you eating enough?"

"She carb-loads like a fiend," Mom elaborates, and I roll my eyes.

I weigh plenty, thank you very much, though if I'm honest, I have more ass and boobs than a girl needs. But I'm not all caught up in the Anorexia Movement. Starvation is not a plan. I eat when I'm hungry and stop when I'm full. But I eat what I want to eat. Unlike my crazy parents.

Mom puts a steaming mug of coffee down on the table and mutters something about the antioxidants in the java.

I slurp, drowning out her wisdom. "Thanks, Mom. Oh my gosh, where's the sugar?"

"We have the whole-leaf liquid stevia," Dad offers, coyly not mentioning the sugar I know they keep around.

No. I trudge over to the glass dish on the kitchen counter, lift the lid, plucking a raw sugar packet from the bowl, and close the lid. After a pausing, I turn back around and get a second.

Dad covers his eyes. "I can't watch."

"Don't." I breeze by, ripping the top off the packets, unceremoniously pouring the entire load into the black goodness.

"Real cream." Mom plops a small carton down in front of me. I pour some into my coffee, stirring until the color is exactly what I like. I take the first critical sip then moan in pleasure. "This is definitely the life."

Dad harrumphs and sits at the table.

They're so traditional, my eyes ache watching them. Mom dishes Dad up and pours sugar-free syrup over his pancakes. She flounces back to the kitchen and gets my pancakes, which look better, full of carbs and fluffy. She's a short-order cooked today.

I dig in.

Somehow, between bites, Dad gets all the same info out of me that Mom did last night when she stopped by.

He thinks the arrangement is as weird as she does.

I explain that it was something implemented after my hiring.

"Dad, I just have to give up thirty days of my life so I can get back to what I love doing when September rolls around." I stab a bite of pancake then lift it high. "I do get to continue for the summer if the students need more work or if I like it." I plop the yummy morsel in my mouth and chew.

"Extra money." Mom lifts a shoulder, sipping some whole milk, which leaves behind a slight moo-stache. "You've talked about wanting that."

I nod. "I'm lazy and want my summer free, but it'd be great to have the extra. *If* it worked."

Dad nods. He threads his fingers through his thick hair, and I notice the light silvering at the temples. "That's key. If you don't care for the position, then you're only stuck for a month. You can do anything for a month."

He takes a swig of coffee, and our eyes meet over the cup's rim.

"For sure." I shrug. "What's a month?"

We laugh.

I take care with my outfit today. This isn't little kids that are forgiving of my light makeup or casual Friday attire.

These are my peers, and I have to look professional and ready to play the part.

But I don't want to look like I'm trying, either.

God.

I gaze into the full-length mirror and just *know* that the outfit's a fail.

But here's the thing—it's my third one. I'm pressing my timeline to be at the school because I'm fussing over appearance like a dork.

Starting with my head, I check off what I do like: dark hair swept up into a messy bun.

Check.

Smokey taupe eyeshadow appears to make my eyes smolder like two pieces of brilliant stormy ocean under a gray sky.

The screaming-crimson blouse with tiny buttons down the front completely covers my ample bustline, but doesn't hide my shape. I don't do frumpy. My long skirt is simple with a pattern of bright-red, white, and black flowers. Black ballet flats complete the look.

At the last second, I toss on silver hoops and slender silver bangles.

I smack my deep red lips together and thank the heavens I only wore mascara today.

Not *trying, remember Krista?*

Hopefully, that won't matter. I bite my lip, get lipstick on my tooth, and waste five minutes fixing that. Then I rush out to my burnt-orange Fiat, tear open the door, and chuck my slender black clutch purse and cell inside.

Ready!

I sail off without a care in the world, ready to take on the new students.

Sitting at my desk in Martin Sortun Elementary, I prop my chin in my hand. The school, located on the far east side of Kent, not too far from Meridian Valley Country Club where my folks live, had a different name when I went here.

I tap my polished nails on the desktop and check my roster for the fifty-second time. *Jerk.*

Brett Rife was supposed to be here—glancing at my watch gets my panties in a twist—*nineteen minutes ago.*

I knew this guy wouldn't want to learn anything now, just like in high school, and waste my time.

Hearing a low rumble that sounds faraway, I lift my chin off my hand. I wonder if that could be him.

The sound grows louder, practically vibrating my teeth. Half-standing, I ask to the silent room, "What the hell is *that*?" Then it shuts off abruptly.

I run to the door and peer through a slim rectangle section of glass bisected by a gridded diamond pattern of tempered glass.

A big, beautiful black motorcycle gleams like an ebony dream in the empty lot. School is out for the day, and my sessions for my three students run from three in the afternoon until nearly eight at night.

Brett Rife is the first.

A huge guy dismounts, cleaving himself from the dark machine like he's part of the machine. He appears to take stock of the bike then pockets something before turning in my direction.

I jump back from the door as though caught and race back to the classroom, past the sign pinned neatly to the door that reads Special Session-Reading.

He looked like a felon. Tatted, huge, and muscular. Why would someone like him *need* my class?

That guy didn't look like he needed anything. Or anyone.

Instant shame swamps me. I shouldn't judge. Not being judgmental is one of my best features. It keeps me teaching instead of criticizing. However, Brett Rife was rude to not be on time.

The steady gait of boots with thick tread strike the polished linoleum floor to the beat of my heart, and I sit behind my desk, rustling the useless papers I have in an attempt to look casual.

My stack of phonics books, flashcards, and my beaten-up ruler are stacked neatly at the right side of my desk.

He walks through the doorway—filling it—and stops dead center, his fingers turning white from the grip he has on the half-open door.

Brett Rife is a beautiful man.

Fine scars, in various stages of age, litter the surface of every bit of visible skin.

His skin is magnificent, but it's his eyes that stop my breath, my thoughts, and my forward motion.

They're such a pale green they appear translucent.

He's so tall that there's nothing empty around him, just his body. I stand, because it's physically impossible for me to sit when someone that big is so near to me.

I'm only five foot six, not short by any means, but I feel fragile compared to this monster of a guy.

The more I stare into his eyes, the more I feel I know him. And his pain.

Pain is what I see.

Then the blinders sweep down over the expressive gaze that drills me where I stand. Not before I caught a glimpse of something, though. Something important. It vanishes with his will for it to remain hidden.

"I don't want to be here any more than you do, so let's get the shit on the road."

Blinking, I sit down.

He finds a chair in the front row, seats himself, tosses out his legs, and glares at me from hooded, swimmingly gorgeous emerald eyes.

I jump when the door automatically clicks shut.

He smirks at my reaction.

Somehow, it makes me want to cry. Because that pain I saw? *This* is how he covers it.

I *see* him.

And Brett Rife will learn. Because that's my purpose on this earth.

6

TRAINER

I manage to slip out after an all-nighter at the club without anyone asking me where in the actual fuck I'm going at three in the afternoon.

Could be getting my cock waxed.

Did a lot of that last night. I run a hand over my face. Still avoiding Crystal.

There's something about a girl ignoring me then finally paying attention for reasons that shouldn't matter—I feel like shit for giving in.

Crystal's that way.

I know every rider's had her. Just don't want to. I don't feel that special. And Crystal goin' after me just makes that dim fucking feeling of failure even sharper.

Thanks to Judge, I'm finally getting to a point of feeling neutral at least. Thinking clearer in my head.

Not talking like an idiot every single day.

I straighten, popping my back as I tap the low ceiling of the club and survey the damage.

Lots of shit I used to have to clean up. Not having to do it no more rocks.

Guys are sprawled out like human carpeting with semi-naked chicks draped over them.

I smile when Storm charges in, looking half-outta-the-bag, his kinky reddish-blond hair standing straight up on one side.

"What?" he yells.

A rider rolls to his side, displacing a girl without a top, and she yelps as she falls on the floor.

With an arm swoop, he hauls her back onto his lap.

I ignore the make-out session and turn to Storm, slipping my smartphone into my back pocket.

"Why'd ya text, Trainer?" Storm is checking out the female flesh on display, barely paying attention.

"You're on cum fest duty."

"No—shit! Come on…I'm hung like laundry. Barely keeping my chow down."

Know that one. *Never mattered*. "Don't matter. Gotta get outta here and see ta something. Get cleaning."

I turn around and walk toward the door, feeling kinda bad that Storm is doing the detail I was on barely a month ago. But I don't tell him that. I got a duty. That was made clear. Once I got patched in, that shit goes to the prospect.

Hard though. I feel like I should still be doing that shit. Like I'm not good enough to be patched.

Noose comes in as I'm leaving. He looks at the carnage over my shoulder and snorts a laugh. "Nice."

I nod.

His eyes take in my seriousness, and he says so quietly that only I can hear, "Ya off to the teaching?"

I nod again.

He claps my shoulder, moving sideways to get through the door. We're about the same size. He works at it, whereas I'm just this way without much gym time.

Been working my whole life. Got the muscle of survival to prove it.

Noose turns again and studies my face. "See ya later."

He raises his fist, and we tap knuckles before he walks away without looking back, hollering something at Storm.

Noose doesn't have any problem ordering prospects around. I smirk. *At all.*

The sun strikes my face, and I stand in the ray until it passes, liking the warmth, the reminder that I'm still alive.

But I'm putting off the teaching by stalling in the sun like a cat taking a nap.

My bike sits with the others, gleaming because I wax her every other month. I copied Noose and got a Road King. Not that I'd ever say. Not many MC guys have these. They're mammoth and difficult to move.

Don't care, though.

Road Kings are built for two. Comfort. And someday I'll have a lady who will ride with me. Maybe.

Being ballsy getting one. *Like a lady would like me well enough to be with me.*

My fists clench, and I stride to my bike, give it a rough start, and pull out.

Better get this over with. I'm late as fuck.

The ride's great, late afternoon in early June that's unconvinced summer's around the corner. Don't like hot weather anyways.

Clicking on the left blinker, I pull into the Martin Sortun parking lot. The words on the signs are all just jibberish, but I know the place.

I kill the engine then listen to the ticks as it cools.

Don't want this. This learning shit.

I hike a leg, swinging it over the seat, and give a light bounce off my ride. Pocketing my keys, I walk toward the entrance to the school. I see a flash of something and slow, holding my hand over my eyes to shade them from the late-day sun.

Must've been nothing. I guess. But I'm not much for seeing shit that's not there. Always had sharp eyes.

I blast through the door, kicking it so hard that it hits the wall and bangs back.

As I move through the school, the smell brings back pretty shitty memories of being teased for being slow.

Judge doesn't miss a chance to remind me that the way I was raised made me believe I was stupid, and that I'm not *actually* don't have shit for brains.

I go to the door marked with a sign. I look at the email that Judge sent and carefully check the letters there against the ones posted on the door. They match.

Grasping the handle, I open the door then step inside.

A beautiful girl sits behind the desk, and my heart-beats go pear-shaped, splitting and dividing, having erratic babies in my chest.

I clamp down. Hard.

But my eyes do their work, moving from a head with loose curls that spiral down to a small waist, great big tits, and what looks like a nice spread of ass.

This lady, my teacher I guess, is too pretty to exist.

So I do what I do when I'm scared. I get mad.

She moves to stand, and my earlier glimpse confirms everything I thought. Perfect.

"I don't want to be here any more than you do, so let's get the shit on the road," I say more harshly than I mean to, but there's no taking it back.

Lumbering to a desk, I plop down, kicking out my legs, and cross my shitkickers at the ankle.

My heart's racing so hard, it's giving me a dull throb in my head.

Her eyes are the same color as Noose's, but deep like a stormy ocean, and they don't look at me with hate. The way most eyes do. The ones that misunderstand me.

"My name is Krista Glass."

Her voice is throaty, like she practices sounding sexy.
I look away.

Maybe she just is sexy, without the practice.

The rustle of a skirt has me turning. Big flowers
move with her as she walks toward a long rectangular
table with two chairs.

Krista carries a large stack of cards, books, and other
shit and sets it carefully at the corner.

"Those seats are for students during the day, Mr.
Rife—not adults." She stands patiently by the chair
that's hers, fingers lightly holding the back of the
empty one.

For me.

I stand then wade through emotional quicksand to
reach her.

She's a tiny lady. Maybe a foot shorter than me. But
she's not afraid of my size. I can tell.

I like that she's not afraid. Don't need to be.

I don't hurt women.

Krista pulls the chair away and sits in the one I
thought was mine. "Here, you take the end one. That
way you don't have to squeeze behind me."

She smiles again.

I notice the table has us against the windows, facing
the only door to the room.

I like that too. Wanna see who comes and goes.

"Why don't you tell me a little about your situation?"

My face heats. "Can't read. That's my fuckin' situation."

Instantly, Krista says, "You can't read because you weren't taught or because you can't recognize letters?"

My head jerks to her, and for an agonizing moment, I forget all my internal shit. A near first. "What do you mean?" I ask before I think about it.

"I think you know." Her eyebrow rises, and my gaze caresses the slight arch.

I shrug. "I know what the letters are. I mean—I know that's a K," I say with great hesitation, pointing to a flashcard that has a picture of a kangaroo with the letter K.

My head starts to pound, and I rub my temples.

"Headache?"

"Yeah."

"Is that normal when you try to read?"

I look at her again. "Are you testing me?"

She nods. "I think I know why you can't read."

"'Cause you think I'm dumb." My voice is a low bass growl.

Krista leans back, and my eyes go to her breasts then to her eyes.

Everything is so beautiful, I don't know where to look first.

Her lips curve into a smile. "Classically, people with dyslexia are pretty bright. But the disability can mask that."

"Hang on." I hold up a hand, and she waits. "Dys-what?"

"Dyslexia. It's where people see letters in the wrong order or direction. Often, teachers don't know enough to recognize the issue, and the child gets labeled as slow or learning disabled."

My mouth softens, and her eyes crinkle at the corners.

Another thing I like about Krista Glass: her smiles are real, and they reach all the way to her eyes.

"Can you…" I look down at all her books, flash-cards, and paper and softly close my eyes, measuring my breaths. "Help me learn to read?" I finish on a whisper.

Hate asking for anything.

"Yes, Mr. Rife, I can."

I open my eyes, and she's still staring at me.

She's an unguarded lady. People could hurt her because she doesn't see it. Krista's not had the pain.

The bad.

That makes me happy. That there's a person in this world who hasn't. Gives me hope that not everyone has Arnies in their life.

My eyes travel her face.

I'd kill an Arnie that touched her, I decide easily.

"Sorry I came on so strong." I hike a thumb back at the door.

Krista shakes her head with a smile, and soft rich brown hair tumbles around her shoulders. "It's okay. To tell you the truth, I'm so nervous to do this new job, it wouldn't have mattered what you said."

I jerk my head back. "Why?" How could anyone like her be nervous of anything? *How can she admit how she feels?*

"I've only taught young kids. I don't know if I can do as well with adults my age. But"—she puts her palms out, and I fight the urge to take her hands—"I love trying."

There's that smile again.

I'm trying really, really hard.

But being next to Krista smelling so good makes me think of eating her from the pussy out.

Pretty fucking distracting.

I like the learning, though. I suck at it, and the process makes me kind of start a sweat goin', but for the first time ever, I understand words. Some.

"See this sight word?" Krista asks, pointing to a jumble of letters.

"Yeah."

"Remember what I told you about sight words, Brett?"

I haven't told her I'm MC yet. My road name will be on the way out of here.

I glance at the clock. Five minutes left. Feels like that's all the time I've been here.

Goes fast next to Krista Glass.

"Yeah. They're words that can't be sounded out. Gotta memorize them. The combinations."

She smiles.

I'd kill to see that again. I'll dream about her smile tonight.

"That's right," she exclaims, lightly touching my shoulder. The contact makes my dick get hard.

Not now, I tell it. But it has a mind all its own. Stays hard.

Great.

"I don't want to overwhelm you for your first day. Actually, I believe you don't have a very severe case." She appears pensive for a moment, rolling her bottom lip between her teeth, and I hold back a lustful sigh. "I'm wondering why no one picked up on your dyslexia for all those years. It's puzzling."

Probably because school wasn't a priority. I went when the Arnies weren't around and stayed home when they were.

Someone had to protect Mama.

"Don't know," I answer honestly enough.

Krista stands. "Got to wrap this up. I have Corina next, and she has more challenges than you."

I lift my eyebrows, and she grips my bicep. "You'll be reading inside of two weeks, Brett."

"Actually, my name is Trainer."

"Oh…" She seems flustered, looking at some scribbled words I can't read on a sheet of paper on the long table. "I didn't get that nickname. I'm sorry."

"No big. It's what I like."

Her eyes meet mine. "I won't forget, Trainer."

Me, either.

Krista Glass is unforgettable.

We walk to the door. I feel light, like I'm floating.

A mousy chick opens the door just as I reach to open it, and her breath catches at the sight of me.

She's got a massive tick in one eye and rushes in, practically running to the same desk I sat down in.

Krista and I exchange a glance, and I get what she was saying before. Everybody's got something.

I move to step out, and a tall dude in a suit almost runs into me. I sidestep, gracefully avoiding a crash. For a big dude, I move like liquid.

"Excuse me," he says. His voice is cultured. Formal. Smart.

All the good feelings I had with Krista fly away like released pigeons.

He doesn't notice. Too busy checking out Krista.

"You look beautiful."

Krista's skin flames to a deep pink. She seems uncomfortable.

I hesitate. It's crystal clear she knows this guy.

But, my instincts fire off. Don't know why. Never mattered much. They've always been spot on.

"Thank you, Allen."

Stupid name.

He cocks his head at me. "Would you excuse us?"

Krista glances inside where Psycho Tick is sitting, looks at me, then looks at Allen.

"Um, this is Br—*Trainer*. He's a student, and Corina is waiting for me inside. It's not the best time, Allen."

"I see," he says.

I know that tone. He's pissed and doesn't see anything. Nothin' at all.

"Since when did you start teaching adults?" Allen turns and studies me like an insect tacked to a science board.

Don't like this fancy dick.

"Allen, this is all pretty sudden. Maybe we can talk later," Krista says, putting her hand on his arm.

Don't like that, either.

He pulls away.

"I don't appreciate not being in the loop, Krista—and the audience." Allen angrily hikes his chin at me.

"It's not Trainer's fault. He's within his rights to be here and be taught. I'm on teaching time, and I have to begin." Krista wrings her hands. "It's my first day," she adds in a low voice.

"Okay." Allen clenches bright, perfectly straight teeth. "Call me later."

"I will," Krista says, and Allen the Dick charges off, slamming the school entrance door behind him.

"Sorry about that," Krista whispers. She turns and pokes her head inside the door to her classroom. "I'll be right in, Corina."

"Don't matter," I say, though it does. It matters that there's a dude who doesn't *see* her, sniffing around in her life.

'Cause I do. I see all of her.

"Allen doesn't intend to be like that. He gets all fussy when I don't communicate."

I frown. "Communicate what?"

Krista lifts a shoulder. "What's going on. But this time…" She laughs a little. "I didn't know the direction my life would take until three days ago. Hell, my parents hardly knew."

Her eyes widen, and she covers her mouth. "I'm sorry," she mumbles behind her hand. "I have a bit of a potty mouth."

I grin. Nothing compared to mine.

"It's okay. See ya tomorrow, Krista."

She nods.

"You did well today, Trainer."

I keep walking toward the door her controlling boyfriend just went through.

"Trainer?"

I turn, hating to see her one last time—because I want it so badly.

Our eyes meet, and hers are solemn. "You did well," she repeats.

My face gets hot again, and I know I'm fucking blushing. I don't say nothin'. I just nod.

Safer.

7

KRISTA

Allen has me rattled. I can barely enjoy my time with Corina. She reminds me so much of Trainer. They're hugely different, but at the core, they're the same: misunderstood.

I don't know why, but somehow, the students are always so clear to me. It's like I've got x-ray vision or something.

I see them.

I *get* them.

They hide because they've had to. Saying I'm a great teacher wouldn't be accurate. I'm great at being intuitive.

It's my strongest asset…and my greatest fault.

My gaze goes to Corina, who's saddled with this horrible tick. She's also a non-traditional learner. Her learning was a fail before she ever made first grade.

Thankfully, I always get the squirmers and people that can't sit still. Her tick doesn't register with me. It's just a part of who she is.

"Who was that?" Corina whispers. She dips her head, letting the curtain of her dishwater-blond hair hide the eye that jumps around all the time.

I don't answer the question. "You don't have to do that with me," I say.

She looks up, startled. "Do what?" Corina momentarily forgets about her eye, and it twitches. Self-consciously, she puts her hand over her eyeball and stares at me out of a beautifully flecked greenish-brown hazel orb.

"Hide the tick in your eye. I don't care about that."

"Ah-huh," she replies, clearly unconvinced.

"I need you to use your finger, so you're going to have to let the eye jump." I lift my shoulders in a dismissive shrug, telling her it's no big deal.

Corina bites her bottom lip almost hard enough to draw blood, but she slowly lowers her hand.

The eye twitches, and a defeated sigh whispers between us.

Corina waits for me to do the expected. Look uncomfortable. Laugh. Turn away from noticing. Whatever.

I don't. I stare at the jumping, twitching, leaking eye.

"Thank you," she whispers.

"For what?" My eyebrows knot.

"For not caring," she says instantly.

I smile, feeling the expression reach my eyes, creasing the corners. "Oh, I care. More than you know."

Then I turn away. To my work.

Our work.

I can't return to my condo.

I'm fit to bursting. The day was a-fricking-mazing. All three students did well—especially the socially awkward guy at the end, Dwayne.

I did well.

This is my purpose. The reason I was meant to be alive.

I twirl on the way to my Fiat, like Eliza Doolittle in that old film, *My Fair Lady*, that my parents used to watch. I spin with happiness.

I *have* to tell Sam. She's going to die.

And someone needs to know how inappropriate my feelings are toward a certain, tall, dark and dangerous.

Dangerously vulnerable.

That's what Brett Rife—Trainer—is.

I grasp the handle on my car and pop in, locking the doors out of habit.

I wonder how Trainer ended up with that name, then shrug. He seems like he has deep reasons for things in his life. Secrets.

I'm curious to know them.

After tapping out a quick text to Sam, I wait for her to ping back.

She does within seconds.

Coincidentally, I'm sitting in the parking lot of the school where we first met.

In kindergarten.

We've lived mirrored lives with boring parents who stay together and affirm their offspring.

Unheard of.

Hells yes, come on over, Sam texts back.

I start my car and travel the five blocks to her house. Her parents were killed in a twenty-car pile-up after we graduated from high school, and Sam inherited their house in Kensington Heights.

And a set of new parents. Mine.

I take a deep, cleansing breath.

Samantha Brunner is a court stenographer.

She refers to herself as a fly.

As in, *on the wall.* We giggle over that.

"I'm just nosey and want to hear all the juicy tidbits," she'll say.

Her honey-colored hair is a mass of dark gold curls that whip around her shoulders as she pulls open the door when I've barely had time to knock.

Sam's hair is actually quite long, but it's so curly, the length is hidden in springiness.

Saying Sam has energy is an understatement. She likes to write off her excessive exuberance by saying, "I sit on my ass all day, so I'm rearing to go when I'm outta there!"

Deep-chocolate eyes with a rim of bright navy blue greet me.

"Okay, I want all the details of this new 'job.'" She puts air quotes the last word, and

I roll my eyes. *Like I have a choice?*

"And Allen showed for the first day of this new gig? Holy crow—what a colossal *ass*."

Sort of.

"I'm fucking grief-stricken I introduced you two." Sam mock-slaps her forehead in disgust. "Come in here!" She jerks me inside and shuts the door, hitting the locks.

I follow her inside the dim interior and get a melancholy pang. It's been five years since Sam's parents were killed, but she hasn't altered the interior much.

The inside of the house has a mild shrine-ish feel.

Sam doesn't need to work. Both of her parents had healthy life insurance policies. Since she does work, she has the money to refurbish the place. Give it her own personal stamp.

She hasn't.

I guess Sam needs more time.

"Can you believe this shit?" she says, scooping up a pile of mail at the edge of the beige-colored laminate countertop.

She wags the letters around for a few seconds then slaps them on the counter.

I pick them up.

They're addressed to her dead parents.

Morons, I think, disgusted with the powers that be for not getting their facts straight, five years post-mortem.

"Don't they *know* they're dead?" she asks in a thready voice.

Sam always gets strung out toward the anniversary of their death.

I know it by heart. It's next week.

Moving behind her, I wrap my arms around her small body. She's terribly tall but as thin as a whip. Sam always says she wants my ass and boobs.

I don't think so; grass is always greener.

Sam looks like a model. Her dad was a mixed-race black man, and her mother was a porcelain doll. They made a beautiful daughter together.

A sad one.

Sam perks up, turning in the circle of my arms and wiping her eyes.

"Enough of this bullshit!" she whips a finger in the air. "How'd I even get here, anyway?"

"Assholes sent mail for your dead parents."

She scowls, wrinkling her perfect brow. "Yeah, fuck-wits," she mutters.

We laugh, and the sounds melts away the sadness.

"Wait, I need coffee for this."

I move over to the couch that still faces a humungous room-length fireplace—classic 70s style. Real masonry to the brick foundation, it's sort of cheesy now. The house was the last one built in the development and faces Clark Lake, which is more pond than lake. But the area behind the house can't be developed, so the house has a pretty view of a permanent greenbelt.

Trees I don't know the name for fan out where four picture windows rise from floor to ceiling, framing silky fronds tipped with delicate pink blooms.

Spent blooms from the large ornamental weeping cherry tree at the corner of the small yard litter the ground like pink snow, and a large boulder is beside it like an anchor. A chain-link fence divides Sam's property with the low maintenance park that runs immediately behind it.

It's peaceful. Unlike Sam's life.

Sam looks in the same direction my gaze is turned toward, taking a sip of black coffee that she just made with her Keurig.

"The trees seem like they're talking among themselves," she comments wistfully.

I close my eyes, listening to them rustle through the kitchen window that's cracked open a couple of inches.

The forest reaches down to the easy shores of the glorified pond, and lots of the trees appear to be nearly a hundred years old.

"Second mature growth," I say aloud, guessing the area was clear cut a century ago and these are the babies of yesteryear, all grown up.

I'm a tiny bit of a tree hugger. Love nature. Love what it provides me. Beauty, peace…hope. I can name the evergreens, though the names for the deciduous trees right in Sam's yard are harder to remember.

"Huh?" Sam gives me a look. "You're getting all day-dreamy. 'Kay, so before the brain fog rolls in"—she taps the rim of my cup, and I shoot her a dirty look—"tell me how your day went. And I don't want to hear about Asshole Allen first. That text saying he did the asshole-show-up slayed me."

I hide my smirk. When Sam introduced me to him, she was only acquainted with him as a lawyer she'd met at work and didn't know him well enough to thoroughly vet his character.

Allen's fine. He's just…Allen.

I tell her everything. She stops me a dozen times to ask about Trainer.

"Did you look at his penis?"

"No!" I reply emphatically. She replies with raised brows, calling me a liar.

And she's right.

"Was there chemistry?"

"He's a student," I reply.

"So?" Sam says, brows popping. "He's over eighteen. You're not pulling a Mary Kay Letourneau."

So creepy.

"He's *definitely* over age. It's not that. I want him to trust me, not jump on his bones. Besides…" I shrug.

"Don't give me one word about Allen. You're not into him anymore, Krista. I mean, when was the last time you slept together?"

It's been a while—like nearly a half year. I mean, Allen was a nice guy, but he's gotten kind of possessive lately. He seemed to have a sixth sense that I was pulling away…which made him push harder.

The fact is, we just have lousy chemistry, and he's not really on point with what gives me pleasure. He just wants to stick me and get off, but I'm not a human pincushion. I want *more*. He's only my second boyfriend, and he's the worst at meeting my sexual—and emotional—needs.

"He's a limp noodle in bed." Sam's thoughts echo my own.

I feel like I owe Allen, somehow, and I hate that obligatory feeling.

"I didn't tell you that, Sam."

She rolls her eyes, sitting down on the same couch as me and curling her legs beneath her. "Ya don't have to. There's no fire when you talk about Allen. It's more like distaste." She wrinkles a pert nose. "Like you tasted a piece of fruit going bad and want to spit it out."

A laugh bursts out of me. "That bad?"

"Uh-huh." Sam nods vigorously then winks. "Hells yes."

I give my head a little shake. "God, you're something."

"Yep." She wraps her fingers around her mug, warming her hand. She shoots a scowl outside. "It's effing cold for June."

I glance at her partially open window, tilting my head toward the kitchen, and restate the obvious, "You're letting all the cold air in."

"Fresh air," Sam qualifies with a slight shrug.

We sit in companionable silence while I drink coffee with enough cream and sugar to qualify the concoction as something other than actual coffee. I only hope I can sleep tonight after the extra caffeine jolt.

Sam's takes hers black. Like punishment.

After a minute or so, Sam says, "So Trainer?" Her full lips curve like a Cheshire Cat.

I can't help the blush that makes my cheeks hot. "He's really rough around the edges," I try to repeat what I've already said.

"Bad boy," she sings then adds, "*Not* like Allen!" Sam slaps her thigh then spins her index finger in a circle. "Love that whole program."

I laugh. "You're no help."

"Help for what?" She sets her empty cup on the sofa table behind us.

"You said he swore at you and stomped around the class."

"It's just bravado and self-defense." I lift a shoulder. "He's never had anyone care or look too deeply at why he's illiterate. Like a lot of dyslexics, others assume they're stupid. When actually, it couldn't be further from the truth."

I glance at my half-drank coffee. Cream has made it beige. "His eyes. God, Sam—his eyes."

I look up as her brow screws into a delicate frown. "What? You said they're all clear green. Hot."

"Wounded," I correct. "There's pain I saw there before he shut me out."

"Listen to me, Krista."

My gaze rises to meet hers.

"You *cannot* save everyone. You're a teacher, not a shrink."

My face turns to the window again. Watching the tree branches caress each other, I hear their whispers. I hear one of the learners I teach even more clearly.

What do I do about Trainer?

The one I hear the loudest.

8

TRAINER

I stare at my cell phone screen for a long time.

The text I sent Storm is a memorized phrase. One of many that I've saved on my phone so I can pretend better.

People don't know how lucky they are to see letters and understand what they mean.

Mama didn't know I couldn't learn. Course, Mama wasn't paying attention to much except whichever Arnie had her on her back.

I look away from my cell, gazing into the deep woods that surround the club like a battalion of green.

Something I do a hell of a lot—like thinking about shit alone.

I release a pent-up exhale, digging my hair out of the tie at my nape and re-doing it.

Mama loves me. She just don't see *me.*

Rubbing my chest, I can't get rid of the tightness there. Never been afraid before. Except when I was too young to be anything but hurt by the Arnies.

Now I'm afraid.

So afraid my teeth are numb in my mouth. That teacher—Krista Glass—she fucking *sees* shit to my toenails.

Gotta keep my distance. Gotta take the class in case I go to court for the turds whose asses I kicked.

Remembering that fancy prick who was a jerk to Krista when I was standing right there...makes the distance harder. Want to find out what *kind* of a prick he is. He might be an Arnie.

Fancy suits don't put me off none. Anyone can be that kind of man. Seen 'em in all shapes and sizes.

In the end, they're the same.

"Hey, bud," Noose says, plopping down on the wide back concrete step of the club where I'm perched with my uneasy thoughts.

"Hey," I say, not turning.

He claps me on the back. Noose was a taskmaster when I was a prospect, but he was fair. Never talked down to me.

Never treated me like I was dumb, even though I probably acted the part.

He bangs out a cig and, stuffing it between his lips, asks a muffled question, "How'd it go?"

I let the silence drag out. Gives me time to work over a reply.

Noose waits, which is his way.

"Embarrassed. Angry," I say truthfully, staring at my scuffed boots.

"Fuck it." Noose springs the lid free from his beer with his tungsten wedding band and rolls the chilled glass bottle across his forehead.

After a couple of minutes, he says, "Gonna miss this cold snap. Always fucking hot as hell."

I smile. True. Us guys run warm-blooded.

Which makes me think of Krista.

I take a pull of my own icy beer. Need to figure things out. Not used to having to. I like the club. It keeps things simple. My mind zones, and I can do what I'm told and get loyalty and respect in return. Road Kill MCcompletes me.

Krista, and my obsessing over her, screws up all that small amount of peace I lucked into carving out for myself.

"What else?" Noose asks causally.

Noose isn't casual. He's always rooting around for answers, wanting to know the why or what behind things. It's just him.

I'm not an actor. Never been good at keeping a straight face. So I don't bother. Besides, Noose has taught me a sort of fragile trust in the last couple of years.

Could've been the first time he knocked two guys' skulls together because they called me dumb.

Began there, I figure. Me loving him.

Guys don't love, they say. But when you haven't had any, the emotion sneaks up on a man, tackling him when he's not expecting it.

I'd go to the ground for my brothers. But I have a soft spot for Noose.

Even if he did have me clean up after the orgies. *Fucker.*

I give a rough exhale. "There's a girl."

"Figured with that moon face ya got." He sips his beer, issuing a quiet snort.

I frown.

"Go on," he says, spinning the bottle of beer hard enough that some slops out the top. "Fuuuucker!" he barks, licking it off his hand.

I laugh.

His lips twist into a trademark grin, half-menace, half-humor.

"She's the teacher." I yank the stubby tail of hair at my nape.

Noose whistles. "Nice."

"It's not like that." I glare.

Noose shakes his head, kicking a small pebble with his boot. "It's *always* like that." He chuckles. "Got sweet butts coming outta our ears, and then complicated pussy walks by, and suddenly, a man can't think. The only thing thinking in that is"—he grabs his crotch, sets down his beer, and puts his other hand on his chest over his heart—"the little head and this beating mess inside our chests."

So maybe he gets me, some.

Here goes nothin'. "She said I could learn."

"Fuck, yes, you can, Trainer."

I nod. "You looked into me."

Noose gives a single nod. "I know what I read on those papers. But I also know"—he taps his temple—"all the bullshit that's between the lines. Undocumented." He takes another pull from his beer, grimaces, then threads fingers through his longish hair. "Think you did well only killing the last guy." Noose adds with a bark of a laugh.

I slowly pivot to face him, elbow planted on my thigh, and my beer dangles from my hand. "What do you mean '*last* guy'?"

"I mean, that your mom didn't suddenly decide to invite that loser into the house when you were seventeen. At least that's not how it worked where I grew up." He splays his fingers against his chest, dark-blond eyebrows hiked.

Letting the silence eat up the space between us is easy. Talking about this shit is painful. The thought closes my throat and makes my guts feel like they're gonna fall outta my ass. A few heartbeats of time stack between us before I answer, "No. He was the tenth guy—I don't know—twentieth. It all blended, Noose."

I take another pull, and the brew sloshes in my gut, not settlin' shit. Stomach is still a churning mass.

"Yeah," he agrees softly then drains the rest of his beer and digs the bottle into the dirt beside the step. "What kind of chick is your teacher?" Dipping his head, Noose cups his hand around a cigarette he lights with the old one. He parks the butt of the spent cig inside the bottle.

That's an easy one. "She's the kind I don't deserve."

"Probably the perfect one for ya." Noose nods, as though agreeing with himself.

We look at each other.

"I can't stop thinking about her." My fingers wrap my beer hanging between my thighs. I study the bottle instead of the man before me—or his words.

"There's plenty of pussy here, Trainer." Noose jerks a thumb behind him at the club.

I nod. *Yup.* I lift a shoulder. "You know how much I love the ladies."

Noose smiles, sweeping his hand to my crotch. "If I had a foot-long cock, they'd love me too."

I turn away, shamed by yet another difference.

"Hey, don't get your boxers in a twist, pal. That's not a little factoid the bitches keep quiet about. And let me tell you something, they say size doesn't matter, but I've never met a chick that wouldn't like some sizable meat when presented." Noose gives a satisfied chuckle. "Hell, if I were you, I'd hang out my tile and have it read 'Come and get it.'"

He starts roaring, giving a sharp slap to his thigh. "*Come* and get it. Love that."

I shake my head, and he claps my shoulder. "Listen, Rose was out of my league. Didn't stop me from wanting her. And she's not complaining. Hell, Lariat's married to a lawyer. Maybe there's certain women that need something different than the simp fuckers running around being all sensitive and shit. Maybe they need a protector, a man who will die to please them."

Noose straightens, putting his boot on the step he was just sitting on, and stares off into the darkness of the woods that look more black as night blankets the day. "Or just die, brother."

Yup.

"Did some looking into this Krista chick." Noose slaps down a stack of papers and photos in front of me.

The letters laugh at me, daring me.

I meet his eyes. "Not too good at reading, Noose," I admit, like I'm a slow reader.

Not the real truth: that I can't read. At. All.

He shrugs. "I read through the shit. Not much to worry about. Krista Glass, age twenty-three, five feet six, one hundred thirty pounds. Mom and dad still hitched, normal childhood, no siblings."

He spreads out glossy eight-by-tens on the table.

My teeth grind when I see a picture of her with that dick Allen.

His hands are on her body, leading her into a restaurant I could never take her to.

Not for lack of cash. But because I don't belong there.

"He's a problem." Noose points to the dick.

No surprise to me.

"Lawyer." Noose's reason is not the same as mine.

But still…Shit.

"Gotta mind your shit in this situation. Word has it she's dating this mouthpiece, and we don't want him digging around, maybe paying attention to you, causing trouble because he somehow sees you as a threat to the teacher."

"Krista," I correct softly.

"Fuck, Trainer. I want you to be fixed and fucked and loved just as much as the next brother. But between offing Daddy of the Week and this new mess with those fucktards you put in the hospital, I won't lie—you're skating on thin fucking ice, dude. Ya gotta do this class and do Teacher later." He cocks a brow.

And I'm somewhere between agreeing and wanting to punch him.

Just trying to save the ladies. My mama and the blonde I never got the name for—I was just trying to save them.

Now there's Krista. And Noose is telling me to keep a distance that's closing like one of his famous ropes around my neck.

I'm sitting on the same concrete step again. Next day. Different beer.

Noose sinks to his haunches, his eyes piercing mine. He taps a knuckle on the stack of photos that lay atop papers I can't read. "Just finish the school. Go after Teacher when that's done and the possible trial is over. Don't let your big dick think for you."

I take a deep breath then let it out.

Noose stands. "What? I know when you got to say something." He rotates his neck, getting the kinks out in a series of small pops exploding between us.

"I don't like this guy."

"Pfft. Figured. He's sniffing around Teacher."

I glare up at Noose.

He raises his hands, palms out. "Hey man, get off my dick." He chuckles. "Can't resist. Like when Snare married his sister." Noose cocks his head, blowing out another smoke ring in an endless precession. "Come to think of it, I am being an asshole."

I say nothing.

"All right…shit." He stomps out the cig. "What I'm saying is: yeah, you don't like this guy. I wouldn't, either."

"No, I mean, I got—" Frustrated, I yank my hair tie from the back of my neck, and my hair swings forward, hiding my face. "He feels like an Arnie."

Noose frowns. "You mean like the douches that worked your mom over all the time?"

"Yeah."

Our eyes meet.

"I don't know. This dude…" He flicks the photo with the lawyer in it. My eyes latch on to the big hand at the small of Krista's back. I know I'm gonna have a lot of "restraint issues," as Snare calls it.

Noose continues, "He's got money, education, and no motive. He's not a pimp." Noose has lit another cig, and he talks with it, nodding as he speaks. "He isn't after a hooker, doesn't look lit on meth and other shit, and has an alarmingly hard white-privilege angle." Noose squints through the smoke.

I snort. Oh, the shit we smack.

Noose's ash on the tip of his cig is an inch long. He spreads his arms away from his body, and the movement causes that tail of incinerating gray to fall like dirty snow between us.

He takes the cig out, frowns, and uses it to light another.

I raise my brows. "What is going on with the chain smoking?"

Noose's eyes narrow as he waves away the veil of smoke. "Anxious as fuck."

Now that's something I never thought would cross his lips. *Noose is anxious for nothin'.*

He clamps the cig with his lips and roughly assembles his hair at the nape, savagely twisting it through a buff-colored hair tie.

"Rose is knocked up again."

I smile. "Congrats, man."

Noose lifts his fist, and we touch knuckles. "Thanks."

"Why do ya sound like someone just kicked your puppy?"

Noose gives me a look like a drowning man. "Twins, fucker."

I stand in a stiff stagger. "What the fuck?" I breathe out.

Noose gives a sage nod. "So forgive me if I don't think you having the hots for Teacher—" His face swivels to mine. "For *Krista* is worth worrying about. *Jesus.* I just look at Rose, and she's full of babies again."

Now it's my turn to comfort. Not something I get to do or know how to do that good.

Clapping his shoulder, I say, "Aria's like two, right?"

"Yeah," Noose says mournfully. "Early trainer. Doing all her business in the potty now." He shakes his head.

In the potty?

"This time next year, I'm going to be up to my earlobes in diapers and leaking tits." Noose gets a half-smile. "That last isn't such a bad thing."

He takes a long drag.

I blink.

Noose cocks his head, giving me a speculative look. "Maybe TMI for you, pal."

Maybe.

"Anyways, pretty stoked it might be a couple of boys. Sure have a full house, though. Charlie will be eight, and

Aria will be three. Yeah…" He tugs at his short ponytail. "I feel sleep deprived just thinking about it."

Yeah. I repress a shudder.

"Love the fam. Love Rose. I'll get through it."

He looks at me again, squeezes my shoulder. "We'll get through all of it."

Noose walks off, leaving a trail of smoke, the photos, and papers behind.

I scoop up the stack and trudge to my bike.

I stuff the shit in the trunk and lock it up tight. Gonna ride home and look over everything, use my scanner that translates words to audio. Then I'll know what those letters say about Krista Glass before I see her again.

Better to know more.

9

KRISTA

Tuesday, Trainer shows up, and we begin the tedium of memorizing sight words.

I suck in my breath when his hand accidentally brushes mine every few minutes.

By Thursday, I know it's no accident.

When Wednesday rolls around and every time I look at him, he's looking at me, I feel myself cave degree by degree. To him.

To the temptation that is Trainer.

Thursday's session is different. I receive a text from Corina saying that she'll be a half hour late, and her delay gives me more time with Trainer.

Time we can't use during the learning process to get acquainted.

He starts out with, "Got bad shit to tell you, Krista."

I know. Knew it all along. Inside, I fortify myself. "Okay."

He nods. "Love my mama."

The intro surprises me, especially a little boy's endearment out of such a masculine guy.

"She picks men. Bad ones."

I don't say anything. I've heard something like this before. Lots of my kids are from broken homes where their disabilities are tolerated very little, or not at all.

But Trainer's not a kid. He's a man. A man I'm very aware of.

Terribly aware.

My gaze sweeps his bare arms, where tattoo sleeves don't hide the pockmarks of abuse caused by branding and beatings.

His eyes take in my face, searching it for disparagement, disbelief, or some negative emotion.

I take a deep breath. "I'm still here."

He gives me a rare smile. "I know."

Trainer looks out the window, translucent eyes bleeding almost to white as he gazes into the trees circling the building.

When he finally speaks, it constricts my heart. "They beat us pretty regular-like. The men." He takes a deep breath then adds, "The Arnies."

My heartbeats begin a punishing rhythm. I don't want to hear. To know. To understand this beautiful, wounded man was once a fragile, inquisitive boy who couldn't see letters in the right order.

And was beaten for that. And lesser things—while watching his mom get beaten too.

I put my hands over my eyes, though the tears squeeze between my fingers.

Trainer picks me off the chair beside him and hoists me onto his lap. My hands fall, and he looks deep into my eyes. I suck up his unique fragrance of clean male, vague leather, and engine.

"Never told nobody this stuff. Don't mean to make you cry."

"I can't help it," I say against his neck. It's so inappropriate, but I can't pull away now. He's telling me what's so difficult to say.

I won't reject him by creating a physical distance, though I know that's not my only reason.

His large hand winds my nape, each finger a brand of erotic heat against my skin.

"So when I wanted to get help learning, people made fun of me. When they tried to talk to Mama, the Arnies made her quit caring."

"Or they'd hurt her," I guessed.

"Yeah," he answers and squeezes my neck. The strength in the gesture lays between us, unrealized. That violent potential that Trainer has.

When he's touching me like this, it's hard to remember what he's been put through, what he's capable of.

The moment is now. Him and me. The world a distant place that surrounds us, yet we're not a part of it.

"So that's why I'm dumb," he states as fact.

I pull away sharply, my wet eyes searching his dry ones. "You are not dumb in any way, shape or form, Brett Rife." My voice is a reflection of how I feel inside: convicted, filled with absolute surety and belief.

He nods. "That's why I can tell you, Krista. I can tell you the horrible shit."

Feeling my brows pull together, I ask, "Why?"

"Because you believe."

I put my hands on his broad shoulders for balance. "Of course I believe you're not dumb." I give an indignant snort. I never thought for a second that he was stupid.

Trainer shakes his head and lifts my palm to place a hot kiss in the center that leaves me breathless.

"Nah. I already knew that." His green eyes rise to meet mine. "It's the other thing you believe in."

Another kiss has me biting off a moan.

"What?" I ask, voice breathy.

"Me," he answers simply, laying a chaste kiss on my unresisting lips, "You believe in me," he ends on a whisper.

FRIDAY

Shit.

I glance at Allen's text for the twentieth time.
We need to talk, he says.

I roll my bottom lip between my teeth and chew on it. Finally, I tap a response, breaking my run of avoidance—the inevitable.

How about we meet at Starbucks—8ish?

My feet shift restlessly on the floorboards of my Fiat. I'm still sitting in the nearly empty parking lot of the Elementary school.

Momentarily, I'm distracted by a deep bass that rumbles through the car, thrumming through my seat.

Turning, I see a great big bike come rolling in.

Black. The machine shines in the June sunshine like a giant ebony pearl.

My cell vibrates with a reply, but I'm riveted, like I've never seen a bike before.

Of course it's Trainer's. And that makes it different from all the others.

He must have seen me sitting in my car. If there's one thing I've learned in the four days of teaching him to read through the struggle of the mild dyslexia he's saddled with, it's that Trainer's naturally inquisitive *and* smart.

Somebody—or something—squelched that natural childlike curiosity. *Hard.* Of course, now I know part of the why.

Trainer's learning a new skill set that includes trust and hope. Plus, he'll have to muster enough drive to learn after that natural impulse was amputated by sadists before he could cultivate it.

I know that desire is within him, buried underneath all the steel-plated armor. I'll have to find a way to pull that eagerness to learn to the surface.

That's complicated by our growing sexual chemistry, though, like the way we crossed the line yesterday with that kiss. It didn't go further, but it doesn't matter. It's not *if* it'll go further, but when.

I saw the sexual tension in how his eyes crawled over my body. In the soft way he said my name.

The invisible heat has smoldered between us from practically minute one.

I wipe sweating palms on my shredded jeans before adjusting my messy hair knot.

Trainer rests for a minute on the bike, and I take in his solid form.

He's a big man, and an intimidating one.

For some reason, he doesn't scare me.

I suspect Trainer would be tender and compassionate where he could, despite his terrible background.

Just a feeling.

The flat of his feet planted on the ground, he swings one leg over, scooping a half-helmet thing off his head. Resting it on the passenger seat, Trainer peers at the sky before leaving the bike, and I just know he's looking for rainfall.

Seeing a rare, clear day, he leaves the helmet where it sits.

His icy, green stare finds me in my car, staring at him like a dope. I'm helpless to look away.

Trainer begins to stride toward me with purpose.

My heart hammers against my ribcage.

Quickly, I check the text.

I'll be there. I barely have time to say *kk* to Allen's cryptic response before Trainer is standing outside my driver's door.

His dick is in plain view.

I mean, it's behind dark denim jeans that are skin tight, but I swear I can see the outline.

Oh God.

Shutting my eyes, I know there's no amount of self-chastisement that will stop me from thinking about him sexually. Imagining us together. Yesterday's confession and interlude saw to that.

I hate that *we've* been set in motion.

And I can't stop it.

Opening my eyes, I find myself staring into his green ones, with only the glass of my car window separating us. They're so close, I swear I can see the darker green ring surrounding his pupil.

Trainer doesn't speak.

My hand shakes as I grasp the handle, and he takes a step back to allow me to exit.

Standing, I turn to grab my purse and planner, then pivot to face him.

Still silent, he eats up the step he retreated, right into my space.

His raw size engulfs me, and I think to shut my door, but he cages me with both hands, effectively shutting it before I have a chance.

My butt hits the door, and I look up, clutching my stuff like a shield. Maybe I can salvage some scrap of distance. Doubtful.

"Hi." I clear my throat and repeat the lame greeting.

"Hi," Trainer says back, but his eyes are on my throat…and lower.

They sweep up suddenly, dark brown lashes framing those gorgeous irises. Though they're prettier than a girl's, there's no mistaking Trainer for being anything other than all male.

"Why were you sittin' in your car, Krista?"

I look down at the cell still clenched in my fist and brush his chest as I slide it into my purse.

We simultaneously suck in a breath at the contact, and my peripheral vision watches his fingers curl against the Fiat's roof.

"Just answering a text before our time." I try on a smile. It falters because Trainer's looking at me like a dessert he's been denying himself.

"Gotta tell ya something else, Krista."

His words from yesterday flood my brain, but I nod stupidly, managing, "Maybe after class."

He shakes his head, and a long piece of chestnut hair escapes from a tie at his nape, falling forward to cover one of his gorgeous eyeballs.

I have an insane urge to put that chunk back, and clasp my hands together over my things.

He gives a sharp jerk of his head, and the tendril settles behind his shoulder. "Gotta talk about more bad shit. Be honest."

My heart goes into overdrive at this point. His nearness. The smell of him.

More? My heartbeat speeds. "Have I done something wrong?"

Somehow, he knows how I've been feeling—probably all the moaning when he was kissing my hand then kissing him back yesterday. Maybe I stared at him too long, flirted, or led him on. *I don't know,* I agonize. I hadn't been that obvious. I mean, before he told me…what he told me.

We'd made progress. He had his twenty basic sight words memorized. Trainer was sounding out words without clenching his fists, as of yesterday. Victory.

We did get something done besides all the other stuff. But now?

"Kinda," he says. "But I figure it wasn't your fault, just one of those things that happen."

Oh *shit.* "Gonna touch you now, Krista."

What? Oh—touch *me.*

His eyes ask permission, though his words leave no choice.

A sigh slides out of me, and my purse drops to the ground between us.

My chin dips in acquiesce, but a moment later, my eyes rise to meet his.

I don't have the first clue what he'll do.

Then he does it.

One large hand lifts from the roof of my car and cups my chin, running a thumb along my jaw.

"Soft," he whispers. "So soft."

"What?" I ask just as quietly, then he takes me in his arms and presses me against the front of him. My head tilts back, and he captures it with the hand that just caressed my face.

His fingers dig into my hair, loosening the messy bun I carefully coiffed to look good for Trainer. Much to my shame.

Trainer turns my head, forcing my face to where he wants it to be, and kisses me.

Hard. *Well.*

Sucking and pecking at my lips, Trainer grinds the front of himself against me.

His stiffness presses against my belly, and I groan.

Losing it.

He takes that sound for what it is and wraps me tighter, eating the lustful noises as fast as I make them. I couldn't escape his hold if I wanted to.

I don't.

His tongue licks along the seam of my lips, and I part them for his entry. Trainer plunges in; our twining heat is all that I hear. All I know.

All I want.

A car door slams, and we reluctantly break apart, our chests heaving and gazes locked.

I turn to look at the intruder then cringe internally. *Allen.* Nothing awkward about having a guy you've slept with catch you making out with another man.

Nothing. At. All.

He's striding our way.

"Is he a problem?" Trainer asks, lust thick in his voice.

"No," I answer automatically, because…well, I never thought a lawyer could be capable of anything the "dredges" are.

Just shows how little I know.

Allen slows as he comes nearer, taking in our flushed faces and swollen lips.

He smirks.

"Is this what we're going to talk about, Krista?" Allen swings a palm at Trainer.

Trainer stands with his boots planted wide and arms crossed, saying nothing.

I hate the way Allen looks at Trainer.

Like he's worthless.

That type of behavior is part of what's wounded Trainer in the past, and I don't want Allen, who has been given so much, to cause more harm.

I can't stand it—now more than ever.

Though I didn't notice at first, Trainer's taken a semi-protective position in front of me.

Allen's not a threat. But Sam's right: he *is* a colossal ass.

I touch my mouth where the heat of Trainer's kiss still lies, then let my fingers fall. "It's not what it looks like."

It's *exactly* what it looks like. But I feel like I owe Allen an explanation. We're not officially broken up, yet.

"This isn't your business," Trainer says.

Allen's eyes slim to daggers pointed at him.

The big body in front of me tenses.

Shit.

I quickly step around Trainer, meeting Allen halfway. "Things got carried away here, Allen."

He folds his arms, eyes still on Trainer, and I can feel his anger like molten lava behind me, running over me to get to Allen.

"Really?" His smirk widens to a smug grin. "I'd say him jamming his tongue down your throat while he dry humps you against your car is really *carried* away."

I nod. Yes, it was a dumb move. A move I gave permission for.

Why?

Because I'm weak. And if I'm honest, I want to sleep with Trainer.

Save him. Both.

I shiver. Maybe I already love him.

Clenching my eyes shut, I ask Allen without opening them, "I thought we were meeting at Starbucks tonight?"

"I thought you might need this before tonight. You left it over at my house." He shoots a triumphant glance at Trainer, at once dismissive and informative.

My eyelids fly open, and he's handing me a bright-red peacoat, which I don't really need because it's June.

I want to hate Allen for his asshole behavior, but I realize my actions have brought out the worst in him.

Allen's just peeing in corners, giving me tangible reminders that we're still a couple. Even though we haven't been on a date in a month or slept together in six.

He could have handed that off to me tonight. Hell, Allen could have given it to me when he stopped by unannounced at the beginning of the week.

Now it's Friday, and he's back again. Doesn't seem smart. And Allen is a bright guy.

"Thanks." I feel embarrassed, caught and exploited in a miserable emotional lump.

"You're welcome." His pure-blue eyes peg Trainer. "If you couldn't figure it out, we're dating, Krista and I." He wags a finger between himself and me.

There isn't a handy rock to crawl under, but I wish one would appear. Now.

"Doesn't look like she's dating you no more, *Allen*."

Allen smiles like a shark.

Oh, my God.

"Okay, I already told you I'll see you tonight, Allen. It's Trainer's time now."

"Yes, it does appear very much like it's *his* time."

Jesus. I push my messy hair behind my shoulder and take a deep breath. "Allen, it's not professional for you to drop by whenever. Not again." I finally stand up for myself, despite my guilt.

Allen cocks his head. The sun backlighting him makes his champagne-colored, carefully styled hair glow. Not in a good way. Like he's on fire.

"Professional," he muses, tapping his square jaw.

"Fuck off," Trainer commands.

Shit! I had this handled.

Keeping the brittle smile affixed on his face, he turns his attention to Trainer, and I can see he's not through.

Not by a long shot.

Allen spins on his expensive heel and strolls off. Casually.

Like he didn't just see me making out with a student in the parking lot.

As though the whole exchange was no big deal.

Allen hops in his bright-red Porsche and spins out of the parking lot, spraying loose gravel from the pavement.

Watching him go, I begin to shake as his sports car becomes a red dot in the distance.

When the tears start, I can't shut them off.

Trainer moves behind me, wrapping his arms from behind and crushing me against his body. "Don't cry, Krista."

"I'm so sorry," I say, meaning it. I have some fit of hormonal shit, and I—what? Try to *fuck it out* with my student? He's supposed to be able to trust me. Gah!

More tears cascade.

Trainer turns me in the circle of his arms, and I can't look at him.

Shame rides me like a deranged monkey. "I'm sorry," I whisper again. "You trusted me, and we were learning so well together…"

"Hey." He puts his finger beneath my chin and lifts it. "I can kiss you and still learn."

I shake my head.

Then he's kissing me again.

Oh God.

Then I'm kissing him back.

I pull away, drowning, trying to stop this thing that's between us. "No," I whisper.

"No to me?" He cradles my face, kissing the tears and bending down to rub his face along mine like a cat.

"No—I mean yes to you. No to…" Then Trainer's dragging me to the classroom.

When we're through the door, he locks it.

Then he hits me like a ton of bricks.

What do I do?

Fall.

10

TRAINER

I gotta tell Krista that I killed the last Arnie. Need to tell her why I'm even one of the students she teaches. That it's to look good for the courts.

It's not all about the stupid dyslexia. But for the first time, it feels good to know that there's a reason I couldn't read. Can't see shit right. Letters look out of order to me.

No fuckin' wonder.

Still, the learning part is hard to really get, to take in, since I'm older.

Krista tells me I'll absorb it naturally. "Don't be surprised if you dream about it," she said a couple of days ago.

I dream about her instead.

Kissing her and touching that soft skin I got a taste of yesterday, moving in her body.

Showing her what I want and need without words that fail me and don't say how I feel. That come out all jumbled.

My body doesn't lie. And I want it to speak for me.

I think Krista wants it.

I catch her looking at my goods. Seen that look from plenty of ladies.

But never from one that I wanted something more outta.

I pull in to the elementary school parking lot and go through my day.

Gotta go with the boys for a gun run tonight. Need to tell Krista the mess that I'm in. That I don't want her in…but I want *her.*

It's a fucked-up mess of words, and my head aches with the effort of getting them all out in the right order. With the right…bullshit that goes with it. Don't know if I can.

But Krista and Judge have made all that a tiny bit better.

I catch sight of Krista's car and wonder about her being in it instead of the classroom.

She looks tense.

I search the lot, and nobody's here but me and her. I let the engine cool and think more about the words.

Fuck it, as Noose would say.

I swing off my ride and set the half-helmet, which I take tons of shit for wearing, on my seat.

Mama asked me to wear it when I saw her half a year ago.

I do it for her.

Haven't been back to see her, though. Can't.

Figure I might kill the next Arnie too. Got a taste for it now.

Putting my hand over my eyes, I squint at the sun. Don't look like rain.

My eyes find her car again, and I think I can make her out, looking at me.

As I make my way toward her, my dick gets harder with every step. Not gonna be easy. This word thing.

When all my body wants is to show her.

Been trying to show her in small ways all week. Almost died yesterday with her on my lap. Thought my boner would snap off, it was so hard. Had to jack off twice at my place to just calm shit down.

Coming to stand beside her car, I look down. She's got her cell clenched in her hand.

She doesn't turn and look at me. That's fuckin' weird for Krista. She's so open, I don't want her without me around. Maybe people see all that I see on her face.

Everything.

I don't want them to. Don't trust others. Bending down, I peer inside, and Krista's eyes are closed, like maybe if she doesn't see me, I'll disappear.

Or maybe that's the Arnies whispering in my head. Sometimes they don't stop buzzing, and I want to cover my ears and squeeze my hands together until my skull smashes, so I won't hear them no more.

Then her dark-gray eyes open, and she stares into mine.

I mean to talk, but I can't get much out.

Because Krista's right here, with soft skin and beautiful hair that smells like peaches or somethin', wearing just a T-shirt and ripped-up blue jeans.

No fancy clothes today.

And that's okay. I want to see her naked anyway. Don't care about packaging.

I slam her door shut, softly pushing her body against the car.

She seems nervous when she tells me hi, clearing her throat.

"Hi," I say.

She says hi again.

When I tell her that I gotta come clean, she says we should talk after class.

I don't think I can wait that long.

But damn, I lean in and take a whiff. She makes my cock hard.

"Gonna touch you," I say. But my eyes still seek an okay from her.

Thought she wanted me pretty good yesterday, but some ladies give a man mixed signals. Especially a man like me who always thinks *go*.

The only time I'm really free to be gentle or tender is when I'm with a lady. Their bodies beg to be taken but not hurt.

I allow myself that time 'cause I don't have it any other place in my life. No room for soft in my life. Never before. Not much now.

Her fragile jaw sinks a little, and I don't wait for words. I wrap her against me in one motion and kiss her.

Krista Glass tastes as good as the first kiss—better.

Diving in, I tip her head back, carding my fingers through hair like wavy silk, and push my tongue into her mouth.

Krista meets me, twining hers with mine, and I press my hard-on against her, helplessly pushing and pulling against her smaller frame. Afraid I'm gonna come in my jeans. But when a car door slams behind us, I gently set her away and spin, my cock a raging, thumping nightmare, but softening as I take in the fucker who interrupted me and Krista.

It's that lawyer guy. *Allen*.

My hate swells.

Mainly because I don't know what they are to each other. Not for sure. Second, I get from Krista she's done on him.

But why is this dog still sniffing around?

I tuck her partly behind me.

Don't know what he wants and like that even less.

His words are the same as all the Arnies'; they're just fancier. He's one of them in a suit. Doesn't make him better.

Allen doesn't think much of me. No big fucking deal.

But I don't like the way he looks at Krista, like he owns her.

I really don't like that she's meetin' with this fucker tonight while I'm running guns for the club.

When Allen leaves, I make a decision.

Pretty easy after Krista falls apart and starts freaking out.

I kiss her and take her, caveman style, back to the classroom to fuck her brains out.

I think we'll both feel better after.

I turn away from locking the door and take in her flushed face and untucked t-shirt. For once, thank fuck, I manage words that make sense. "Tell me no, and I leave."

Tears streak her face.

"Because I want to fuck you, Krista. If I can't have ya, I think I'm gonna die."

Or my dick will fall off.

"Ya understand what I'm saying?"

She nods.

I wait, cock pounding, blood boiling.

"Yes," she says softly.

I rush her, get to her in two point five seconds, and pick her up as I walk. Her legs wrap my waist. We get to the long brown table, and I sweep all the shit off then lay her down.

God. I suck a labored breath in.

Her hair's come completely undone and I have to...I scoop a handful off the table's surface and smell it. Bite back a groan.

Smile.

Krista gives me a tentative smile back.

I move to the waistband of her jeans and unsnap them, jerking them and her panties down to her ankles.

She makes a surprised yelp.

"Gonna treat you good." My eyes meet hers, and her face turns deep pink.

"I know."

I unsnap my own jeans, freeing my prick, and it practically shrieks its relief.

My eyes skate her warm pink pussy, and I slide both hands under her hips and yank her forward. Bending over, I lift her pussy to my mouth, sealing my lips around her wet heat.

I dig in.

"Ah!" Krista screams, latching on to my hair.

I don't stop. I know ladies like this part and the screaming is for pleasure, not pain.

But Krista tastes different. Sweeter. Juicier. I lick her up. Can't get enough.

My fingers bite into her ass cheeks as I suck on each one of her pussy lips—delving my tongue deep in her cunt.

Moving hard, in and out.

I give her entrance one last lap with my tongue and strike her go button. Hard.

Her hips buck, and she gives a hoarse shout, "Trainer!"

Like my name from her. Like it when she screams it. Makes me want to fuck her even more.

Feeling her pussy pulsing around my tongue makes me want to come, but I think about cleaning up after orgies and shit, and I hold it back.

Barely.

Jerking my jeans down, I lean over, tear off my shit-kickers and toss them. My jeans are off in the next second. Krista lifts her arms and I strip her top and bra off.

"Don't want to hurt ya. Hard not to."

This is the point when my dick is a real problem. Some ladies haven't wanted to fuck me 'cause of the size.

Can't blame them. They call me the "bitch splitter." Don't want to be, but there's no denying I got a big cock.

Krista's eyes widen when she takes in my size. "Go slow," she says, then swallows.

I can see in her eyes that she's afraid.

"I can make it feel good," I promise her. A drop of precum oozes onto my tip, and I drop my head with a shudder, throbbing for release.

Fuck, gonna blow before I can get inside. I lick my lips. The taste of her is still on my mouth.

Krista's eyes track the movement and she opens her legs wider for me.

I lie down on the table between her thighs, and my dick homes in on her wet pussy with zero trouble.

"I haven't been with anyone in a while. Actually, I've only been with two guys."

Don't like hearing her confess to being with another man. But I've been with plenty of women.

Krista's a saint compared to me.

I set the first part of my huge cock in that first bit of delicious wetness. I grit my teeth, wanting to drive my prick home.

But there's been no woman that I could do that with. Ever.

And Krista's tight.

So good.

I drop my head to her chest, listening to her rapid heartbeats as they thump against my forehead, and my body is curved, the first part of me inside her.

Then I move to push-up position, sliding more of me inside her.

"Ah!" Krista says, face screwed into pain.

I still, dipping my chin and looking back at her. I'm so much taller that being on top puts me above her face. But I want those eyes. Wanna see what's in 'em. "Don't wanna hurt ya."

She puts her hands on my ass, and my jaw clenches as I about come on the spot.

"You feel so good, Trainer...but you're...large."

My lips curve. "So I feel good?"

I pump another inch into her tight pussy.

Krista's eyes round. "God yes, but I feel like you could break me in two."

I nod. Heard that before.

I kiss her, whispering into her ear, "I won't. Wanna make you come again, though."

Leaning back, I search her face. Looking for permission to press on.

Krista spreads her legs, and I hook them over my arms, rocking forward as far as I can. Some of me remains outside of her body.

That's normal.

"I think you're bottomed out, Trainer." Krista giggles softly, and her pussy strangles my cock.

"Don't," I breathe through the sensation. "Don't do that, Krista."

"Sorry," she says.

I look at her face. She doesn't seem very sorry.

Punishment. That's what Krista deserves. I slowly pull out, her pussy gripping me, trying to suck me back in the whole way.

"What's that face—*ah!*" She arches her back, and we groan together as I shove back in. Her body resists, and Krista's hips rise, easing me in deeper.

I rock forward, surprising myself with how deep I can fuck her body. Almost in the whole way.

Love how she feels. How wet and warm.

I start moving inside. Then out.

Back and forth. Until she's slick and my dick can begin a light pounding. Always, I think about not hurting.

I give a gentle plunge, and Krista moans.

"Hurts?" I ask, a drop of sweat falling between breasts I tore the bra away from.

"No, *more*," she whispers.

Thank God.

I speed my rhythm, the effort to not pound like I want to is hard as fuck, but this is Krista.

She's special.

"I'm coming again," she says through her teeth, but I hear her, frantically raising her hips with my hands. I feel my balls clench tight against my body, and I plunge as deep as I dare, unloading my come.

Throwing my head back, I bark my release. Haven't come like that in forever.

Krista's head lolls to the side with the soft clenches of her pussy gradually slowing, and puts a palm between her breasts. "Oh my God."

My dick gives a final nod to stiffness before softening, and I gently pull out of Krista.

I watch her lie there in a sexy tangle of limbs.

My heart swells at the sight. That tight feeling that's always in my chest loosens.

It's like I can feel a chunk of it floating away. Where does that missing piece go exactly?

Krista smiles at me, holding out her hand. I lace my fingers with hers, and I know where.

11

ALLEN

Bitch.

No one dumps me. I'm Allen-goddamned-Fitzgerald. Old-money people. There isn't any *nouveau riche* in my family tree. My smirk is carved on my face. I leave it there, like perma-scorn.

Even though Krista Glass's family does not, in any way, shape, or form come close to the thoroughbred lines mine does, she is gorgeous and respectable. And from her own lips, she's only had sex with one man before me, making her only *slightly* spoiled goods.

And I need to marry someone not from the echelon I rub elbows with.

Marrying Krista Glass is the way to go about that. She has all the more common folk credentials. Appealing ones.

I'd give my left nut to understand why I can't marry within the circle of acceptable women, but my father's will stipulated that I shall marry before thirty years of age and provide a Fitzgerald heir in order to obtain my inheritance. My father's obsession that his future progeny not come from the upper echelon is an odd one, and it means I cannot select from the pool of "American royalty."

As an attorney, I understand the terminology and parameters of the will intimately.

There's no foiling my father's carefully laid foundation.

And I've invested nearly two years into this ambivalent bitch.

Further, I turn twenty-nine next week.

Now, why can't I just entice any bitch to the Fitzgerald name? Because my wealth is not set until I marry before the magic thirty years old. As far as Krista knows, I'm simply a lawyer. My income is high compared to most, but it's a penance compared to the billions I stand to inherit. Krista Glass is too naive to have looked closely into who I really am. She's too indifferent, probably, to even perform a Google search.

And she's fucking late to meet me.

I rub my forehead, feeling the telltale vein throbbing in response to my seething anger.

Catching her with that moron, kissing what's mine, almost made me internally combust.

However, that won't do.

I need her.

And that big imbecile biker will not stand in my way. Or I will have him removed from the picture.

Running my palm over my tie, I tap my other fingers on the stained wooden Starbucks table, a step above similar coffee houses.

Plush couches face a large fireplace, where flames burn brightly. Normally, it would be shut off in the first week of June, but abnormally cold weather has been with us the entire week.

A bell jingles, and Krista walks through the door, wearing the same ratty trendy jeans from this morning. She has on a different shirt, I see.

Pondering that, I stand.

She meets me. "Sorry I'm late."

Bitch.

I smile down at her. "Don't worry about it, Krista." What I'd really like is to throttle her. Eyeing her slim neck, I envision my hands around it…squeezing.

Her eyes guiltily skate away, and I'm reminded, on a physical level, I could do worse.

Plus, I love her tight cunt.

"It's this damn new job. I only have three students, but the allotment per is an entire ninety minutes. I had to come up with teaching material and a plan on the drop…" She reaches up, tightening her hair knot.

I glance at it.

All of that will change once we're married. Allen Fitzgerald does not abide top-knot coiffing. My eyes run to her legs as she sits at the chair opposite me. Her jeans have more holes than fabric.

My eyes sharpen on her face. "I interrupted something disturbing today."

Krista knots her hands together, probably to stop the fidgeting.

I continue my unflinching gaze on her face.

"Yes." She shoves a loose strand of hair behind her ear. "One of my students has developed a crush on me, I think."

A deep flush creeps up her face, coloring her high cheekbones a light pink.

She's lying.

I am an expert liar, and I can spot a non-truth a mile away.

It's more than that biker having a crush on her. Krista hasn't perfected the art of a blank face or feigning indifference with any degree of proficiency.

Casually, I lean back against the seat of the chair and loosen my tie. Then I fling my arm along the seat back. I appear comfortable, but because I'm six feet two, my limbs are equal length and there's simply insufficient room to balance that arm.

I leave it where it lies, feigning a casualness that is opposite of the internal war that rages.

"The interlude seemed more two-sided from where I stood."

Krista looks down, putting her clenched hands in her lap. "I didn't come here to talk about my job, my students, or anything like that." Her eyes rise to meet mine.

I know what she'll say before she's said it, and my body reacts in a physical way. The rage mixes with embarrassment, causing nausea to surge in an acidic geyser in my gut.

"It's about us, Allen."

Of course it is. I say nothing, silently wanting to kill her as I plunge my dick in her body. Finally, I say, "Oh?" The acid in my stomach burns, but I keep that fucking smile affixed like my life depends on it.

It doesn't. Hers does, though. Krista Glass will never know how close she comes to dying.

"I've been thinking."

She doesn't think. I do all of that for both of us.

"We've grown apart in the last month or two, and…" The little bitch musters courage at this part. "I want to take a break."

Nobody breaks from a Fitzgerald. No one.

I lean forward, taking her hands in mine. "I understand."

Her dark eyebrows jerk high. "You do?"

"Oh, yes." I give her hands a light squeeze before falling back against the chair again. "I know how much I've pressed you lately."

"Yes." Guilt flashes across her eyes again.

It must be that moron she was bunny humping against her crappy little car this morning.

Pouring on the charm, I continue, "It's just—you know how much I love you, Krista." I duck my head, pretending as though it's a painful admission, when really, I'm hiding my eyes before the lie.

She nods. "You've told me. And you're a gorgeous guy, Allen. You're smart. You say all the right things."

My smile hurts my face, though I glow underneath the flattery of her words.

Then what is the fucking problem?

We are clearly on the same page. She sees how perfect I am.

I frown.

"But I need more."

You'll get more, you stupid bitch. Stick around until the money comes in, then you can teach all the imbecilic children you want to.

She'll learn a few things about obedience too.

Traveling her fragile neck, my eyes leave the fingerprints of my intent behind.

Krista Glass has no idea how careful I've been with her.

Just ask all the dead whores I've gone too far with, or Abbi, my personal assistant and so many others. Those messes took some extreme measures to tidy up.

I look down, schooling my expression.

"What more could you need, Krista?" I ask softly, behaving like the wounded suitor, when all I yearn to do is reach across the table and choke her until her face blooms like a plum.

Beads of sweat spring to life on my upper lip.

"There needs to be chemistry." Krista waves her palm between us. "That indefinable something that tells me we can't be apart."

"That soul connection?" I arch my brow. "Is that what you're talking about?"

Krista gives a small shrug. "Probably."

"It's a fable." I lift my chin, looking down my nose at her as I shut the notion down hard.

She takes a fortifying breath, and I check out her fine tits. "And there's the issue of our sex life."

My jaw jerks back. *Keep it together, Fitzgerald,* my mind commands.

My hands become fists, flex apart, then fist again.

"What issue?" I manage between my teeth.

Krista meets my eyes. "You don't seem to care about what I need. It's all about you getting what you want, and not caring about my pleasure," she finishes on a whisper.

Of course I fuck her and get off. I restrain the urge to roll my eyes. *She has* got *to be kidding.* I'm not going down on any woman. I don't care if she ever has an orgasm.

Krista Glass, like all women, is a sperm depository. There's not a simpler truth.

"I didn't realize you felt that way."

Now Krista looks slightly irritated. "I've said what I need before."

"Not in such precise terms."

She slaps the table, clearly losing patience. "Allen, you're a grown man, and almost six years older than me. I should not have to give you a blueprint of what a woman likes in bed."

Several people pause their conversations to stare at us.

Heat suffuses my face, which I know manifests as a blotchy, unattractive ruddy color on my neck and face.

My hands ache to strangle her.

"I'm sorry," Krista says, looking around at the keen observers in this public place, where she basically just told me I don't know how to fuck.

Aloud.

"I shouldn't have said that."

She's right—she shouldn't have.

I stand, and she does too. Walking toward the door I know Krista will follow me.

It's time for some prime manipulation. The effort hurts my already-battered ego. After opening the door for her, I follow her out.

We stand, staring at each other. "Give me another chance to show you what I can do, Krista. We've been dating for almost two years, since Samantha introduced us." I tack that last part on to sway her.

Krista closes her eyes.

I lick my lips, forcing my fingers apart and to lie loosely at my sides.

She opens them. "I want to, Allen, so much—but I think there's too much between us to try again."

Krista turns and walks away to her car.

She believes it's over.

But it's only begun.

12

KRISTA

I close the car door then slap the lock. Knitting my hands together, I pin them to my lap then bend over to rest my forehead on the steering wheel.

I believe I escaped something awful.

Where is the relief I should feel?

My heartbeat's erratic, my mouth is dry, and my palms are damp. Telling Allen he wasn't meeting my needs in bed is so true. He says everything he ought to say, all the right things.

But there's this small part of me that feels like he just says what he thinks he's *supposed* to, not what he really means. I can't shake the gut feeling.

Shivering, I remember his eyes on me, like pools of ice skimming a lake. When I first met Allen through Sam, I thought he was the most handsome man I'd ever seen, with golden-blond hair and azure eyes the color of the Caribbean Sea I'd never visited. He has a strong jawline and a tall, athletic build. He's smooth with words, articulate, and apparently sincere.

Because I was so excited to be on the arm of a man like that, I didn't see his flaws right away. Then as I got to know him, his true colors would show up in unguarded moments. He was critical and judgmental, and he always thought about himself first.

That was never more apparent than when we were in bed together. My God, he didn't even get me ready. He just used lube and pushed his way inside. He told me to get on the pill because he wasn't going to wear a rubber.

When he wanted it from behind, he ordered me to get on my hands and knees.

Like a dog.

There was never that sense of intimacy or connection.

The couple of times I asked for him to do something a certain way, so there would be a remote chance of me having an orgasm, Allen said he would take care of it.

He never did.

My vibrator was the only relief I got. I swear I went through two Costco packs of double-A batteries.

His flaws piled up, and our relationship sparkled less as time wore on. The lavish parties he attended with people not from his work, his dad's mansion, his wonderful, designer clothes—they made me start to wonder... who *is* Allen Fitzgerald, exactly?

I became more distant, and Allen began to sense my slow withdrawal. Somehow. The last time we were in bed together, I knew our relationship was over.

He was rough—too rough—like he wanted to fuck me into staying. The sex seemed desperate.

Painful.

I was dry, and he didn't care. Allen pounded when I said it hurt.

My vagina felt abused for two days afterward.

I didn't tell Sam what had truly ended it emotionally for me. I was too ashamed.

But why don't I feel proud now? Now that I've terminated an unsatisfying relationship?

Allen seemed hurt—that's why.

I lean back in the driver's seat and take a sharp, sucking inhale. Letting it out slowly, I grip the steering wheel with both hands.

Well, he hurt me too.

And that's the bottom line. Treating people like you don't care too many times makes them stop caring too.

So I did. Allen says he loves me, but his chilly eyes don't agree with his words.

Then there's Trainer.

I groan out loud.

Trainer did for me in one hour what Allen couldn't do in nearly two years of dating: shared glances, hand holding, sex, eating together, socializing…

I wasted all that time on Allen, time I can't get back, in hopes that Allen had potential.

Trainer has more potential in his pinky finger, though.

My pussy gives a little sore pulse of agreement, and a giggle escapes me. The idea is so juvenile but true. Trainer has a monster-sized penis. When I saw that thing coming for me, my heart just about stopped.

But the look in his eyes told me I had to trust him.

I couldn't let this fragile connection that had started between us be snuffed out because of my fear of death by cock.

Another bursting laugh flies out of me. *God, I need help.*

I sober up when I realize that despite all his bad-guy attitude and manner, something deep down told me I could trust Trainer. He's not a predator. He's a protector.

So I welcomed him inside my body—and my heart.

I close my eyes again.

It'll be nothing shy of a miracle if I can finish what I set out to accomplish with him as a learner, which is how I think of my students.

But I don't know. The way he had held me after—until we were dangerously close to when Corina would appear—was every tender thing I'd never shared with Allen.

Then there's the simple fact that I sexed him in an elementary school, on a table. Completely unlike me.

"Out of character" doesn't cover what we did and *where*. How come I even took that risk?

I'm not sure I can be his teacher *and* lover.

I don't even know if I have a choice.

There are things I don't know about Trainer. And the scary part is that I'm not sure I care.

I wasn't planning on hurting Allen or having him run into me and Trainer dry humping against my car in the public parking lot.

I put my face in my hands and think about how I fucked things up.

On top of that, I remember how earth-shattering sex with Trainer was. It changed everything. I couldn't remain the same after what Trainer and I shared.

A rapping of knuckles on the glass startles me into making one of those annoying girl noises. I yank my eyes to the window. Even in the poorly lit parking lot, I can see who it is.

Trainer.

Frowning, I crack open the door. "What are you doing here?" I ask quietly then give an uneasy laugh, adding, "You scared the shit out of me."

His crooked smile melts me on the spot. "Heard you tell Allen you were meeting him here."

That's right.

"Had work to do for the club, thought I'd come by after and see that you were okay."

My brows pinch together. *Of course I'm okay.* "I'm fine."

We sort of stare. The silence isn't exactly comfortable, but it's not bad, either. I think Trainer's just not a huge talker. Even if he was born that way, it wouldn't have lasted long with his family life.

Trainer's eyes search the parking lot restlessly. They find me again.

"Ya still wanna be with me?"

Oh yes.

The crystalline green of his irises pierces the night like emerald shadows.

That's the Trainer I'm beginning to know. No pretense. Just straight talk without inhibition or filters.

"Yes," I answer softly, heart in my throat.

His smile is as luminous as his eyes. Radiant.

Trainer opens my door the rest of the way. "Get out."

Okay. I slip out of my car, reaching for my small clutch purse and turn.

He shuts the door and tows me into his body. "I was worried, Krista."

I pull away slightly. "Worried?"

"Yeah. Don't like Allen." His serious eyes search my face. I can see why he doesn't like me seeing Allen since Trainer and I sort of made us "official" with the christening of my teacher's table.

"Not that," Trainer says intuitively, eyes still everywhere. "He reminds me of somebody...somebody bad."

I don't know how to respond to that. Allen made me uneasy too—especially tonight—even though he didn't say one wrong thing.

And maybe that's why it's so noteworthy. Allen should have been pissed, sad, or something. But he just wore this expression of resignation—like a mask. He was neutral. Too indifferent. Too pleasant. Pleasantly creepy.

"We're through," I announce.

Trainer stares into my eyes for another intense moment then dips his chin in a decisive nod. "Good." He pauses for a second then asks, "Wanna go for a ride?"

Huh? Oh. I find his bike only two spots away from the Fiat, sitting there like a dangerous metal bullet. It's engine is still ticking from cooling off.

Why not? Slowly, I nod.

For now, I feel as though I'm waking from a deep sleep, like I was dreaming during Allen and I'm waking up to Trainer.

His smile is back. I can make it out in the discs of light thrown by the streetlamps.

Trainer takes my hand and tugs me toward the waiting bike.

"So I'm gonna give you the five-second lesson."

Oh? My lips twitch. "Five-second lesson?"

Trainer gives a solemn nod. "Take a lot of shit for wearing a helmet, but my mama made me promise to wear one. I don't break no promises."

"I don't break any, either," I agree.

Trainer leans forward and kisses my forehead. "I like that about you too, Krista."

He cups the mound of my pussy, and my breath sucks in with a hiss.

Holy *shit*.

"And this." His thumb cleaves me between the thin folds of my fashionably ripped jeans, and my pussy gives a deep hiccupping pulse in instant response.

"Ah," I breathe as he watches my expression.

"Like that noise." He leans forward to kiss me deeply as his finger presses harder on my clit.

I don't care about lessons anymore. I just want to be taught by Trainer.

A total role reversal.

He breaks away. "Anyways…" His hand leaves my heat, and he turns, pulling a brand-new helmet from what he calls the trunk of the motorcycle. "I got one for ya." Fine sparkles throughout the deep-violet paint glitter underneath the streetlamp. "It's pretty."

"Safe," he says, though he ducks his head as if he's shy about the compliment I gave him.

"Yes, safe." I put it on and tighten the chin strap.

"When I do corners, you move your body with me. One body, one movement."

"Got it."

He continues, "When I stop, just rest against me. We're taking a short ride, out to Orting. Prez has a place up there I'm borrowing. Guys have scraped—uh…forget it." His hand rakes over his dark hair. A few strands refuse to lie down, and he flicks them back, re-tying the entire thing into a stubby ponytail at his nape. "I'll tell ya more when we land."

He gets on and turns his face so that half of his profile is lost to the night and shadow. Trainer nods.

I approach the bike and place a hand on his shoulder. Whipping my leg around, I seat myself snuggly behind him.

Thankfully, I forgot to take the pea coat that Allen returned out of my car, so I won't freeze during the ride.

Trainer hands me a hair tie.

With deft fingers, I quickly braid my nearly waist-length hair then tap his shoulder, signaling that I'm ready.

The bike starts with a roar, making me jump.

Trainer shifts slightly, and I put my hand to my heart with a little laugh.

He grins, turning back to the front of the bike. He'd backed into the parking slot, so all he has to do is take off.

But Trainer sits there for a moment. And I definitely get the feeling he's a still-waters-run-deep kind of guy. He's not reactive and thoughtless. Though I think if the right circumstances presented themselves, Trainer might react very decisively.

He takes my slightly chilled hands around his flat stomach and covers them in leather…and him.

My fingers have to be like ice, but he doesn't seem bothered.

Trainer warms them with his body as we speed off.

13

TRAINER

Feels good to finally have a lady on the back of my ride. A real one.

Not a sweet butt for the night, or one of a ton of club whores I can have. Krista's not like them.

She's got real class. She went to college to get that degree that lets her teach. Noose says she has a good family.

Dated that Allen prick. I scowl at the thought as the cold wind blasts the uncovered parts of my face that the helmet doesn't cover. I smile in the next moment—she dumped his lawyerly ass.

Maybe for me.

Not sure.

We'll sort shit out tonight. I want to fuck her again, and I figure we got the whole weekend. But better than that, I want to tell her about Arnie and the court shit. The reason why we even met.

Krista's gotta know who she's with. I'm not a classy, slick guy who can bring her home to meet my parents.

Mama is a whore.

My dad was some dude who probably doesn't even know I exist. At least, he split before I was outta my high chair.

I work as a mechanic for the club. They don't care that I can't read. And the place before that didn't care, neither. But most jobs are gonna care. A lot.

As near as I can figure, I don't have much to offer a lady.

But the brothers have put some cash in the kitty to build me a small house in the foothills of the Cascade Range. Not too far from where Wring, Snare and Lariat live. It's not much, but it'll be mine.

I got money—plenty of money—but it's wrapped up for this court thing that might happen. So I gotta save the cash, just in case.

The brothers are fronting me. I pay them back when I can.

It'll be good to permanently get outta the dump of an apartment I was living in. Vipe's been good to let me stay at his cabin digs out here, but…I wanna start fresh. Have my own spot.

Rolling up the long, gravel road, I slow down to keep the dust from flying up. It's been rainy the last week, so the dirt's not up. Don't want Krista sucking grit.

The headlamp illuminates the ribbon of green grass that bisects the driveway as it climbs the quarter mile to the Prez's small cabin.

How many fucking Sundays did I ride up here and mow the grass? With a small shake of my head, I answer my own question: too many.

Now grass duty belongs to Storm and whatever guy's dumb enough to sign on. Course, Road Kill MC took some getting into. Being a prospect for eighteen long months was torture. But I can't think of where I'd be without them.

Probably nowhere.

Carefully, I maneuver around an island of plants, carefully laid river stone, and a thick-trunked, towering evergreen tree. "Probably been there since the cabin got built back around 1900," Viper said.

Wish I could have a place just like this. Don't need much. It's got a bedroom, a bathroom, and a large area with a couch and a fireplace.

Kitchen's in there somewhere too.

Feel the crooked smile on my face—simple is good.

I park in front of the ancient wooden steps and look up. Pine needles shaken loose by the light breeze fall like rain all around the bike, smelling vaguely like fresh-cut wood. New growth isn't visible because in June, all the new stuff is just coming on.

Old stuff sloughs off when the wind kicks up. No sounds. Just the tick, tick, tick of the engine, still hot from the ride.

"Wow," Krista says from behind me, inhaling deeply, then releases her breath on a sigh.

I hike up on my pegs, half-standing, and give her room to dismount. Krista sorta awkwardly falls off, catching herself on my shoulder. Laughs. I've never been with another girl whose laughter makes me think of music. Or crystal tinkling. Or some other awesome shit.

Flicking my foot forward, I swing the kickstand out and settle the ride. Dismounting gingerly, I watch Krista.

She spins slowly, trying to see everything, though it's so damn dark, I doubt she's having any luck. The breeze continues, lifting all the fine hairs that came outta her braid during the ride.

A rare clear night reveals stars above us. I gaze upward, enjoying the solitude. It's just me and nature.

And Krista.

"Is this your place?"

"For now," I say, looking away.

"Hey," she calls softly, and I turn, watching her walk back from inspecting the house. "I love it. Doesn't have to be yours for me to love it."

Then Krista moves my legs apart with her hips where I lean against the bike, pushing her way between them. "I'm sorry, Trainer."

I wrap an arm around her and tilt my head, eyeing her up. "What for?"

"I want to teach you. I'm meant to. But I also want to explore what this is between us."

I nod, think of a joke, and feel so great about coming up with it that I can barely hold it in. "It's my cock, right?" I ask slowly, making the words crisp.

Krista bursts out laughing, small hands flying to her chest. "Well, it's not a bad thing!"

I draw her to my body, loving the way my words made her eyes twinkle. "Nope, like using it in ya."

I feel Krista's smile against my chest.

"That makes two of us."

She snuggles her face in deeper, and we stand there for a minute. Then I ask, "Ya cold?"

"No." She shakes her head at me, only my heartbeats between us.

"Wanna go inside and talk?"

Krista leans back, studying my face for a sec. "Among other things."

I feel a slow smile spread across my face. Hot *damn.*

I press the strange push-button-style light switch with my index finger, and with a snapping sound, a center ceiling fixture bursts to life. It illuminates the space, leaking light into the cramped kitchen.

"This is so cute!" Krista says, walking to the large river-rock fireplace that spans nearly the entire wall, leaving only a door at the end, leading to the single bedroom.

"Local rock, I guess," I say, remembering Vipe telling me that his great-grandparents built this place by hand. Hauled the rock to make the hearth and surrounding fireplace.

People worked in those days. For every piece of their lives. The puzzle of their existence wasn't put together without sweat and tears.

Krista's palm runs along the polished stones in various colors of tan and gray. Some of the rock is black and jagged, giving the hearth a rough texture.

Never paid a lot of attention to stuff in here. It was comfortable, neat, and met my needs. Seeing it through Krista's eyes is interesting.

"You said something about your friends helping you out with building something?" Krista asks, turning to study me.

My eyes sharpen on her. "You don't forget much."

Krista shakes her head. "No. The important things stay like barnacles on my ass." Her lips curl.

I chuckle. "You're funny too. I got lucky, Krista. Meeting ya."

She turns, resting a hand on part of the hewn old-growth log that is now a mantle for the massive fireplace. Viper said the tree was felled to build the house and that piece was probably just a sliver of the original. Every piece of wood used in the cabin's construction came from just the one tree.

Hard to believe.

"Not as lucky as me, Trainer."

Krista's words bring me back to now. I need to get the rest off my chest. *Now or never.* I study my boots. "So, I gotta tell ya something."

Krista glides to where I stand. "Do I need to sit down?" she asks with a little laugh, obviously trying to make the moment less serious. Her gray eyes seem deep with only the center ceiling light to illuminate them.

My eyes hold hers. "Maybe."

We walk to the couch and sit down. "So the reason I gotta take this reading thing with you is because I might have court come up soon."

Krista's dark-brown eyebrows pull together. "This is a first time thing for me too, Trainer. I mean…" She whips the tail of her messy braid behind her back. "I've only taught early elementary before now, and the details of your past, and that of Dwayne and Corina, have been purposely kept from me. I just know I *need* to teach." She takes my hand, and I fold it inside mine.

Actually, her hands are so small, it's a joke—her holding my hand. I turn her hand over and cover it with my own.

"You don't have to tell me anything, Trainer. I feel like I do about you just because."

She smiles, and that wonderful look of happy climbs right up to her eyes.

"Just because."

My inhale is harsh. "Gotta come clean, Krista."

She squeezes my hand. "Okay."

"So there was a hot chick in a bar…"

Krista's brow rises in a delicate arch.

Yeah. Better rip off the Band-Aid. "And we were gonna hook up."

The other eyebrow rises, joining the first.

Shit. I rake my hand through my hair, tearing out the hairband thing and snapping it. "Anyways, long story short, I tore into three guys in the parking lot that were making her do a bad thing." I look up again, and Krista has a soft look to her face. "Somethin' she wasn't wantin'," I add.

Krista squeezes my hand. "Go on."

"So I hurt 'em pretty good. Next thing I know, about a year later, they start talking about how the lady was willing."

Krista cocks her head, giving me a look I can't figure. "Was she?"

"Fuck no!" I explode off the couch, breaking our hands apart. I stalk to the window, place my forearm against the wood that wraps the glass, and stare into the black canvas of night. "She wasn't wanting it, Krista. I can't take that. Love the ladies, but only when they love me back. That's how it should always be." I grind out each word. Just thinking about those fuckers makes me pissed off all over again.

I hear Krista steal up behind me before her perfect embrace comes around my waist, and I cover her hands with mine. "Hey, Trainer, I believe you."

Turning, I look down at her, grasping her forearms. "Ya do?"

Krista nods. "You're that kind of man." Her eyes run over my expression, and whatever she sees there causes her to nod. "The kind of guy who'd hurt someone if they harmed someone who was defenseless."

Or kill them. I open my mouth to confess about Arnold Sulk.

Then snap it shut.

Can't. Too many truths, too fast.

Instead, I say what I can. "The courts think it looks good for people like me to try to improve themselves." I lift a shoulder then wrap my arm around her shoulders, pulling her in close. We practically touch noses. "So me coming to you for learnin' reading was for that." I touch her face, feathering my thumb along her jaw. I add slowly, "Me being with you is for somethin' completely different."

"Oh?" Krista replies, her hand cupping the side of my face. "What reason?"

Love, I figure.

But I can't say that. I'm falling hard for this lady. Like I waited my whole life for this moment, the only moment that mattered.

Here. Right now.

With Krista.

Instead of pressing me for the answer that's on the tip of my tongue, Krista grabs my shirt and pulls me closer.

Our lips meet, and I use my other arm to set her against me as hard as two people can be and not be one.

With a hop, Krista wraps her legs around my waist, and my hands latch onto her lush ass.

Boner goes full tilt.

"So much for talkin'," I say, moving toward the small bedroom.

Krista is already biting and kissing my neck, driving me insane. She shoots me a sly smile.

"We've done enough talking for now."

I look down at her, pausing in the open doorway, the ancient nightlights sputtering their shitty glow just well enough to see her face. "It's my cock, right?"

I ask it lightly.

Krista nods. "Oh yes. It is." Taking her bottom lip between her teeth, she grins too hard to do it right.

Then she straightens inside my palms, making herself taller, and kisses me deeply.

Hot. *Wet*. Full. I gently spread her beneath me on the bed, admiring how right she looks. How right she feels.

Krista sighs.

It's the melody I've been waiting to hear.

The tune of desire.

14

KRISTA

I arch off the bed as Trainer does the thing with his tongue down low, taking a long, wet pull down one side of my labia. In the next moment, he works himself up the other one.

Again and again. Pausing only to flick his tongue on the bundle of sensitive nerves in the center.

Gripping the bed linen between my fingers, I pant, heart racing. *Coming,* I have time to think and buck my hips hard.

Trainer holds me still with a forearm as I yell an orgasm that sounds painful.

It's not.

I've just never been with a man who wants to pleasure a woman like he takes his next breath.

His face pops up from between my legs, and he's licking my juices from his lips.

Our gazes lock for a moment, and I give an exhausted little laugh.

Climbing up my body, Trainer plants his forearms at either side of my face, using his hands to press all the loose hairs against my temples that had been scattered by my flailing.

"You made me come about four times," I say in a semi-dazed voice.

Trainer nods. "Like it." He kisses my lips softly.

A lazy smile lifts the corners of my mouth. "Yeah, you do." Sliding my hand between us, I grab hold of his mammoth penis.

His breath catches, and it's my turn to watch Trainer's expression go hard with lust, where it was soft on me before.

"Krista," he grinds out between his teeth.

I'm so evil. "Yes," I whisper, nipping at his bottom lip like a she-demon.

"I…" His head dips, and he rests his chin on my chest. "I gotta…"

I push him over, momentarily letting go of his hard length, and Trainer rolls over on his back, looking up at me with eyes gone liquid with desire, colorless in the gloom lit only by weak nightlights.

I don't ask permission or give much thought. Bending over Trainer, I wrap my fingers around the base of him and bring the tip of him to my lips. After licking him, I plunge downward.

He groans, grabbing the back of my head.

Uncertain, I pause.

"Please," he says. Wetting my lips again, I slide down the length of his cock again as far as I can without gagging, which is barely a third of the way. Tightening the seal of my lips, I draw back up him, smacking hard at his tip.

His large hand guides me back.

Establishing a rhythm, I add my hand where my mouth can't go and work up and down, glossing my hand with spit to make it smooth.

I know Trainer's mine when his body stiffens.

"Gonna come," he whispers, dropping his hands to fists at his sides.

Lots of women have probably done this for him. Trainer's obviously experienced.

But I bet not many of them have stayed where they were for my reasons.

His big cock grows impossibly harder, and a subtle vibration lets me know seconds before it happens.

Hot come shoots from the tip of him, filling my mouth, and I swallow it—more like choking and gasping for air.

I get every drop. Savoring him down.

When everything's gone, I lay his spent penis gently down, and he half rolls over on me, big hands caging my face.

"Whadya do that for, Krista? I don't need nothin'."

I search his eyes in the gloom. "You give me so much pleasure, Trainer, it seemed only natural to give some back." I cup his jaw, feeling the rough texture of day-old stubble peppering his strong jaw. "I wanted to," I add in a voice barely above a whisper.

He leans close. His kiss is soft, like breath and warm air above my lips. I smell me and him mingled in that gentle press of flesh.

Trainer laughs, and I raise an eyebrow.

"Don't think I can finish you off again."

His palm sweeps toward his crotch. His penis soft after what I did.

"Was that even a possibility?" I laugh.

His face goes solemn.

Taking his hand, I do what Trainer did to me the other day: I kiss the middle of his palm. "*This* is better than sex for me."

"Really?" he asks in disbelief.

I nod. "I've never…" Stopping, I think about my words then start again. "Having sex isn't always about a man putting his penis in a woman. Sometimes, it's sharing each other's' bodies and exchanging pleasure. That makes it 'real' sex, right?"

Trainer stares, trailing a finger down between my naked breasts. "Felt good to me."

His smile is shy, and I capture his finger. "And it might also have something to do with the fact that no man has ever, ever, done the things you do to me." I feel the blush, but bravely hold his eyes through the shy feeling, adding, "For me."

The amber light from an old nightlight partly illuminates his face, and I swear I can make out his answering blush.

Trainer begins to pull away, and I haul him closer by the finger I grabbed.

He could get away if he wanted. Instead, he gives me that bashful, wounded gaze I caught a glimpse of only last week.

"Ya sure, Krista?"

Placing my face against his hand, I whisper, "Oh yeah, *so* sure."

We lie together, legs and arms entwined, for a long time after that.

Intimate.

Just in the way I always wanted, and thought I could never have.

TRAINER

My lady fell asleep inside the curve of my body.

Makes my chest feel liquid hot to watch her sleep. Not like the sweet butts. I knew what I was to them.

They didn't want to sleep with me, and I didn't want to sleep with them.

I wanted to sleep with a lady who'd want me. Sleeping's different than fucking.

Giving a hard swallow, I allow myself to think the forbidden wish I'd never let myself hope for:

Having a lady for forever.

I been wanting a woman of my own since I could think it up. Not a whore like my mama, but a lady. A girl who would be mine. Only mine.

Deep down, I always knew I was too dumb to deserve it.

Searching Krista's face as she sleeps, I can't see the shit I see in so many people's faces.

Deceit.

How is it that Krista escaped the lessons of lying everybody else learns so good?

A single hair crossing the bridge of her nose lifts with each exhale, and I pluck it from her face, gently adding it to the rest of her dark, soft hair that cascades across my pillow like a fan of exotic silk.

Darkness spills like grease into my thoughts, coating them with questions.

What if Krista finds out about Arnie?

It's a sealed case, Judge told me. *"Nobody knows because you were a minor."*

So why doesn't that fact make me feel better? Krista isn't the kind of girl to blow off a murder. And Arnie wasn't dead after a single blow from that ashtray. I came back and did it as many times as it took to finish what needed doin'.

Until the little bit of brains the fucker had washed up on the rank carpet like the tide from a gray ocean.

Watching Krista, I can't help thinking that I'd do it again. Kill a dozen more Arnies.

Judge is right. I have a taste for killin' now. Not just anybody. The right somebodies.

Krista groans in her sleep. Shifting to her side, she buries her face against my chest, and my throat constricts with emotion.

Trainer doesn't cry.

And the kid who was Brett Rife knew better.

Why would the urge come over me now, when my life has a glimmer of hope? Of being happy for fucking once.

Then it comes to me: *Because I didn't think it'd ever happen.*

I was hopeless.

Then I found Krista.

KRISTA

Rolling over, I find myself not in my own bed, but next to a warm body.

Eyelids springing open, I meet Trainer's slitted gaze. His translucent green eyes seem to glow like a cat's in the pale morning light seeping around the edges of a filmy drape that hangs from the single window.

"Hey," I say.

Trainer grins, not saying a word.

"My, aren't you the cat that ate the canary?"

He frowns at the expression, and I want to kick myself. "I mean…" I stammer, slightly flustered. "You look satisfied."

Trainer nods. "I am." Upon closer inspection, I see that his eyes are slightly bloodshot. Frowning, I ask, "You didn't sleep well?"

He shakes his head. "Nope. Too busy watching my lady."

"Oooh…" I flutter my eyelashes at him. "I love the way you say that."

Trainer kisses the tip of my nose, and I suddenly think I need to get my ass in a bathroom and brush my teeth, take a pee—*ick*. "I'm going to use the bathroom." I draw away, not wanting to contaminate the moment with all my morning goodness.

Trainer lies back down, palm to chest and the other hand tucked behind his head. "Sure. Have at it all. Got a extra toothbrush in there too. Club prospects stock extra toiletries."

"Oh." I don't know what he means exactly, but I'm super happy for a potential toothbrush.

And the possibility of a shower. Like now.

Padding across the living room, I take in the spartan space, which looks like an antique bachelor's pad.

Clicking on the light for the bathroom, I'm guessing it was put in when indoor plumbing came to the area.

Like in 1930.

Wow, the fixtures are museum-worthy. The pedestal sink with chrome-covered solid brass taps is complete with a steady drip, drip into the basin.

I check out the shower, and it's tiny, with only glass block and a small opening to slide into what looks like a porcelain enamel basin.

The toilet is no different. The tank is huge and wall hung, separated from the bowl by an elephant-trunk pipe for refilling.

I smirk at the archaic thing. Bet that's not a one-point-six gallon flush.

Turning on the shower faucet to hot, I get to brushing my teeth. Checking myself out in the mirror, I decide I don't look too bad. I laugh. *No, Krista, just put away wet.*

Shutting the door to the bathroom, I spit then rinse and repeat. When the water is finally steaming, I step into the shower. Using a neutral-smelling shampoo and soap sitting on a built-in tile shelf, I wash up my finely used parts, twice.

I know that they want to be used again. My pussy gives a happy little anticipatory pulse at just the thought.

Soft rapping comes at the door when I've just wrapped my hair in a worn towel.

I open it.

Trainer stands there naked, arms crossed against a muscular chest as he leans against the jamb. "Feelin' better now?"

I should say so, but I'm silent. Instead, I swing the door wide, letting the towel covering my body drop to the floor.

Apparently, Trainer's not worried about morning anything.

Scooping me against him, he swings me into his arms. "Do I need to shower too?"

Heart speeding, I shake my head. "No," my voice sounds like a thread.

"Good." Trainer doesn't hesitate, going straight for the bedroom.

"I guess we can't do this *all* day," Trainer says. "Gotta get some fuel eventually."

Running my hand over a stomach like flat muscled cobblestones, I reply with a question in my voice, "Looks like you're pretty cut. Do you eat a lot?" My eyebrow quirks.

"Cut?" Trainer shakes his head, his face doing an *ah-huh* moment. "Don't do gym time. Eat a lotta food, though." He smacks his hard belly.

He's so lean. Not skinny like some men who are naturally that way. Trainer's got broad shoulders like a swimmer, an eight pack, and heavily muscled arms.

I'm not much for exercise and I consider hearing about others doing it my vicarious exercise. *Probably doesn't qualify*, I guess.

"A lot," he says with a smirk, and heat whips across my face.

He went after my pussy again, first with his mouth, then with his cock.

"Yeah," I say softly, "maybe have to take a day's break."

Trainer stares into my eyes, that fleeting vulnerability making a showing again in his green gaze. "Did I hurt you?"

I shake my head. "No, but you're built big, and"—my eyes move away then back to him—"I love how you feel inside me, stretching me."

God do I. Rolling my bottom lip between my teeth, I let it pop back out. I shouldn't tell him. Then I do. "I love how big your dick is."

"As long as you don't think I am one."

Covering his lips with my hand, I say, "I'd never think that. But I'm afraid I have to prove the cliché correct: size *does* matter."

Trainer laughs. "You said you don't need…" He pauses.

"Penetration," I insert.

"Yeah."

My smile feels bright on my face, like I captured a star of happiness. "With you. No. I don't need it."

I take Trainer's hands and cup them against my heart. "But I love it."

Trainer gathers me against him for the second time in a day.

When we finally eat, it's later than ever.

Because there were more important things to do than food.

15

ALLEN

He *will* die.

The old coot who spawned me—who's decided to withhold my rightful inheritance because I haven't married a sniveling, do-gooder, bleeding heart, tree-hugging cunt like Krista Glass—will eventually succumb to age.

Yet, for now, my ass-kissing days are not behind me.

I raise the brandy snifter, filled with a perfectly delicious sacrilegious cider beer with a bright, crisp taste, and stare at my wretched father over the fine crystal rim.

"Cheers," I say without enthusiasm.

"Allen," Orson Rothschild begins with a tone of voice I abhor, "if you were to partake of the beverage that server was intended to hold, you would sound merrier."

Father's smirk is the same, pushed into a surgery-enhanced face.

He considers himself a Hugh Hefner lookalike and dresses in velvet and expensive lounge sets. He's smoking a horrible pipe in the lavish drawing room where we meet.

After having called me like a dog to heel to quiz me about who I've decided to permanently tolerate.

Jesus.

I turn away from my father's penetrating stare, hiding my sourness, and stare at the lushness of Lake Washington. The mansion's many windows face the sparkling depths.

Father lives in Medina, an expensive neighborhood that houses the rich of Washington state. Though Bill Gates could arguably be among the richest of the world, he resides here, as well.

Today is gray, like many days in the Pacific Northwest, and though rain doesn't fall, the outdoors are pregnant with the potential.

I take another sip, staring at the waves, painted an angry gray to match the sky—and my mood.

"So how is lawyering?" Father asks casually.

I know from raw experience that he is the least casual person of my acquaintance.

"The same. Tedium."

"I see."

I give him a sharp look, thinking that if I have to slice and dice my face to remain youthful forever, as my father has, I might as well die now and get it over with.

"And your marital prospects?"

My exhale is hate on breath. "I'm working on that." I lean forward, letting the crystal snifter dangle between my semi-slack fingers, dangerously close to empty.

I'd need ten of these to numb me before my father's scrutiny. The old fucker is consistent, I'll give him that.

"I'm desperate for grandchildren, you know."

"Yes." I don't look at him.

"Allen, look at me."

My eyes rise reluctantly, finding a shade exactly like my own. Bastard.

"Your mother and I…" Orson spreads his hands.

"She's not my mother, as you damn well know." Heat suffuses my face.

Orson nods. "True, however she does stand in her stead."

My birth mother died due to a rare complication when I was born. There's been a precession of blonds with perfect teeth, tits, and tight asses since.

Because Orson Rothschild was not picky about anything else. He had a wife, and he didn't take another until last year.

The bitch was my age and hopelessly stupid, like the others.

"I liked the potential surrounding the young teacher." Orson taps his chin.

He should like her, he originally brought her to my attention then encouraged Samantha Brunner to make the introduction.

"Kristin?"

I hate him, and a simmering loathing threatens to boil over. Like his puppet, I swam to the bait like a hungry fish.

He absolutely remembers Krista and his own involvement, but he also enjoys his theatrics.

No one else does.

"Krista Glass," I bite out. Hell, he practically chose her.

Orson snaps his finger. "Ah yes, fine girl. A girl from a very different family, circumstance, and social circle than our own." His smile is secretive, as though something only he is privy to amuses him.

Orson's smile makes me think, *Shark.*

Wouldn't he love to know I've fucked every girlfriend he ever had? Some weren't so willing.

I fucked them anyway. I wanted Daddy Dearest to have my sloppy seconds. The slut girlfriends were always too scared to tell Orson Rothschild he had a rapist for a son. It'd be my word against theirs. And how could a fifteen-year-old boy act on those impulses, surely?

Easily, as it turned out.

A flutter of adrenaline beats through my veins, and dissipates just as quickly as it came.

It's the quiet defiance that keeps me going. The little *fuck yous* I sprinkle about like fairy dust allow me to survive these cock-tug soirees. If it weren't for all the small deviant acts I committed behind my father's back, I never would've lasted without killing him. *But then I wouldn't have the money…*

I lift a shoulder, smoothly entering back into the game. "She's had a change within the parameters of her teaching. We've not moved forward because she's busy."

Actually, the little bitch just cut me off with a "let's be friends" line, as though I'm a cartoon character she no longer wants to look at.

Orson's eyes, so like my own, glitter like the tropical seas I've visited since I was a boy. I've been everywhere on my father's expansive yacht.

All the sights that allure most leave me cold. I will marry Krista Glass, chuck her overboard, and entertain female harems with my father's billions.

After she's birthed a few children, of course. A fleet of nanny's can take care of the brats while I have my fun.

"Allen?"

I jerk my face toward the sound of Orson's voice.

He must have said something, but I missed it while scheming my future. That pastime has, of late, consumed my thoughts.

"Apologies, I was a million miles away."

"Yes, you were." Orson clears his throat. "In an effort to protect my assets"—his eyes pierce me, seeming to look directly into my treacherous, black heart—"and you are my most precious."

I maintain a straight face by imagining losing this elusive fortune and am pleased to discover how well that mental imagery works.

Orson continues, "I have contracted my team to investigate Miss Glass thoroughly."

Rage and defeat sing through me like the thrill of adrenaline did just moments before. But this—Orson digging around Krista's background—is the final insult.

I move to stand, and he throws up a palm. "She is the perfect choice. I don't want another girl."

"Why can't I marry one of the women from our own inner circle?" I beat the armrest, nearly slopping the remainder of my beer over the fine crystal rim of the snifter.

"That's not something I can divulge at this time, Allen. However, suffice it to say, when you have recouped your rightful inheritance, all will be brought to light. Or if need be, sooner."

Orson leans back, artfully tugging the heavy silk pantleg at the knee and crossing his legs. After setting his brandy on a nearby table, he steeples his fingers, staring unblinkingly at me.

How I despise him.

"What if Krista doesn't want to take the next step?"

Orson spreads his fingers. "That is not my issue. *Persuade* her."

For the first time, I see a glint to Orson's eyes as he emphasizes that word.

Right then, an epiphany strikes me—perhaps, the apple doesn't fall very far from the tree.

Who knew?

The documents are delivered by courier.

Inside are things about Krista Glass that even she might not know about herself.

Tapping out a message to my personal assistant, I chuckle. Oh, what monetary resources can provide. Excellent. My assistant answers immediately with the only response I require:

Yes, of course.

Reading the handwritten note from Orson for a third time, my eyes stutter over the message: *Use this information to woo, Allen. I do expect a degree of creativity.*

Her parents aren't really her parents. That's a biggie. And the tidbit about her "scholarship," that she supposedly earned…I snort.

There is no way in our current climate of diversity handouts that Krista Glass, Miss Caucasian, would be awarded the type of scholarship she enjoyed at the University of Washington. That is precisely what she and her pseudo parents have been led to believe, though.

I'm uncertain how this information helps me woo her. But if knowledge is power, then I can at least blackmail her into becoming my wife.

The third item, and the most puzzling, is what I hope to use, but don't know if it's significant to Krista.

A sex trafficking ring has their eye on the elementary school where she teaches.

In particular, they hope to acquire certain children from neglected and underprivileged environments.

Just the type of imbeciles Krista teaches.

Though her current students certainly do not belong in that particular category.

Brett Rife. Corina Style and Dwayne Carson: three morons, all illiterate adults. They have nothing in common except their stupidity, which is plenty for me.

However…

I type out an email, encrypt it, then press Send.

I will use my own expensive team to flesh out the character of those three.

The more you know. I hated that one big idiot on sight, for thinking he could have a woman far above his station. Brett Rife is nothing more than an animal posing as a man, probably employing every manipulating tactic because he's got the hots for teacher.

And Krista is far too soft to tell him she has me, a real man, who can actually provide something for her.

It's probably a dalliance, which will be easy to stop.

Permanently.

I shoot a predatory smile at my female assistant when she walks in.

Naked.

Orson hired her. She fucks on demand. As long as I don't come inside her honeypot, I can do what I want.

"Yes, Mr. Fitzgerald." Her voice only quakes a little.

I get a painful erection just hearing that small shiver of fear in her tone.

"Hands and knees."

Abbi turns, showing me her back. Faded bruises meet seamlessly with new.

I love my work.

I watch her rear end go up like an offering as she takes her hand, as I've instructed, and parts her pretty pink pussy lips.

In my haste to drop my pants, I almost trip. Finally, I manage to kick them off and drop to my knees directly behind her. I pull out the lube I carry in a small tube always in my front pocket. The shape and size mimic lip balm very closely.

After loading my cock with the slimy stuff, I stab myself inside, and Abbi bites her lip to keep from screaming, which is also a major turn on.

I pound her unmercifully, until her forehead touches the carpet of my luxury office, and she's mewling.

When I'm close to coming, I say hoarsely, "Turn."

Abbi knows the drill.

I tear out of her, my cock aching, and she rolls over and opens her mouth, tipping her head back.

I gag her with my prick, shooting my cum down her throat.

"Ah!" I yell into my office, grabbing her head and ramming it to the bottom of me, lips to base.

She doesn't fight.

Abbi knows where that leads.

"So good," I say, still pumping inside her wet mouth. Finally, I drag myself out from between her lips.

She stares at me, her disgust and disdain plain to see.

But we both know who that's for. Her.

Orson Rothschild pays her well to keep my demons at bay. God knows it was a challenge to not let them take over when I've been with Krista.

I smile down at Abbi. She's Krista's surrogate.

But the real thing is *this* close.

I can taste it.

"Get out," I tell Abbi.

She leaves, nervously licking the remnants of my cum off her lips, and I wait for my team's intel on Krista's current students.

16

TRAINER

I try not to stare at her.

Not really managing it.

Adjusting my cock, I steal another glance. She's back to dunking a salty fry in her shake.

We're at a diner because Krista says it's her favorite. Since she doesn't seem to ever lie, I took her at her word.

"You not gonna pretend to be on a diet and have a salad or somethin'?"

All girls are on diets. The sweet butts are always trading secrets about how to stay skinny.

"Hate green food."

No salad, I guess.

Krista laughs, dragging a soggy fry out of the shake, then slides it in a mouth that was on my dick an hour ago.

I try to shake the image but can't.

Can't hide my huge boner that well underneath the cheap cafe table, either.

"I'm not into exercise, really," Krista says.

Can't hold back my smile.

Krista's face turns red, and I know she's thinking about what we just did.

What we've been doing for a solid day.

She puts down the shake, and flipping both hands over, palms facing the ceiling, she leans forward and slides her hands toward me. My big hands engulf hers.

I lean forward too, until our faces are an inch apart.

"I love the exercise we do together," she admits in a hushed voice.

Me too. But I'm not sure I should say shit like that. Saying how I feel got me beat. Yelled at.

Told I was dumb.

The shit I been through hardened my feelings; the memories tough to shake.

Krista's hand leaves my hold, and she cups my jaw. The tight spot deep inside my chest starts to burn.

"You can say what you want to me, Trainer."

I want to say so much more than Krista knows. Probably things she doesn't wanna hear.

Bad shit.

Like some of the bad shit I already told her.

Haven't told her about Arnie yet.

I take a deep breath. "I like you a lot," I say on the exhale, and realize how bad that sounds.

But Krista's smile is worth it.

"Thank you."

Thank you for liking me, her face says.

How could I not? She's this hot girl who treats me like I'm the only person in the world who matters. Krista doesn't just fuck me. She *loves* me when we're together.

And. I might love her. A little.

Nothing is more dangerous than that feeling I'm starting to get for Krista Glass. Makes me want to run.

Makes me want to never let go.

Our hands are laced together as we stand in the movie theater line.

Don't have to read good to watch a movie.

I open my mouth and catch a piece of popcorn Krista tosses at me.

I crunch it, asking through a buttery mouthful, "Do you always eat like this?" I'm impressed by a girl that can keep up with my large eating habits.

"Only when I'm happy," she says.

Our gazes lock, and I jerk her against me, squishing the popcorn bag. Kernels ooze out the top and scatter to the ground like buttered snow.

My chest swells. The burning there begins to melt my guts. I know what the feeling is. Not had it much, but I recognize it.

Happy.

This girl I'm starting to trust is the reason.

But the feeling might not stay. And I can't say how I feel. Words don't come easy.

"I know." Krista rises on her tiptoes, pressing her fingers between our lips.

She kisses her own fingers, and I swear I feel the heat of it through our flesh, lips tingling.

Krista rocks back on her heels, grinning up at me. "I *see* you." Her hand goes to her heart, and that's when I realize that my muddled words aren't necessary.

Krista Glass doesn't need them.

She gets me.

KRISTA

This is so wrong.

Then why does it feel so right?

My eyes follow Trainer until he's a black rumbling dot disappearing out of sight.

Hugging myself, I let myself in my condo then slide the dead bolt behind me. He followed me after I picked up my Fiat from Starbucks all the way home.

Now he's gone, and I feel empty.

Silence greets me from the barely lit space. I didn't turn on the heat, but because June's been so cold, that wasn't the smartest move. With a small shiver, I twist the thermostat knob, kicking it to seventy-two. Grabbing a hoodie off one of the five hooks hanging on the wall, I toss it on.

Without Trainer's heat to warm me, I feel cool. Cold.

My body remembers Trainer—and his touch.

Heat suffuses my body as tactile memory sinks in for the long term.

I told Trainer I had to get home because I have class the next day. I can't go back to casual with Trainer— we're so much more than that now. But I need to *teach* him too.

I head to the kitchen in my tiny condo and set the kettle on to boil. I grab a Good Earth teabag from the tin and get a teacup from the cabinet, setting it on the countertop by the stainless sink.

The water won't boil faster if I watch it, so I turn my back on my kitchen and make my way to my dinky bedroom.

When I open the door, a big guy is sitting on my bed.

That alone should have made me pee my pants, but *this* man? My second-long perusal says he's as big as Trainer, but he wears menace like the leather vest he's got on.

Whirling, I sprint through the house on the way to my front door.

The teapot whistles a shrill tone, splitting the air, and at that precise moment, my feet lose contact with the ground.

He's got me.

I swing my head back, giving myself a teeth-shattering jolt as the back of my skull makes contact with his forehead.

"Fuck!" a bellow comes from behind me.

He drops me.

I spin.

Then I'm against the door by my throat, and pale-gray eyes are fixed on me like twin slits of iced smoke.

"So you're *Teacher*?"

What? I try for words, but my throat's pretty much not working because this crazy man is holding me up by it.

"Ya gonna try to head butt me again, scream, or ball kick?"

Actually, I was kind of contemplating all three.

He clearly sees the direction my wheels are spinning.

"Don't like hurtin' women, but I'll sure as fuck subdue ya. I'm hell on wheels at that."

I believe him and give him a jerky nod, and he slides me down the door.

Pressing my palms against the wood panels, I say, "Who are you?"

It doesn't come out intelligibly because my throat's still messed up. I clear it then repeat my question.

"My brother, Trainer? He's got the hots for you."

I'm super confused now. "So you hide in my bedroom and strangle me?"

Crossing my arms, I glare at the man I thought was an attacker. "You make zero sense. I guess you won't kill me, but I need to understand *why* you broke into my house to wait in my bedroom." My fingers go to my throat, and I try to quell the racing of my heart.

"Yeah…" He rakes his dark-blond hair into a pony-tail and ties it off at his nape. Out come some cigarettes, and he makes like he's going to smoke.

"You are *not* smoking in my house!" I yell. "Who the hell are you? Forget it—get out!" I point at the door as my fingers circle the knob.

"Nope. Got shit to discuss." He stabs an unlit ciga-rette at me. "And you're gonna listen."

"Really?" I spit out, raising my eyebrows. *Unbe-lievable.*

"Can you shut that fucking thing up?"

Tossing him a second glare, I move quickly to the stovetop and take the screaming kettle off the burner.

I turn, and he's striding to my small sliding glass door. He unlocks it, yanks it open, then steps onto the Juliette balcony. Just like the name implies, it's a one-butt accommodation, little more than a perch.

This dude doesn't mind. Leaning up against the rail, he lights the cigarette, shooting out three successive rings so quickly, they collide.

"Huh," I say.

"Better?" he asks, waving the cigarette around.

"Yes. I don't want my house polluted with that garbage."

He snorts, taking another drag, and smoke streams out in a clean line with his next exhale, muddying the air between us to an opaque wall.

"So Trainer is my brother."

I frown. I hadn't gotten the sense Trainer had family, except for the "mama" he referenced a few times.

"We're club. Motorcycle club."

I'm not a big TV watcher, but everyone's heard about *Sons of Anarchy*.

Of course I'd seen Trainer's bike and the vest with the colorful patches, but I hadn't put the pieces of this particular puzzle together. *Probably too deep in lust.*

"Okay." I touch my slightly sore throat then fold my arms again. "So tell me why you're hiding in my house and strangling me."

He winces. "Had to calm your shit down so we could talk."

"Could you have knocked on the door maybe?"

He shakes his head, eyebrows hiked. "Don't figure you'd let me in, would ya?"

Silence. *Absolutely not.*

He nods as if my silence was just what he expected. "My name's Noose."

"You know who I am, I suppose."

He nods, tapping his temple. "Know a fuckton now." *Great.*

"How do you feel about Trainer?"

I've been trying like hell not to examine my feelings about him because I know if I get too introspective, I'm going to come up with something really uncomfortable about myself.

Meeting him was like one of those rehearsed, love-at-first-sight things that I've heard about and never believed. And I sure didn't believe it could ever happen to me. I didn't love Trainer on first sight.

Not first.

But probably second.

"I've known him a week," I answer cautiously. Do I really owe this guy anything? He breaks into my house, chokes me, and *what*—expects me to just spill my guts?

My eyes roam his vest, finding it to be nearly identical to Trainer's. I've got a feeling they're not handing those out at the local department store.

Noose puts the cigarette out on the thick tread of his boot and carefully sets it on the wide metal top piece of the balcony rail.

"That's not what I asked ya. I know how long you guys have known each other."

He begins to stalk toward me, and I do what any reasonable person does.

I back the hell up until my ass hits the door.

Noose stops about two feet from my position and looks me over from the top of my head to the tips of my toes.

I blush under that unyielding scrutiny.

"Like what you see?" I snap.

He shakes his head. "Got an old lady. Don't need other tail."

I blink. *Do people actually talk like this?*

"Trying to figure out what Trainer sees in you."

Well, that's fucking flattering. Stick a fork in me, I'm done. "Get out." There's brusque, then there's just plain rude.

Noose puts a palm on the door.

Right beside my head.

"Nope, I told you who I am. Now you're gonna listen."

He turns away from me, and I fight the urge to kick him in the ass and run like hell.

As though he has an uncanny sixth sense, Noose turns, fixing eyes like flint on me.

"Trainer isn't like the other brothers. He's unique. Can't read. Guess that's why he's going to you."

I'm not allowed to discuss my students, so I say nothing.

"He's not a dumb dude."

We stare at each other. "I know that," I snap.

"Good," he replies in an abrupt word. "'Cause I don't need some bitch tearing his beating heart outta his chest and grinding her stiletto in it."

Appalled, I let my mouth pop open.

Noose chuckles. "You should really learn to control your face. Read ya like a book."

Spluttering, I say, "I've got nothing to hide."

"I know—looked into ya."

My mouth remains open. "What?" I yell.

He winces, putting a finger in his ear. "Shit, settle."

"No." My hands shake. "I'm not a bitch, and I don't play people, you—you *jerk*!"

Noose looks amused instead of insulted.

"I don't know what's going to happen with me and Trainer, but you can't warn, scare me, or whatever other plan you had."

Noose nods. "Good. Because your lily-white background might not work with Trainer. You know he's doing this reading gig to get gussied up to look dandy if this court thing goes through for the attitude adjustment he gave those assholes last year?"

After a second-long pause, I say, "Yes. Trainer mentioned that."

Noose perches his denim-encased butt on the back of my floral couch and rests his palms on his thighs. "I'm asking you to do your job and not crush his heart. He's been through some shit."

I'm not betraying Trainer's confidence by acknowledging information he told me during our more intimate moments together. However, advertising what I know would be a betrayal. So I say, "A lot of my students come from less-than-ideal circumstances." *There, that's broad.*

Noose nods then waits.

I let the silence go on without volunteering anything.

Finally, after a full minute of scrutiny, he says, "Good. Now about this lawyer boyfriend ya got."

I shake my head. "No. We're through." My face gets hot, and I put my hands against my cheeks. "I broke it off with him." This is beyond awkward.

"Ah-huh. Don't like the guy."

I jerk my chin back, remembering Trainer saying the same thing. "I don't see what Allen has to do with Trainer."

"He out of the picture, like a clean break?"

"Yes, he took our break-up really well." My brows knot. "Wait a second—why am I explaining this to you?"

Noose grins, oozing a crude sort of charm from every pore. "Just that kinda guy, I guess. Father confessor."

I roll my eyes.

"Can't find anything on him. He's like a void in society." Noose tears fingers through his hair, messes it up, and reties it. "Had my ear to the ground, and Allen Fitzgerald should have left more of a trail." Noose shrugs. "I guess it's no big if you cut the guy's nuts off."

I snort. "There was no surgery. It was a coffee and a 'let's just be friends' conversation. If you must know." My eyebrow arches.

Noose nods, cupping his chin. "I must." He gives an infuriating smirk. "So you teach Trainer. You fuck Trainer. You don't hurt Trainer." His voice drops dangerously low. "And you definitely don't get back with that fancy mouthpiece, Allen Fitzgerald."

Our gazes hold.

"You don't fool me, Noose," I finally say.

"Not trying to."

"You're smart and manipulative."

He shrugs. "Yeah."

"Doesn't that bother you?"

Noose doesn't even pretend to give it thought. "Which part?" He laughs, then his face grows serious, eyes like sleet. "No. Do anything for a brother. But Trainer's special."

Standing, he heads for the door.

Now it's me pursuing the guy who broke into my condo. "Why?"

Noose turns, hand on the doorknob. "Because I know what he's been through. And I know he's got nobody but us."

"That's not true," I say. "He's got me."

Noose nods, eyes hooded as they search my face. "Figured." He opens the door and steps into the hallway. "And that scares the shit outta me."

Not exactly a vote of confidence.

Noose checks out my door and lifts his upper lip in disdain. "Get some fucking real locks. These blow. You're a sitting duck in here."

His boots thunder down the stairs, leaving me alone. With my thoughts.

17

KRISTA

"Oh. My. God—I'm going to have to say *no* on this one, Krista."

I was afraid Sam would nix Trainer.

"I think I'm a little in love with him," I admit quietly, eyes on my knotted fingers.

Sam stares at me over the rim of her coffee cup filled with gross black coffee. "Or maybe it could be that stupendous appendage swinging between his legs." Her eyebrows pop, and a smirk takes up permanent residence.

I choke on my creamy coffee, slapping a hand over my mouth, and say between my fingers, "I never thought I'd say this."

Sam arches her eyebrow.

"Size does matter," we say at the exact moment.

Giggling reigns supreme.

"Okay, okay…" Sam slaps her thigh, picking off a piece of lint as she does. "Seriously? We're so juvenile."

I flop back against one of the worn swivel chairs that faces the tall windows overlooking the forest. "Of that, there is no doubt." I whip up my finger. "In fact, there's substantial proof."

"So let me recap." Sam sets her mug on one of the square beveled glass pieces inset in the coffee table. "Trainer spent the better part of a day and a half making you come?" Her eyebrows shoot up.

My face gets hot, and my hands go to my face. *Damn.* "Denial is not a strong suit of mine."

"Only because you can't get away with it," Sam counters with a knowing smile.

"True." I laugh. "Go on."

Sam smiles, ticking off point two of about one hundred twelve on a bird bone of a finger. "Then you get home, and a hulking guy sort of chokes you while putting you on notice?"

I nod, remembering the strange encounter. "Well, kind of."

"I'm scared. What scares me most is how weirdly calm you are about all of it. Please, convince me."

"Okay—so it makes me feel better about existing to know there's actually another human being out there that sees Trainer. Who he really is. Who he was meant to be."

Sam frowns, pouting her lip—a sure sign she doesn't get it. "So…choking guy?"

"Noose."

"Oh, great—nice. A guy that chokes a girl against a door and has the name Noose. Makes perfect sense."

I put my face in my hands. "I know it sounds bad."

"Yup," Sam agrees instantly.

"Shit."

"That's what I've been saying all along."

I meet her light-brown eyes. The navy ring stands out in stark definition. "But you had to be there."

"When he was choking you?"

"God." I study my screaming red Chuck Taylors for a second then look back at Sam. "I have a good feeling about Trainer."

"Well, he's a feel-good kinda guy," Sam says sarcastically. Her eyes sweep my face, and she must see something there because she leaves the couch. Sinking to her haunches in front of me, she takes my hands. "Listen, you look so crestfallen, but I don't care about anything but your well-being."

"You sound like my mom."

"Good—*damn*. You need some sense."

Sam stands. "This is a full-pot-of-fresh-coffee night. No Keurig." Sam strolls to the u-shaped kitchen, grabs coffee beans from the freezer, and pours a portion into the grinder. I listen as the shrill grinding takes up the sound in the open-concept living room and kitchen. When she's done, she pours the grounds into the pot and kicks it to on.

At the bar that separates the two spaces, I pull out a comfy chair and sit.

Sam faces me behind the counter. I park my chin on top of my fists.

"Listen, at least you dumped Allen."

A prickling unease starts up in my chest. The tightness resolves to an almost-electric tingling. Not in a good way.

Sam sees my expression. "What?" The coffee finishes brewing, and she turns to fill our cups. She takes time to put just the right amount of cream and an obscene amount of raw sugar in mine.

Sam slides the mug across the three-foot-deep bar. I grab the thick ceramic, letting it warm my suddenly cold fingers. "Allen said all the right things. He really wanted to still try."

"But him being gorgeous and rich is not enough?" Sam winks.

"No, he's—I don't know. Most women would be all over that. What Allen has to offer. And I don't know if he is personally wealthy, but I have the feeling his family is swimming in money."

"Then there's the question of Allen's one critical inadequacy." A gale of laughter erupts from Sam.

I roll my eyes. "I don't care about dick size, really."

"Really?" Sam says.

Grinning, I say, "Really. Trainer is so great at all the non-penetration things—so loving and tender—it's just a great bonus."

Sam walks over to the four-seater kitchen nook table and sinks into one of the seats facing me. "Wow, does he have a twin?"

I shake my head. "He's so unique, like Noose said."

"So Allen's history." Sam pretends to wipe sweat off her forehead.

"I guess."

Sam leans forward, resting her mug on a slender knee. "You sound unconvinced."

I shake my head. "I don't know...he seemed so reluctant to let me go, like we were unfinished somehow."

"Slow learner. Especially for an attorney." She waves her hand. "Anyway, whatevers. So just teach Trainer. Don't screw him too. It's just going to complicate things. And find out if this Noose is legit. If Trainer knows him, and he really is part of this biker gang, then there's another layer of complication to consider. Beyond the obvious one of him being a student."

"Adult student," I say, slightly defensive.

"Very, very adult."

We laugh.

"This is a tough call. I mean, you've only had a couple of serious boyfriends." Sam huffs a breath out, moving a long wisp of spiraling hair behind her ear. "I'd still like to kick my own ass that I introduced you to Allen."

I lift a shoulder. "Why? I mean, he's just what you said: gorgeous with money. He really does and says the right things." *Except for things that matter.* I roll my bottom lip between my teeth.

"You've thought of something."

I nod. "You know what the real problem with Allen is? It's like he wasn't really present when we were together."

Sam gives me a hard look. "That's deep."

"Yes. I'm not much for self-examination or anything."

"But you're practically psychic."

I give a little self-conscious laugh. "Intuitive is more like it."

Sam nods slowly. "Maybe, but remember when we were little and our parents still had landline telephones?"

"Yeah!" I laugh, getting an instant visual of the big lump of square plastic.

"And you could guess who was calling."

I forgot about that.

"And how when we got our licenses, you'd know what song was playing on the radio before I turned it on?"

"Yeah." I'm not smiling now. "Not all the time, Sam."

"Mostly." She flips her hand, glancing a finger off the mug in her other hand and almost tipping over her coffee. "Oops—" She catches a drop off the rim and sucks it from her finger. "Don't freak. I'm not saying you need to join the Psychic Friends Network or something. I'm just saying, when God was handing out the goodies, you were first in line for intuition."

"So I should listen to my gut?"

"Essentially, yes." Sam gives a trademark small twist of lips, her version of a smirk. "Besides, you've never sung your praises as a teacher. You've always said your *instincts* made you see the issue for the student, and how it could be fixed."

Sam jerks her shoulders up as if to say, "Duh."

"That's all true, but I don't know how my skill at getting to the root of why somebody can't learn is going to help me know if someone's bad news."

"Trust your feelings. You feel weird about Allen—don't get back together with him, no matter what bullshit he pulls."

After Trainer, I don't think I could have another man's hands on my body. "Don't worry about that. *Pfft.*" I repress a shudder.

Sam winks, "That bad, eh?"

What can I say? "It was pretty easy to break up when faced with returning and having only what Allen wanted in bed."

Taking a swig of cold coffee, she grimaces and winces. "Yuck—shit, this is like ice."

"We're too busy hashing through everything to drink our coffee."

"Important girl talk."

"Yeah," I answer softly. I know what day is coming up this week. I bring out the pink elephant like a circus trainer. "So I want to come with you to visit them."

Sam doesn't miss a beat. "I'm fine." She lifts her mug, remembers her coffee's too cold, and sets it on the kitchen table again.

"I know. I still want to come with."

She turns her head, swiping at her eyes, refusing to look at me. "It's been five years."

"I know."

"I love your parents, Krista," Sam confesses.

"But it's not the same." I believe down to my soul that she thinks about her parents every day.

She throws her arm out, stiff.

I stand, taking the hand she offers. "I miss them."

"I do too."

Sam gives me a sharp look, her eyes more amber in the dying light of the day that slants in, making her irises blaze, shimmering with tears yet shed.

"You do—why?"

"Because they made you, my friend. And because of them, I have you."

Sam stands, dwarfing me with her height. "I love you, you sensitive, emotional, gorgeous thing. Love you."

We hug tight over the counter, bellies pressing against the edge, like we're drowning.

"You're so fucking needy, Krista."

We both know it's a lie.

But I don't need to deliver the truth.

Sam's head is at one end of the eight-foot couch, and mine's at the other. Our legs are side by side.

"I'm going to explode."

Sam's head pops off the armrest. "If you didn't eat your body weight in pizza! As a matter of fact, you should be a fat sow by now."

"Metabolism still works, I guess." I feel a lethargic smile spread my lips.

Sam knocks my legs off the couch.

"Hey, ya bitch!" I jerk up, rubbing my eyes.

She waggles her eyebrows. "Woke you up, though."

"I didn't *want* to be woken up," I pout.

"But if I asked if you wanted dessert…?"

I don't even need to wonder; it's easy. "I'd say yes."

"See? My exact point. You're a junk-food addict."

I curl a strand of hair around my finger. "Yeah. I blame my parents."

Sam snorts. "Agreed, they're health nuts. And you're clearly rebelling."

"Clearly," I answer in a droll voice and lie back on the couch, squeezing my legs next to Sam's again.

"You've boxed me in. I can't get to the freezer for ice cream now."

I roll my eyes at Sam. "You're too lazy to bother, and you're hoping I do it instead."

"Yes."

Rolling off the couch, I slouch over to the freezer and tear open the thirty-year-old door.

Ben and Jerry's. The Tonight Dough.

Holy shit!

I squeal, and a curly head pops up over the sofa table. "What?"

"The Tonight Dough!"

Sam sinks back down, hiking her feet on the back of the couch. "Hells yes."

"Can we share a pint?" I ask, digging around between the frozen food, sausage, and ice cream bars.

"No. Get your own pint."

"So selfish." I'm grinning.

"Yup."

Carrying two pints of my favorite ice cream on the planet, I swipe two spoons out of the silverware drawer then walk back to the couch. I plop down, and Sam swings her legs over and plants her feet on the floor, curling her toes in the worn high-pile carpeting.

"What?" I ask, handing her a pint plus a spoon. "You can't just lay around and spoon it in?"

Sam shakes her head, lifting the spoon to make her point. "I have to draw the gluttony line somewhere."

"Not me." I scoot against the armrest and draw my knees up, balancing the cold pint on my tummy. Digging for my next spoonful. I groan in relief from the flavor burst. *Yum.*

We eat in silence for a couple of minutes, then Sam asks, "What's Trainer's real name? You said that guy that busted into your condo was Noose. Why do they all have weird names?"

"You've seriously never seen the MC show, *Sons of Anarchy.*"

"No, I like to be non-conformist. You know this." Sam stabs her spoon in the melting ice cream, doing a slow spin, then loads the utensil. "If lots of people like a show, I don't want to be common."

The bite disappears.

"No fear there," I mutter.

"I heard that." Sam licks her spoon then drops it inside the pint, setting her carton on the slim wood table that runs behind the the couch. "Halftime," she announces, hand to her flat stomach.

"His name's Brett Rife, but he corrected me early on. I've been using Trainer since the first day I met him." I stare down at my empty pint—impressive, even for me. "I've got more appetite."

"I wonder why?" Sam asks, voice as dry as the Sahara Desert.

I cock my head, giving her the wide-eyed innocent look, setting my empty carton next to her half-eaten one.

"Brett Rife," Sam repeats, ignoring my feigned innocence as a faraway expression takes her attention elsewhere.

"What?"

She gives a small startle and shake of her head. "Nothing. Thought the name sounded vaguely familiar."

"Well, he does have a court possibility."

Sam shakes her head a second time. "Nope. Don't know about 'possibles' or dates that futuristic or vague." She shrugs, tucking a curl behind her ear and bending her knee to join her thigh. "It's nothing. I hear a ton of names in court, and sometimes, they get scrambled."

"Brett Rife isn't a super-common name," I remark.

"No, but Brett's pretty common." She gets that distant expression again. "I don't know…something about the combo." Sam shakes her head again, curls bouncing. "Weird."

A quick check of my cell says it's already eight o'clock at night. I groan. "Why am I doing this?"

"The teaching?"

I nod.

"Because you help people. And there's Trainer."

"Who you don't want me to date."

Sam laughs, and I look at her. "The jury's out."

"Cute."

"Just be cautious." Sam's face crumples. I wrap my arms around her, speaking to air. "I'm not going anywhere, Sam."

"I can't lose you too, Krista. I couldn't survive it."

I know that. "I'm not going anywhere."

"Be more careful for me, since you have no self-preservation instincts."

I pull away, scowling. "That's not true."

Sam searches my face. "You've always trusted everyone. Just because you see them, doesn't mean they see *you*. It's about perspective, and so few share yours, Krista. So few."

"I'll be okay."

But her words follow me all the way to the condo.

Like a portent.

18

TRAINER

"What the fuck?"

Feels like my head will explode.

Noose betrayed me. He went to Krista's place and scared her.

"Calm down, Trainer."

I can't. Feels like my blood is boiling. I feel sick. I trusted him. "I thought we had each other's backs."

Noose rakes a palm over his hair, screwing it six ways to Sunday, as Vipe always says.

"Fuck yes, we do. That's why I went over there—had to set her straight."

"No, you fuckin' didn't!" I yell, pacing away from him so I don't murder the big fucker. "She's innocent, Noose."

"No woman is innocent, Trainer. Look around."

I don't look through the one-way glass of the church room to where I can take my pick of clubwhores. "Those ladies have a goal. Krista just wants to help people." My hands fist.

"That's true, Trainer. But listen to me. She's got some history with this mouthpiece I don't like."

"Allen." My hands loosen then clench again.

"See? You're already wanting to pound this guy's brains in."

"Not funny."

Noose grunts. "Sorry, I wasn't thinking about the stepdad."

I turn my head back toward Noose, giving him my profile. "That's too good a name for him. He was just the latest guy."

"Gotcha. Lived the same deal."

Facing him now, I look him in the eye. Maybe I have him by a half inch, but we're close. "But your mama wasn't in the mix of my horror story."

Noose spreads his hands. "Don't remember her much. Died before I got grown."

"Was she…" I look down. I can't say *whore*—not about Mama—though it's the bald truth.

"Yeah." Noose doesn't make me finish.

My shoulders slump in relief. "All I'm saying is, stay away from Krista." I add through my teeth, "Please." Because I really want to sock him for messin' in my life.

"I'm lookin out for ya, is all."

Our eyes meet. "When it comes to her, don't."

"You got it bad?"

"What?" I ask, having a sense of what he might be fishing for.

"Pussy fever."

I shake my head. "Got plenty of ladies around to help me with that."

"Trainer."

"Yeah," I answer, half-barking.

Noose smirks. "Got news for ya. They're not ladies." He swipes a hand over his nape, giving me a look that says, *"Get real."*

Probably. I meet his eyes, still wanting to defend my thinking. "Krista's a lady."

Noose keeps staring at me. "Had a good weekend?"

"Amazing," I admit in a whisper.

He snorts, checking out my crotch and giving me a chin lift.

I frown.

"Simmer down, pal. If it feels like you want your woman permanently impaled on your dick, you got it bad."

A visual rises inside my brain of Krista riding my cock all the time.

Gives me a boner.

Sorta embarrassing. "Some limitations with that."

Noose shouts out a laugh from his belly, folding his arms. "Not literally, Trainer. Just feels like that'd be any guy's dream woman."

I flick my eyes at his then look away. Swallow. "That how ya feel about Rose?"

"Yeah."

That's what I like about Noose. He doesn't complicate everything with a bunch of words that hurt my brain.

Krista uses lots of words, but they don't punish me.

"Came on pretty strong with Krista."

I glare at him.

"Didn't hurt her, but she's got fire." Noose chuckles, lighting up, and jets a stream of smoke toward the ceiling.

"Vipe's gonna kill you if he catches you smokin'."

"Yup." Noose starts popping rings. First one large ring, followed by a medium ring with a tiny ring floating inside.

Sometimes simple things get my attention and hold it prisoner. When Noose does rings, I never think of what the Arnies did with their lit smokes.

Noose is the first smoker who doesn't remind me of those freaks.

His gray eyes slim to razors on me. "What?"

"Nothin." Not talking about those demons. Even with Noose.

"Chill. Not asking about shit you don't want to talk about."

Tension slides out of me. He never presses.

"You coming over for pancakes before church?"

I nod.

"Bring Krista. Rose won't give a fuck."

Rose is nice. I especially like the kids. Charlie shows me his toys and never makes fun of how I talk and shit.

He reads. An eight-year-old kid.

I take a deep breath. Krista promised me I can learn. Hard not to go over our first twenty sight words.

I remember again how she said I'll dream about my learning pretty soon. Didn't tell her I was dreaming about her instead.

A smile curls my lips. Probably don't want to tell her that.

Krista will think I don't want to be taught. I didn't at first, but she's made me want to be something more.

A better man.

"What's that shit-eating grin ya got goin'?" Noose asks.

My head jerks up. "What? Oh, nothing...I—" I scratch my head then drop my hands next to my ass that's leaning on the solid wood church table. "Just thinking that I'm doin' okay on the learning part, but Krista's helping, but not helping."

"Pussy fever," Noose repeats, folding his arms over his built chest.

I cross my arms, matching him. "Well, yeah, I like that." I look out the one-sided viewing glass, watching Crystal walk by, hot as ever, and I'm not that into her. "Love that, actually."

Noose is quiet, snuffing out the last cigarette and lighting another one.

He watches the girls.

"Do ya miss fucking the sweet butts?"

"It was easier," Noose admits, and I look away from Crystal and turn my attention to him.

"This loving shit is complicated. But at the end of the day, there's no choice. And the good parts…they're so fuckin' good." His voice lowers to a wistful thread.

"Like what?" Never had a normal family life. Weird to think there's something different out there.

"Like when your flesh and blood falls asleep on your chest." Noose takes his free hand and folds it over his heart. "And the baby smells like new life and powder and soap and your wife, all rolled up into this fucking awesome scent pill. A man never gets tired of that. Then there's this fucking awesome chick that gives an actual fuck about what you say. Remembers where your bike keys are when you've been searching around for ten minutes. Puts just the right amount of blueberries in your pancakes." Noose looks at me. "And never seems to have a headache, if ya get my meaning. Fucks like a goddess."

He smooshes the cig into a Road Kill MC ashtray at the edge of the table.

"So to answer your question: do I miss fucking them?" He jerks a thumb behind him. "Not anymore."

Then he walks out.

Noose doesn't make speeches.

Unless he's got something important to say.

I review his words for the next half hour, committing them to memory.

He has more experience. Life experience. Not in the bad shit. We're about equal there.

But the good stuff.

His words give me that second seed of hope.

The first was given to me unexpectedly.

By Krista Glass.

ONE WEEK LATER

"Ya don't call the bitches right away." Storm erupts from the chair he was sitting in.

I shake my head, leaning back in my seat, and lace my fingers behind my head. Storm's over reactive. Has been since the first day I met him. And kicked his ass. "I've got class today. There's no playing Krista right now, even if I wanted to." *Which I don't.* "She's gotta teach me, Monday through Friday."

"Damn, you're like a captive audience, dude."

Yeah, but that's one audience I wanna be a part of.

"She hot?"

I think of her beautiful deep-gray eyes, hair so dark brown that it borders black, and the way her pussy looks. *Tastes.*

I lick my lips. "Yeah." The one word is deep.

"Holy shit in a sack. That *face*."

I shut down my expression.

"Never seen you look soft, man—that's all I'm saying. Hope you're not looking at the bitch with that face."

The legs of my chair kiss the ground, and I stand, scooping Storm across the table, neck cranked back hard. Tightening my fist, I strangle him with his shirt collar.

Church goes silent.

"Don't fucking call Krista a bitch."

"'Kay," Storm squeaks.

Too much air. Not enough lesson. I know about lessons. I tighten my grip until I feel his Adam's apple flattening.

"Let him live, Trainer," Wring says dryly from his usual corner. "He doesn't have the smarts to appreciate restraint from a brother, but it'd be a mercy." His voice is low, cutting like a dull blade across the red field of my vision.

Slowly, I release Storm, and he slaps his palms on the table, coughing up a lung.

I straighten my vest and fling my ass back in the chair.

"Gonna live, ya 'tard?" Noose says, helpfully slapping him on the back.

Looks like clubbing, actually.

The gavel bangs on the table. "If we're completely finished with the drama, let's talk about that gun run that Noose and Trainer took care of." Viper narrows his light-blue eyes on Storm. "You're taking up precious real estate on our table. Get your ass down."

Storm crawls backward, gets to the opposite edge of where I sit, and sort of falls off the edge.

Lariat grabs him by the seat of his pants, near the belt loop area, and hauls him backward into a seat. "You never refer to a potential old lady as a bitch. Trainer about killed you on principle, yeah, brother?"

Lariat's dark eyes sweep toward me like black high beams. I can see the question on his face 'cause he wants me to.

"Yeah." I nod my agreement.

"Jesus, I got it! I'm doing all the work, slopping through clean-up detail that makes me puke, watching all the females that—somehow—are the most compli-cated tail on the fucking planet, and now my partner for almost eighteen months is a brother and about kills me because I called his teacher girlfriend a—"

"Don't," Wring commands, though he's back to cleaning his nails with a switchblade he is never without.

Storm's mouth snaps shut.

Hell, I remember with crystal-clear clarity when I was right there with him. Didn't whine as much, though. I don't think.

Viper turns to me. "So those guns were a special acquisition. We needed the capital for the next venture."

Judge has been working with me, and even though Viper is the prez of one of the most aggressive tristate MCs, he sounds pretty smart, uses words like Judge, who told me that I have to listen to the words around the ones I don't get and the meaning of the phrase will come to me. Krista called that "contextual learning." She says everyone does it, and its how kids learn new words and their meanings.

Just thinking about her makes me want to leave church.

But there's pancakes, and I'm so nervous about having all the guys meet Noose and his family—Lariat, Wring, and Snare.

They're all the family I got. I have Mama, but she's messed up. And Judge said I can't go near her.

He knows I might kill another Arnie.

Probably right. And I don't want to leave Krista for prison. I know that now.

Had nothing to live for before. But now I got plenty to live for.

Family has never been this close.

"Hey, you awake?" Viper says, not unkindly, but I'm disrespecting him by not giving my attention to his words.

"Sorry, Viper. Got my mind on stuff."

"Well, get it off stuff. We got another gun run. Bigger— fueled this fucker from the proceeds of the last one. Meeting our Oregon charter. Just a hand-off, but they'll give us an advance because they have a solid buyer lined up."

"Sweet," Noose says, fingering his smokes inside the interior pocket of his vest, almost like they're a lucky charm.

"Don't you fucking light up in here, Noose. Smells like shit even without you smoking."

I don't look at Noose, but it's not easy.

"On to other news—everyone has their tasks for the gun run?" Viper looks at the front men: Lariat, Noose, Wring, and Snare.

He includes me. "You're going again. Noose said you did well."

"Okay," I say.

"What's the time?" Viper cups a palm behind his ear.

I sigh. "Friday night, eight p.m."

"That's right. Pussy will have to wait. Club shit first."

We stand, and everyone taps knuckles. Road Kill MC always comes first.

But a part of me—a part I didn't know I had—wants to be with Krista, and I don't like making up shit as an excuse to not be with her.

Unless she'd be my old lady.

Too soon. Just thinking about putting myself out there for a lady makes my pits sweat.

Even if she's the only lady I want.

19

KRISTA

It's a dream.

These past two weeks have been the best of my life.

A man did this, made me feel this way.

Blushing, I think about what that man does to my body, for my body.

We haven't committed another sin on my teaching table, thank God, but we committed plenty between the old cabin Trainer stays in and my condo.

Every surface christened, many positions explored.

And Trainer read his first sentence Thursday. A little flutter stirs inside my belly like a trapped butterfly as I remember the moment his face lit up, realization that *he* alone recognized the words and knew what they meant. Coming from his own mouth.

I was so proud, I cried.

Trainer hugged me, genuine happiness opening his expression. I swear I saw his soul that day.

Not pieces of it, but the whole.

Looking in the mirror one last time, I decide I'm stalling. I feel as though I'm meeting his parents today.

But I'm meeting his biker family. As Sam says: the biker gang.

If Trainer chose them, and he has no other family, except the elusive "Mama," then that's good enough for me.

I've been teaching him for two weeks—but he's been teaching me too. And his lessons are the best I've ever learned.

Smoothing my hands over my short-sleeve blouse, I eye the form-fitting charcoal tunic. Finally, early summer has arrived, and Kent is having a rare clear, cloudless sky. My lightweight leggings are black—as are my flats with a line of little black gems scattered across the toes. I left my hair loose, its natural waves flowing just shy of waist length, though I'll need to braid it for the bike ride. My jewelry is simple, with gun mental-colored hoops and a wide sterling band on my middle finger.

Okay, Krista, get your ass moving.

Walking to the door, I grab a cropped jean jacket off the hook for the ride.

I turn the knob and swing the door open.

Allen stands there, arm raised as though to knock.

"Hi!" Startled, I jump a little, hand to my heart.

"Hello, Krista." His turquoise eyes roam my form.

I feel uncomfortable with my door standing open and Allen having a view of my condo. And me.

We slept together in this place, but those moments feel almost sacrilegious now that Trainer has been here. It's as though he wiped away the stain Allen left here, the bad memories of crappy sex and lack of intimacies, like an eraser to a chalkboard.

I have a clean slate. Or at least it felt that way until Allen appeared at my doorstep.

Tucking a strand of hair behind my ear, I try my best to hide my irritation. "What are you doing here?"

Allen smiles, and my own expression falters. He looks slightly predatory, like a shark scenting blood, or maybe I'm just imagining that. "I thought we'd let enough time go by. Maybe we can revisit our earlier chat."

I don't know what to say to that.

Stepping through the door, I turn to close and lock it. Slipping my key into my small, cross-body purse.

I don't want Allen in my condo. I don't want him here when Trainer picks me up.

Pivoting to face him again, I find Allen is uncomfortably close. Anxiety crawls up my throat, but I stand my ground, flicking my eyes over his shoulder. Besides, there's nowhere I can move. The door's at my back, and the stairs are behind Allen.

I'm trapped.

I swear I can hear Trainer's bike in the distance. *Great.*

Allen's eyes move to the locked door at my back. "I was hoping we could talk inside your place."

No way. This is not the clean break I bragged about to Sam. I didn't tell her about my instincts regarding Allen. She would feel even more guilty for introducing us.

I want to protect Sam from more pain, more grief. Those are already things she has too much of.

"Allen, I just want to be friends."

He laughs, and the brittle sound echoes in the strange acoustics of the open stairwell.

He takes a step back, spreading his hands with a jerk, and I notice he chose a shirt that matches his eyes. Of course. "The friend speech? We're more than friends, Krista."

Okay. *How could I have dated him for two years?* He's clearly a narcissist. "We *were* more than friends, yes. But we didn't have any chemistry, Allen. I thought we went over that at coffee."

I cross my arms beneath my breasts, searching his eyes, and see anger, denial, and something I can't identify. Maybe I don't want to.

Sam says I'm practically psychic.

Right now, my sixth-sense alarm bells are ringing from here to Oregon.

I know I can't get Allen to leave before Trainer shows up. And that has potential to be a disaster.

Allen reaches for me, and I pull away, my butt cheeks pressing against the door. He moves in, grabbing my chin in a painful hold. "I had all the chemistry I needed with you, Krista."

My heart tries to beat out of my chest. *Thump, thump, thump.* "You're hurting me."

Allen gives me a gentle smile that causes icy adrenaline to pour through my veins. "No, this isn't pain, Krista."

I can definitely hear the bike now, and my palms dampen.

"I had plans for us, Krista. And I'm not going to let some slumming infatuation curtail our future together."

Crazy. Allen is certifiable.

"Let go of me."

His hand slips off my chin, and my exhale is full of pure relief. I've never been threatened by a man before.

Stupidly, I thought that only happened to other women. Nope. I'm not immune.

The familiar sound of a bike rumbling into my condo complex parking lot reaches us. The engine shuts off.

Allen's creepy smile grows.

How could I have never seen this side of Allen?

"Krista." Trainer's voice, low and careful, floats up from the bottom of the stairs.

I shut my eyes. My earlier joy drains from me, and like a tire with a hole, I'm deflated.

Allen turns, literally looking down at Trainer from the landing that tops the short flight of stairs from my second-story condo.

Trainer's not looking at Allen.

He's looking at me. That beautiful green gaze glitters with the beginnings of wariness—and anger.

"You okay?"

Not really, but I don't want to inflame the situation any more than it is. "Allen and I were just talking." *And he was just going,* I add to myself.

Trainer shifts frosty emerald eyes toward Allen. "Time to go, Krista," he says to me, but his gaze never leaves Allen.

I nod. Yes, I totally want to get the hell out of here.

Allen tips his head back, folding his arms and planting his feet wide. "I know all about you, Brett Rife. And you're not good enough to polish Krista's shoes."

Trainer says nothing, but if it's possible, his eyes turn colder, like frozen glacial pools of rage.

I'd be a fool not to see that kind of talk is a big trigger for Trainer.

I turn to Allen. "I've been reasonable, Allen. But I don't appreciate you putting down one of my students."

Allen turns back to me, planting the flat of his palm against my chest and shoving me the short distance against the door, pinning me.

The abbreviated scream is torn from my throat. I'm more startled than frightened, but the sound incites Trainer, as Allen knew it would. My peripheral vision catalogs the motion of a big man taking the stairs two at a time.

"The student you're fucking," Allen grits next to my ear, voice soft and low.

Terrifying.

Then Trainer engulfs the limb that pins me to my own door and swings Allen hard.

Allen is trained in martial arts and uses that now.

This time, my scream is loud and alarmed.

My ex uses the momentum Trainer just gave him, sweeping his foot under Trainer. His arm snaps out, punching Allen in the nose as he fights falling. *Crunch.*

I flatten myself against the door.

With wide eyes, I watch two men I've been with—in different ways, but so much the same—beat the shit out of each other.

It's not like on TV, where it's pretty and organized, perfect for viewing.

Trainer will lose, I think, my heart in my throat, choked with grief, with anger at Allen. Trainer is bigger and stronger than Allen, but Allen likes being a master at all things. He feels like a big man because of his expertise in defense.

It doesn't take long for Trainer to realize that his own strength and momentum is being used against him. Allen tries to capture any limb that gets near him, putting Trainer in painful holds.

"Allen, stop!" I scream, covering my mouth with my hand as Allen bends Trainer to his knee, ready to dislocate his shoulder in what I recognize as a classic martial arts hold meant to incapacitate.

Allen's bright eyes meet mine, shining with triumph that makes the orbs appear to glow in the shadowed alcove.

Trainer grabs Allen's nuts in that moment—and twists.

Allen bellows a sick shout of pain and begins to sink, releasing Trainer. He crowds Allen as he goes down, blood dripping from the various wounds Allen's inflicted.

I catch sight of the imprint of Allen's class ring on Trainer's cheekbone as he puts a forearm to Allen's throat, driving him to the ground.

Allen suddenly bucks, slamming his forehead into Trainer's on the way down.

Trainer staggers backward, then with a brutal kick, centers a lucky strike on Allen's face.

He falls backward, smacking the concrete hard with his palms. His ironed button-down shirt, once royal blue to match those arrogant eyes, is now covered with liquid rust.

Then, impossibly, with nothing but brute force, Trainer gets over the top of Allen again, blood raining down his jaw and dripping on Allen.

"Stop!" I scream at them.

"Don't you ever"—Trainer whips his face to the side, splattering blood across the rail that runs down each side of the staircase—"ever"—he slams Allen's head on the pebbling concrete on the landing, making him groan— "touch her again." Trainer releases him, and Allen falls back, chest heaving.

Trainer stands. "Krista's mine."

I am?

I am.

Trainer sways.

I rush to him, wrapping my arms around his waist. He ignores me, sliding out a cell.

I watch a list of phrases surface on the black viewer after his thumb presses it.

He taps the one that says *need back up.* When Trainer hits Send, the symbol of a hangman's noose comes up, and I know who's coming.

The guy who broke into my place.

Allen sits up, and I almost laugh, though nothing about this entire situation is remotely funny.

But he's always got himself in complete order. Not a hair out of place, outfit mussed, or word misplaced. That's not what's going down anymore.

He looks like shit now.

"Perfect." Allen spits out a wad of bloody phlegm.

Trainer puts me behind him, and I peek around him as Allen drags himself to his feet.

Trainer and Allen stare each other down for an impenetrable moment. "You'd never best me in a dojo, loser."

"Don't have to. Just bring it when it counts. Don't need no dojo to protect Krista."

Allen laughs, grimaces, then spits again, narrowing his eyes on Trainer. Then his gaze shifts to me. "*This* is what you want?" Allen sweeps an abraded hand at Trainer. "A Neanderthal to add to your 'tard-wrangling acquisitions?"

My mouth gapes.

"How *dare* you?" I seethe. "Speaking about my students that way!" I move to go around Trainer, and he says, "He's just baiting you like a coward."

Allen sneers, "You're less than nothing, *murderer*."

I stop in my tracks, staring at Allen. "*Now* what are you accusing Trainer of?"

"Trainer? Oh, yes—his biker gang name. Great company you're keeping, Krista."

"Brett Rife is a murderer." Allen looks at me, and whatever he sees there tells him what he needs to know.

He smirks at a silent Trainer.

"I'd bet my Fitzgerald fortune this big idiot never told you." Allen throws his head back and laughs, which devolves into a coughing fit. He wipes off his mouth with the back of his hand, knuckles wiped clean of skin and freely bleeding.

"Trainer?" I ask in a small voice.

He turns only partway in my direction. I guess he's not allowing himself to be vulnerable with Allen around.

Our eyes meet before his flick to Allen then away.

"Tell her, moron."

Trainer's face hardens. "I'm not dumb," he says without giving Allen a glance.

Allen's golden eyebrow whips up. "Smart enough to stick your dick in Krista."

We ignore him.

Trainer's eyes move to mine. "He's tellin' the truth."

"You murdered someone?" I ask incredulously.

Trainer nods. No explanation. No anything.

The deep, purring rumble of another bike landing beside Trainer's barely registers. Probably because I'm stricken by his confession.

"Why?" I ask, barely able to speak around the lump in my throat.

"He needed to die." Trainer lifts a shoulder, and I want to cry at the abuse all over him, courtesy of Allen—courtesy of people who came before I knew him.

I step back from both Trainer and Allen, looking from one to the other, painfully confused.

Noose trots up the steps, hanging on to the rail, and looks around at the carnage, bruised faces, and a terrified *me*.

He lifts his hand, and it comes away bloody.

Noose grins, nodding. "Class-A clusterfuck. Thanks for inviting me to the party," he throws in Trainer's direction, but his eyes are on Allen.

Leaning against the wall, I fight passing out, concentrating on evening out my breaths instead of the ragged sucking inhales that saw in and out of my lungs. "All of you—leave," I manage.

Noose gives a slow, emphatic shake of his head. "Nope. Think shit's gotta be worked out."

"Fantastic. Neanderthal II." Allen glares at Noose.

Noose's head swivels toward Allen. "Don't like you much, pal. Just a first impression. But I suggest you shut the pie hole underneath your nose unless you want round two with my friends Left and Right."

Noose raises first his left hand then his right, smile broadening.

"Fuck. You," Allen says with perfect clarity then smiles.

Oh no.

I push off from the wall at the same time Noose steps toward Allen.

Bad move, I realize later.

20

TRAINER

My heart sinks when the fucker, Allen, calls me a murderer.

'Cause I am.

Killed Arnie dead. Made sure of it. Just wasn't ready to tell Krista yet.

Because of the way she's lookin at me now. Like she doesn't know me, confusion and hurt etched across her face.

But I *can* tell her, she knows me better than anyone. I oughta know—I let her in.

Second by second, I watch her face shut me out. Grief slashes at me, bloody fissures reopening old wounds.

Then Noose appears, and I know shit's gonna get ugly. Not just because Noose is here, but because that Allen fucker is a baiter. He wants to beat people. It's who he is. Knew that the first time I met him.

I wait until Noose dresses Allen down. Because that was gonna happen. Noose dishes out shit to the deserving.

And sure enough.

"Fuck you," Allen says, crusty blood around his nostrils.

Noose's expression doesn't change, and that's when I know he's gonna blow.

What I don't expect is Krista charging him. I was so focused on the men, I forgot the woman.

"Stop!" she yells then jumps on Noose's back.

Reactively, he dislodges her as I'm already moving, and Krista tumbles over the rail.

Falling the six feet to the ground.

I'm already airborne, slapping the rail and flying over the top right after.

Too late. I bend my knees as I land like a cat.

Krista shrieks from the ground.

Fuck.

I sink in one motion, scooping her from the ground and lift. She's a small girl, so it's no problem.

Krista holds out her hand, her eyes finding mine, and tears seep out the corners of her eyes. "Trainer, it hurts."

"I know." I trust Noose to deal with fucker up above as I find out how my lady is hurt.

Doesn't take long. Broken bone bulges at her wrist, threatening to poke out through her skin.

That knot in my chest comes back like an old friend.

Our eyes lock. "Is—" She chokes back tears. "Is it bad?"

I nod. "Yeah."

"Hospital field trip?" Noose asks from the landing, having been watching Allen and listening.

"Yeah," I repeat, gently cradling Krista.

"You'll need me to take her," Allen states.

We all look at him. His cruel smile is all for me.

In that moment, his potential Arnie status isn't in question anymore. He is one. Fancy clothes and words don't matter. Deep down, he's an Arnie.

"You have to remember, I know *all* about you, Neanderthal."

Casually, Noose's hand flies out, swiping the back of Allen's head. He stumbles forward, catching himself on the railing.

"No fucks given about who ya are, what ya are, or any happy ho-ho shit like that. Don't disrespect a brother, fuck nuts."

Allen turns, hating Noose with his eyes. Seen that expression enough in my life. "I don't *need* you. Krista must go to the hospital because you threw her off the balcony—classic move—imbecile."

Noose stiff-fingers him in the chest. Allen moves into him, and I size the men up. The attorney has a steely core, I'll give him that. He acts smart, but anybody who goes toe-to-toe with Noose has a death wish.

"Your brother"—Allen cocks his head in my direction—"is on probation for a second derelict offense. If he takes an injured woman to the hospital, how will that go for him? Think it through, if you're able."

A flicker of uncertainty washes over Noose's face and is instantly gone.

"That's right," Allen says with soft, triumphant menace, just loud enough for me to catch.

Loud and clear.

"Fine." Noose says, stepping out of range.

Allen smirks.

"But I go with. I'm not letting you alone with Trainer's girl, no matter what bullshit slides out of that hole you got for a mouth. It's all brown and stinks to me."

Allen's face tells me he's up to something.

But Noose will see it.

Krista takes ahold of my ruined shirt already stiffening with blood. "Don't leave me alone with him."

The urge to cry sweeps through me, like smelling rain before a storm.

I bite the inside of my cheek. Pain rushes in where agony was a moment before.

I gasp out an answer, filling the void caused by emotions I'm not used to having. "Noose will be with you." Never had physical pain from words before.

Krista searches my face, and I see the defeat in hers.

Holding the stare is the bravest thing I've ever done. Keeping my eyes on a face I love, not sure if it loves me back.

"Because you murdered someone."

There's more to it than that. But words aren't there in the front of my brain like everyone else's. So I use the simplest one. "Yeah."

"Set me down, Trainer."

I do, carefully—like she's made of glass. Krista yelps, cradling her arm as new tears stream down her face.

The men walk down the stairs. Allen first, I notice.

Noose's eyes meet mine. "Gonna be okay, Trainer."

"Doesn't feel like it," I admit as Allen breezes past me like we didn't just go hard.

Only fought a few guys who put the judo moves on me. Didn't expect it from this douche. Packaging doesn't match the man. Sneaky fuck.

Keeping my arm around Krista, I reluctantly hand her off to Noose.

Her skin is pale like chalk.

Noose takes one look at her. "Shock." He knocks her off her feet with a well-placed arm behind the knees, catching her and lifting at the same time.

"Hey," she protests weakly, "I can walk."

"What's wrong with her?"

Noose looks at her wrist. "Spiral fracture. Lots of pain. Slipping into shock."

Allen glares, spinning on his heel. He strides to a BMW.

My soul flares like a sun spot. I recognized the letters. I mean, I knew it was a BMW using what Krista said is memorized visual cues. But to read it?

In the middle of this mess, with my girlfriend's wrist busted—I can read.

I jog after Noose and Krista.

Grabbing her good hand, I whisper, just for her, "I read something just now."

The corners of her lips pulse once before her eyes flutter closed.

Straightening, Allen and I lock glares over the roof of the car. "This isn't through."

No it ain't. I back away, wanting to be with Krista so bad, it's a well of raw pain.

Glancing back at Allen, I realize I want him dead more.

Noose sees our silent exchange and jerks his head to the right. "Head to the club. Tell the Prez what's what."

He bends, sliding Krista into the back seat of the BMW. She curls into a fetal position, and he carefully shuts the door.

Noose moves around the back of the car, eyes his ride sitting there next to mine, and sighs before slipping in next to Krista.

Noose being there or not, it's so hard to watch that prick back out of the slot and drive away with my lady.

It should be *me* taking her to the hospital.

Because an Arnie is in charge, and people get hurt with Arnies.

And I got a feeling Allen Fitzgerald is a really bad one.

KRISTA

Lifting my arm, I admire the ugly cast. They gave me a choice of color, and I chose charcoal gray. I'm pretty sure it's going to look filthy pretty quickly, so the dark color seemed the best option for the almost two months I'll have it on.

Sam says, "Sit still."

Carefully, she prints her name after the phrase she put on my cast.

I read it, letting the thing drop onto my lap. "It's a good thing that a lot of my students can't read well."

Proof that I need to watch where I'm going is printed neatly across the longest and flattest part of the cast. In light-colored, metallic ink.

I groan.

"Hurt?"

I shake my head. "Well, yes. But they gave me joy juice." I lift my other arm. Clear tubing runs from the crook of my elbow to a bag of happy liquid hanging from a tall metal hook thing with wheels.

"Where's the prick?"

"Allen?" I whisper back.

Sam nods, her topknot of thick curly hair bobbing with the motion. "Of course *him*." She caps her pen, slapping it on the side table that serves as both tray and nightstand.

"He's out in the hall."

Sam's lips curl in satisfaction. "I like Trainer's work on his face."

I look away. I can't face telling her. Just when I thought I'd found someone extraordinary...

"Okay, so tell me what happened. I just got the *Reader's Digest* version."

I take a deep breath, and Sam helps me get water from a bendy straw before carefully setting it at my bedside table when I've had enough.

It takes me a half hour to do the total gut spill.

Sam slumps in the chair. "I couldn't make this shit up. It's like a reality show."

Frowning, I shake my head. "It's my *life*, Sam. I mean, I knew about the thing with the guys—the possible court date—the very reason why Trainer needed to 'improve himself.' I got all that. I knew he was rough around the edges. That's not unusual with my students, really."

"But you don't judge people." Sam flings a palm out.

Annoyed, I exhale loudly. "No, a big character flaw, I guess." Allen comes to mind. I should have judged that one a *lot* more.

"No." Sam takes my hand. "It's your best trait."

We sit quietly for a time.

"Now what?" Sam asks.

"Trainer being a murderer isn't probably something I can move past. I'll finish our schooling—there's still four weeks left. But beyond that, I can't do romance. Not with all that. I'll be like a heroine in a bad soap opera."

Sam winces, clearly visualizing it.

"I'm sure you've already considered how weird it was that Allen knew about Trainer's past."

"He must've looked into it," I say, playing with the sky-blue silky trim of the hospital blanket.

"And that's not weird?"

Lifting my eyes to Sam's, I reply, "Yeah. But I think we've already established that Allen is…"

"Has a screw loose. I mean, he shows up at your house, wanting to talk again." Sam raises her eyebrows. "Unless you were just glossing over details with me, and you actually *didn't* make a clean break."

Lifting my good hand, I cross my heart. "I was crystal clear."

Sam inclines her head, causing her curly topknot to flop forward. "Okay, so Allen comes by and wants to ramrod his agenda to get back together, and you're not into it."

A small laugh slips out. "So not into it."

"He gets rough."

I'm silent.

Sam's eyes sharpen on my face. "Has he been rough before?"

I don't know what to say.

"Krista?" Her hushed use of my name tells me she understands I've not been completely transparent about Allen and me.

"The last time we were…together—he hurt me."

Sam's face morphs to horror.

I try to clear this part up. "Ah, I mean it was consensual, the sex. But the rough stuff, I told him to stop."

I swipe a tear, not realizing until just that moment how much I hadn't wanted what he did that night.

"Why didn't you tell me he was a fucker in the sack?"

I laugh. "I think he's just a fucker. Period."

"Duh," Sam says softly, her eyes brimming with sympathy, which makes me have a mini pity party. "God, I didn't know."

I lift my shoulder. "It's over. And after the ugly things he said about the kids I teach—and Trainer—I know how he really feels inside. He doesn't respect me, what I do, or what I'm trying to accomplish. Allen thinks he's the smartest person in the room."

"In the world," Sam corrects, heaving a disgusted sigh.

I can only nod.

"But he knew something about Trainer." Sam gives me a pensive look, chewing her lip. "I can find out the details of this."

We exchange a heavy look.

"It doesn't really matter in the end. Whoever Trainer killed, he didn't think I was important enough to tell. He should have."

Sam shakes her head. "But his *actions*, Krista. He's like this big defender of Krista—the biggest—besides me." She blows on her fist and pretends to polish it on her shirt above her breastbone. "He's beautiful and strong, vulnerable and honest. He's all this yummy maleness, and you'd say *no* to that because of this past event from a long time ago?" Sam's eyes roll to the ceiling. "I guess *event* doesn't cover it, right? It's murder."

Definitely a deal breaker. I wipe more tears. "No, I'd get rid of him because Trainer didn't think I could handle the hard truths."

Sam huffs. "Not pretty lies."

I nod. "It's something my parents always told me. Ugly truths is what we want."

"Not pretty lies," Sam repeats like a mantra.

"Yeah," I agree softly.

"This is going to be hard," Sam says.

"You have no idea."

Sam silently takes my hand, and with her free one, she closes the space between her thumb and index until they're almost touching. "A little idea."

We don't talk anymore. Sam gives me the silent comfort she's so great at.

She leaves when Noose enters. He scowls at Sam as they pass each other, and Sam sticks out her tongue when she's nearly to the door.

Noose snorts.

Then he turns to me, and I almost can't meet his gaze. But I do.

21

TRAINER

Noose leads me down the narrow hospital corridor, as far away from Allen Fitzgerald as humanly possible.

Noose slings an arm around me. "Listen up, ya morose fucker." His eyebrows hike. "Why are you here, for starters?"

"Can't stay away. Allen's here, and Krista's hurt."

Noose nods. "Solid, but ya gotta think, man. What would Judge say?"

He'd be pissed. "He'd tell me to stay away so I can't be tied to this."

Noose steps back as he spreads muscular arms away from his body. "'Kay. So you're *here,* why?"

I huff out a frustrated exhale. "I wanna explain shit to Krista. She doesn't know *why* I murdered Arnie. Allen's a fucking prick. He wants her, so he tells Krista just enough info to make her think I been holdin' out, being dishonest. Krista don't like liars."

Noose grips my shoulders. "I love ya. You know this. But get the fuck outta here, Trainer. Let me handle shit with Krista."

I stare at him. "She told me how you handled stuff. I don't like it."

Noose squeezes my shoulders hard then releases me. Shooting out a raw breath, he hunts around for cigarettes, finds them, and sighs again, probably realizing he can't smoke in a hospital. "Yeah, coulda gone better. But here's the thing: you know I gave her the talk because I don't want some broad workin' ya over, yes?" Noose studies my face to see if I'm gettin' his motivation.

I nod.

"It's better that I'm here when that fuck Allen is too, right?"

Hell, yes. "Yeah."

"Figured there had to be something good in this shit mess. And Allen is a cunning fuck. Girl doesn't want him. He presses, she gets in the mix of shit going down. Accidental, but the facts are: Krista's hurt, and we don't know enough of what went down between them before me"—he thumbs his chest—"and you"—he lightly taps my sternum—"blew in there."

"I know it ain't good." I hesitate for a sec, thinking of her face when I got to the top of those stairs, when Allen had her pinned against her own door. "And she's scared of him."

Noose looks at me. "What's your gut tellin' ya? Because this prick is smooth. He convinces juries every day that his criminals are innocent. Fitzgerald is smart. And very, very rich."

I raise an eyebrow. Sure he is, being a lawyer.

Noose nods. "Got some feelers out. Not enough to know the whole story. Pretty cloaked, his history. But he comes from a family who has *billions*. That little factoid is not well known. Uses his mother's maiden name."

"But *you* found out."

Noose hikes his shoulders. "The devil's in the details."

Cocking my head, I give him a razor-sharp stare. "Does Krista know?"

"Doubt it. Lover Boy doesn't want people knowing he's related to Tycoon Daddy." Noose smirks.

"I don't want to make Krista sound bad," I begin.

"Can't," Noose says. "Got her vetted. Nice girl from a nice family. Kinda a Pollyanna type, but there's worse shit to be guilty of."

I smirk. "But I gotta ask—why wouldn't a lady stay with a guy for all that money?"

"Most would."

But not Krista. My eyes move down the hall to where I know her room is.

Noose and I exchange a glance. "Maybe we need to find out why she dumped Allen. Because she's only dated him and some other guy from high school. Girl doesn't get around."

Heat climbs my neck, and I grab my nape. Talking about Krista feels like a breach of loyalty or something. Hate it.

"Hey—settle, Trainer. Krista's a nice girl, but we're boot deep in shit right now. We got a possible court date for you because of those assholes you worked over. You *gotta* finish your class."

True. "Yup. That's not up for negotiation."

Noose's eyebrows pop at the fancy word I used, realizing it wasn't so hard after all. "Excellent. So we're together on this. You get the fuck outta here, let me handle Krista, set shit straight because you being here—it's suicide. If I were that prick, Allen? I'd already have called the cops and tried to blame you for Krista's broken wrist."

The first wail of sirens breaks out like a symphony in the distance.

Noose whirls. "*Damn!* I hate being right all the time." He shoves me through a side entrance to the morgue. "Storm's outside in the club truck. Get in there and lay down!" he hisses.

I run for the hammered pick-up. Storm's eyes widen in the rearview mirror just before I yank open the back door and heave myself, Superman-style, onto the long bench seat.

Storm cranes his neck around. "What?"

"Shudup," I hiss.

"Oh shit," Storm says as cops begin to pour into the hospital I just came out of.

"Yeah, that."

"I'm gonna take off," Storm announces, beginning to back out.

And they think I'm *the dumb one.*

KRISTA

Cops file into my hospital room just as Noose perches on the narrow rolling stool Sam occupied at my bedside.

"What?" I ask, sitting straight up in bed. "What's going on?"

"Brett Rife?" A cop bellows, placing his right hand on the butt of his weapon.

"Nope," Noose says, crossing his arms and slowly spinning in the stool. His eyes hood as he stares at the lead cop.

I don't have any idea how Noose has made it this far. He seems to relish in unraveling people.

"ID!" a second cop commands.

Noose takes his time, searching every pocket until he gives a sardonic grin. "Oh yeah, must be in my back ass pocket."

"Where everyone else's ID always is," one of the cops mutters sarcastically.

"This man isn't Brett Rife," I say.

The cops look at me for a full second then bring their attention back to Noose.

He flips the wallet out and chucks it at the cop with a hovering hand above his gun. Deftly catching it, he gives Noose a withering look before reading whatever's in there.

"Sean King, age thirty, six feet four inches—" he gives Noose swift appraisal—"two-forty."

The cop throws it back.

Noose raises his hand, and the wallet sort of folds into it from thin air.

He's got the reflexes of a cat.

The cops exchange an uneasy glance after that little maneuver.

"Do you know Brett Rife?" one asks.

"Trainer? Yeah," Noose says in a bored way, relaxing into the narrow stool.

"Did Brett Rife harm this woman?" They look to me then back at Noose.

Unbelievable. I raise my hand. "Hello?" I wave it back and forth, and the cops turn their attention to me. Finally. "I'm 'this woman.' For the record, my name's Krista Glass. Trainer's my boyfriend. I fell. I was not pushed, and Trainer didn't physically assault me."

The cop appears almost disappointed. "Did anyone physically assault you, Miss Glass."

Allen, my mind offers. "No."

The cop picks up on my one-second hesitation because they're trained to do that. What I *didn't* expect was Noose's subtle acknowledgment of the same thing.

Tension that had been building suddenly begins to dissipate. "My ex-boyfriend, Allen Fitzgerald?"

The cops exchange another look. "Yes?"

"What can I do to arrange a restraining order against *him*?"

They tell me.

I'm going to do that the minute I get out of here.

I should be scared of Trainer because he's a murderer.

But Allen scares me more.

The cops are finally gone.

They couldn't find Allen, either. Noose had signed me in, and Allen disappeared in the meantime.

For now.

"This Allen is a real prick," Noose states the instant the cops have left the building.

I fold the paper the hospital printed out for them: instructions to file a restraining order.

"The irony that I'd have to file a restraining order against an attorney." I shake my head, using my good hand to bring my ice water to my mouth and use my index finger to guide the straw to my lips. Cool water slides down my throat, and I breathe a contented sigh, settling back against the plumped pillows. The dull ache of my wrist is beginning to get through all the meds they're giving me.

Noose snorts. "Yup. Too many freaks. Not enough circuses."

"Wow, you're so easily amused," I say, crossing my arms and getting a jolt of pain. I can't so easily twist and move my arm like I used to.

"At least it's your left," Noose says, winking, "can still wipe your ass and eat a helluva lot easier."

I flop back on my pillow again. "You know, I'm not sure about you."

Noose leans in, carefully folding his hands at the edge of my bed, almost prayer-like. "All you gotta know, honey, is that Trainer is my brother, and I don't want him fucked with."

The unspoken threat settles between us, like déjà vu of the last time we met.

I give him the look he deserves, serving up all my frustration, pain, and doped-up intellect in a single stare. "You already told me that—the *first* time you threatened me."

Noose blinks. "That was *not* threatening you. You'd know if I threatened you." He chuckles. "If ya lived—though I take pause with murdering chicks." Like it's an afterthought, he adds, "Kids too."

"Is this some kind of schtick?"

His golden-brown eyebrows pull together.

"An act? A routine? Scare the poor teacher, and she's going to quake."

Noose's lips thin. "No." His face is like granite.

Maybe he's not playing around by acting tough. *Maybe Sean King isn't acting.*

"What do you want then? Besides to show up and beat up my ex-boyfriend and tell me that you and Trainer are tight? Because I'd be stupid not to get that by this time."

"Wanna do more than I have," he confesses. "That sperm stain needs to stop breathing." Noose rests his elbows on his knees, seeming to contemplate a thought. With a heavy sigh, he continues, "But, got bigger fish to fry, much as I'd love Fitzgerald coming to an end."

"I wasn't saying I want him dead."

"You weren't saying you didn't," Noose points out, brow cocked.

Nervously, I tuck a strand of hair behind my ear with my good hand and change the subject. "Trainer murdered someone. Allen said so, and Trainer admitted it."

Noose says nothing.

"You know what happened," I state.

Noose nods.

"Tell me."

"Not my story to tell. And a bit of advice?" His eyes peg me to the hospital bed, and I realize they're as light as Trainer's, just gray instead of green, like dirty glass.

Fine scars are scattered across his face, and one especially ugly one seems to be newer, crossing the bridge of his nose. The imperfections keep him from being truly handsome.

But I suspect a man like Noose is comfortable with his flaws.

Noose doesn't wait for me to answer. "You like Trainer. You guys do okay fucking, and getting along, right?"

My mouth drops open. "Gah! You *can't* talk like that. It's awful!"

Noose grunts. "Just did. Now hear me out."

"Is there a choice?"

"Nope." He smiles, oozing that weird charm again. I can't decide if I like him or I'm offended.

"I'm a captive audience anyway. I'm too drugged to go anywhere, and I tossed myself over the railing, so there's that."

"Technically, I tossed you."

God.

He lifts a shoulder dismissively. "Anyways, so what's a little killing between lovers?"

That hurts. I feel a scalding tear slide out of my eye, and I angrily flick it. The drugs have squashed my inhibitions, and I hate it.

"No to waterworks. It's where I draw the line."

I glare through my tears. "Not tough enough?"

He glowers back.

I smile. "Here's what's between us, Noose. Trainer didn't tell me he was a murderer." I arrange my face in an expression that says, "So explain *that.*"

I move to fold my arms again and think better of it.

"Let me tell you something, sweetheart. Trainer can barely talk to me about dick, and I'm the best friend he's got. Me, Lariat, Wring, Snare—we're his wingmen. Guys that don't have anything at stake for hangin' with 'im except having his back. We're just there. You get me?"

I nod, thinking of Sam, who's not a superficial friend like a lot of women. She's been there for me no matter what.

"Yes."

"He's never gone into any details with me. I know stuff because it's my job to. But Trainer didn't barf the deets out for me all nice and neat."

"Sounds sloppy." The corners of my lips lift despite myself.

He chuckles. "Yeah, I guess it does."

We sit there for a moment, and it's not awkward. Probably because we're both thinking about the same man.

"Trainer didn't come clean with you because he can't. And if I know him—as much as any human being can know him—Trainer was afraid you'd walk away."

"I wouldn't."

"Oh, really? What's this talk about? You deciding shit. Judging."

I study my knotted fingers, not even able wring my hands properly with this stupid cast. The dull ache in my arm grows sharper.

"Don't lie to me, or yourself. Thinking about ditching Trainer because he killed someone is an excuse to forgo the potential for something really fucking awesome. Look in the mirror and ask yourself if *you're* the one who's scared to see it through. Because Trainer's brave as fuck, confused as fuck, and before you showed up—hopeless as fuck."

Noose stands, towering over me. His eyes are piercing, nearly translucent in the odd mix of hospital fluorescents and ambient light filtering in through the lone window as the sun releases the day. "Don't you fuck him up more, Krista Glass."

Tears come, but Noose has already left me with my decisions, shredded heart, and uncertainties.

And the self-examination is worse than the broken wrist.

Far worse.

22

TRAINER

"I'm glad you came here today, Brett."

"I screwed up," I admit after I just spent the last half hour filling him in.

Judge lifts a palm, and I notice his reddened knuckles are swollen, the skin around them stretched tight. "No. Don't apologize for love."

I lean back in a patio chair that's all-wood, a "lounger," Mama would have called it. "I didn't say I loved her, Judge."

Didn't say I didn't, either. Without answering, he takes out his pipe from his silken robe and places a bit of tobacco in the bowl. After lighting it and taking a few experimental puffs, he settles comfortably against the chair.

That uncomfortable woven shit is MIA. Don't miss it.

The smell of Judge's tobacco makes a good feeling come over me. Solid. Unshifting.

"Don't expound to Eleanor about this little noxious habit I maintain. I'd never hear the end of it."

This is like Krista told me. I get what Judge is saying, even if I don't know all the words. It's okay.

Learning isn't so bad no more.

"So the ex-boyfriend was already at her residence when you arrived?"

"Yeah. Shoved Krista into her door."

"Hmm. What is this fellow's name?"

"Allen Fitzgerald."

Judge puzzles over that for a half minute. "Doesn't ring any bells, but that doesn't mean he wasn't just starting out as I was finishing. However, by that time, I was a judge, and no longer an attorney."

"Which job was your favorite?"

Judge chuckles. "Neither." Smoke flows between us, but I still make out the twinkle in his eye. Hard to know when Judge is yanking a guy's chain.

It's just his way.

"This Fitzgerald seems a bit disheveled around the edges with conduct like that. I'm surprised a man of that caliber would be caught manhandling women."

"Any man can be caught doing the wrong thing to a lady, Judge."

Our eyes meet.

"True, so true…my apologies, Brett. I forget with whom I'm speaking."

"It's no big."

After a few more puffs, Judge rests the pipe in a holder made just for it. Another thing I like about Judge is how precise he is. There is a purpose and a reason for everything he does, everything around him.

That's part of why I know I'm okay.

Because he wants Brett Rife as part of his universe. The Judge Hammerstein universe.

"I think your friend…Noose?"

I nod.

He smiles, continuing, "Your friend Noose did you a good turn, showing you the door at the exact moment law enforcement arrived. It would have been very bad timing had you been there, given some of the issues we face."

Leaning forward, I plant each foot on either side of the lounger thing and clasp my hands. I don't wince, but they still hurt from using them on Fitzgerald.

I'd do it again if he were standing in front of me.

"I didn't do nothin'," I say.

Judge inclines his head, picking up the pipe for a few more puffs. Frowning at the pipe, he picks up a square silver lighter, with elaborate script that I can almost read. Flicking the lid open, he dips the flame inside the pipe bowl, relighting it. He puffs then sets the lighter on the small glass-topped table beside his lounger. "I know that, and you know that. But where there's smoke"—he lifts his pipe—"there's fire. Those police officers would have connected you because of your presence, nothing more, truly a circumstantial coincidence. One we do not need."

"Allen Fitzgerald is a bad dude." I look down at my hands, consciously forcing myself to stop hanging on so tight. "He's an Arnie," I say so low, I'm surprised to hear Judge's reply. Almost as surprised at his words.

"I know. They come in many shapes and sizes. You might think to ask Krista what happened to cause her to terminate the relationship."

I make a noise of disbelief. "None of my business. She doesn't make me confess all the chicks I've…y'know—been with."

"Oh, I think it is very much your business."

Lifting my chin, I meet Judge's stare. His eyes remind me of Noose's a little. Not the color, which is sorta boring brown, but the determination in them. "Krista Glass chose you. This Noose has said you're her third boyfriend. And the last was an attorney." His eyes narrow with intensity, and his voice goes deeper. "You're a young man with outstanding moral fortitude, from a debilitating childhood, who cannot read—yet. Why would any young woman in her right mind take on a male with those challenges unless she sees who you *really* are, as I did? The man behind the traumas, so to speak."

My heart begins to race. Judge is saying so much of what I've been thinking, but couldn't find the words for.

250

"I thought she did, ya know—see me. It's why I gave us a shot."

"I know she does." Judge sounds so sure.

"What do I do?" I struggle to rein in my emotion and fail. Fisting my hands, I plunge them against my burning eyeballs, hating my bullshit, the barrier that's always been there.

"Brett."

I can't do this.

"Brett," Judge repeats.

I drop my hands, ignoring the small wetness on my skin, the feeling like I'll blow up any second and fly away like leaves on a torrent of wind.

Relentlessly, I focus on staring at the lake. Sunlight glints off waves, and everything around me is happy to soak it up.

I don't think I deserve it. Soaking up sun, being happy. Living.

Finally, I look to Judge.

"Don't let the Arnies steal her, son."

Choking emotion begins to suffocate me—having Krista and the Arnies sharing the same space in my head.

I make an inarticulate noise and try to stand. Can't see. My hand flies out, and I touch the cold glass of the sliding door that leads into Judge's house as I fumble around for the handle to escape myself.

Warm arms go around my torso, and I try to shove away.

They grow tighter.

"No, son—let it out. I won't leave you. Let it out."

Those cracks in my chest grow wider.

Then break.

My chest heaves, and a broken sob tears out of my throat.

Wrapping my arms around the smaller man, I cry like I'm gonna die.

Feels like it.

Great hitching sobs spill out of me, one after the next. I see my life rewind like a movie.

The beatings.

The burnings.

The words used against me like weapons and the ones I couldn't read.

In the end, when I'm a spent, useless mess, shaming my ass to the point of no return—I see Krista like a mirage inside my head.

I see her so good.

"Let him sleep, sweetheart."

I hear Judge's voice, but I ignore him telling Eleanor that I'm okay, that I just need rest.

My phone's been blowing up with texts all day.

I sent a two-word memorized phrase text to Noose. And I could read the second word, accepting a brief moment of victory through the haze of releasing a life-time of bottled emotions.

I'm okay.

Feel like an empty husk. Like shit. Empty. Withered. But at the same time, I think I know what I want.

And if Krista doesn't want me like I want her, at least I know I tried for it.

For that happy thing everyone tries for.

I feel like the luckiest man alive that I had it for two weeks. But now I know how it feels to be happy. I ache for another taste. The smell of her hair. That smile she gets when she thinks I'm smart because I learned more letters. Or because I try. Krista says even if I don't get it right then, I will.

Krista believes in me, and her believing changed how I felt about me.

Made shit look different.

When I finally stopped bawling like an infant, Judge told me I've experienced a perspective shift.

Didn't have to guess at that one. Pretty easy to figure out. Shit was always the same. Krista came into the picture, and suddenly, all the old shit looked different. New shit became interesting in a good way.

I gotta face the club first. The brothers have to know I'm throwing down for a woman even if she won't have me.

Just making the decision to come clean with the brothers makes me feel better. A load off.

Haven't spent the night at Judge's house in a long time. They keep a room for me here.

Why do I feel so unbalanced when something good might actually happen?

Maybe because happiness is so new, I don't know what to do with it. Bad is so familiar, it's automatic on how to deal.

If Krista says yes to me, I'll have her stop by, meet Eleanor and Judge.

She'd like them.

I know it.

I shovel Eleanor's pancakes down, chasing the entire load with a glass of milk, and remember at the last sec to use my napkin.

"My, you do have a fine appetite." Eleanor's grin takes up her entire face. She loves that I eat good. Never had trouble with food. Me and food get along fine.

Judge gets a secret smile on his face, looking at me over the top of a small fancy glass of OJ gripped in his arthritic hand.

Setting the half-empty glass down, he looks at a wristwatch. "Brett slept—ten hours." His eyebrows quirk.

Judge doesn't reference my pussy meltdown. His only comment is, "Brett is lighter today. Aren't you, son?"

"Yes." I am so much lighter. I know what I want. Who I want. And reading is important for shit other than just improving myself for some distant court date. And that feels way better than it outta.

Maybe I just want to be something. Maybe I want to be what I would've been if I'd had a mama who cared.

I duck my chin, guilt sweeping through me.

Mama did her best.

A horrible thought moves through my mind. Maybe Mama *didn't* do her best. Maybe she just got by and let those men beat on me because she was too broken to do what was right.

"What is it, son?" Judge grips my forearm, sharp eyes on my face.

The words that form aren't perfect, but I have more than usual. "I think Mama didn't make so good of choices, Judge."

He bursts out laughing, and I cock my head. Don't know what's so funny.

Judge sobers up, like a drunk without a drink. "It's okay to love your mama, even though she made bad choices. Sometimes folks make the only choices they can see. To some people, there's only a few choices. To others, there's an infinite number."

I get what he's saying, and that feels great too. "*I* think there's more, Judge."

Judge's smile broadens, and Eleanor walks to stand behind him. They look proud of me, and I feel my face get hot with an emotion I can't name.

But I got no reason to feel dumb or ashamed. I got something to say, and I know it. Feel it. "I *see* more choices."

Judge spreads his hands away from his body. His next words make me feel like I could fly. "You always did."

23

ALLEN

"Look at you," Orson says with a disgust so pure, if I weren't so accustomed to my father's insults, I would flinch. His finger waves indifferently toward my face, my taped nose.

I don't react.

Not bothering to answer, I pour myself another shot of eight-hundred-dollar-a-bottle scotch.

"Have I not instructed you on how to play the victim?"

Exhaustively.

"Then do that."

"I've ruined it. Got overeager."

"Did you?" Orson struggles with clear impatience. "Have you hurt Krista?"

I shake my head. *Goddammit.* "I did shove her against the door, instead of through it, like I wanted to."

"Imbecile. Not only have you damaged the only thing you're good for—the good fortune to be born looking like a Greek god—you've made the perfect bride candidate as skittish as a colt."

Fuck. "She doesn't *want* me." That's unbelievable, but true. I shoot the expensive whiskey down my throat without tasting it, setting my belly on smooth fire.

"Of course she does."

I turn, facing Orson. "Krista has her eyes set on some moron she's teaching during a forced sabbatical."

"Explain."

I do, in great detail.

Orson captures a jaw artificially unsoftened by age between a curled index and thumb. "This poses a problem."

I jerk my head back, snorting derisively. "Don't pretend you care about me gaining your billions."

Orson hits me with a look of disgust. "It's not about the money, fool. My fortune has always been a tool of manipulation to perpetuate the family lines. There are very few females who will do."

I search his face. He's bluffing, but about what isn't clear. Suddenly, a slow realization dawns. "This is about the *family* fortune. If I do not marry a predetermined female, *you* lose the money too."

His silence tells me I'm right.

Having the upper hand for perhaps the first time in my life, I move in for the metaphorical kill. My experience as an attorney is no small thing in tightening the rope around his neck.

"What clause or loophole is attached to our family's money?"

My father turns on his heel, moving to a thirty-foot-long set of custom-built bookshelves that span the entire wall. A ladder that reaches ceiling hooks onto a solid copper rod across the top of the bookshelves. Instead of climbing the ladder, Orson rolls the wheeled ladder out of the way and pulls out the Holy Bible about halfway up.

As the books spine tips outward, the entire bookshelf slowly swings open to reveal a dim room.

Sudden brightness bursts to life as minuscule LED lighting illuminates a huge vault. I follow Orson across the threshold.

Curiosity killed the cat.

The room appeared bigger from the vantage point of the library. However, since it's use is nothing more than a vault, the space doesn't need to be large.

The darkened area is roughly circular, perhaps fifteen feet in diameter. Vaults of many sizes run floor to ceiling, touching one another in a more or less jigsaw array.

Some look antique. Some modern.

"What is this?"

Orson says without turning. "What does it look like?"

Secrets kept. Out loud, I guess, "Something I won't like."

"Oh, I don't know. I've come to admire the precepts of our ancestors. Though it does cause certain dilemmas."

I don't know what the fuck he's talking about, but Orson has always spoken in riddles. It's probably the singular thing that made me such a gifted attorney. My God-given bloodthirsty nature didn't hurt, either.

"You ask why it's so critical that you marry Krista Glass."

I just stare at him, waiting. Orson adores the sound of his own voice, so I'm certain he'll answer all my questions when he's ready.

He turns back to the oldest-looking safe in the room and with a few practiced turns of his wrist, he silently opens the smooth, round door.

He extracts a single rolled piece of paper.

Striding to a table that sits in the exact center of the room, he carefully unties the ribbon that surrounds the middle and unfolds it.

I was wrong—it isn't a single sheet.

There are many of the same size.

"These are copies, of course. The originals have faded but were copied over a hundred years ago to preserve them."

"A fucking family tree?" I laugh. Not a small chuckle but a genuine belly laugh.

"Foul language doesn't become you, Allen."

I roll my eyes. "Your good opinion doesn't matter. You've made that abundantly clear."

Our eyes meet, and I don't shift mine away. He's made me what I am, and he can deal with it.

"I pay for your playthings," he states.

I feel a cruel smile take over my face. "It's kept precious Krista safe."

Orson's chin rises, and even in the artificial lights of the strange room, his eyes appear to be lit from within.

That used to spook me when I was younger. But I'm all grown up now and am a diagnosed sociopath.

Orson should be intimidated by *me*.

"Take a look." He taps the family trees.

I step forward and peruse the oldest. *Blah, blah blah. Johnny begat Samuel who begat...*

Wait a second.

The same surnames come up over and over again.

Quickly, I move the oldest sheet aside and scan the next. Then the next.

And on.

Seven sheets later, I raise my eyes to Orson.

"This was done on purpose."

Orson nods.

"This is the most fucked up scenario of history I've ever seen."

My father's shrug is a practiced roll of shoulders, an answer without answering.

My fist pounds the table once, and the injuries sustained from dealing with that idiot Krista is fucking sing through to my shoulder. "I see the last name is Krista's?"

Orson nods.

"What kind of sick fuckery is this, *Dad*?" I say with thinly veiled sarcasm.

"You share the same father."

I blanch. I have slept with a relative? I glance back at the family tree—with branches so incestuous I can't follow them. Essentially, it's a tree without branches. Finally, his words hit me like a sucker punch. "You are Krista's father?"

Orson nods. "Yes, and we cannot let a drop of Rothschild or Fitzgerald blood escape."

"You were trying to get me to marry my half-sister."

Orson lifts a shoulder. "I was not so lucky. I was married to your mother, and she was only a second cousin."

"Lucky?" My voice holds a hysterical shriek.

"Calm down, Allen."

"I can't *calm down*. There are almost four billion women for me to choose from, and you directed me toward a relative, a close one."

"It is the way it has always been since time immortal." His eyes peg the seven sheets. "Centuries are represented here, Allen. This gives tradition new meaning."

I blast my fingers through my hair. "Why?" I demand. "Convince me."

"Do you want to inherit over fifty billion dollars?"

"Yes," I answer instantly. "What kind of inane question is that?"

Orson is silent.

"You mean I have to marry and have offspring with my own sister?"

Orson nods. "It shouldn't take much to convince her. And what is very nice is that I went outside of family lines to impregnate her mother, thereby insuring a certain"—he waves his palm in a loose circle—"longevity to the lines."

"No, that's not it," I say slowly, "it's more along the lines that you didn't want the potential for recessive calamity to take us all down."

Like insanity or inherited disease risk. Ten fingers instead of ten toes.

"You're sick," I hiss from between my teeth.

Orson smiles. "But very, very rich."

"Why would our ancestors want a tree so polluted by the same blood?"

"We feel..." Orson chuckles, placing a tender finger to the oldest sheet. "That our family is superior *because* of our pure blood."

He lets me think it through. Seconds pound into long minutes as I review Krista and what she has to offer:

Billions of dollars.

A fine, fuckable cunt. And wasn't that delectable fear I saw in those perfect charcoal eyes? Yes, *yes it was*.

"Fine," I bite out. "I'm in."

"Magnificent," Orson says, his face brimming with my inevitable answer.

"One question."

His eyebrow rises.

"Is Krista the only relative I can have? Are there any more female bastards out there running around without knowing they carry the precious Fitzgerald or Rothschild bloodlines?"

Orson's chin hikes arrogantly. "None. And so you're aware, every woman you've put your seed inside is dead, save one."

This revelation should surprise me.

But it doesn't.

Father had hundreds put down like dogs. Because they didn't have the perfect genetic stock.

"Who was Krista's real mother?"

"That's two questions," Orson smiles, but it's more a baring of teeth.

"Yes," I grit.

"She was a very distant cousin. A Rothschild. A woman who thought she could escape our family." He tsks.

"How'd that work out for her?"

Orson's glittering eyes meet mine, and we smile at each other.

"Badly."

24

KRISTA

Noose was dead wrong.

Having my left arm in a cast is still a pain in the ass, regardless of my wiping abilities. Yes, I can do all the basics, but it's like hauling around dead weight.

I feel klutzy, because I am.

Not only that, I'm also nervous. I'm going to see Trainer today, and I haven't worked out how I feel.

Noose put me on notice, *again*. I filled out the paperwork for the restraining order, but I haven't had the time to drop it off at the local police station.

And even though I completely understand my broken wrist was an accident, a niggling part in the back of my head tells me that if Trainer and I weren't involved, it wouldn't have happened.

On the other hand, that might be an unreasonable dot I'm connecting. Allen's true colors showed in part, only because of my new relationship with Trainer.

But what if there wasn't any Trainer?

What if I'd chosen to overlook Allen's dull performance in bed and given him a second chance?

Remembering the expression of disgust and disdain on Sam's face, I decide a second chance never would've worked. Allen didn't respect me the last time we made love. He'd just taken from me. Actually, looking back, he never respected any of my feelings or choices. I was living in Allen's World.

I have enough respect for myself to know that his behavior wouldn't be acceptable long-term. There's no apologizing his way out of our last sexual encounter. Mainly because he doesn't get it. And if I have to explain it to him—well, that defeats everything. He'll never see his issues—or ours.

Shifting my weight in my chair, I dump my forehead in my good hand and huff out a pissed-off exhale. I'm still angry about all the things he said about my students. Allen might be an attorney with a nice bankroll, but he's ignorant of what I do for a living, though I've talked about my work extensively.

That just means Allen never listened. Not really. He wasn't motivated to because he didn't care.

The fingers of my left hand dangle out of my full-hand cast, and I make small circles on the long, banquet style table.

My stomach's in knots.

I haven't talked to Trainer since yesterday. I'll never forget his eyes as they watched Noose put me in Allen's car.

I understand why he couldn't be at the hospital with me.

But my heart ached with his absence and the unanswered questions.

It's none of my business, really. But Allen made it my business when he blurted out the *M* word.

Murderer. I sweep my eyes over the empty classroom, noting the familiar items: whiteboard, erasable markers, and a world globe. That ubiquitous smell that permeates every school covers them all.

I got here the minute the Martin Sortun emptied. I needed time to get my head cleared before Trainer comes. My plan's not working, though.

The door bursts open, and my eyes fly up as I jump in my seat. I groan as the movement jars my arm.

Sam runs in. Tiny diamond stud earrings wink as her hair falls away from her face and her vibrant purple tunic-length top floats around her hips.

She's out of breath, eyes frantic. "Krista!"

This can't be good. "What—what are you doing here, Sam?" I ask, slowly rising. I know for a fact she's got court today.

"I remember him."

My eyebrow flies up. *Huh?* "Who?"

"Brett Rife."

Oh. "Tell me." I wince when my fingers grip the edge of the table, zinging pain up my arm.

I let the cast drop to my side like a log.

"His records are sealed, but *I* was the stenographer." Sam hops up and down like a jumping bean. "I don't think I would've remembered, except it was my very first case after graduating." She pushes her wild hair behind her shoulders.

"I *knew* I knew that name!"

Should I wait to ask Trainer? I glance at my watch. *Half-hour until he walks through that door.*

I bite my lip and meet Sam's eyes.

"You're *killing* me, Krista," Sam says, inhaling deeply and letting it out in a rush. "Don't you *want* to know what really went down?"

I do. So badly. But like Noose said, it's Trainer's story to tell.

"Just answer me this," I say finally, after we've stared at each other a full minute. "Did the guy deserve it?"

Sam gives a vigorous nod. "Twice."

The air seeps out of me like a popped balloon.

"Brett Rife is one damaged dude, Sam. I love what you tell me about him, and what he does for you, but his history goes way beyond not being able to read."

Heaving a sigh, I realize I never slowed down long enough to examine our pasts. We worked—meshed or just had general compatibility—and now my lack of concern is going to bite me in the ass.

Especially since I'm pretty sure I love him.

"His mom's a prostitute."

My chin jerks up. "What?"

"Yeah, a real class-A winner, jumped from guy to guy his whole life. He never had a dad. It's all in his file, the testimony his lawyer gave."

My mind's eye flows over Trainer's muscled skin, littered with the scars of past abuse, and I close my eyes, leaning my fingers against the table as my head droops. When I open my eyes, my vision is clouded with tears begging to be released.

"His absentee record for school is shocking. It's no wonder he can't read. It's a wonder Trainer's functional at all."

An image of him raised above me, pumping into my body with single-minded purpose makes my panties wet. My heart races, and my hands dampen.

Trainer is *so* functional. In all the ways that matter. The ways that count in life.

Sam walks over to where I stand, my eyes glued to the faux-wood tabletop.

I don't lift my eyes, but her words strike me like blows.

"You can't keep him for his big cock, Krista—like an exotic pet. He's a murderer, even if the latest jerk his mom picked deserved it."

A noise has my eyes shifting to the door.

Trainer fills the space, his big body taking up every inch. His presence uses the oxygen I need to breathe.

And I can't breathe...

Sam stares at me. "Oh shit, he's here," she says quietly, eyes riveted to my face.

I give a sad, numb nod. "Yes," I whisper.

Needing to fix this mess, I move around the table. "Trainer."

Trainer holds up a hand. "That's okay, Krista." His icy-green eyes drift to Sam. "I guess you're gonna believe whatever your friend says."

"No!" I cry.

Sam gives me a sharp look.

I split my attention between the two of them. *Damn.*

"I mean—I listen to Sam, but I was going to ask you directly."

"You didn't, though, Krista," Trainer states.

He's right.

I should have just told Sam to hold back until I could speak with Trainer. She could have filled in his version with whatever he needed to say then or later. I walk to him slowly, reaching for him with my good arm, and he pulls away, hurt etched in his eyes.

I put that there.

Talking to Sam shredded his trust.

Then I think of Allen and how that might seem. Him being at my condo. Us "talking." Maybe it all looks like I'm just playing him. It might add up to him in a bad way.

"I'm not playing you," I blurt.

Trainer nods, then he turns his attention to Sam. "Guess you told her about Arnie. That you know somethin', somehow."

Sam shakes her head. "Not exactly."

"I'm gonna tell you what you need to know."

I wince at the tone of his voice. Obligation. Resignation. The warmth that is usually reserved for me is absent—like he knew all along we weren't going to last and this moment was inevitable.

No. "You don't have to explain," I rush out, putting my hand forward.

Trainer angles his body so my contact can't land as his eyes skate to mine. Uncomfortably, he holds my gaze. "Yeah, I do."

His eyes move back to Sam. "You don't make me sound too good. But you got a lot of shit right. I *am* a murderer. I ain't no dog." He scowls at her, obviously referencing the "exotic pet" comment. "And my mama's a whore." His gaze levels on her, glittering with anger. "And my cock *is* big."

Heat suffuses my face, and I fight not putting my hands to my hot cheeks. I've never seen Sam blush. With her dusky coffee-and-cream complexion, it'd be difficult to see. But it's not difficult to see now.

Trainer pauses, his big hand coming to rest on the doorjamb, though he makes no effort to enter the room.

Sam stares at her feet, clearly ashamed by the words he bore witness too.

But she's not more ashamed than me.

His beautiful green eyes, rimmed by thick, chocolate-colored lashes turn to me.

"But there's shit you both don't know. I own it."

My hand flutters to my throat, where a thudding pulse beats as though a bird is trapped within the confines of my flesh, searching for a way out.

"I own it. All of it." He squeezes his hand into a fist, briefly touching the part of his chest where his heart lies beneath.

My eyes shut, and a tear squeezes out. *Oh my God.*

"I never knew what day I'd eat, get beat, see my mama, or be free of all that. Never knew. My life was a big mother-fucking Russian roulette. Always spinning," his finger shoots up, making lazy spirals.

I fixate on that digit symbolizing his horrible childhood—a circle without end.

"Then I found these guys that are as fucked up as me, and they don't care how fucked up I am. They see me—really see what I am. And I'm relieved, because I finally have acceptance, and I don't have to be starved, burned, beaten, and screamed at to get it. I just work hard and be loyal, and it's there for the taking."

I open my eyes, and his next words are a weapon, each one a bullet to my heart.

"Then I meet this beautiful girl." His eyes rove my face, and the tears come faster now. "She's so beautiful, it hurts to look at her."

Sam's soft sobs are the only noise in the room.

"She doesn't tell me I'm dumb or make fun of me. She teaches me. And when I hold her, all that shit that happened fades away to nothing. Like it didn't never happen. That she made that nightmare go away for good."

"Trainer—"

"Shut up!" he bellows, his breath blowing the hair that's come loose from my messy bun. "You wanted to *know.*" The last word seethes out from between his tight lips.

I cringe back, and Sam sobs.

"But she'd rather believe everyone else but me. Her fancy ex. Her best friend. Because they think they lived what I lived."

He steps in so close to me, I can feel the heat of his breath on the top of my head.

My fingers ache to hold him. What he's mistaken for distrust is really just confusion, the result of miscommunication and bad timing.

"They didn't live a minute in my shoes."

My bottom lip trembles. "I know, Trainer."

His fingers cover my lips, and I suck in a sob. "What—?"

"Don't talk. I'll learn how to read, Krista."

My eyes widen as his finger traces the contour of my bottom lip, his fingers saying goodbye. I feel it down to my toes.

"Just not with you."

"No!" I yell.

Trainer spins on his heel, striding toward the entrance to the school.

I chase after him, leaving behind the classroom where we made love, where I taught him he was smarter than he knew.

Turns out he was smarter than all of us.

Trainer slammed the door, making the glass shiver inside the frame. He clearly isn't going to talk to me, so I watch him stalk to his bike, jump on, and roar off. When I can no longer see his figure, I trudge back to the classroom, where I sort of fold myself into one the classroom chairs. I bang my knee in the process.

It hurts, I guess.

But I don't care. All I can think of is Trainer and how I blew it in a bunch of small ways.

They were all ways that mattered, though.

"Krista…" Sam says helplessly.

I don't look at Sam. I just sit there, staring.

A tissue box lands on the desk, and I suddenly become aware of the wet heat of my tears cascading down my face.

Lifting my cast, I study it, as a fresh wave of tears bursts.

"This is my fault," Sam cries, plopping down beside me.

I shake my head. "Nope, it's mine. I should've just gone to that cabin last night after they released me from the hospital. Shouldn't have waited even a minute." Angrily, I swipe away the tears. "Trainer coming in on your comments was just cementing his feelings that he was second in my heart. That trust was last place. He's too fragile emotionally to deal."

I put my head in my hands, and my arm gives a painful squawk. "God."

"It's a mess," Sam says.

I nod.

"And I didn't even get to the part that he referenced. The judge let him off. I guess there was so much history of abuse that Brett's hospital records were like the Dead Sea Scrolls. This was just the latest pimp that took out all his awfulness on the son of his prostitute."

Air squeezes out of my tight throat. "Figured that. I mean, Trainer's not a cold-blooded killer. But I have always sensed a willingness to protect others." In a low voice, I add, "Except for himself."

Sam and I exchange a loaded glance of remorse, sadness, and emotional exhaustion.

"I was going to say that despite all those facts, there's a counterpoint to it all."

"Except the cock part." My smile is rueful, my heart heavy.

A sad little laugh slips from between Sam's lips. "Yeah," she says softly, "that's not up for debate on being a negative attribute."

She takes my hand, and I give her a bone-crushing squeeze back. "You're not mad?" she asks.

Sam meant well. It was just bad timing, and I don't have the heart to come down on her, even if I didn't want to accept responsibility. It's too close to the anniversary of her parents' death. I don't know if she could handle it all.

Shaking my head, I wrap icy fingers on my forehead. "No, I feel like kicking my own ass, but never yours."

"He loves you," Sam says. "Even I could see that, and I was last in line when they were handing out intuition."

My sadness is so vast, I can hardly speak past it, but I do. "He did."

Past tense.

25

TRAINER

Don't care if I die.

Don't care if I live.

Thought I had somethin'.

That's what I get for thinkin'.

The Arnies' words from the past crowd my head, and I pour on the speed. *Gotta get to the club.* Touch base.

Touch something.

Can't get Krista outta my head. Her face lingers there in my mind.

Sadness.

Confusion.

And a fuck ton of *sorry.*

Can't get past those words from Sam. How could I?

Pet. Big cock. *Murderer.*

That's what I am to them. Some dude who walks around killin' people, fucking women, like I'm no better than a dog.

Okay.

Had enough of that attitude growin' up. Don't need no more of it.

Turning off the backroads highway, I hit the long road leading up to our new club. My bike eats up the pavement Vipe just paid a shit ton for. The club's more like a fortress. None of us are complaining. Me and the brothers take security to a paranoid level.

Kinda natural for me anyway.

Ripping into the vague temporary outlines of parking stalls, I have the kickstand slapped out and the bike settled in less than two seconds.

I jump off and jog to the front door, bang it open, and scan the dim interior.

I see Storm first.

"What the fuck?" he says, taking me in.

Not explaining nothin' to him. "Noose around?"

"Hey, man, maybe just chill before you go bustin' in there."

"Fuck. Off," I say so quiet, I'm not sure he hears me.

Storm retreats, hands up, palms facing me. "Hey, man, whatever the fuck—your funeral."

Yeah.

Then the guys are coming out of church with lots of loud talking, back slapping, and the general brotherhood of being Road Kill MC.

"Beating the shit outta me isn't gonna make it better, Trainer," Noose says, spitting blood to his left.

My abraded fists drop. "I—"

Noose's drop too. "Ya done?"

"Wasn't trying to"—I rake my hand through my hair—"do what I done."

Noose grins. "I know that."

"You're idiots," Lariat says, shaking his head.

"You got something to say?" Noose asks.

My eyes flick to Lariat and Wring. "Fuck it, you guys need some uterus time? I gotcha," Lariat says.

Noose rolls his eyes, grabbing his package. "Yeah, so fuck off. We don't need an audience."

Wring gives a chin lift, then he and Lariat walk off.

"Not here," Noose says, gingerly moving his jaw as he whips his head toward the back of the club.

I realize we'd fought all the way to the front.

I follow, knowing I fucked things up even more than usual.

We're at our post where we normally jaw shit, asses on concrete. 'Course, that was back when Noose and I were talking a lot.

I had Krista for the last two weeks, and haven't been doing much talking back here with Noose—or thinking. I've been with my lady.

Didn't need Noose. Had her.

Noose glares at me, cocking his head to the left, and I can just make out his profile from twilight fading to dusk. "'Kay. Spill your shit."

I open my mouth then close it. Don't have the words.

Noose helps, even though I don't deserve dick.

"Gotta be about pussy to make you beat the shit outta me." He chuckles.

I nod. "Krista."

"What happened now. She blaming you for the ass-over-tea-kettle that broke her wrist?"

"No."

"Give it to me then." He cups his fingers toward himself in the classic gesture of *come on.*

Tying my hair back, I wince at the new aches in my body. Ones I gave myself for going after Noose.

"Sorry, Noose," I whisper.

He hikes a shoulder. "Fuck it."

I look at him, and clear gray eyes stare back. No bullshit.

"I don't know why I—"

"Whatever, tell me the problem." He digs his cigarette pack out of the interior pocket of his vest, flips the lid, plucks a cig out with his lips, and lights it in one fluid motion.

"She's got a friend, Sam."

Noose dips his chin, scattering smoke between us. "Yeah. Know who she is. Folks were creamed on a highway five years ago. Not getting over it. Court stenographer."

I blink and reply slowly, "The lady who keeps the record during the court crap?"

Noose nods, blowing a stream of smoke. His jaw partially flattens, and I know he'll toss a ring.

He does.

Memories of the Arnies broadside me. Taking a deep breath, I look down at my boots, trying to level my shit. Sometimes the past sneaks up on me when I'm not expectin' it.

"What?" Noose says.

I suck in a couple more breaths. "The men used to do smoke rings."

"All of 'em?"

No, just the worst one. "No."

"Shrinks call that a trigger."

I give him a sharp look, surprised out of the horror of my past for a sec. "Trigger?"

"Yeah, see something that reminds ya of bad shit that happened before. Makes a man feel sucker-punched. Depending on the shit."

Noose blows another ring, and the ghost that haunts me dissipates.

"Gotta face that bullshittery."

I nod, kicking a pebble of the square of concrete at the base of the steps. "Hard sometimes."

"It'll go. Rose makes that shit better." His lips twist, and he crosses his arms, cig sticking out of his mouth like a flag, the ash lengthening.

"So Krista…"

"She believes her friend. Said Krista couldn't keep me like a pet with a big cock. And that I was a murderer."

"Ya are."

My head jerks up.

Noose shrugs one shoulder again instead of saying anything right away. He takes a drag and tilts his jaw back, pushing out a flat stream like a wedge of opaque white. The smoke hits the air and shatters into tiny spirals. "Me too. You're in good company." He chuckles. "Ya got a big cock. That's no well-kept secret."

He kicks his head back and props it on his shoulder, giving me hooded eyes. "She dig your junk?"

I frown. "Yeah."

Noose sweeps his palm out. "So that part's good. What's this pet thing?"

"I don't know, seemed kinda like Sam was calling me stupid, and Krista was believing her."

"Nope," Noose says in crisp reply.

"Why do ya think?"

Noose shakes his head. "People that teach kids who need extra work don't choose to do that because they think they're dumb." Noose taps his temple. "Think that through. Doesn't make sense. She's a big-heart type, wants to make the world better and that shit."

I laugh. Can't help it. "You have a way of putting words together."

"I'm not wrong."

No.

"So you think I should have stuck it out, seen what was what before I got the hell outta there?" I rest my hands on my knees, letting them dangle between my legs.

"I don't know. Not much for an audience, and her BFF was hanging around, talkin' about your cock and killing like she knows something. If a man's got something he wants to get off his chest, comes out better with just your girl around. Just sayin'."

"So I handled it wrong." *Fuck.*

"No, you handled it the best ya could for the time and situation. Maybe there was some shit you misinterpreted."

"You and Krista"—Noose uses his cigarette to point at me—"seem pretty pure, like you two just"—he slaps his hands together, and more ash flutters to the rough concrete between us—"happened."

"We did," I admit. "I mean, I wasn't thinkin' I was gonna be strung out over my teacher. Or any lady."

Noose chuckles. *"Annnd…*that's how *that* ball bounces."

"Listen, now that you got all your aggression out"— he jerks his jaw to the right—"for today, maybe you go by Krista's place and hear what she knows, fill in the shit she doesn't with your version. The true version."

The seconds tick by, and after a minute or so, I ask, "How did you know what I needed?"

Noose grins, smoke swirling around his face. "Cut from the same cloth. When I can't handle shit, figure it out fast enough—whatever—I just get pissed off and want to lay my hands on something and shake the shit out of it."

That's how I felt.

"Some men don't do feelings," Noose says, briefly touching his chest. "I'm not in touch with the feels." He snorts.

"Me, either," Trainer says.

"Yet, we're the kind of dudes that when circumstance forces us to get in touch with it, we fight for our lives so we don't have to."

Sounds right.

"So how can I, ya know, not beat you up every time I can't get the emotional stuff in control?"

"Fuck if I know." Noose's smile flashes back like a wink. "But let me know when you figure that shit out, ya hothead."

After putting out his smoke on the tread of his boot, he sticks the butt in his pocket, muttering about Rose kicking his ass for tobacco pockets. He stands in front of me, his eyes roaming over my body.

"You look like shit."

Probably.

"Clean up here and go to your girl."

"I don't know if she'll listen."

Noose grips my shoulders. "I think she will."

"How do ya know?"

His eyes flick to mine for a minute then away, he drops his hands from my shoulders. "Gut instinct."

Good enough for me.

26

ALLEN

Krista walks out of her little friend's house.

I'm certain she's bent the cunt's ear with a battalion of sniveling. *"Oh, my wrist,"* and *"I have a biker cock now"* and *"Allen is so mean."*

Yes. A bleeding heart like Krista would feel obligated to carry on about her lot.

Her lot's about ready to get a good deal better, though.

Oh my, yes.

Rotating my stiff neck, thanks to that freakishly large parasite she's fucking, I shut the door of my Aston Martin. Wasn't feeling the BMW today.

The click of the door closing breaks the bubble of quiet as I cross the street to the sidewalk in front of Samantha Brunner's house.

Actually, it's hers by default because of a handy little accident five years before.

Krista fumbles awkwardly with the door handle of her Fiat, and some sixth sense warns her of my presence.

Her head comes up, and the body that was so soft a moment ago goes tense.

I'm practically hanging out in the middle of the street, but it's not well traveled. As a matter of fact, Sam's house dead ends at the loop of a cul-de-sac.

"How are you, Krista?" I say in a low voice that I know from experience carries well.

I take a step forward, close enough to see the knuckles of her fingers pale to white as she tightens her grip on her key fob.

"What do you want, Allen?"

"I'm not the bad guy here." I spread my hands inoffensively from my body and take another step. Her car is just a few feet away.

"I'm filing a restraining order against you," she announces in a flat voice.

Stupid bitch.

I smile instead of sailing over the roof of her car and strangling her with my bare hands. "That's not necessary. After all. It was that Neanderthal who charged *me*." Spreading my fingers, I place them above my chest, attempting to appear wounded. After countless hours in front of the mirror, I believe I'm quite good at it. "He drew first blood." I stuff my hands inside my pockets and rock back on my heels, affecting a contemplative demeanor.

Krista has let her hair run wild, and it whispers over her full breasts, hanging nearly to her waist.

My mouth waters with the thought of holding all that hair while I do things to her—things she most certainly wouldn't like.

My thoughts take charge of my brain, and I find myself with a huge grin for the second time today.

Instead of smiling in return, Krista frowns.

Why must *I* always be the amicable one. Sighing, I take another step. I'm so close to her car, I could stretch out and tap the roof.

"There's definitely something I want to get straight with Trainer about everything." Her hand rises and shoves the hair out of her face. Opening the door, she readies herself to slide inside.

"Trainer?"

Krista's chin lifts. "My boyfriend."

"Ah. The murderer. Oh, Krista, the company you keep."

"I don't need to say anything more to you, Allen. Not everything was your fault, but things aren't right between us, and I don't like how the tide's turned. The way you're behaving."

Krista's dark gray eyes suddenly find me over the roof. "The creepy way you show up wherever I'm at."

The GPS tracking device my people put on her car works like a charm.

I guess it's now or never, as they say. "I have a proposition for you, Krista."

"I'm not listening, Allen."

Of course, the stubborn twat. "You'll want to hear what I have to say."

Her face creases into doubtful lines, and she crosses her arms.

The low drone of a car approaching causes me to pause. Our eyes touch on it as it passes, then I look back.

"I am worth a lot of money."

Krista actually laughs at this. At me. Keeping my expression neutral takes monumental effort.

"You must not know me, Allen. I'm not about the money."

"Billions," I say in a low voice.

That gets her notice. A dark brow slowly lifts. "Even if that were true," Krista says with slow enunciation, "I still wouldn't be interested in a man who doesn't even care about me."

"Does the name Orson Rothschild mean anything to you?"

A burst of surprised laughter shoots out of Krista. She gives a vague nod. "Of course—who wouldn't know Orson Rothschild? He lives in Bill Gates's neighborhood, for God's sake!"

"He is my father."

Krista unfolds her arms and opens the car door wide. "I've had enough of your games. You live in Allen Fitzgerald Fantasyland, and I'll just do me."

I take away the last of the space.

We face each other over the roof of her car. "I took my late mother's name. She was a Fitzgerald."

Krista has one foot inside the car, her palm resting on the roof. "This is all so interesting, Allen," she says sarcastically.

That's when I know I won't be able to stop from hurting her—at least a little. I suck in a strangled breath then say with precisely clipped tones, "I must marry someone by age thirty, or I will be stripped of the family fortune, as will my father."

Shock registers across her pretty face.

Finally, a reaction.

"How is any of this my problem?" she asks, placing her fist with the keys against her chest. "You're not winning me here, Allen. You're making me more determined than ever to get the order against you. There's just something not right about all this."

I play my last card.

"You were adopted. You're not even who you think you are, Krista."

"Okay, talk to you later. I call bullshit and everything else I can." Her eyes are troubled when they look at me. Like I'm something to feel sorry for or be feared.

She's got that last part down perfectly. "Don't you want to talk to me about how the path of least resistance for you, dear Krista, is to marry me, inherit billions, and stop having to work with all the Dumbs?"

Krista steps out of her vehicle and slams the car door. She walks around and moves right into my space.

Excellent.

Her bad arm has a dark gray cast, and she doesn't lift it. She uses her good finger to point in my face. "Don't you ever call my students dumb. They"—she stabs me with her finger with surprising force—"are. Not. Dumb!"

Krista pivots on her heel and strides around the back, heading to driver's door again.

I flick a surreptitious glance around and see no witnesses. Then I do what I've been yearning to do since nearly the day we met. Grabbing a fistful of that thick, luscious hair, I wrench her backward with a satisfying pull that nearly takes her from the ground.

I clamp a hand over her mouth and squeeze down so she can't bite me.

When I slam her head into the roof of her car, a muffled cry escapes her before she slumps.

Almost too easy. I hike her over my shoulder, fireman-hold style, then casually trot across the silent street.

Whoever said quiet neighborhoods are safer?

TRAINER

I feel my brows come together. *Where is she?*

Not waiting around for you, moron.

Putting the flat of my palm on the solid wood door, it's like I'm almost feeling for a pulse.

But the windows are dark.

Not a sound.

It's only been five hours since I took off from the school, leaving Krista and her friend, Sam.

Still, wanted to make things right. Explain shit.

Maybe even listen.

Taking out my cell from my interior vest pocket, I thumb it open.

I've got a picture for every number, so I don't have to read.

But I can read now. I know what the letters are and can even sound out a few. If I wanted to.

Don't, though.

Need to straighten this mess out with Krista.

My finger hovers over a photo of judge.

I hesitate then hit his image anyway.

"Brett," he answers right away.

After the polite stuff, I dig in, telling him what went down. I change some stuff so I don't have to talk about my own dick.

Judge understands, though.

"So to reiterate," he begins, "Krista is uncertain about some key things in your past, her friend is playing advocate, and you waltzed into the middle of their conversation without them knowing."

I think through what he said, using stuff Krista and Judge have both taught me. "Yeah."

"Had it occurred to you that Sam was speaking quite baldly, leaving all the niceties off. After all, from what you've said, she is Krista's most-trusted friend."

"You mean they were thinkin' it's just them and not worried about audience."

"Yes. It sounds to me as though Sam censored nothing. If she'd known you were there, I'd wager she would have had a different tone, certainly a softer delivery."

"They were puttin' me down, and…" I can't finish.

"No, I don't believe that was her intent whatsoever. Nor do I think she was inferring lack of intellect."

I love Judge. He skirts around the *D* word. For me.

"Now you've come to your senses and realized there could be two sides to the story. You've sought Miss Glass out, and she's not at home."

"No." He goes silent for a second then asks, "Is there something you're not telling me?"

"I still don't like the ex."

"Of course not."

"No, I mean…" I shake my hair out and press my head against Krista's door. "I mean I got a bad feeling about him."

"Do nothing more, Brett. He is an attorney, and from what your associate, Noose, says, he must be very wealthy."

"That's the thing. He doesn't make sense in this equation."

"How?" Judge asks in a sharp voice. "Because you have unique insights, Brett. Your environment made it such."

"Allen Fitzgerald feels wrong. Krista is smart and beautiful and all this great shit, Judge. But he could be hobknobbin'. Why did he go with Krista, a school teacher?"

Teacher of dumb kids.

I squeeze my eyes shut. Hear the ghost of Krista's voice. Feel her silky skin underneath my fingers.

"Brett?"

My eyelids spring open. "Yeah."

"I called your name three times."

"Sorry, I can't stop thinkin' on this."

"Do you love the girl, Brett?"

I didn't want to. 'Cause it's scary.

"Yeah."

"Then you owe it to yourself to sort this mess. Tell all the truths, even if they're dirty and ugly. Because a lie is never pretty."

Judge is right. But to be laid bare, for Krista to know about Mama and the Arnies…

"Okay," I whisper into the phone.

"Brett?"

"I said okay."

"It'll be fine. You'll wonder what all your anxiety was once you come clean with your past and the way you feel about her. And I'll tell you something, son. Even if she will not have you, it doesn't mean that you'll shrivel up and blow away. Other people don't define us. We define ourselves."

"Then how come I give such a shit?"

"Because that is who you are Brett. It's who you've always been. It's as though you were meant to be part of a different family and were placed with yours by accident. And now the cosmos, or whatever force governs our lives, has seen fit to bring this fine young woman into your life. Though I don't approve of your biker gang, I approve of how they support you. It's about time you were able to live without fear of reprisal and have the potential for joy. It's about damn time."

I don't understand everything Judge says, and he promised to never talk down to me, but I know the bottom line is he thinks I deserve Krista. And I had to go through the fucked-up childhood to get her.

If I'd been born rich and privileged, I'd never have met my brothers in Road Kill MC. Never have met Krista. I'd just be another dude with a regular life. Krista could have that fancy prick, Allen, but she chose me. At least, she wanted me before the whole murderer thing. So I must be worth something to her.

"Thanks, Judge."

"We're here for you, son."

I squeeze my eyes shut and say goodbye.

With a light tap, I push off the door and jog down the half dozen steps striding to my bike.

The hell with it. I'll ride over to Sam's house.

Noose told me where she lived. She'll probably think I'm a stalker, but I gotta know Krista's okay.

Gotta know if I have a chance at that joy Judge talked about. Maybe permanently losing the weight inside my chest.

I want more of the warm Krista gives me.

A lot more.

27

KRISTA

Initially, the pain wakes me up, then awareness and consciousness seep in because of my awkward pose.

Pins and needles stab me everywhere, like microscopic sleet rocketing off my body.

My eyelids crack open, and my gaze combs the space: concrete walls and floor. No windows. My heartbeat picks up the pace.

A dangling bulb, like the kind in horror movies, swings from the ceiling. Pushed by a source of wind I don't feel, it bounces frenetic light over my body.

Looking down at myself, I notice my legs are neatly arranged.

They hurt.

So do my arms, since they're strung up over my head, with my cast making a horrible, painful thump in time with the beats of my heart.

A whimper slips out before I can help it. Memories rush in like a river finding a new fork.

Allen did this.

The last thing I remember was yelling at him, disgusted with whatever his last comment was. I strode around the back of my little Fiat, distracted by the thought of desperately needing to talk to Trainer.

I'd made up my mind that he's my boyfriend.

Of course he is. There's no way someone with a soul like Trainer's doesn't have a great explanation for why he committed murder.

Was it cold-blooded? Could Trainer even commit something that was?

No, is my silent answer.

A tear plops on my black leggings, making a wet spot, and I tell myself to suck it up. Now is not the time for wallowing in regrets.

I'm in the care of a madman.

Using whatever I'm strung to, I pull myself to my knees and stifle a scream when my arms move out of the position they've been held in. My broken arm feels as though it's re-broken.

My arms have probably been in this position since Allen bashed my head into the car. At least, I assume that's what he did because the font of my skull throbs along my hairline, though I don't remember what caused the injury.

Leaning against the cold wall, I hike my knee and plant my right foot.

Dizzy, I stand.

My breath fizzles out, and I suck in a deep inhale, trying to steady myself.

The room swims in front of my vision.

Quickly, I shut my eyes against the spinning concrete walls and flatten my body against the cold stone.

My arms are bound, but I'm no longer hanging from them. Big improvement.

I groan as blood pours into all the spots that the circulation had been cut off from.

Hissing through the pain, I open my eyes again as I hear a key being used in a door I didn't see on my initial perusal.

Allen steps in.

I tense.

The smell of his cologne almost gags me.

"Well, hello, Krista."

"Untie me. Now," I say through my teeth.

Allen shakes his head as though saddened by my plight. "I think I much prefer you this way. Helpless. Compliant."

Bull *shit*.

"I am neither of those things." I frown, and the movement causes pain to swarm my head. A dull pounding starts in my skull. I wince and note that I can't touch what hurts or explore how badly Allen injured me because my hands are tied.

Allen's eyes go to my head. "Sorry about that." He snickers. "I got a little carried away."

"Carried away?" I ask in a thick voice. "You bashed my head in."

Our eyes lock.

"Do you think if I wanted to 'bash your head in,' I wouldn't be able to?"

I don't say anything, cold terror slicking my insides. Yes, I do think Allen's capable of that. And more.

Whatever's on my face tells him exactly what I'm feeling. "Fear keeps you malleable, Krista. And I require cooperation in the extreme."

"I'm not cooperating with anything." My knees weaken, and I mentally let go of Trainer, telling him goodbye. "Just kill me. Then you can move on to whatever woman you want. Just so we're clear—I'm not *her*."

Allen saunters over to me.

He reaches out, and I flinch, cornered. Squeezing my breast, he pinches my nipple and twists. Hard.

I scream. Tears of pain spring to my eyes.

Reacting instinctively, I raise my knee between his unguarded legs.

It's a glancing blow but has the intended result.

Allen sags.

Planting my right foot, I raise the opposite knee and slam it into his taped nose.

Blood bursts from his face as he falls backward.

I watch Allen writhe on the ground. Between his broken nose and his wounded balls, I figure Allen's out of commission for a while.

Not so.

After twenty minutes on the floor, Allen sits up, his crystalline eyes looking all the bluer for the red covering his face.

Those eyes hate me, glittering with a bottomless rage. And I'm tied.

Oh God.

Then he smiles. "You think you hurt me?"

I'm clearly stupid and have a death wish. "I know I did. Now kill me." Maybe if I goad him, he'll make it a quick death.

I don't want to die, but I don't want to live through what Allen has in store for me, either.

Allen shakes his head, grimaces at the motion, and stands. He gives his balls a delicate adjustment and casually slides his cell out of his pocket. After tapping a few things on the screen, he puts the phone to his ear.

"Abbi," he barks when someone has answered. "I need you."

A terse five seconds go by.

His face screws up into a rage, and his curt reply is nearly instant, "The basement."

"You're going to drag witnesses into this?" I ask incredulously.

"They're only a witness if they live to tell about it."

My heart beats into my throat.

One minute.

Then two.

Three minutes pass before the soft knock at the door. I scream, "Don't come in." My voice is so loud, it hurts my own ears, and my throat is instantly abraded from the force of my shout.

Allen doesn't react. He calmly walks to the door and lets a woman in.

The term *cowering* isn't quite accurate to describe her demeanor. Like a dog kicked once to often, she scuttles into the room, and Allen jerks his head toward the center of the space.

My eyes move to where Allen indicated: a drain in the center of the floor.

The bare bulb continues to spin slowly, stirred by a current from the door's motion, casting thin light over the two of them.

"As usual, Abbi will be your surrogate." Allen bestows his version of a tender smile on a girl who has to be close to my age.

My bare skin pebbles at his words. "No." I can't think of anything else to say to stop the horror I feel building like vile steam inside this place.

Abbi's wide, dark eyes flick to me.

"Don't look at her. She will be my wife, and you will take and do the things I can't do to her."

"Yes, Mr. Fitzgerald."

"Hands and knees," Allen says.

My swallow is painful. "Allen, don't do this." I try to jerk from the restraints holding me. Thin metal encircles the narrowest part of my arm, exactly over my wrist bone. The circle over the cast of my left arm is bigger. My eyes travel up, until I see a solid metal ring held by another embedded in the wall.

Thin chains conjoin the two.

My head whips back to the scene in the center of the cold, dank place with four concrete walls and no window.

Abbi slowly lowers herself to the cold floor.

Allen slowly unbuttons his slacks. Tearing the belt through the loops, he lets it fall to the floor, where the buckle clanks against the cement. Abbi flinches.

Allen pushes his underwear and dress slacks to his feet and kicks off one pant leg.

He stands, naked from the waist down, with an erection.

Allen's hand climbs beneath Abbi's short skirt, and the sound of material tearing is loud within the confines of the space.

Lace is tossed aside.

"What the fuck are you doing?" I yank at the chains again, and pain shoots from my wrist to shoulder, and I'm certain I've re-injured my arm, but I don't care. I have to stop this.

Allen ignores me, picking up a small tube of something that must have fallen from his pocket.

He pops the cap and squirts gel onto his palms then slathers his penis with lube.

So familiar, I have time to think before he kneels behind Abbi. Gripping her hips roughly, he stabs himself inside of her without warning.

She bites her lip and doesn't shout out.

He's done this before. A dull resignation sweeps across her features.

"No," I breathe.

Abbi's clearly being raped, but not reacting as though she is.

Allen doesn't hold back.

And I thought he was rough with me.

I want to look away—but I *can't.* The sounds of their bodies slapping together is deafening.

Allen is awful, but predictable, and I know when he's getting close to release.

The girl moves as though to disengage.

"No," he commands in a hoarse voice. "Stay."

He grips her hair, yanking her head back so her neck is cranked at a painful angle, and tips his head back, releasing inside her with a final grinding thrust.

The sight is burned into my brain, churning my gut. *I'm responsible for this.*

Allen's trying to…I don't know what. Hurt me by hurting someone else?

Because he knows that will hurt me worse.

Allen pulls out of Abbi, and she tries to salvage some dignity by pulling down her dirty skirt.

Semen stains the ground beneath her.

Allen stands, planting his foot in the middle of her rear, and shoves.

Abbi sprawls out on the concrete, painfully cracking an elbow on the way.

She yelps, rolling over, and tries to gain her footing.

Allen stalks after her.

Oh no. "Allen!" I scream with what's left of my voice.

Allen leans over, scooping Abbi up by the waistband of her skirt, and sets her on her feet.

As soon as she's righted, Allen retreats a step then punches her in the stomach.

She folds, gasping and obviously in pain.

"Stop!" I beg in a wail.

"No," Allen says in a good-natured voice. "She'll get everything I want to do to you, but can't."

"Please, *please*, Allen. No!" I jerk against the chains. They clink their awful music, my cast making the motion awkward and painfully numb.

Allen shoves Abbi into the wall, and she yelps, biting her lip again.

Then I notice all the bruises, old and new, pockmarked on whatever skin is revealed.

"Run!" I scream at her.

She stays.

Allen punches her in the face, and I hear a crack.

Finally, she staggers more or less toward the door.

Allen laughs, causally walking after her.

He trips her as blood pours from her face.

Abbi barely breaks the fall with her palms as her knees smack the unforgiving floor.

As she turns her head slightly, I catch sight of a bubble of blood filling her right nostril.

Abbi raises a delicate palm as if to ward off Allen's next move.

He kicks her face, and Abbi falls over, rolling onto her back with a moan, then goes still.

"No, no, no," I gasp.

Allen hops on top of her, straddling her body. He places his palm on her chest. "Still warm," he says with satisfaction and stands again, feet on the ground and on either side of her chest. One foot still remains inside a pant leg, and he gives an irritated fling with his leg. The pants skitter a couple feet to the right.

He lowers himself to between Abbi's legs and tears the skirt up.

I'm light-headed and feel my vomit rising.

"What are you doing, Allen?" I ask in slow revulsion.

Allen grins at me. "Viagra, Krista. It's the wonder drug. Let's me fuck on demand." He winks.

I try to keep my gorge down, but when Allen begins to rape Abbi a second time—and she's either unconscious or dead—my breakfast erupts out of my throat. The whole time I'm throwing up, I can hear Allen's ragged panting as he uses the woman beneath him.

Wiping my mouth against my shoulder, I finally look at this man I dated for almost two years.

Strings of saliva hang from his mouth as his hands wrap Abbi's slender throat.

With a hoarse shout he finishes, his fingers tightening around Abbi's neck.

I don't have to guess if she's dead now.

No one is that still in life.

It seems naïve, but as the hours pass and Abbi's body remains broken, battered, and saturated with Allen's bodily fluids, I realize I never knew what a dead person looked like.

Abbi was pretty.

Now the rosy color of her life has bled away, to be replaced slowly by ashen skin.

Her dark eyes stare at nothing.

I stare at her.

How did I ever dare to stand in judgement of Trainer—when I just murdered this girl in front of me? That was what Allen said when he walked over to me, pantless, his spent penis making a fleshy slapping noise against his thigh.

Grabbing my cheeks in his hand, he squeezed them together until I resembled a blowfish.

"Now," he said, inspecting me like a prized bug, "that's what happens when you're naughty." He waves a vague hand behind him to indicate Abbi's corpse.

"There are a million Abbi's." He grinned, and I recoiled.

"You will marry me, or I will do this to countless more people. Beginning with your parents." He made air quotes around the last word. "We both know they're not bio. However, you do care for them. And next on my list will be the giant imbecile Brett Rife. He's probably loved fucking your tight cunt." He enunciated the *T* hard enough to create a dot of spittle at the corner of his lip, and I stared at it to avoid his crazed eyes. "I will enjoy baiting him with a few choice crumbs, and he'll come running!"

Allen suddenly released my face and paced a few steps away. "That would be very rewarding. But not so rewarding as forcing your compliance. You marry me, I get my rightful fortune, and Mommy, Daddy, and Fuck Stud shall remain unharmed."

He halted, turned sideways, and swept a palm toward Abbi's body. "Or what I did here will look like a day at the spa compared to what I do to your mommy and Mr. Rife, the Dumb."

"He's not dumb," I whispered with my last thread of defiance.

Allen frowned, walking back to where I leaned against the wall.

His hand came out, and I screamed, clinging to the concrete, as though it would offer me protection.

Gently, he flicked some of the hair that came loose from the braid I had it in that morning. "Is that my answer? Because I have the means to make everything I just outlined a reality. Your new reality."

I couldn't breathe. My lungs had frozen. I didn't want anyone else to get hurt. My eyes were drawn back to Abbi. A dead and broken doll.

Then my gaze shifted to Allen's, his insanity etched on every plane of his face.

Finally, I nodded.

"What?" Allen cupped a hand behind his ear.

I can't kill anyone else. I might not have been the weapon, but I was the motivation.

"Yes."

Allen jerked me against him.

I moaned as my abject terror loosened my bladder, and I peed myself.

He smirked, diving in next to my ear, and nipped the lobe. "Good."

Shoving me against the wall, he took a look at my soaked pants.

"I think you can lie in it." He nodded to himself then looked at Abbi's corpse.

"Abbi will keep you company."

Hot tears started to run down my face, blurring my vision, but I could make Allen out perfectly.

He was the one leaving with all the hope, happiness, and humanity, taking it all with him.

28

TRAINER

Sam's wide eyes take me in, from the top of my head to my scuffed-up black boots.

"Krista's not here," she says instantly.

I frown.

Gotta be. I jerk my thumb over my shoulder. "Car's out front."

Now it's Sam's turn to frown. "What?" She turns, stuffing her feet into bright-red plastic shoes with holes over the toes.

Sliding past me, she leaves the door standing open and walks out to where Krista's car's parked.

"She just left…" Sam bites her thumbnail, and I glance quickly inside the front door then close it, following behind her.

Dread coils inside my guts.

Sam makes a slow circle around the burnt-orange Fiat.

I watch her, hands to hips.

When she gets to the driver's side, Sam stops. "Trainer," she calls urgently.

Striding around the front of the car, I see it too. Hell, I can't see nothin' else but the chocolate-colored strands of Krista's hair, stuck to where roof meets door…by scarlet glue.

My lady's blood.

I stand beside Sam, and we stare at the damning patch, the evidence that someone hurt Krista.

Then took her.

"Allen," Sam guesses.

"Yeah." Nothing else—*nobody* else—makes as much sense as him.

Knew he was an Arnie.

Sam looks up at me, eyes shining with tears. "I introduced them."

My stomach does a slow turn, and I know exactly what I need to do. "Gotta make a call." I move toward the open courtyard near Samantha's front door, where wooden beams cut the view of the sky above my head.

Scrolling through my contacts' images, I find the hangman's noose then tap the icon for a telephone receiver.

Ringing starts.

Noose answers in his chatty way, "Yeah."

"Gotta a problem."

"What kind?"

"Somethin' I can't talk about over the cell."

"Got ya." Then after a few seconds, Noose asks, "Where you at?"

I tell him.

"Hang tight. Be there in a jiffy."

With a grim nod he can't see, I blank the screen, pocketing my cell. I walk over to an old wood bench with its legs embedded in pebbled concrete that sits directly before the entryway to Sam's house.

"What are you doing?" Sam asks slowly, coming to stand in front of me.

"Waitin'."

"Ah—maybe you're not aware, but that fucker Allen has brained Krista and taken her somewhere." She folds her arms.

Sam needs to eat, I think randomly then say, "Got my friend coming. We'll come up with somethin'."

I know better than to go shootin' off half-cocked without my brothers as backup. Might get fucked-up. Can't help Krista then.

"Right." Then her face lights up like she's thought of something. "Is this the dude that came by and choked Krista, put her on notice about not hurting you?"

My face whips to hers, and I stand, towering over her, though she's a pretty tall girl. "*Choked* her?" Noose didn't mention that, only admitted to giving her a talking to, which I was mighty pissed about anyway.

Sam nods vigorously, curly hair bouncing around. "Yes, held her to the door by her throat." Noose's motorcycle roars in the distance.

We're gonna have words, then he's going to help me get Krista.

Noose is sprawled on his ass.

My knuckles throb from being used so soon after the my last beat-up session with Noose.

"What the *fuck*?" Noose says, popping to his feet. "That hurt, fucker!"

"Oh shit," Sam mutters in the background.

I swing my jaw toward where Sam stands behind me. "She told me you choked Krista."

Noose's hooded eyes move to Sam, who shrinks back, then back to me. "Not really."

"Not fucking really?" I say, flinging my arms wide.

"Yeah, broke into her security-breach condo, and she freaked out, tried to take off." He shrugs. "Got her at the door before she could get out and alert the media." He chuckles.

I glower at him.

"Listen, didn't leave a mark on her." Noose slides his jaw left to right, eyes tightening with pain. "Twice in twenty-four hours. Hurts like a bitch now," he mutters, shooting me a glare.

Noose wags his finger. "I can do that shit, ya know."

We all know. Noose is a master at hurting where it shows or doesn't—his choice. Still don't like him putting hands on Krista. "Don't ever touch her again."

Noose's eyebrow quirks. "Let's make that possible by finding her first, eh?"

"Yeah." I'm still pissed. My hands fist, and I ignore the pain at my knuckles.

Noose gives me the weight of his hard stare. "Save it for the fucker who took her."

"Wait a second," Sam says from behind me, and we look at her.

"I wouldn't suggest you just go over to Allen's and demand Krista."

Noose snorts. "Why the fuck not?"

"I'm really trying hard not to be intimidated by you right now. But I have to say, you scare the pee out of me."

He smirks, taking time to smack a cig out of the ever-present pack he carries, and lights it. Tipping his head back, he shoots smoke rings.

"Yeah, I get that a lot."

"Well, why don't you just try? You know, to tone back"—she waves her palm around at him—"this whole bad-ass act."

Noose doesn't answer.

I do. "It's not an act. Noose is always legit."

Sam's brow stitches in a small frown. "Well, that's just frightening."

Yup. Good man to have on your side, though. That's why I called him up.

"So where's the evidence?"

I jerk my jaw toward the Fiat. Noose slides from the seat of his bike and follows me to the car.

He flicks his half-burnt cig, and it lands near the front tire of Krista's car, smoldering.

Noose bends down and smells the matted tuft of hair and blood.

"That's weird."

I shake my head at Sam. She mimes zipping her lips gesture, but rolls her eyes.

Noose rubs a strand of hair back and forth between his index finger and thumb.

He straightens, staring at the spot of gore on my lady's car.

"Looks bad."

"You think?" Sam says with that bitchy tone some girls get.

Noose looks at her.

She shuts up in a hurry.

He strides to the front of the car, about where the center of the hood is. "She was walking away. He grabs Krista, then drags her to…" He stuffs his freshly lit cig back in his mouth and takes three steps to where the blood is, jerks the cig out, and with both hands, cages the evidence of her injury. "Spins her and brain dusts her on the car."

That knot's back. The tight thing I've lived with my entire life. Back like it never went away.

I rub the spot in my chest and ask Noose, "He snuck up on her and did this?" My voice cracks, and Noose gives me a sharp look.

Not losing my shit.

"Nah. She knew he was coming—I'm betting—just not his potential for violence."

"I knew it."

Noose dips his chin, smoke sliding out his mouth as he answers, "Yeah. Knew he was a class-A chode right outta the gate."

"I introduced them," Sam says a second time, mournfully.

Noose laughs.

Nothing's funny right now. *Nothin'.*

"Good call." His lips twist, and he puts out his smoke on his boot sole.

Sam bursts into tears, covering her face.

Shit. Noose exchange an uneasy glance with me.

"He's a lawyer. Follow the law. Call the cops." Sam looks between the two of us, wiping her running nose and sniffling. "Krista said she was going for a restraining order."

"She was." Noose says.

"Yes, she's been putting it together recently that Allen's more unstable than she realized."

Sam twists a spiral of hair, lets it bounce back, then does it again. "Are you sure it's him?"

Yes.

"Know anybody else that wants to beat the shit outta a schoolteacher and kidnap her?" Noose looks at me. Puts up a palm.

Sam shakes her head.

"Okay," I say, "think we all know it's Allen. Not gonna call the cops. They'll see his fancy shit and figure we're the bad guys. It's how that shit always goes down."

Sam looks like she's going to argue that.

But she and I both know what I am and where I've been. I know what I'm talking about. Cops don't care about the invisible people like Mama and me. Cops don't see prostitutes, or their bastard kids, as people.

They won't see me now when I say my girlfriend's been taken by a psycho lawyer who's got a bankroll.

They'll see *him. Not* us.

"Trainer's right. Cops don't look past the patch." Noose points to the one-percenter patch—a solid red diamond with the number and symbol for percentage inside its borders.

We tap knuckles.

"That's why we're club, so we don't have to be under their authority."

Sam takes a deep breath. "What can you do? Nevermind, maybe I don't want to know."

She walks over to us and takes my free hand and Noose's. Tears well again in her eyes.

"Save my friend." Her eyes narrow on me. "And pull the penis off Allen. Slowly."

Noose chuckles, pulling his hand away. He grabs a tissue out of his pocket and hands it to her. "Remind me never to piss you off."

Sam dabs at her eyes. I never let go of her hand. Holding Sam's hand feels like I'm a little closer to Krista.

Sam cries for us both.

She tilts her head back, searching my eyes. "You love her." It's not a question.

I nod, because anything else is a lie. I fell hard. I fell fast…I'm still falling.

Squeezing my hand, she lets it fall. "Don't get dead, Trainer."

I shake my head.

She smiles. "You don't talk much."

"No."

"You're going to kill him?" Her eyes skate nervously between us.

Yes.

I don't say anything.

Noose and I walk away, mount our rides, and slap kickstands into position.

We pull out, and I don't look back at Krista's friend. Instead, I look forward.

29

ALLEN

"Even I will have a challenge cleaning up this mess, Allen."

My father's ass is perched on an expensive table he and wifey picked up on holiday from Italy.

I sip my cider beer. "Krista needed to be encouraged."

"Did you have to kill Abigail? She was a spectacular mule. I paid her well. She withstood your savagery in fairly good humor—it was a good marriage of greed versus perversion." Orson's smile is clever.

How I hate this man.

"Krista Glass did this to your face?" His eyes run over my taped nose.

I throw him a sour look. "Yes," I hiss.

The corners of Orson's lips tweak. "She might take some management in the future, Allen."

I ignore his thinly veiled insult. "I can't undo Abbi, now can I?" Releasing a frustrated exhale, I continue, "Besides, I think Krista will do anything I ask now. She wants to protect her adoptive parents and this ridiculous thug she's fucking."

His steely brows rise. "I prefer the term 'sexing.'"

I sip my beer, hating his inept attempts to appear relevant. "Fucking, fucking, fucking, fucking," I murmur.

Orson doesn't take the bait. He merely glowers at me with cold eyes. "Are you through with your juvenile antics?" One eyebrow rises again.

I sneer. "For the moment."

"I will dispose of Abigail, and you get Krista Glass cleaned up."

"Why?" I lean forward, gripping the table's edge.

"The wedding, of course. Let's strike while the iron's hot. Don't give her any time for introspection or choice."

I laugh. Cocking my head, I raise the fine brandy snifter in salutation. "Because your fortune hangs on me wedding and bedding this particular girl."

Orson nods. "Your half-sister."

Gives me a semi-boner just thinking about breaking that bit of news to Krista—her familial role and the horror behind the knowledge.

Nasty perfection.

"First decent suggestion you've had."

His smile becomes predatory. "I have everything in place for a lavish ceremony. The story will be you traveled to a romantic destination and eloped, then wanted to share your joy with a large, post-nuptial celebration."

"It won't look odd."

"Exactly." My father takes a sip of his brandy.

"Get her cleaned up, and I will pull a favor from a dear old friend of mine."

"I didn't think you had those." I feel a suspicious eyebrow elevate.

Orson sets the crystal snifter down. "I don't, but this particular fellow owes me a favor."

I frown. "He'll perform the ceremony on such quick notice?"

He nods. "Judge Hammerstein will do whatever I want."

That type of favor piques my interest. Not only is the judge's name somehow familiar, but I also wonder why he would be so indebted. "Did he do something wrong?"

Orson laughs. "No, that's the irony. He did something right."

His secret smile infuriates me.

"Wakey, wakey," I murmur beside Krista's ear.

She's probably sat in her own piss long enough.

With a start, her head whips back, cracking hard against the concrete, and she groans. "Go away."

"I don't think so."

I use a small key to unlock the metal circlets around her wrists. They clank against the cement wall.

Krista begins to lean, listing to one side. Her cast is much worse for the wear after having hung like a plaster sausage from the chain.

Grasping her shoulder, I tilt her upright. "Can you stand?"

She blinks, her gaze moving to where Abbi's body laid for more than thirty hours.

It's gone now.

Though a few blood spatters remain, and the room smells decidedly *not* fresh. It suddenly occurs to me I might have fucked her corpse that last time.

Hmmm. I'm not especially bothered by the idea.

My gaze travels over Krista, noting the strange pallor to her skin. She's not eaten in nearly a day and a half, and only gulped down the water I allowed her.

She pissed in fear and pissed again in desperation.

I loved Krista having to sit in her own waste.

After all, she's responsible for Abbi's fate. If Krista had not chosen to smash my nose and knee me in the nuts, I might have spared Abbi.

For a time, anyway. Abbi's eventual demise was inevitable. Being married to Krista will test the levels of what little self-control I possess, and Abbi would have suffered in Krista's stead, at least until Krista bore my children. I'll need another Abbi. I tilt my head, tapping my chin with a finger. *Maybe two.*

Hefting Krista up by her armpits, I wrinkle my nose. She smells like BO, piss, and putrid vomit breath.

"Let go of me," Krista gestures weakly, feebly attempting to get away.

"Shut up, or I do something worse."

She stills, grabbing onto my shirt. I was smarter this time and wore a T-shirt instead of decent clothes.

Krista would bleed, pee, or vomit over anything nice, I'm certain.

"I'm going to get you upstairs, where you'll be bathed, dressed, and fed." She leans away from whatever expression is on my face. "Then we'll have our nuptials."

"No," she whispers, her stormy-colored eyes growing wide.

"Oh yes." My eyes slim on her face. "Or I go after Mommy and Daddy and the big doofus."

My eyebrows hike as I await her reply.

Krista says nothing, her shoulders slumping in defeat.

TRAINER

"How long's it been?" Viper asks, splitting his attention between me and Noose.

I shrug. "Not sure. Sam wasn't paying attention to time when Krista left her place. All she could give us was a window of a couple of hours." I flip my palm back and forth.

Viper looks at his watch, and Noose gives an amused smirk. Nobody wears watches anymore. Time's on the cell.

"It's been every bit of ten hours. Daylight's fading." His brows come together, as his gaze takes in the fading light outside the one window in the space.

I know. That's why we're all in emergency church.

Vipe gives a frustrated huff. "This fucker's high pro-file. Noose did a quick look into him, and he's from old money. Dad's loaded."

Not a surprise.

"His inheritance is murky, though. Noose couldn't get a bead on that. Right now, he's just worth whatever his lawyering makes him." This shit don't matter. "Don't know what his money-bags status has to do with any-thing." Just know he's hurting Krista. Makes my mouth water to kill him.

I think of Judge and how he'd want me to let what-ever was gonna happen, happen. *Save yourself, son*, he'd say.

But I can't. There's that piece of me that won't be reasonable.

Ever.

And it's right here. Right now. In this moment.

The piece that's usually buried has resurfaced. Because of Krista.

I never cared about no lady—even Mama—the way I do her.

"What I'm saying," Viper continues in a soft voice, "is that I know you want to get to Krista. You already threw down for her. We fully appreciate your feelings." Mutterings rise at his words, backin' me. "But"—his voice drops impossibly quieter, and every brother at the table leans forward to catch what he says next—"this particular snake has got a lot of rattles. He's not an obvious slimeball with a criminal record that goes on for miles that nobody's gonna miss if he disappears off the face of the planet. He's connected, and from what Noose says, well-spoken, dressed, and understands whose palm to grease."

"So we gotta be careful," I state.

Vipe nods. "Yes."

"I can't wait." I barely keep the frantic note outta my voice.

"We'll send in Lariat, Wring, and Noose with you. They can go in and SEAL it out."

Noose rolls his eyes, but Wring looks up from the corner, taking a break from cleaning his nails with his switchblade. "I'm in."

Lariat raises a hand, saying nothing, but his black eyes glitter his yes at anyone botherin' to look.

Viper turns his attention back to me. "See what shit's going down, if anything. I repeat, do not dust this guy without reason."

I turn to Noose, seeing a bruise growing on his jaw. "We kill him if he's hurting her."

Noose grins.

TRAINER

Normally, jealousy is something other people suffer from. I never had nothin' and never thought *things* or how much shit I had was gonna make me happy. I was too busy surviving to wish on material shit.

But rolling into the exclusive gated community on top of the East Hill of Kent has me kinda pissed. We slide by the ritzy houses then go back down into the valley between the east and west hills of Kent. We park Noose's slightly beat-up Nova in a dark alley.

Krista fucked Allen in that fancy house. When I craned my neck to get a look, I let my eyes roll over the outside, where two houses flanked his. The view of the valley was glowing neon lights swathed in surrounding darkness, keeping true light pollution at the edges of the valley.

Noose taps my arm, and I look at his painted face, pulled from my thoughts.

First, we Google Mapped the place, then did a drive-by. Now, were on recon, as my brothers call it.

We crawl up the ravine leading to the high fence surrounding the small neighborhood of million-dollar houses. Noiselessly, we move through yards. Any dogs that bark are silenced by tranquilizer.

"Can't move quietly enough for a dog not to notice," Noose said after he nailed the second one.

"He'll be okay," he added when he noticed my lingering look at the unmoving dog.

Don't like hurtin' animals, women, or children. Goes against the grain for me.

With his assurance, I nodded and followed.

The hike was easy at first, then went to sucking ass pretty fast. Every bit of strength went to climbing up the steep ravine—*quietly, w*hich seemed to be the worst part. We poured sweat, all of us shaking our heads to part the sweat from our flesh.

When we reached the fence, Noose tapped me again. "Gonna do a little recon, Trainer."

His voice was so quiet, the light breeze stole most of the sound, but he used the hand gestures he taught me before.

I never been in the military. Couldn't have passed squat for any kind of test. But Lariat, Wring, and Noose seem to speak their own language. I understand it more naturally than I should. Probably comes from a lifetime of not being able to read and having to count on body language to understand shit goin' on around me.

I'm grateful they brought me along. Would've come anyway. I smirk. *They probably knew that.*

Digging his elbows into a hard and narrow trail that surrounds the entire length of the fence, Noose drags his body forward with hard pulls. Wring and Lariat watch him.

When he's near the gate, Noose rolls onto his back, pulling something out of his pocket. He rips it apart with his teeth and puts the small circular object against the bottom part of the gate.

After a full minute, Noose gives the signal to follow.

When we reach his position, I want to ask what he did. A small black disc is attached to where the gate latches against a post. All metal.

Looks locked up tighter than a drum.

Noose stands, and we remain on our bellies. With a thumb pressed deliberately on the latch, Noose lifts his other hand, which holds a small aerosol can.

He sprays the latching mechanism and pushes the gate open. Soundlessly.

Jogging along the fence, Noose sidles to an obvious security system portal then jams a sharp object in the side, where a key or tool should be inserted.

The numbers on the viewing screen blink randomly then go black.

Noose turns his head. Only his teeth appear, like a slash of white in his painted face.

We come.

Noose's restless gaze covers the interior quickly. "Clearly, Fitzgerald isn't here, and neither is Krista."

"Smells stale," Lariat comments, lifting his nose.

"Nobody's been cooking in these swank accommodations for a long time." Wring looks around. Wipes a gloved hand over a surface. Lifts his finger. Even in the darkness, I can see dust.

"Where the fuck is he then?" I whisper-hiss.

"Chill," Noose says absently, looking over everything. "Losing your shit means a case of soft brain."

He's right.

I don't see everything Noose sees, but I do see money: the TV set above a rich-boy fireplace that has a hearth full of expensive lookin' stone running the length of the wall.

I stalk away from the guys, moving to the bedroom.

Flinging open the door, I stop. Noose almost collides with my back.

It's covered in photos of Krista. Seeing her large gray eyes and open face makes my palms sweat, and that weight inside my chest grows. The photos were obviously taken without her knowing.

Pervy fucker.

Finally, I look away and start jerking open drawers on a wide dresser.

I paw through shit, finding a drawer that's filled with only lube. Like thirty tubes, stacked with a creepy sorta OCD.

The guys stare inside.

"Guy that needs that much lube isn't doing the work to get a chick ready." Wring chuckles.

No. But a dark part of me likes it. He had to use this shit with Krista because he couldn't turn her on.

Not so perfect after all. I snort, blowing off the wealth of his place. Who cares how fuckin' rich Fitzgerald is if he needs shit like this?

"Whoa—what's this?" Lariat looks to Noose and holds up a piece of paper.

Frustrating letters crawl across it. I can read some, but not most.

"Birth certificate says Rothschild, not Fitzgerald."

"Yeah," Noose says, ransacking the other drawers without looking up, "Took his mother's name. Father's got money coming out of his ass. Different last name."

That strikes me as weird.

"Why though?"

"Who the fuck knows? Richies have their own set of rules. Makes sense to them," Wring says, setting the piece of paper down.

Slowly, I close the drawer filled with lube, a grim knowledge eating at my brain. "He wouldn't take her here."

Lariat, Wring, and Noose look at me.

"What do ya mean?" Noose frowns. "You know something I don't?"

I quickly shake my head. "No, but Fitzgerald is about himself. And he wants to keep things separate. I bet you he's taken Krista somewhere that's easier to hide his sick brand of shit."

I wipe damp palms on my black pants. Getting worked up again, thinkin' about Fitzgerald having Krista.

Wring's face lights even as his glacial eyes narrow. "Daddy's."

"Bingo," Lariat says, slamming the drawer.

"Field trip," Noose says, and claps me on the back as he makes his way to the bedroom door. "Way to make a leap of logic, Trainer."

I tense. "You sayin' I'm smart?"

"I'm saying I never doubted it."

30

KRISTA

My legs dangle as Allen easily carries me upstairs.

I recognize his father's house. I've been here a couple of times in the nearly two years we'd been dating.

Allen doesn't have to do much work to get me upstairs.

The elevator does most of it.

I watch the bright blue-white light of the LED numbers tick off from *B* to the third floor, then a sharp ding tells me we've arrived.

Allen steps out, and another man steps forward.

I'm too weak to flinch, but I know a bodyguard—or just plain guard—when I see one.

He holds his arms open, and Allen transfers me to him.

"She reeks."

"Yes." Allen gives me a tender smile, and I shiver. "Our Krista needed a little lesson."

The guard's pockmarked face, riddled with the evidence of teenage acne, puckers in obvious disgust. "I'll have a girl get her cleaned up."

Allen shakes his head.

"You do it."

The guard raises his head. "I don't know if Mr. Rothschild's duty list expands to cover washing the piss and puke off this woman."

I listen to them discuss me, but don't even have the strength to be embarrassed.

Allen lifts a shoulder. "That's not my concern. Mr. Rothschild said he wanted her cleaned up."

Shutting my eyes, I groan. Every piece of me hurts, and this stranger is going to see me naked.

Allen is going to try to marry me. No—he *is* going to marry me.

Fear coils like a slick snake inside my belly. Sweat breaks out on my forehead.

He's evil.

And he said he'd kill my parents. *Trainer.*

Swallowing past my fear, I croak out, "I can do it myself. Just make him…" I suck in a breath and let it out. The guard turns his face away from my breath. "Stand guard or something."

Allen reaches out, pinching my nipple, and I cry out. The pain is so miserable in combination with everything else, I fight tears of frustration and despair.

"Don't make suggestions, Krista."

I stare numbly at him, not able to comprehend where my life is now headed in just two short days.

"Take her, Simon."

The hulk rolls his shoulders and drives his legs toward the few stairs that lead to a single door.

With a hard turn, he twists a solid brass knob, and swings the door wide.

Allen pushes past us and opens the bathroom.

Marble covers every surface. It's austere and Romanesque.

Cold, like a mausoleum. *I'll die here*, I think.

My eyes already hunt for a blade. If I can get my hands on one, I could fill that huge claw foot tub, stranded like a lost ship in the sea of ivory marble, and slice my life away.

Allen would return, and his terrifying idea of marriage would be washed away in a tide of my blood.

He meets my eyes. His own twinkle in perverse delight as he smiles.

Allen anticipates me. Maybe he always has.

Defeat swallows me whole.

Allen watches Simon. "Undress her and make sure she gets cleaned up." His voice lowers. "You lay a finger on her, and I'll cut it off."

"I don't need kidnapped tail, Mr. Fitzgerald."

Allen grins. "Yes, I imagine Abbi serviced you very nicely, as well."

Simon frowns, setting me down.

I bite back a moan. My body so weak, I can't believe I was contemplating suicide just two minutes ago.

I look up at the guard, feeling even more hopeless. He's a huge man. His suit fits him badly, too tight across the chest and back, like his time at the gym makes all the clothes he wears suffer to accommodate his bulk.

"I don't require Fitzgerald seconds. I get my own women, on my own time."

Allen's lips flatten, and my body tenses.

"Clean. Her. Up."

"Yes, sir."

Allen's lingering gaze roams my body and with a purse of lips, he spins on his heels and leaves.

My entire body collapses in relief.

"Dickhead," Simon mutters.

Our eyes meet.

"Please," I swallow again, "get me out of here."

Simon sighs, shaking his head. "No can do."

A tear spills from my eye as Simon tugs off one of my shoes. I realize the other is somewhere down in the bowels of this house of horrors.

He gently takes off my socks. "Hate to be the bearer of bad news, but you do smell awful."

More tears follow. "Yes, I do. It might be the...I don't even know how many...hours I spent chained with a dead body for company." I practically spit in his face.

"Or maybe it's because crazy Allen is holding me prisoner? I don't know—take your pick!"

Simon's dark brown eyes flick to mine. "The pay's good."

I cover my face with my hands, listening to him stand and move somewhere.

When my palms drop, he's brought me some water. I gulp it down until it spills out the side of my mouth, then I wipe my grimy face. "Thanks."

"More for me than you," Simon replies, setting the glass on a shelf behind the tub with gleaming chrome faucets. "Your breath stinks."

Have I been talking to a wall all this time? "Right," I reply, weary.

"Roll over."

I lie on the floor, and he unbuttons my jeans. With a quick, practiced jerk, he slides them past my hips.

Seeming to remember something, he turns, cranking the hot water tap of the tub. Steaming water splashes inside the porcelain as my eyes remain on the ceiling.

"Can you move yet?"

I try to sit up, and a wave of dizziness sweeps through me. I grip the rolled porcelain rim of the tub. The tile's cold against my nearly naked lower half. "No," I whisper.

Simon slides his hands under my pits, hoisting me to standing.

I lean against him.

"Can you take your underwear off?"

More tears slide down my face as my humiliation is complete.

I manage to hook the fabric at the side and tug past my hips as Simon holds me upright.

Kicking my panties off, he lifts me into the tub.

The water's too hot, and I hiss.

With one hand, Simon turns more water on from the cold side.

"Better?" he asks.

I nod, gripping onto him though I don't want to.

"I'm putting you in the water. Lift up your arms so I can get the rest of your clothing off."

My tears join the rushing water from the faucet as he gently slides me into the water, and I lift my arms.

Simon unravels the foul-smelling top over my face and tosses it.

The bra, he expertly unhooks and says, "Arms."

I raise my arms, nipples puckering in the cooler air outside the steaming bath water.

"Lie back."

I yelp when my back touches the frigid porcelain above the waterline.

Simon stands, surveying my nudity. With a curt nod, he shrugs off his ill-fitting suit jacket, finally resorting to kind of tearing the thing off his limbs. "Dammit," he mutters.

Arm muscles are growing babies on his arms, and I blink, knowing I can't fight him off.

I'm beyond starving. I was hungry the first day. Now I just want to sleep.

Rolling up his sleeves halfway up his forearms that would rival Popeye's, he walks across the bathroom then returns with a basket of toiletries. He pulls a stool from underneath the tub and plucks a bar of soap from the basket. He dunks his hands into the water, slowing lathering.

"I'll bite you," I warn him, feigning more bravado then I feel.

"Hungry?" his smile is warm, belying our situation where a strange man will handle me intimately.

"Pissed as hell."

Simon inclines his head. "Don't make me hurt you. I'll do it where they can't see it. Where others can't notice."

His eyes slide to mine.

I see the evidence of what he's done in those eyes. They're not soulless—yet.

It won't be long before they are.

"I don't love him. I don't want to be here. This entire thing is against my will."

"Uh-huh." His hands slow. "Go underneath the water and get yourself wet. Stand up and spread it."

I gasp. "You mean?"

Simon nods. "It'll be my head if I don't get every crack and crevice."

Fresh tears join the old. "No," I deny softly.

Simon leans forward so our noses are almost touching. "If I tell you a secret, will it make you cooperate?"

I shake my head. "I don't know." I hitch back more tears, angrily swiping at my eyes while fighting lightheadedness.

"I'm gay," he says in a flat voice. "You're"—he moves back, sweeping a meaty palm at my body—"female bits do nothing for me. You can spread your cheeks, and it's nothing but a chore."

I blink. "Really?"

He shrugs. "Packaging doesn't match, right?"

Slowly, I nod, my eyes running over a brutally masculine face and physique. "Boss doesn't know. Don't figure that'd go over well."

His eyes search my face. "You're an open book." Then Simon's face goes serious. "Better?"

It's all bad. But having a man who won't molest me while he washes me takes away some of my fear. "Some."

"Good," he gives a brisk nod. "Now do what I said."

Slowly, I dunk under the water.

When I open my eyes, Simon's wavering image warbles in the water between him and I.

What if I could drown? I'm dragged from the shallow depths of my imagined grave, my cast soaked.

I weave where I stand.

"No drowning, Krista," Simon uses my name for the first time. "Turn away from me, grip the edge, and spread your legs."

343

Heat climbs my body, and I want to barf.

A person has to have food to do that, though. But my body still tries, dry heaving in great whoops that arc my body while nothing evacuates.

"Take your time."

His hand falls on my back—offering clinical reassurance.

Shaking, I wipe my mouth and stand there.

"Let's get started."

I tense.

Then he does.

"Sip it slowly," Simon instructs, bulky arms crossed over his barrel chest. His shirt and slacks are covered with dark wet spots from bathing me.

I slurp the broth, and its flavor explodes in my mouth, quieting my weakness. My hand still shakes as I lift the spoon.

Simon shaved me. Soaped me. Shampooed me. Rinsed me.

I'm technically squeaky clean.

But I feel filthy.

Ready for Allen Fitzgerald to marry. *Rape.* I'm not deluding myself. He'll have to force himself on me for sex to happen.

I finish the first bowl of chicken broth, and Simon puts another in front of me, inclining his head toward it.

"Why are you doing this?"

"Feeding you?" he asks.

I shake my head, feel nausea sweep through me, and grasp the edge of a small table within my new prison. Shut my eyes, I wait for the sensation to pass. "Not hurting me?"

Anyone who would work this closely with Allen has to be awful.

"Thought I'd get there faster with a few mundane moves."

I give him a sharp look. "Like what?"

"The gay thing." He chuckles.

My heart begins to race, flooding my system with adrenaline. "You're not?"

"Fuck no. But I'm not stupid enough to do anything I'll get nailed for." Simon taps his temple with his index finger.

His cold smile ices my heart. "Enjoyed the show, though." He tips an invisible hat my way.

Tears run down my face, and I turn to my meal, trying to see the broth through the wash of my tears.

"Don't bother with the waterworks, honey. It'll all be over with soon. Dickhead will marry you, get what he's after, and you can live somewhere separate, enjoying his billions." He quirks a brow. "It's not a fate worse than death."

My narrow-eyed stare seeks him like a missile set to destroy. "And you'd like your freedom being stolen from you?"

345

His smirk fades. "For the rich life you're gonna have?" He snorts. "Might bat for the other side for real for that kind of cash."

Simon lifts his chin. "Eat." His tone implies there might be pain if I don't.

I eat, but allow my eyes to hate him for lying to me. I don't know what I expected?

The truth?

Never.

31

HAMMERSTEIN

Closing my eyes, I pinch the bridge of my nose. I'd hoped this call would never come.

During all my years of being in justice, I never took a bribe, never accepted one or gave one.

Except this one.

Because emotion had been involved, of course. Isn't that always the case?

Six years ago, Brett Rife's life was on the line, and I knew down to my marrow that his situation was a perfect example of life's cruelty. I simply could not let him be condemned.

The judge was sympathetic, nearly. However, the jury was split.

I reached out to Orson Rothschild, a man who attended the same exclusive boarding school I had when we were adolescents. He'd said if I ever needed anything once he came into his fortune, it would cost me only the price of a favor, no more.

Now the proverbial check has come due.

"Does this make what is between us square, Orson?"

"Perfectly," he croons.

I had forgotten how much his smugly entitled arrogance irritated me. Certainly, it was even more of an annoyance when I was obligated to endure his attitude solely due to my indebtedness.

Eleanor touches my shoulder, and I drop my forehead into my aching hand, pressing the fingertips of my free hand against my temple. The beginnings of a fine headache begin to thump mercilessly in time to my heartbeats.

I stare at my cell, sitting on top of the acre of quartz countertop in the kitchen.

"Then I will see you around three o'clock at my residence," Orson says.

Eleanor raises her eyebrow in question.

I give a slight shake of my head, and our gazes return to the cell, listening to Orson Rothschild on speaker.

"I'll be there," I say softly before ending the call with a light tap of my finger.

The screen goes dark.

"I loathe that man," Eleanor says for us both.

I nod. "He's a necessary evil."

Eleanor's face turns to mine, her jawline only slightly softened by her sixty years walking this earth. "He freed Brett."

"Ultimately, yes."

We hug each other, trying to console ourselves.

What's one marriage done in secret? It's a small penance.

However, I know if this is the favor Rothschild has called in, there is a high price.

One that might haunt me forever.

TRAINER

"This isn't that stealth shit you are about," I say to Noose.

He shakes his head.

My eyes run over his fucked-up clothes.

"Don't," he warns.

Can't say much. I look awkward as fuck too.

Running my hands down my old clothes—or should I be saying, my pre-MC clothes—feels like I'm putting on things I've grown out of. Like this shit's the stuff I wore when I was a kid, and now I'm tryin' it back on, and it don't fit—even if it does.

Bottom line: we're missing our cuts, and that just feels wrong.

"Vipe says we can't kill the fuckers," Noose repeats, as though talking himself out of what he wants.

We're about a quarter mile from Rothschild's mansion. Noose works out his tension with cigarettes. I don't have nothin' for mine. The cold anxiety sits inside, simmering like a pot of water that won't boil.

"Gotta push some line like we're concerned friends, haven't seen Krista. That kind of classic bullshit."

I raise my eyebrows at Noose. "Aren't we gonna get a butler or something?"

Noose chuckles. "I got ways past that."

Probably.

Noose flicks his cigarette, and it lands by a bush in the deep woods where we hang. He crushes the smoldering butt, then kicks dirt over it.

"Gonna get your shoes messed," I say, looking at the cowboy boots he borrowed from me.

"Fuck it." He winks.

Then we turn toward the Rothschild mansion. We're strolling, when all I really want to do is run to where Krista is.

After a few minutes, a long sweeping driveway unravels to the right, and we take it.

I'd thought Fitzgerald's place was for the richies, as Noose calls them.

This place looks like a slice of heaven has fallen to earth.

That feeling of not belonging moves through me, and I ignore it. Don't matter how perfect a place looks.

It can still be filled with Arnies.

They don't have to be poor to be evil.

KRISTA

"Remarkable." Allen nods in satisfaction as he makes a slow circle around me.

A dress in gauzy white had been laid out for me, short-sleeved, as though my cast had been considered. Tea-length, it grazes me at mid-calf and I pluck at the itchy and low-cut bodice.

He tilts his head, studying me like a unique bug specimen. A slight frown mars the perfection of his forehead. The tape he still wears on his nose is a nice touch.

I bite my lip to keep the sudden urge to laugh hysterically from erupting and grip the sides of the lightweight dress with my fingers.

"Her eyes are red."

Simon nods. "Yes, Mr. Fitzgerald. That's because of what she's been through. She keeps crying."

Allen smirks. "Oh well, maybe Krista can keep it together for the ceremony."

"Don't know. Got her prepped. Like I was told to do."

Allen's hand snakes out, and he pinches my breast. Again. I don't give him the satisfaction of reaction.

Pretty easy. I'm numb, and my nipples are getting there.

Allen appears pleased by my silence. "You'll react later, love." His bright-blue eyes gleam with intent.

I shudder.

Simon rolls his eyes when Allen isn't looking, and I glare at him.

Liar.

I jump when a doorbell rings, playing a tune I almost recognize.

Allen's face whips to the sound, his vague frown becoming a scowl. "Fucking hell. Who could this be?" He strides to a window, peering out. "You'd think Daddy Dearest would want this day free of interference."

His gaze pierces me. "Bring her downstairs. The judge will be here in two hours."

Simon walks over to where I've been forced to sit for Allen's sick perusal. Not that I was strong enough to stand. "Can you walk?"

I stand, attempt to take a step, and sway.

Simon wraps an arm around my waist.

"Don't touch me."

"Sorry, sister—no can do."

I realize how stupid I was to think I had a chance to get away. Forget Allen's threats of harming the people I love.

I'm not physically strong enough to break away.

And I'm sure that was part of his plan. With a huff, Simon bends down, places his arms beneath my knees, and lifts me easily. "Simpler to carry you."

My head rests against his chest, and he says, "For the record, I do feel kind of sorry for you."

"Not enough," I whisper.

"Yeah," he agrees with the faintest tone of regret.

I shut my eyes, listening to the whoosh of the elevator doors open then close.

Then the dinging of the floors.

Suddenly, the doors open, and a hand has encircled my wrist. The grip is painful enough to make my eyelids slam open.

An icy-blue gaze meets mine. "Your fucking thug-on-demand boyfriend is here."

My eyes widen. *What? Trainer?*

Fear thrills through me.

"Set her down."

Simon does.

Allen jerks me forward, and I moan from the pain of my casted arm slamming against my hip, and topple forward into Allen's hateful body.

"I'm going to fuck you until you come apart. But I might make it easier if you put on a little show right now. Academy Award time, bitch."

He shakes me, and I open my eyes, head tipped back. His manic stare sears me. "Brett Rife is here. Tell him you don't give a shit about him, that you're with me and can't wait to begin our new life together." He shakes me again, and Simon covers my mouth as I open it to scream in pain.

"Take it easy, Mr. Fitzgerald. She's barely hanging on."

Allen incinerates Simon with a glare.

"You can give me all the dirty looks you want, but Krista can't do both. You either beat her and she doesn't show her face—*or* you don't, and she performs the circus act you're demanding." Simon lifts a strong shoulder. "One or the other."

Allen's teeth grind, as he clearly decides. "Fine."

Jerking me against his side by my good arm, he whispers fiercely, "Slap a smile on that pretty face, and stop acting weak and doped up."

Biting the inside of my lip is the only way to keep another round of tears from sprouting. *I'm not acting.* I couldn't beat my way out of a wet paper bag right now.

How will I keep from bawling when I see Trainer? How will I be able to force myself to not run to him and throw myself at his feet, begging to be saved from the misery that will soon be my life?

Because Allen will hurt Trainer if I do that. He has the means to do it, and Trainer can be made to disappear. His background will assure it.

Dragging me behind him, Simon follows Allen. We walk what seems ten miles to a giant vestibule area, the part of the mansion with which I'm most familiar.

We stop short before a huge sitting room. I know that's what they're called but this is so large it seems like a laughable distinction. One wall holds nothing but glowing wooden shelves with books stuffed inside.

I decide it isn't too challenging to put on the act.

Allen stops so abruptly, I have to cling to him for balance. A light sweat coats my forehead, and my stomach is empty of everything but the one and a quarter bowls of soup I slurped down. My heart races, fueled by adrenaline.

Trainer stands quietly next to Noose.

He's wearing clothes I've never seen before: a button-down shirt with pearlized buttons, tight jeans and beautiful hand-tooled boots.

No club vests in sight.

First, I wonder how he found me. Second, the longing inside my chest is so profound, I can't breathe—or think. How will I ever lie convincingly?

Trainer's eyes aren't vulnerable or tender. They're hard as they run over my hand clinging intimately to Allen's arm.

It's not what it seems, I yell mentally.

Yet, I say nothing. Instead, I swallow my desire, fear, longing...and love like a bitter pill of unrequited want.

"Well hello, Brett." Allen's lips curl in a triumphant smirk, as he pets my hand clinging to his arm.

Trainer says nothing, his eyes on me and only me.

"Krista's car was dumped in front of Samantha Brunner's house. Nobody's seen her for almost forty-eight hours," Noose explains.

Allen slides his arm around my waist, subtly pinching my side. "Well here she is, safe and sound."

So unsound. So unsafe.

I hitch a breath. "I'm fine," I bark from a throat I've not spoken out of very much in the past two days.

Noose frowns, as does Trainer, their eyes giving me mirrored sharp looks. "Blood was found on your car."

I lick my lip. "I fell." My free hand goes to the two stitches I received before I woke up, then falls. "Allen saw that I received medical care at the ER."

I try on a smile of reassurance, and Trainer's face tightens at whatever expression I've managed. He looks from me to Allen then finally asks in a low voice, more a growl, "Are you all right, Krista?"

Tears flood my eyes, but I nod, not letting a single one fall. "Yes."

Noose moves toward me.

Don't! I shriek inside my brain.

Simon intercepts him, hand to chest. "Close enough, tough guy."

Noose's lips curl, and the expression chills my blood.

Simon's face hardens.

Noose's pale-gray gaze studies me, missing nothing. "You don't look so hot, Krista."

He presses against Simon's palm.

Simon staggers back a step from the pressure.

"I got a concussion," I say, figuring the truth is better than any fiction I can contrive.

Suddenly Trainer is there, a gentle finger tucking underneath my chin, and his eyes meet mine. "Has he hurt you?"

So much.

"No," I lie softly. "But he's the man I love, and we're getting married."

I feel blood burst from my heart, flooding my system with a grief so terrible it threatens to kill me.

In that moment, a broken heart is not just an expression.

Trainer moves back as though struck by my hand, and Allen's expression is frozen on his face.

It says it all: *I've won.*

Trainer's bright-green eyes have turned from wounded to devastated.

There's nothing I can do to take it back. Not without Allen hurting him.

Trainer will get over me. But he'll be alive.

Noose makes a sound of disgust and slaps Simon's hand away. "Come on," he says to Trainer, "leave her with this winner."

Noose's disdainful eyes rake over me, with the certainty of my eventual disloyalty. "They deserve each other."

Trainer nods, giving me another parting glance, then all I hear are the echo of his boots striking the marble floor as he walks out through the expensive, double front doors.

Out of my life.

I cry then. No one can stop me.

At least I could save Trainer.

But not myself.

32

TRAINER

I slow as I descend the steep, winding ribbon of asphalt that leads away from the mansion.

"Something ain't right," I announce to Noose.

He slides his jaw back and forth. "No shit. Probably starting with that bitch stomping on your heart. Talk about wearing stilettos while doing a tap dance? Fuck *me*!" he nearly shouts, tearing fingers through his hair and ripping out the tie, only to redo it in the next second.

"No. I mean…" Hell, I don't know what I mean. "She didn't *look* right. Krista looked hurt." Besides the obvious cast on her arm and the gash on her head.

Noose stops, gives me a hard look, then whips his head back to the mansion. "Fuck it." Yanking a pack of hard-top cigs outta his back pocket, he taps one out and nips it between his lips. He raises the lighter to his mouth, cupping a hand around the flame as it sprouts from the tip.

His gaze pierces the fog of smoke he creates, finding me easily in the haze. Tipping his head back, Noose shoots a cloud into the air. "Surprised they let our crude asses into the house."

I was too.

His face turns in my direction, only the profile showing.

My eyes sweep back to the mansion, then toward the end of the long driveway. No one can see us from the house, and they can't see us from the gated entrance, either.

"Blind spot," Noose comments, tracking my thought process from my face alone.

Been told I don't wear my feelings much. Noose is sharp. Watches everything. "Good." Don't want none of 'em seeing me and Noose chew on the shit that just went down. I feel shaky. Off balance. Not throwing Krista over my shoulder and dragging her outta there took almost more grit than I got.

"I say let it go. She's not into ya," Noose says.

Seemed that way. Left my guts up there in that house at her feet.

But there was something there.

I shift my weight. *Fear.*

I know pain. I know scared. Seen it.

Lived it.

Got a nose for it.

Krista didn't have the look of someone at ease. "Krista didn't seem settled."

"What does that mean?" Noose asks, quirking a brow and tapping an ash to the ground.

I shrug. "Seemed like she was saying something, but her body and face didn't agree." I shake my head. Can't explain shit good. "Maybe I'm such a pussy, and I want her so bad that I'm thinkin' there's still a chance." My eyes flick to his, then quickly look away. "When there ain't none," I end quietly. "But her saying she's gonna marry that fucker?" I shake my head. Doesn't add up.

Noose's slow grin has me getting pissed off. "Don't you fuck with me."

My hands fist.

"Not."

"Then what's with the look?"

I plant my hands on my hips, ready to gouge his ass like the bull with a red flag waving.

"Krista Glass might be up to something besides wanting that dumb fucker up there." Noose jabs a thumb over his shoulder at the mansion. "I suppose it's possible. She seemed pretty convincing, though, hanging all over that perverted fuck."

We agree on that at least. "Yeah."

"But what angle is she playing?" Noose spreads his arms wide, his heavy muscles bunching, and he does a slow spin, cig bobbing from his lips. He takes the butt outta his mouth, joint style, and says, "Thinking it's time for round two. Just to be a thorough mofo."

My heart starts to thump hard. I want Krista away from fucking Allen and to talk to her without other people around. "How could he make Krista lie? I mean—" I suck a tortured inhale. "If she *is* lying." Maybe I'm off on this. Maybe Krista's like every other back-stabbing human being walking around.

"Got something on her?" Noose shrugs. "Blackmail is the sweetest motivator."

"You said it yourself, she's a schoolteacher. Don't seem right."

Noose slowly nods. "Might have a checkered past."

I cross my arms. "You said she came from a good family, normal childhood, and all that shit."

"Yup. But Fitzgerald might have something. Holy fuck, he's got the means to dig up the world if he needed to. Look at it all." Twisting my neck, I take in every square inch of the manicured grounds. "Yeah," I agree quietly.

"Something stinks," Noose says, tapping his nose. "I can smell a growler of bullshit in an empty stadium."

I can't help but laugh, then I swallow hard. "Does this stink?" I ask, ashamed of the hope that flares deep inside me.

He shakes his head. "I guess I was willing to believe the worst of her."

I wanted Krista so bad. Loved her. Know that now. I didn't even have to work myself up to wanting to kill Allen.

Natural as breathing.

Noose gives a brisk nod. "Reeks like ass, garbage, and ten-day-old rotten meat." He smirks. "First impression was she dumped you for Allen's money and associations. But now…I think your gut might be right after all."

My shoulders sink. "What do we do? Got the place guarded like Fort Knox. And there's that big fucker in there…"

"Fuck him. Goliath will go down hard. Those big suckers always do."

I want to hug him. My emotions are shredded. Instead, I raise my fist, and he bumps knuckles with me.

"Gonna get the boys on board, then cruise back and get Krista alone. She'll talk. If Krista really wants Fitzgerald, we'll bow out. But I wanna hear it straight, without that weasel up her ass."

Noose dumps his spent cig, crushing it with the heel of his borrowed cowboy boot. He checks out the instep. "Nice shoes." Noose winks, striding down the hill.

I follow.

Fear for Krista keeps my heartbeats rapid. I can't help but feel like we left her there in a den of wild animals to be torn apart.

I feel like a coward.

But Krista claimed she wanted Allen.

My head hurts with all of it.

Except for one thing that makes me believe there's a chance. Krista can't act worth a fuck.

And her eyes begged me to go. Not for Allen. Could have sworn that look was all for me.

Like she was protecting me from somethin'.

That look alone would have had me coming here again.

For her.

KRISTA

I slump against Simon, and he props me against a couch.

"That was a miserable performance." Allen cups his chin, gazing critically at me. "I think the idiots bought it anyway. Sure didn't kick up a fuss about us showing them the door and the news of our impending marriage."

Allen chuckles as I fight throwing up for the millionth time.

"All right!" Allen rubs his hands together. "The judge should be here in about…" He checks his wristwatch, a smug smile curling his lips. "One hour."

"I think it's safe to give her some real food," Simon says. "The threat is gone, she'll be your wife in an hour, and her being able to stand during the ceremony is a plus."

Allen gives me a withering look, and I cringe. "All squeaky clean, but you have an empty spot in your belly?" His voice is baby-talk condescending, and a rush of anger boils up inside me.

I hate him.

I hold my breath, saying nothing. Visions of Abbi's death flow through my brain with a chaser of Trainer's decimated expression for extra torment.

Whatever it takes, I *will* kill myself. At least I won't have to be with Allen. And I won't be alive to live in fear of his threats against my family and friends.

Tears run as I think of never seeing the wonderful faces of my students again.

My parents.

Trainer.

I weep, loud hitching sobs erupting out of me.

"Shut up, Krista."

I can't stop. It's like a faucet's been turned on without any end in sight.

My head rocks back as his open-handed slap stings my face.

Tears dry, and sadness separates me from my body.

"Boss," Simon says.

"Shut up. She's a wreck, and needs to pull up her big girl panties and deal with her imminent role."

How did Allen fool me for two years? Oh yeah, he took out all his sadistic urges on Abbi. With my good hand, I wipe the wetness and snot off my face.

Maybe he was the only one I couldn't see.

Simon wrinkles his nose. "Better get her fed. Don't want the judge to get the idea of not going through with things."

"Fuck," Allen curses.

Simon picks me up by my armpits and half-drags me into the kitchen.

It's outfitted like a hospital. Every surface is medicinally white, lacking all warmth.

Simon grabs a tissue box and sets it down in front of me. I honk out a few blows and toss the crumpled tissues on the sea of pure white marble.

An older man sits at a grand table.

A servant dressed in immaculate white clothing places several dishes at his elbow. With a small shake of his head, followed by a subtle nod, dishes are added and subtracted.

His eyes catch mine, and hope surges. *Maybe this man will see reason.*

"Hello, dear," he says, turning the tines of his fork upside down and delicately stabbing a morsel of food off the fine china in front of him.

Allen watches us quietly, arms crossed, mild scowl affixed to the serene insanity I've played witness to for the past two days.

Licking dry lips, I implore him, "Please, sir, please help me."

He chews slowly, as though contemplating what I asked. "I'm afraid Allen is your future."

My attention shifts from Allen's smirk to the other man's grim resignation. "What? Are you all insane?"

The older gentleman inclines his head. "In an effort to keep that possibility at bay, we've taken careful measures to see that potential diminished." He raises his fork. "However, one can't predict genetics. They are a wily part of the equation." He chuckles, capturing another bite.

Anger has my head up off my folded arms, and my eyes sharpen on the older man. "You're not making sense." Tears of frustration fill my eyes.

He bestows a benevolent smile on me. "Allen is my son."

My eyes shift to Allen. He raises an eyebrow and dips his chin in acknowledgement.

"So?"

"I am Orson Rothschild."

I shrug. "We've met before. I remember you. It's been forever since I saw you, and it was a brief introduction."

"Not as brief as the moment when you were born."

My mind spins, trying out all kinds of reasonable explanations for this newest insanity, attempting to solve his strange comment. Nothing fits.

"Dear old Dad loves his riddles," Allen comments in a bitter voice.

"Too true," Orson concedes. His sharp eyes find me. "Have you solved your part in our elaborate puzzle, my dear?" He takes a careful sip of ruby liquid from a crystal stemware.

"No," I whisper, but I'm sure it will be awful. I'm so sure of it, my body aches with dreadful anticipation.

Orson looks at Simon. "Leave us."

Simon nods, glancing at me with a look of sympathy, and backs out the door.

The solid mahogany plank of wood swings back into place and stills.

Orson dabs the corners of his mouth with a cloth napkin, folds it neatly, and lays it on his mostly empty plate.

"I am your father," he announces in a bland voice.

I laugh. "I *have* a dad, and he's great." The unspoken *you're not* hangs between us.

"I know." Orson's smile is a ghosting of lips. "They were handpicked, your parents."

Blanching, I say, "Allen tried to tell me I was adopted. It's untrue." My parents keep no secrets from me.

"Don't fault them. It was part of the contract of your adoption. If they were to ever speak of your true lineage, their guardianship of you would be terminated, and you'd be relegated to state care. They were bound to silence because of their love of you. An excellent and circular manipulation. Very effective."

I open my mouth then close it.

Childhood memories float around like dust motes inside my brain.

Things begin to come together: small oddities that when taken individually, mean nothing. But taken as a whole, they add up.

Then the implication of what he's told me crashes into my brain.

I stand, adrenaline slamming through my body in a rush so heady, the sudden onslaught makes me nauseated and lightheaded.

"You're claiming to be my father?" I say incredulously, looking to Allen.

"I've seen the proof," Allen offers, his lips twisting with dark pleasure at my reaction.

"I am—I am," I sit back down. Actually, I fall on my ass where a stool happens to have been tucked underneath the solid marble countertop. I flick my eyes to Allen.

"You're my half-sister," Allen says in a voice devoid of emotion.

Orson chuckles, looking between us. His gaze touches Allen briefly. "Apologies. I did not intend to steal your thunder. I thought you would have told our Krista already."

Allen rolls his eyes, pushing off the island. "All in good time, however, now she knows."

I jerk to a stand again, staggering away from them, and before I've gone three steps, I'm spilling the broth onto the floor with all the delicacy of a firehose.

"Disgusting," Allen hisses from behind me.

"Judge Hammerstein will be here shortly. We can't have him perform his duties in the middle of a pool of vomit, Allen. Get control of this."

This? Oh, he means *me*. Like I'm some kind of commodity.

Turning, I curl my hands into claws, then go for Allen's face. "You fucking creep!" I scream hysterically.

Simon throws open the swinging door, and it smacks the wall as he wades into the fray.

Deftly skipping over the puke, he lifts me by my waist and back steps over the regurgitated puddle of barf.

Allen's breathing heavily.

"Pervert," I spit at him.

"*Loved* fucking you, sissy."

I mewl, horrified by a lifetime of memories being put on their ear by deft words delivered by an insane Allen and his father. Nothing I believed was true—*is*.

I clench my eyelids shut, feeling the weightlessness of my body as Simon carries me away from the men who own me.

I'm not even who I thought I was.

I am nothing.

33

HAMMERSTEIN

Eleanor puts her forehead against mine. "I love him too, Richard."

"I can't say no to this. It won't go our way. Orson was a force to be reckoned with when we were just youths. Now, with that fortune at his back, he has the means to take Brett and find a loophole of his own creation, to ruin the boy."

Eleanor looks up, her hand cupping my face. "He's a man now."

I nod, covering her hand with my own.

She turns my hand over, gazing at my swollen knuckles. "Are you stoved up today."

"No more than usual."

I try to fist my fingers and wince. Before noon, my hands are always so stiff that I can hardly move them. Knuckles like golf balls.

⬛⬛⬛⬛⬛

Rheumatoid arthritis is a bitch, and then an old fool like me will eventually die.

Gently covering one hand with the other, I can feel the heat of my swollen knuckles like hot coals beneath my touch.

"I won't talk you out of this, but I'm scared."

Settling my hands on my wife's narrows shoulders, I stare into eyes I've gazed into a thousand times before. A thousand moments. Disappointments. Rewards.

"I have many regrets, but saving Brett Rife from a split jury was not one of them. And…" I chuck her beneath her chin. "He has a girl that he loves, I think. He's afraid to trust it, but she's quality. She *sees* him, Eleanor. When no one else does. So saving him wasn't for naught."

She nods, but the first tear falls from her eye. "I hate this."

"As do I."

I turn away from her and pick up the papers that are needed to be an officiant to a ceremony so secret, there will be no witnesses. I can't deny the dread slowly seeping into my soul.

However, I don't let it dictate my steps to my car. Or the drive that follows.

Or the illicit event I will orchestrate.

I'm not deluding myself that this task is moral. If Orson Rothschild is asking for this to be done, the event is corrupt.

Like the man himself.

And now me.

KRISTA

It's a sham. I'm wearing a dress I did not choose, and vomit coats the back of my throat, despite the superficial minty teeth that Simon supervised the brushing of.

They made me eat, and like a robot, I did.

Simon watched as I brushed my teeth a second time after my first meal in forty-eight hours. Ensuring the deed was done.

Now I stand here, waiting for some judge to tie a knot that feels like a hangman's noose.

Of course, that thought leads to Trainer and Noose. Thank God he believed my stupid words about Allen.

Sam invades my psyche, and the urge to die roars forward, threatening to make my feet run to the kitchen, pick out the sharpest knife, and stab it into a heart that's no longer beating anyway.

The only think I can feel good about in this insane mess is my sacrifice for those I love.

And I have no doubt of my love for Trainer.

Allen turns away from watching out the window and strides toward me. I flinch when he reaches in his pocket.

He smirks at my reaction, extracting a small box. He flicks it open and pulls out a slim, diamond-encrusted band.

He's got to be kidding. "I don't want that."

His eyes meet mine. "Tough titty."

"Allen," Orson says from the corner of the room. At two in the afternoon, he's holding an expensive-looking brandy snifter.

Allen sighs, heaving his eyes in their sockets. "He's against some of my cruder expressions."

Like any of that matters?

"Let's worry about words when my life is ruined," I say.

Orson's eyes narrow on me. "My dear, you stand to be insanely rich. I would marry Attila the Hun if I could gain that kind of fortune, even if only through association."

"I don't care about money. I care about freedom and not being married to a sexual sadist."

Allen's eyebrow quirks.

"That is why I went so far out of family lines and impregnated a second cousin."

My face moves to look at Orson. "My bio-mother was your second cousin?"

He gives a serene nod. "I was not bound on first-degree familial ties for lineage, only that it was a relative. A proven relation. Not that I see how Allen's interests have developed, I think that choice was a wise one. Because your future offspring would be impaired had I chose a closer relation."

"I'm already his half-sister."

"That part could not be avoided."

I step away from Allen, nearly colliding with Simon's chest. Feeling suffocated, I shift on my feet. The crazy urge to run almost overpowers me. "Why do you care? I mean, you're worth millions."

"Billions," Orson clarifies.

My mind can't even really quantify how much billions really is. A lot. "Okay?" Then a lightbulb clicks on. "You stand to lose something if this doesn't go through." My heart begins to race as I crawl through the sludge of almost-enlightenment.

Allen laughs. "She's not stupid."

I give him a sharp look, and Orson's expression turns sour. "So...Allen needs to marry me so he can get some trust fund or something, and if you don't ensure that outcome, then you lose too."

Orson spreads his arms. "You caught me."

"He's here," Simon's alert voice comes from behind me.

A black Cadillac crawls up the driveway. As it rounds the perfectly landscaped circle at the top of the drive, it comes to a stop.

We all watch a slightly stooped man extract himself slowly and what looks like painfully from the luxury car.

He gathers a folder and lifts his hand, shading his eyes from the summer sun that's finally come.

It occurs to me then that I missed visiting Sam's parents' graves. My guilt isn't rational, but I can't shake it. I've never missed the anniversary.

Then I realize I'll never be there again. That day at Sam's house was the last.

The judge shuffles in as I contemplate what little remains of my life.

He's tall and gaunt. He doesn't shuffle, but that's all an act. This guy, though older, has something wrong with him that makes moving painful. With a gnarled hand, he shakes Orson's. My last hope of this judge rescuing me flees. He can't even keep the tightening of his eyes from flashing as his hand is clasped between Orson's.

His pain is there on his body. He can't help me.

When his dark eyes meet mine, I'm surprised. They're kind, without an ounce of the menace shared by the three men who move me around like a pawn on a chessboard.

"Hello," he says to me, smile lines crinkling the corners of his eyes.

"She doesn't need to know who you are," Orson says before the man can introduce himself.

The old judge turns his head and with a sigh. "Of course." Dull ruddy color blooms on his nape and cheekbones.

He's embarrassed.

What is all this?

"How long will this take?" Allen asks impatiently.

The judge narrows his eyes on Allen, and for the first time, steel enters his demeanor, shoulders straightening. "As long as it does. This young woman will have to fill out some forms."

Orson begins to protest.

"It protects everyone," the judge states simply.

"Very well," Orson says, but I can tell he's unhappy with the delay.

"Young lady…" The judge sweeps his deformed hand toward the floor-to-ceiling windows surrounded by thick, elaborate trim, then indicates two chairs at either side of a small table.

"Krista," I say.

His brow puckers, and his expression becomes strange.

I hesitate for a moment, and the judge appears to regain his composure.

He doesn't give me his name.

I sit at the table, the food they force fed me giving my body energy despite my mental lethargy.

Slowly and carefully, I print my name, the date, and all the other requirements of a civil ceremony.

My marriage to Allen Fitzgerald.

I bite my lip, drawing blood instead of tears.

TRAINER

"Vipe's gonna be steaming pissed." Noose drops tiny binocular things into a small black duffel.

"She's in there."

I don't ask for a look through the binoculars. My eyes make out the figures in the house good enough. A new Caddy has shown up at the top of the drive, hiding the tall double doors of the mansion. We came back after the car was parked there.

"They're getting ready to get hitched," Wring says, frowning.

Lariat cups the back of his head, exhaling loudly. "What's the fucked-up rush? I mean—*damn*. Wasn't she just banging our boy, and then she dumps his ass for a pretty boy? Shit's just getting weirder and weirder."

With a clothesline to the chest, Noose stops me from rushing Lariat. "Save it for the fun up there," Noose says, jerking his head toward the mansion.

His eyes glitter on Lariat. "Not helpful, fucker."

Lariat shrugs. "I got it! Fuck, everyone's on the rag today."

"No, everyone's on edge, Lariat," Wring says.

I glare at Lariat.

"Sorry, man. Just trying to work out shit aloud is all. I'm just saying something weird is going on. Maybe it's not her fault, sounds like shit's messed up."

"I love her," I say before I can stop the words.

"We know," Noose says without looking at me. "That's why we're risking the Viper Wrath for your old lady."

"She's not mine."

Noose turns, the heavy branches of many trees casting his face in shadows. "She will be."

He claps me on the back, swirling his index finger in the air. Lariat and Wring bleed into the woods.

I follow Noose.

Like I have since the day we met.

34

KRISTA

Compassionate eyes meet mine.

My gaze skitters away. I'm so ashamed I can barely breathe.

Words come out of the judge's mouth. When he gets to the part where he reads my full name, his chin jerks up.

"What?" Allen asks in a sharp voice.

"Krista Glass?" the judge asks.

I nod.

"Are you a schoolteacher?"

I nod again, a surreal sensation of deja vu moving through me.

Fate is a strange teacher, sometimes throwing a curve ball.

"This has nothing to do with continuing the ceremony," Orson states swiftly.

The old judge turns to Orson. "Humor me. I'm doing what I have to, but I want this question answered." His astute eyes take in me and Allen. "This is clearly not a love match."

At least that much is obvious.

"Do you teach special needs?"

"Yes."

"Adults?"

"Not until recently."

"Get on with this," Allen grits from between his clenched teeth.

"No," the judges answers Allen, then quickly asks me, "Are you acquainted with Brett Rife?"

"Trainer!" My heart sings across the connection, however strange, between this judge and Trainer.

His expression darkens, and he turns to Orson. "Did you manufacture this on purpose?"

Orson shakes his head. "No, but I must admit the irony is scrumptious."

I back away, and Simon grasps my elbow. "Wait—what is happening?"

"I am Judge Hammerstein. I was a lawyer representing a young man who killed another in the defense of his mother."

Trainer.

"The one bribe I ever begged for was to free that young man from an injustice he would have faced. I couldn't bear it."

Oh my God.

Judge Hammerstein face turns to me. "He loves you."

I grab his arm. "I love him too."

"Enough!" Allen roars, shoving me hard enough to send my body flying backward.

I land on my back, head cracking against the polished wood floor.

Stars cloud my vision, black crowding the edges of my sight. At least I'm not married to him. Through the fog, I hear shouts and a loud crash. Dropping from the platform of wakefulness,

I dream of Trainer's face above mine. His crisp, grass-green eyes and deep-brown hair appear for a moment then vanish.

Then I free fall into the deep gray of unconsciousness, hoping I die.

TRAINER

"Wait." I grasp Noose's arm, and he stills without looking at me but instead, where I'm looking. "That's Judge's ride."

Noose snorts. "Fluke of fucking flukes. I don't think I like that."

I *know* I don't.

"Let's roll," he whispers urgently.

We move through the woods as silently as guys our size can.

Noose deftly avoids all the twigs and brush that's dry enough to signal our entrance.

I copy him.

As we sail around the corner of the huge structure, two guards taking a smoke break look up with matching expressions of surprise.

Like a silent locomotive, Noose barrels into the closest one, grabbing the skull of the other, and bashes them both into the side of the house.

Straightening, he adjusts his vest. "Feels good to wear my cut."

That is his comment after the two men lie bleeding at his feet.

"Relax," he says, "you'll have plenty of fun inside, just taking out the sound alarms." Sliding to his haunches, he removes the two slim ropes from his back pocket.

In less than a minute, he's tied the dudes together, nut to butt. He balances their emptied automatic weapons perfectly between their unconscious bodies.

"That's pretty as fuck," Noose comments. Then his eyes slide away.

"Hear that?" I ask.

He nods. "Lots of yelling."

We bolt, going for the back door.

Noose finds it locked.

"Fuck it." He steps backward then kicks the door.

Lock holds.

I push him aside, thinking of Krista in there with Allen.

Giving it all I have, I run at it, blasting my foot through it.

The thing swings wide, bashing against a wall, and crashing into something glass. The tinkle of shattered crystal is like rain hitting the fancy marble floors.

The big fucker I recognize from before doesn't charge us.

Probably because shit's going down in the room where I saw Krista.

We rip through the endless hallway and turn the corner.

Krista's flat on her back, a bubble of blood seeping out of her mouth. Her chest rising and falling.

But what keeps me in place is Judge.

Allen Fitzgerald has wrapped his hands around the only father I ever had.

Judge's face is purple, his worthless hands flailing uselessly around Allen's face like pale flags.

Ginormous is trying to pull Allen off.

My eyes move to Krista then Judge.

Decision made—even if it's the wrong one—has me moving before the first gunshot goes off. The bullet buzzes by my ear. I ignore the searing pain. Gotta get to my lady.

Beautiful gray eyes open. Eyelashes like black lace flutter against too-pale cheeks as they sweep closed again.

"Krista," I say, gathering her close, ignoring the scalding liquid of my blood running down the side of my neck.

Carefully, I stand with Krista cradled against my chest. I turn.

Freeze.

Some old dude has a gun pointed at Noose, who's grinning like he just won a million bucks. "Come on, ya old coot, shoot."

"Noose, no!" I shout, but my eyes go to Judge, who's spluttering, trying to capture breath he can't.

The big bodyguard has Allen against him, pinned.

Not for long, I think before Allen does one of his karate moves and has the guy upside down and flat on his back.

Allen faces me.

"Give me the cunt and get the fuck out of here. She's not worth dying over."

I look down at her. Back at him. "Yeah, she is." My voice is soft and urgent.

Never meant nothin' like I did those three words.

As I watch, Lariat silently moves behind the old guy with the gun.

The rope wraps his neck with a wrist flick and the smooth fingers of his free hand.

When the barrel of the gun flies up, another bullet goes off, and Noose falls to the ground.

I clutch Krista tighter.

Allen smiles.

I never been so torn. Noose is down, Judge can't breathe, and Krista's hurt bad.

Wring appears at my elbow. "Give her to me, lover-boy. You got business with this douche."

Allen doesn't move his face from mine. Carefully, I slide Krista to Wring. Trusting him with the most precious thing in the world.

The old man slumps to the floor with a wheezing last breath, gun clattering outta his limp fingers.

Allen doesn't turn, and I don't stop.

As we charge each other across the large room, Judge fades. The bodyguard. My brothers.

It's just me and this final Arnie. A man who tried to hurt my lady.

He can't be allowed to live no more.

Even if it means I can't, either.

Allen Fitzgerald has already taught me so much. All his dirty tricks and his martial arts shit.

Got it.

Judge told me I was a quick study of humanity, whatever that means.

I understood that I don't give myself over for the same beating two times in a row.

Like now.

Allen does a classic move, trying to grab my arm. I dive at him like sliding in at home base, taking his feet from underneath him and rolling over him. Tucking my arms underneath his pits, I bring my knee up between his unprotected legs and thrust hard. Real hard. Like I'm trying to reach his throat. Fitzgerald makes a strangled sound, I release him and see he's holding a knife.

I bring my fist down on his wrist, chopping hard. He almost loses control, but with a spin, Fitzgerald's close enough to strike my chest, slicing hard.

Blood splatters, raining on his upturned face.

Don't know how bad I'm hurt. I keep working at him like I'm not.

"Trainer!" one of the brother's scream.

My hand reaches out randomly. For anything. Finding something solid, I wrap my fingers around the weight. Lift.

The thing I grabbed musta rolled off a table. Amber liquid still coats the interior, and the cut crystal shines in the light before I smash it against Allen's temple.

He makes a gurgling shout. Heaving the knife, he slices my arm holding the bottle.

Ignoring the new injury, I sit up on my knees, straddling his body. My vision wavers, and lightheadedness tries to stop me.

No!

Allen's form sharpens beneath me again.

I bring the fat, rounded end of the decanter down on his head. Something vital cracks.

My shoulders cave forward. Gray leaks in at the sides of my vision. I begin panting as the room does a slow spin.

I raise my arm. Strike.

Again.

And again.

Shit splashes where Allen's head was, and with a tired smile, I slump to the side, releasing the bottle.

Blinking, I watch the bottle rotate slowly across the floor, stopping only when it hits the body of the big guard.

Guess one of the guys got 'im, I think before passing out, then a final thought threads through me before I give it up.

Krista's safe.

NOOSE

"I assume you brought the accelerant?"

Wring nods. "Hell, yes. Fire does more than keep us warm." He winks.

"Listen, you fuckers. Trainer's bleeding out, and his girl doesn't seem too fucking healthy, either. Stop swapping spit and get it torched."

I sigh. "Hate wrecking nice shit."

"Whatever," Lariat mutters.

"Already tap-danced around the perimeter." Wring inclines his head.

I nod, squatting. I take a long drag on my smoke then touch it to the neat line Wring made. Fire catches, licking the line like a long-lost lover. In a whip of blue and orange, it slides up the gasoline, hitting the accelerant Wring used.

He notes the propane tank. "Let's split. That Tylenol capsule is going to blow."

The white-and-red tank stays silent.

But halfway back to the Nova, I almost fall, nearly dumping an unconscious Trainer on his ass when it blows. I twist his body, taking in the half of the mansion torn away by the blast, like a giant took a bite out of a mansion sandwich.

Lariat and Wring jog ahead of us, knuckle tapping when the big boom sounds.

Evidence gone, I think. *Guess it doesn't matter how rich a person is, if it's your time to go, happens no matter how much cash ya got.*

I jog after them.

Worry creeps in, and I pour on the speed. Trainer's lost a lot of blood.

There's never been a man more deserving of a chance at happiness. I'm determined to make sure it happens.

35

TRAINER
2 WEEKS LATER

I stand between Sam and Krista.

This is a sad place, but I'm happy anyways—so happy I can hardly keep it in.

The graves have flowers. Not funeral flowers that smell like florist and death, but nice ones. I brought some too.

Picked them in a nearby field.

I slide my arm around Krista's waist, careful not to touch her cracked ribs.

Every time I think of Allen, I wanna kill him again. Glad Krista wasn't awake to see me do it.

When she asked, I told her, though. Told her about Arnold Sulk too, finally. After I told her the entire story, as best I could, Krista told me he deserved it.

After telling her about Allen, she said he deserved it even more. The smile on her face was the only hard one I ever saw her make.

Then she thanked me.

Thanked me.

I swallowed the burn of tears. Or I thought I did. Until Krista caught one on my face with her finger.

Then she held me when I cried, her small body cradling my much bigger one.

"I waited for you—to be here with me," Sam says to Krista.

"I didn't think I'd ever see you again," Krista whispers, and I stroke her side as she trembles, leaning her head against my chest.

We're never apart now. Krista doesn't like being by herself. She dreams. The dreams aren't good.

Doc stitched me up good. Only needed ten stitches, but needed some blood.

Felt better after the transfusion.

It was Krista I was worried about. She's not the same after what happened.

Can't tell nobody what happened, either.

The Arnies in that house are dead. But Road Kill could be connected if we're not careful.

The news stories went on about how the billions of the Rothschild fortune hung in the balance. That after their suspicious deaths, the money would go to charity if an heir couldn't be found.

Krista and I hid in her condo. Not because the law was after us, but because we didn't want anything else. The shit between us was gone. And it was just her and me.

The borrowed cabin saw a lot of us too, that is, until my house is finished. Krista couldn't get any time off without making people wonder, and she taught the last two weeks for her other students, Corina and Dwayne.

I got *private* tutoring.

Don't know if I can read any better, but I learned every curve, smile, smell, and tender spot on my lady.

The woman I love.

Sam sinks to her knees beside her parents' graves, and Krista and I watch as she sets six roses between them for every year they've been gone. After kissing each headstone, she stands and takes both our hands, and we face each other in a loose circle.

Tears run down Krista's cheeks, but her eyes are happy. I got that look down now, I think.

"I love them," Sam says, glancing at the graves, "but I think I'll spend more time with the living now. I almost lost you." She looks at Krista then squeezes my hand. "And you." Sam gives me a watery smile. "You big lug, you saved her. And I love you forever for that."

My face gets hot. I know she doesn't really love me. But Sam loves what I did, and that's close enough.

Don't know how I feel about people likin' me or countin' on me. But I'm getting used to it.

Slowly.

Krista and I walk hand-in-hand to the Fiat.

I can't fit inside the fucking thing, so I'll take the Harley.

My eyes don't move off Krista until she's tucked in the car and a dot on the road as she drives away. The kiss I gave her is a promise of what I'll do when we see each other again.

Hanging out on the seat of my bike, I watch the growing gloom as the day gives it up to night.

Twilight settles like a opaque blanket of gray over the headstones, shadowing them against a colorful sky of orange, red, and pink.

Finally, head hung, I know I can't put it off no more.

Swinging a leg over the seat, I slide off, then begin to trudge up the hill, passing the fancy plots.

Keep walking.

Move past the cheap plots.

When the cheapest ones are behind me, I get to a section with only urns.

I approach a plain urn, just left of center of row upon row of numbered urns exactly like it. Mama reduced to a number. *Margaret Rife*, the simple inscription says. Her death date is this June of this year.

She was killed while Krista and I were healin' up.

My eyes stay dry. Not because I don't miss Mama, but because I cried a lifetime *before* she died. Not on the outside, but deep inside. On the outside, I bled a river, wore the burns and bruises of being a living shield for her bad choices.

Choices that left me unprotected.

Haven't told Krista that Mama's gone yet.

It's too much after the shit she found out about Allen and his family messed up her head. I don't need to add my shitty backstory to that. Maybe later.

This fucked-up life of mine might actually be okay for the first time, and I don't want to blow it to bits.

Judge survived. My chest gets tight just thinking about how that coulda gone.

Krista's safe, and she's mine.

My finger traces Mama's name. My heart and mind are together on this. The final goodbye. Because I won't lie to myself. Every day I lived in her house, I said a small goodbye.

At the end of the day, I just delayed what I knew would happen anyway.

I turn away from her state-appointed grave and walk to my bike.

Said my goodbyes when I could.

I miss her.

I don't miss what I had to do for love.

KRISTA

A key turns in the lock, and I know who it is without looking.

I look anyway.

That strong man I love with every beat of my heart walks through the door of my condo.

The condo I'm selling.

His smile is immediate—wide and tender at the same time. I jump off the couch and wince as my ribs give a pang.

The MC doc says they take forever to heal. As I round the couch and head to the front door, I slip my arms around Trainer's flat stomach. The hard muscle beneath flexes as he gently tightens his hold around me.

But my body isn't the worst of the healing. It's my mind that is a festering wound.

Knowing what Allen was—who he was—is more than I can mentally handle.

Noose and the others found a vault in the house before they torched it.

Some really old papers hadn't been put away, and Noose scooped them up before burning the evil place to cinders.

With my real father inside, we confirmed. And my half-brother who was going to gleefully set me up for a lifetime of rape, sadism, and bearing the product of incest.

I shiver.

"Shh," Trainer says, cupping the back of my head and pressing it against his chest.

He knows the terrifying memories are with me more often than not. But I don't think of the horror every single day of my life now. Just every other day. Still, nightmares during my fitful sleep have me waking up and clinging to Trainer.

Noose dug deep into the Rothschilds while Trainer and I were recovering from the abuse of knives, fists, and those moments in Orson's mansion.

But together, we survived.

What Noose found out was terrible: Orson Rothschild's tales were all true. That lecherous family was a tree without branches.

I haven't confronted my parents yet. I don't know what to say, especially without revealing the entire truth and incriminating Road Kill MC.

Trainer would be there. He's always with me now, a loving shadow, my protector.

My arms tighten on him.

"Bad thoughts?" he asks quietly, which is code for *what happened before.*

I nod against his chest.

"It'll get better, baby."

Trainer would know. The things he told me—and I believe his account is only partial—make my blood heat for the undefended boy he was. Probably like so many I've taught.

With a tired sigh, part contentment and part relief, I close my eyes, allowing myself to contemplate extending my sabbatical. I want to teach my kids, but if I'm shattered to pieces because of what's happened, how can I help them when I'm so busy gluing back the pieces of myself?

"Are you ready?" Trainer says, pulling away just long enough to study my face, feathering his thumb against my jaw.

He's expert at reading my expressions, probably because it was a survival tactic. It's what he knows.

I nod. "As ready as I'll ever be."

We take the bike to my parents' house. The bike feels safer somehow.

My mom opens the door, and her eyes widen, taking in Trainer. I always thought the resemblance was because of DNA. I know now it's only coincidence.

She goes to hug me, and I pull away.

Mom frowns.

Dad walks up behind her and tenses at my expression before giving Trainer a thorough look.

He gives a lot of people pause. He's physically intimidating and awkward with his social graces.

I suppress a little laugh. Awkward probably doesn't cover it. But I'm hardwired for awkward people. Unique people. I was made to be the buffer. Their intermediary.

Trainer feels natural to me. He has from nearly the first tense minute we met.

"What's wrong?" Mom asks, taking Dad's hand.

I turn to Trainer and say, "Mom, Dad, this is Trainer."

Dad sticks his palm out, and Trainer gives him a one-pump.

Mom stares. Probably looking at those Easter-grass green eyes and the dark hair.

Tattoos peek from the collar of his nondescript deep-brown T-shirt.

"Hello, Trainer," Mom says clearly. "Nice to meet you. I'm Brenda."

"I'm William—Bill," Dad says.

"Hey," Trainer says.

Dad takes a huge inhale, not really paying attention to the extra person in the room, refocusing on me. "We have something to discuss with you."

Mom gives Dad a small smile. It's sad around the edges.

I have my stuff to say too.

"We were just about ready to text you for a little sit down—"

"Long sit down," Dad interjects.

She nods.

"Then you showed up here. You seem upset, and I want to resolve whatever that is—but, Pumpkin," Dad says, his eyes shiny, "we need to confess something." His eyes flick to Trainer.

I tug Trainer to the large L-shaped couch that takes up half the living room and faces Dad's large screen TV.

He follows my lead, sitting as I do.

"I guess you don't mind if we talk in front of Trainer." Mom looks between the two of us.

I squeeze his hand. Hard. "No, whatever you have to say can be said in front of Trainer."

"Don't matter. I don't talk much. And I don't give secrets away." Trainer lifts his dark brows.

Dad smooths his hands down his dark jeans. "Okay. Pumpkin."

My bottom lip trembles at the endearment. I want to hate my parents for going along with Rothschild and his sick agenda or any part of what his requirements were, but it's so difficult.

"Do you know a wealthy man by the name of Orson Rothschild?"

I nod, surprise flooding my system. I don't trust myself to speak.

"Well recently, he was involved in a terrible accident, as were his son and what we understand to be a few bodyguards."

Mom squeezes his knee. "In any event, his death is tied with what we have to tell you—and why we're now free to do so."

Her smile is tremulous. "We"—Mom's head dips— "are not really your biological parents."

I knew they weren't, but I'm still stunned.

Trainer releases my hand and slides his arm behind my back. Holding me up, he makes small circles on my back. Comforting revolutions of our contact allow me to breathe. Speak.

"What does this have to do with Rothschild?"

Dad sends me a sharp look. "You don't seem surprised."

I give a soft shake of my head. "No." I look at my lap, tears swamping my vision like liquid insects. "I recently came into some information that revealed the truth."

"So you're aware?" Dad asks. He and Mom exchange a resigned look.

"Yes."

Mom's face crumples. "We wouldn't have wanted you to find out this way, honey."

"Yeah, me, either. Why didn't you tell me?" I shift my attention between them.

"Because when we adopted you, the stipulations dictated we never reveal your true biological parents. But now that man is gone, and he can't reach from the grave to hurt you if we come clean with the truth. You were our flesh and blood to us—we didn't care who you came from. We didn't think it would matter, as long as we loved you. And we didn't want to take one chance with you."

"It does matter."

Mom nods. "I know, honey, and we're so sorry. But we couldn't stand the thought of you being thrown into the system if we blew it by confessing everything."

"And there is one more detail," Dad says. "I'd think it would be something to consider."

My brows pinch together. "No, you guys not telling me the truth all these years." I rub my temples. "It's pretty much all I could think about."

Mom winces. "Can you forgive us? We were selfish. We just wanted to keep you and not have anyone else take you, or compromise your safety." Her bluish-gray eyes earnestly search mine.

I can see how scared they were.

Trainer turns to me. "These guys, they're good people, Krista." Turning to look at him, I hear what he's not saying. That I could have been a part of the Rothschild household or maybe one like his by some twist of destiny. Mainly, I was farmed out because Orson Rothschild was hoping to make his sick plans of incestuous lineage continue without anyone connecting anything.

Otherwise, I could have easily been in the care of madmen, Allen within spitting distance my entire childhood.

I repress a shiver and face my parents, who are wearing identical expressions of pensive hope.

"I do forgive you. It was just a shock, is all. And finding out that I wasn't really yours…"

"You *are*," Dad says, standing and moving up to come around to my side of the couch. He kneels, taking my hands. "We couldn't love you more if you'd come out of Mom's body."

Dad touches his chest where his heart lies. "You are part of us, Krista Glass."

Mom nods, sniffling back the tears that flow down her cheeks.

I don't know who moves first, but before my next breath, I'm in my dad's arms, and we're both crying our eyes out.

I'm so relieved, I can hardly breathe.

Dad releases me, and Mom takes over, practically shoving him aside to wrap me in her embrace.

After a couple minutes of happy crying, Mom leans back, and a relieved smile overtakes her face. "We're good?"

I nod, glad Trainer convinced me to face this head on. "Yes." I give a smile only for him and squeeze his hand again. Gently this time.

I feel as if I've reconnected with allies.

Dad shoves his hands in his pockets, rocking back on his heels as he watches our happy faces.

Trainer keeps his hand on my back, and I feel the abiding heat and relax into it.

"So back to my prior comment about what Rothschild's death means to you."

I cock my head, letting the question fill my face.

"Well, they're looking for an heir to his fortune." Dad's eyebrows waggle.

My heartbeats bloom like a ripe flower in my chest, piling up in a stack so high, I fold against Trainer.

I never thought about Rothschild's money. Or what being his biological daughter might mean.

"No," I whisper. "Never considered it."

Mom and Dad grin. "Might want to. After all, there has to be something good to come out of this mess for you, honey." Mom's eyes smile at me.

I look between them, lifting my hands, and they each grasp one. "I do have something good that came out of this, and it doesn't have anything to do with money."

Dad squeezes my hand, and Mom puts my hand against her face.

My eyes are for them both. "You."

36

It feels like sleet hitting my bare back. Hard and unrelenting, birdseed pelts us as we run to the waiting SUV.

The sound of Trainer laughing makes my heart lighter. A rare, sunny early-October day breathes it's deep-blue Indian summer around us, and I'm glad I chose a white wedding dress that was too summery for early autumn.

Then the day came for me to be married, and the sky remained serene—deep blue and perfect, not even marred by a single cloud.

The heavens knew there was someone on earth who had never been happier than at this moment.

The rain of birdseed halts as Trainer picks me up and spins me.

Noose opens the sleek black car door, and Trainer pops me inside without ceremony.

That parts over.

His green eyes sparkle with his happiness, and he bends over my hand, kissing it softly.

"My lady," he whispers in a voice so low, only I can hear.

My hands thread his hair. "My beautiful man," I answer just as softly.

Then he's pulling away, face coloring as he tucks the short train of my dress inside the car, closing the door.

It's a full minute before he makes it to the driver's side—because each one of the fifteen Road Kill riders have to slap his back, shake his hand, and give a few hugs along the way.

My eyes meet those of the other "old ladies," and I smile. They're beautiful women in their own right. Fierce. Loyal. Smart.

Finally, my gaze rests on my parents.

They're crying and hugging.

I turn away from the lovely chaos of the last couple of hours as Trainer hops in, immediately loosening his neck tie.

"Tight as hell. Feel like Noose did it."

"Did he tie it?" I wink.

He shudders. "Hell no."

Slowly, we pull away from the quaint church with its steeply pitched roof and shattered jewel-toned stained glass.

"Glad that's over," Trainer says.

I frown at him.

He grins at me. "Got it wrong, Krista."

Without looking, he picks up my hand and kisses it again. "I've been wanting to marry you—hell, I think I wanted to that first day in class and didn't even know it."

"I don't think *that* early," I say in a dry voice, remembering him telling me we were going to get the shit on the road.

His grin widens. "Maybe not *that* day."

Trainer's grin fades. "You sure ya don't want some big honeymoon."

I shake my head, pulling his hand against my cheek. I turn it and place a soft kiss in the center of his palm. "No. Being in our new home is the only honeymoon I require."

His eyes fall away from the road, looking deeply into mine, then swing back. "You're gonna get me in a wreck."

"You just want to get this dress off."

Trainer takes our hands and puts mine on his substantial erection. "Yeah."

My breath catches. "You have a very large appetite."

"You haven't complained, Mrs. Rife."

Sighing, I lean back in the seat. "I love the sound of that." I squeeze him, and he groans.

"Definitely getting in a wreck."

A half an hour later, we start the trek up the paved drive. After a half mile, we wind around to the front door. The last touches have been put on the grounds.

"It's not too much like his mansion."

Trainer's referencing Rothschild.

I smirk. "Smaller—much, much smaller."

Trainer's eyes darken with desire when he looks first at me and then at the door to our new home.

Built with my inheritance.

Now it's ours to share.

DNA proved me as a relative. Rothschild's efforts at deceit and burying his lineage's strange requirements did not surface once during the process of proving it. Not once.

The FBI investigated the fire. No paperwork or electronic files that mentioned inheritance or relatives remained to be used to compare.

At first, I didn't want his dirty money.

But Mom and Dad convinced me that it was meant to be.

Trainer said he'd want me if I was dirt poor and that the decision was mine—as long as Road Kill MC wasn't implicated.

I never would have done anything to jeopardize them. My saviors. The brothers.

Trainer.

When we reach the door, Trainer swings me into one arm and, grunting, plucks keys from his suit jacket pocket. Once the door is open, he scoops me up once again.

Cradling me just right, he crosses the threshold into our beautiful, brand new home.

Paid for with blood.

Mine and Trainer's.

Trainer is naked, having gladly done away with the wedding outfit finery.

The clothes are scattered like black puddles across the bare, hand-tumbled travertine floors, in a rich, creamy toffee color.

My dress is still on, but he finds the hem and lifts it to my knees, pressing a soft kiss through my stocking just beneath my ankle bone.

Moisture pools between my legs as he makes his way up. Strong hands knead my leg, followed by the same, soft, relentless kisses as they travel higher and higher before sweeping my dress to my navel. He gazes at me for so long, I lift my head, slapping all the layers of dress down to see him.

"Don't stop," I whisper.

"Not stoppin'. Admiring."

"Oh."

"No panties," he says before pushing his finger deep inside.

My back arches off the bed, and I gasp.

"Love that sound." I hear the smile in his voice.

Removing his finger, he places the flat of his palms on each inner thigh and spreads me.

His tongue feathers over my clit before he takes it deeply inside his mouth, gently sucking on it.

When his finger enters me again, he pumps slowly, and spirals of desire unfurl from my core to my fingertips.

I shove my hands in his hair, pulling roughly at the soft strands.

He lifts his head, green eyes blazing at me with passion. "More or less?"

"More," I whisper.

Trainer attacks my pussy, laving one side of my labia then stabbing his tongue deep. His warm breath slides across my entrance, making me shiver with pleasure, and he repeats the hot, wet attention on the other side.

He curls a finger deep inside as he presses his tongue hard against my clit, and I shatter in his hands as my vision darkens and my legs shake, my pussy convulsing around his finger.

"There," he says, rising to his knees, with an erection so big, I'm still amazed every time I see it.

Trainer's satisfied expression changes as he licks my juices from his face and wipes more with the edge of the sheet. "Taste so good, Krista."

Grabbing my ass cheeks, he hikes them high. "Gotta fuck ya now."

"Ah-huh," I reply, dazed, as usual. Trainer never misses tasting me.

He pulls my hips toward his huge cock, and I open wide to receive him.

Cords of muscle stand out as he restrains himself from shoving inside.

We're careful, but the urge to bury himself is there. I know because he's told me.

"So tight," he says through gritted teeth. "But wet for me," he whispers.

"So wet." I spread my legs wider.

"Krista," he breathes, head hung as he slowly rocks inside me.

I meet him with my hips.

"Can't," he mutters, and taking hold of my hips tightly, he takes over, using my body to fuck him. He pushes forward, pulling me down on his length as he does.

"Okay?" he asks.

Pleasure starts to build as he taps me deep inside, while deliciously stretching me wide. "Yes," I whisper.

"More?" Trainers asks.

My eyes fly to his as his taut body moves with an instinctive, smooth rhythm.

"A little," I say.

His pumps go just a bit deeper, and I cry out as he marries his cock to my womb. Exploding, I scream his name, and he pulls almost all the way out, shoving in as much of him as my body can take.

His hot release fills me, and I moan his name again.

Suddenly, Trainer is everywhere, surrounding me, his hair tickling my face as one hand sinks underneath my lower back. He supports me as he plunges in again, and we cry out together. My pussy gives another deep pulse as it milks him of the last of his seed.

Our eyes lock. His are so green, I can make out the color even in the low light of our bedroom, darkened by dusk.

We stay locked, and Trainer's breathing slows then quiets.

"I love you, Krista."

"Not more than me," I say.

"Wanna see?" he asks, getting semi-hard again.

I laugh, my muscles closing around him with the movement. "Will I survive?"

His eyes search mine, ending at my mouth. "I aim to please my lady."

I kiss him softly, smelling me on his flesh. "I know."

We don't leave the bed for a long time.

EPILOGUE
TRAINER
ONE YEAR LATER

Noose has dark circles under happy eyes. His smile reaches that light-gray gaze every time now.

Was slow in coming.

Rose did that for him. Right now, his old lady's feeding a kid on each tit.

And two are running around, throwing ice from the beer cooler at each other.

"Fuck it," he drawls, coming over to sit by me with a weary sigh. He drops his weight on one of the patio chairs and groans. "My ass is more tired with these twins than when I went through BUDS. Fuck, I'm beat."

I'm watching Krista. Her belly so swollen, I can't believe she can walk. Gonna pop any day now.

Her parents are flitting around, worried about her every move.

I don't worry, keep my eyes on her a lot, though.

As if she knows I'm thinkin' of her, she turns.

Gives me a boner when she gives me that look. The yearning look, as I think of it.

We're real careful having sex now. Krista still wants me deep. I just take it slow.

"Man, you got it bad," Noose says, looking between me and Krista. "Yeah," I say, taking a pull on my beer.

Noose grunts, putting a hand on his knee like he's holding himself up. "How's rich life?"

I shrug. "Don't matter. Never needed much anyways."

"Don't take this the wrong way, but with all the money Krista got, seems like you two could've got something really big."

"Yup."

"Didn't, though." Noose frowns, taking in the medium sized house.

"Gotta a pool, though."

I raise my beer, and we clink bottles.

"Yeah, don't know about that one, Trainer. Rains a fuckton here."

The splashing from all the kids playing is a low roar in the background.

"Kids love it," I say, thinking about the one cookin' in Krista's belly. *My kid won't have to worry about Arnies.*

Noose watches me watch Krista.

"Don't worry. You're gonna be a great dad." His lips twist, and he claps my shoulder, picking my thoughts right outta the air.

"Don't know how," I admit.

"Fuck—you think I did?" Noose snorts, taking a pull from his own beer, then clicks the bottle against mine. "Kinda learn-as-you-go gig. Besides, you sure as fuck know what not to do." He snorts.

I agree.

Snare and Wring saunter over. Their women, Sara and Shannon, are holding their children who are too young to be in the water.

Wring glances at Shannon before sitting down.

Snare holds up a beer, tilting it my way. "Missed a lot of action recently."

"Feel grateful," Wring says, leaning back on the fold-out chair and crossing his feet at the ankle. His eyes restlessly move over his family.

"You guys ever relax with the old ladies?" I ask, wanting a kind of confirmation.

"Pretty relaxed now," Wring says without looking away from Shannon and their kid.

"God damn, that kid's blond," Snare says, checking out Shannon and Wring's little boy.

"Toe head," Wring comments. "Not much choice, what with Shannon being Norwegian. My Viking princess," he adds, waggling his brows up and down.

"Nice, fucker, don't ruin the moment with your brand of TMI," Noose says.

"And sometimes that helmet." Wring whistles low in his throat.

Noose raises his hand, giving him the bird.

"Nice, stay classy, guys. There's kids around."

I whip my face to Snare. "Speakin' of—where's Viper? He never misses a barbecue."

"Pussy," Noose says in casual answer.

Wring shakes his head. "As if. Nah—he's found himself someone."

That gets all our attention. "No way," Noose says, violently leveling his beer across his knees and sloshing some onto the stamped-concrete patio. "That bastard is never gonna take another old lady. Lost his girl to cancer years ago—before I was a prospect. No way, no how."

"Saw her. Saw the way his eyes were on her. It's something more than tail." Wring gives us a challenging stare.

Can't imagine Vipe with anyone. He's always pissed about all our "complicated pussy problems," as Noose puts it.

Makes sense.

Though every time I look at Krista, I can't help but think she made shit simpler. And it's not because we have a bunch of cash. Or that the house the guys were helping put together for me is now the new place for brothers to hang if they need a spot for a while.

I see Judge and Eleanor mingling with Krista's parents and greeting everyone.

Then Lariat snags my attention, walking up late. A sheepish expression on his face, he's holding a huge box with dancing lambs on it.

"Hey, fuck nuts," he says, staving off all the teasing that comes with someone lookin' like Lariat, holding a gift wrapped in dancing lambs. Yellow sparkly paper, crescent moons, and baby lambs. Pretty girly.

We start laughing.

He flips us off.

Life is good.

"Angel wrapped it, okay?" He rakes a hand through his dark hair. "So fuck right off with your bullshit."

He plops it down in front of me, and I frown. "What? Isn't this for when the kid pops out? I mean, shouldn't Krista be opening this?"

Lariat shakes his head and lasers a stare at the other brothers. "It's from all of us, but fuck if I knew how to wrap this shit."

"Huh. Okay," I say. "Thanks."

Silence meets me. I pluck the bow, and satiny yellow ribbon unwinds, falling softly to the concrete below.

See, me and Krista are letting the baby's sex be a secret. So the guys straddled the line of blue for boy and pink for girl. Yellow's neutral.

Scoring the paper's edge with a finger, I tear it away and open the box. A bunch of hard, board books for kids are inside.

Silently, I slowly sound out the titles, feeling my lips move through the letters, my mind forming the words.

Goodnight Moon.

Where the Wild Things Are.

There's maybe another eight more. If I try hard, I can make out the titles without too much trouble.

Krista and I do get around to things other than fucking.

Sometimes.

"What do ya think?" Noose asks after they've watched me for a minute or so.

"It's great. This for the kid?" I ask, emptying the last of my beer and setting the bottle on a solid glass table between me and Noose.

"Kinda," Wring says.

Lariat smirks. "It's for you to read to the kid."

My chin jerks up from looking at all the books.

Snare stares at me. "It's for you to read to your kid," he repeats. His voice is significant, deep.

"You fuckers," I say, as a deep emotion rolls to the surface like a tidal wave coming to the shore of the new beach of my mind.

I can't breathe.

My brothers surround me, their hands touching my shoulders—back.

Solace.

That's a word I know now.

They give me that.

"Thank you," I manage as hot tears crawl down my face.

I should feel ashamed at crying like a pussy.

Instead, I just feel grateful. Because I got so many people who give a shit about me now.

Love me.

"Welcome," Noose says, hiding me from everyone else while I have my moment.

"Proud of you, Trainer," Wring says, and the faces of Lariat and Snare dip in nods.

And maybe, just a little, I'm proud of myself.

THE END

Also in paperback:

VIPER
ROAD KILL MC BOOK 8

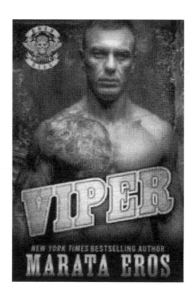

Never miss a new release! Subscribe:
http://blogspot.us3.list-manage.com/subscribe/post?u=
84b2a95b50215894f9cc760c9&id=8c0cadb909

Love Road Kill MC?
_You might also enjoy the sample which follows, also by
Marata Eros...._

THE REFLECTIVE

A REFLECTION SERIES NOVEL
BOOK 1

New York Times Bestselling Author
TAMARA ROSE BLODGETT

THE CAUSE

First: *Right the Wrong*
Second: *Bear No Injustice*
Third: *Change Not What Must Be*

PROLOGUE
TWENTY YEARS BEFORE

The midwife made her way along ancient cobblestoned streets, her shoes catching in the crevices though Principle knew, her shoes were as sensible as they come.

As was her occupation.

She would arrive in the birthing ward at exactly eight a.m. for her twelve-hour shift. Of course, it would not be twelve hours—it would be for however long the woman labored.

And if a Reflective were born ....

Just the thought of the *potential* for that caused a nervous thrill to flutter deep within Florence, as it did each time she worked.

The Reflective newborns must be swaddled in special non-reflective blankets. A baby would not be lost on her shift because it was a prodigy who jumped at a mirror or other reflective surface left uncovered.

Dear Principle. She shuddered, thinking about what the punishment would be for *that.* As it was, midwives couldn't use any surgical instruments that were not brushed stainless steel, and since the last unfortunate incident, the midwives had since moved to an all-ceramic surgical unit.

Florence swept up the massive steps. The rise of the treads was so low the stairs felt more like a gentle slope than true steps.

The sparkling flakes of charcoal that clung to the thick white granite reminded her that the sun still shone brightly, though their version of autumn would soon be here.

A shadow fell over Florence, and she twisted to look at the sky, her foot on the top step, her hand on the solid brass door handle that opened to the birthing center.

A swarm of butterflies, so thick it blocked the cerulean of the sky, dropped false night all around her as they flew through the rectangular vents that fed the ventilation system in warmer months.

The ports were a deliberate architectural feature that allowed entry to the only creature in their world that could identify a Reflective

So many.

Florence stood in stunned wonder. She had witnessed butterflies come to mark the birth of a Reflective, but never in such a great number.

Their importance was such that her world was named in their honor: Papilio, Sector Ten.

Their path created a rainbow of iridescent color, which poured like water through the narrow vents that had been carved in the solid stone of the birthing center.

All who lived in their world were born in similar structures.

However, Florence was one of few birthing center workers who had seen the highest incidence of Reflective births. She had requested placement to this one. After a five-year waiting period, she'd been assigned to the most prestigious.

She snapped out of her reverie as the last of the mingling kaleidoscope of insects funneled through the slits underneath the eaves of a copper roof, now aged a deep verdigris.

Florence tore open the heavy door.

She didn't hear it clank behind her as she ran the length of the corridor to the floor that housed laboring mothers.

Florence burst through the swinging doors as a man and a woman stood over a cradle.

Confused, Florence skidded to a stop.

What is this?

This... appeared to be the parents in front of a babe so new that some of the vernix still coated the wee one, her arms swinging as she howled.

Two nurses, one at the end of her shift and one in training, hung back.

Oh, for the love of all that is good. She stalked over to the newborn.

Florence halted as the sight overtook them all.

Their breath.

Their thoughts.

Everything but the scene itself melted away for those who witnessed the post-birth spectacle.

The butterflies descended, floating in a lazy spiral as the opalescent sunlight washed over their multicolored wings.

The chubby arms of the baby girl swirled and pumped, slowing as the butterflies drew nearer, and her echoing screams gradually grew quiet.

The insects lighted on the rails of the basinet in a portentous group, their wings moving in a steady sweep to maintain balance.

Their appearance froze the parents' breath in their throats.

The moment swelled and grew in the stillness of the nursery, where rows upon rows of cradles pressed against the other. The parents watched the butterflies flutter precariously on the polished sides of the newborn's bed, landing only on hers and no other.

Their appearance was beautiful…final.

Florence strained to hear the mother's voice.

"She is Reflective," she said in a sorrowful tone.

Her mate squeezed her hand so tightly her knuckles turned white.

"Yes," he replied, just as gravely.

Their gaze met in perfect understanding of what the future held for their daughter: a life as mercenary, hunter and hunted.

This was an honor and privilege among their people.

Florence closed her eyes in sympathy. A female Reflective—every parents dream…and nightmare.

FIVE YEARS LATER

Beth shot the plain glass marble across the stretch of earth, watching the glass orb tumble and spin as it met the others she'd shot in a smack of hardened glass. It swerved at the last moment, ricocheting off a shooter, and came to stand where she'd intended.

All the other children her age could play with any marble they chose, but she possessed no mercury-coated marbles.

Beth Jasper was a solitary girl.

But not one who lacked intelligence. Beth had felt the sadness from Papa and Mama and knew she would soon leave for the building that had a big shining silver *papilio* above the entrance.

Mama and Papa had taken her there the previous week to meet with a man who had a nose like the water birds that gathered near her family's pond.

His nose made it very difficult for her not to giggle. Beth sometimes had a problem with laughing when she shouldn't.

Beth had observed and stood watch over her new surroundings, remembering what her adoptive parents had told her.

Beth, you must let us do the talking. Under no circumstances should you volunteer to train for a combative role. There are alternative roles for female Reflectives.

Beth crinkled her face at the memory. She understood all of what they wanted of her, and she would not shuffle papers and sit behind a desk, looking like the dolls she had given up playing with.

All Reflectives were far more mature than their human counterparts from the other twelve sectors.

Beth spoke like a teen, though she was five cycles. She puzzled through things that confounded adults.

She was faster, stronger, and brighter.

Beth was female.

When Commander Rachett of the Reflective Militia, who operated under The Cause leaned forward and delved deep, he tried to pierce young Beth's very soul. She met him halfway.

Her small body leaned boldly toward his, unafraid.

In their people's ancient language of Latin, he posed the question: *What role will you fill within The Cause, young Beth?*

Beth narrowed her eyes, and Rachett's eyebrows raised slowly.

He had studied her, no doubt because she was a half-breed, and female besides. She had met his stare with an unwavering gaze.

"A combative role, of course," Beth said in her child-like voice, though the meaning was very adult, because she understood and communicated like one.

"No! Beth…" her mama said.

Beth swung her legs back and forth underneath the chair. Her eyes drifted to the candy dish poised at the edge of the desk before returning to the commander's.

Beth's stare matched Rachett's.

Rachett had to know what she was: a warrior. The attribute was either present, or it wasn't.

Her papa stood.

"We can't have her fight. She is female…and not big for her gender." Her father's face pleaded with Rachett to see reason.

Commander Rachett wasn't known as a reasonable man.

Rachett steepled his fingers underneath his chin, looking at Beth's adoptive parents. Good people, common folk who were loyal to The Cause, believers in the Principle.

Rachett's gaze shifted to Beth. He scrutinized her face: eyes like crushed brown velvet; hair like a raven's wing; and skin like polished marble, pale but not pasty.

She is too beautiful to fight, he must have thought with regret.

Beth saw that future remorse on his face.

Then he looked at her hands, long-fingered and limber. His eyes shifted back to hers.

"Beth?" he asked softly.

"Yes, Commander Rachett?" Her small fingers held something.

He frowned, obviously distracted from his planned comment.

"What do you have in your hand?"

She opened her palm, revealing a large reflective marble—a shooter coated with hard-laced mercury.

Rachett sucked in his breath.

"That's a locator."

Her parents looked at each other.

"Where did you get that, Beth?" her papa asked carefully.

Beth's eyes touched on the worry that each face held, and she felt her face scrunch.

"They hand them out at the front entrance..." Rachett said thoughtfully before Beth could answer.

Beth nodded carefully. The nice lady had given it to her to entertain herself with.

"Do you know what those are for?" Rachett asked her.

She nodded again.

Beth knew. She liked the feeling of the smooth glossy surface. Her fingers worked over the cylindrical perfection delicately, with reverence.

"It is for those Reflectives who need to find their sector," Rachett explained neutrally.

He smiled down at her.

Beth was certain he understood she wasn't a regular five cycle.

Then his smile faded as he no doubt recalled her gender. Beth was weary of being thought of as lesser because she was a girl.

She'd heard the whispers of the bullying that was so commonplace within the ranks of the Reflectives.

Though, of course, everyone had heard the story of the swarm that had descended on her day of birth.

Papiliones did not lie.

Rachett shook his head, obviously having made his decision. It was safer—for everyone.

Beth narrowed her eyes on the vision of his soft thoughts of her future role.

Rachett stood. As did Beth and the parents who were not of her blood.

"I'm sorry. Beth will be placed in…inter-dimensional communication training. An excellent program and critical calling for the female Reflective," Rachett stated, lacing his hands together, effectively closing the meeting.

"Thank Principle," Beth's mother murmured. She shot Beth a look that let her know she had been naughty for sharing her crazy intentions after being instructed to remain silent.

Heat began to build in Beth's chest. She recognized it immediately: anger.

It began at the core of her body and swam out like molten lava, lashing through her circulatory system in defiance of being contained.

Beth did not want to be a weak female.

She was not.

Then Beth did what all children do—she threw a tantrum.

Beth threw the marble at Commander Rachett.

"No!" she shouted in a clear, bell-like voice that stung the ears and raised the hair on the back of his neck.

Beth's body reacted to her emotions and the spinning ball of glass coated by the forbidden mercury.

It spun, and Beth tracked it automatically, as if it were as natural as taking her next breath. It was part and parcel of being Reflective.

The heat inside her body coalesced, bursting painfully and beautifully, and she gasped as the ball moved toward her, then slammed into her in midair.

Her small body morphed into the narrow strip of shimmering ribbon that all Reflectives become when they jump.

Beth allowed all of it to happen in an instinctual slide of circumstance and raw emotion. Her new form lashed like a shining whip, absorbing into the shell of the spinning glass as it sailed in the air for its two seconds of flight.

Coolness washed away the heat, and she spun with the ball…and went somewhere else, in a falling stream of fire bathed by ice.

Rachett stilled, dazed, as the ball that Beth Jasper had used for transport shattered at his feet.

He and Beth's parents stood stock-still, their bearings gone.

Commander Rachett picked up a shard, and one of his eyes caught in the mirror-like image. He didn't like what he saw there—fear.

His own, and that of Beth Jasper's future within The Cause.

1

JEB MERRICK
PRESENT DAY

Jeb strolled dead center into the group of Reflectives who'd come to attend the finals of the new class of Reflective trainees.

The entire coliseum was packed nut to butt, and the ground beside the ring was standing room only.

It was the female, Jeb determined easily—she was the draw for the day. If he were honest with himself, he would have admitted the same. After all, the last female combative had been killed in action over a decade ago. Jeb had heard of it, but it had been before his time.

This one was different.

For one, she bore the scars of their calling. Her elegant limbs were littered with pockmarking and wounds in various stages of healing. Even with the advanced recuperative powers of a Reflective, Jasper was a mess.

It was such a shame; she was a beautiful female, if not the Papilio ideal. She'd refused to become the he-she that many assumed she would and had retained her femininity, despite the brutal calling of the Reflective. He supposed her gender could be to some advantage in a mission to one of the other sectors.

Jeb found a corner and put his back to it, watching the small group of inductees warm their bodies inside the practice area before the final sparring.

Jeb liked to possess a vantage point that allowed him to see everyone coming through the portals, windows, and otherwise. His height put Jeb at further advantage. With his six-feet-four frame, he skimmed most of the heads in his line of sight.

The ones he couldn't see over were of his kind, Reflective warriors of The Cause.

His eyes instinctively scanned the vast interior of the coliseum. He took in the stands filled with the government of his world. English was not their first language, but it was used in more than three quarters of the worlds they policed. Latin was the primary and native language of Papilio.

All Reflectives were fluent in the primary languages of the thirteen sectors they held as their responsibility. Latin was spoken exclusively by Papiliones.

Jeb stood up straighter, gaining another couple inches of precious visual real estate and caught sight of his own team. At age twenty-three, they were three years past their own graduations.

His team began taking up the remaining corners of the main floor surrounding the ring, while the civilian population moved upward in soaring floor-to-ceiling tiers with marble benches.

The thousands of people who'd sat there before this crowd had worn broad divots in the soft cream-and-peach-veined marble. Centuries worth of observers had witnessed the annual ceremony.

All welcomed the newest recruits. The civilians did not want to know *how* they were protected. They wanted to know only that they were.

Jeb felt a smirk form.

Sometimes he wondered why he jumped.

He grew solemn as he waited, and then he saw *her*—Beth Jasper.

He'd seen her about in the Barringer Quadrant, shopping for sundries and such things—but he'd never been so close. A different woman seemed to have inhabited her body today.

Gone was her softness he'd seen in his earlier observances. Instead, he saw a woman with nothing but hard angles and planes. An indifferent and cool stare met those of her team and those that she would fight.

Not a one had softness for her.

Beth stood alone.

Jeb looked at the five others—all male—and a slight furrow tied his brows together.

She was sorely outmatched physically, though the recruits were all equal in years. Recruits graduated each year in small groups, all at twenty cycles of age, as was tradition.

Jeb studied Jasper, assessing her as all Reflectives could. She stood at five feet two, and curves she couldn't mask, even beneath the bland Reflective uniform, stood in stark relief. Her tight black braid stopped at her waist. An unusual length for a woman of his people, it was an unheard of length for a Reflective.

Perhaps it was a bid for femininity in a role that was exclusively male?

Jeb reluctantly moved his gaze to the other five in turn, searching for his new partner. Jeb found babysitting loathsome but necessary. Otherwise, they would have a troupe of Reflectives bouncing from one world to the next, where they shouldn't land.

Jeb felt his lips twitch. He had been the same when he was twenty cycles: an ignorant hot head. His former mentor had seen fit to beat him into understanding. The Cause did not tolerate ignorance.

It was Jeb's turn to mentor a new recruit since his three-year first partnering was at an end.

The interior lights of the coliseum switched on, spreading the solar-powered illumination to every corner.

It washed the faces of the Reflective inductees in an eerie mockery of false illness, casting a sickly yellow over their flesh.

Reflective Kennet stood in the far corner, exactly opposite of Jeb's position, and lifted his chin in greeting then received one in return. Kennet was wearing his dress uniform. He was on duty. That meant his ass could be snatched to one of the other twelve sectors at any time.

Yet, he was here.

Jeb allowed his eyes to run over his compatriots dress uniform, noting the deep navy, which looked black from a distance. The Reflective crest was the only striking addition.

The butterfly rode high against his left breast, standing vigil over his heart. The iridescent rendering had been executed with real gold and silver, and microscopic jewels were used in the multicolored threading. Only a small shift of movement was necessary for the crest to alert passersby that the uniformed people were Reflective.

They were the slaves of protection for Papilio.

Jeb's musing was cut short as the chime donged six times for the six candidates.

All would fight and be judged in various degrees of worthiness. The illegal betting had been deep and vicious.

Beth Jasper was the underdog.

Humanity had come to see the female fall.

There were only two rules: no blades and no death.

He studied the graceful Jasper as she warmed up. Had he been a betting man, he would have bet on her.

Jeb Merrick understood much could be accomplished without death as an end result. He was profoundly happy that he was not standing in that ring, preparing to beat a female into the mat. Jeb wasn't sure he could have done it.

He understood it for the weakness it was.

Jeb's eyes fell on the favored male in the class, Lance Ryan.

Lance could do it.

Jeb took in the young man's predatory eyes, which were trained on Jasper, tensed without being aware. The idea had seemed fine when he'd entertained attending the ritualistic Reflective ceremony. It was a bloodthirsty hold-over from centuries past. Yet, like many traditions that were no longer necessary, it had flourished.

Jeb unconsciously leaned forward as the first recruit stepped forward and bumped fists with the well-known Ryan. *Well-known for being a jack ass,* Jeb thought.

No one truly liked Ryan, yet he had garnered the respect of many through brute force and jumping prowess.

Respect earned through fear instead of deeds is not truly respect.

Ryan was ferocious in sparring and the martial arts. A keen jumper, he was rumored to be able to jump through reflections as small as a fist—but not while they were in motion.

That was a rare skill.

He had heard of only one Reflective who could jump as a drop of rain fell from the sky. Jeb shook his head in disbelief. Legend…yet, he wished he could have been there to witness such a thing.

The men raised their fists from the greeting then placed them over the plain insignia of their sparring tunics.

They stepped away from one another.

A huge gong sounded, making Jeb's teeth thrum, and the two recruits burst into each other with a smack of flesh and bone.

Jeb couldn't help but be riveted.

Ryan's beauty as a fighter was an awesome thing to behold. He landed punch after punch—all organ strikes—into his opponent.

The other man—Jude Calvin was Kennet's new partner, Jeb vaguely remembered—came in close and took away Ryan's considerable strike advantage.

Calvin wrapped his substantial arms around Ryan's torso, swinging a man that weighed two hundred fifty pounds as if he weighed an ounce, and pile drove him into the mat.

Spectators felt the impact as a reverberating punch.

Ryan shot out his arm and smashed his flat palm into Calvin's nose. Ryan ignored the low *boo* from the crowd.

Blood burst from the offense, shooting like a bright-red geyser as Ryan leapt off the mat, smearing the mess he'd made of his equal.

Jeb's head swiveled toward a female voice rising above the crowd's noise.

"Shoot, Calvin…shoot!"

A small fist swung above her head for emphasis, and the crowd hissed their displeasure at Jasper's coaching from the sidelines.

Calvin shot, taking Ryan's long legs out from underneath him as he sprang forward, his nose bleeding like a sieve.

Commander Rachett stood in the corner of the ring in typical stoic silence, his body tense like a snake before it strikes, as Ryan's body smacked the mat then took a hard bounce, making an echoing slap that silenced the crowd.

Jeb heard the oohs and aahs of low-grade fear all around him.

This time, Ryan rolled Calvin over and twisted his arm into an unnatural pretzel position. *Shit,* Jeb thought, *he's got him in an arm bar.* He'd picked up the classic move from a jump to Sector Three, Earth.

A place he should not have visited yet, Jeb thought with unease. The class-seven world was for partnered jumps only.

Calvin tapped out, hitting Ryan lightly on the leg behind his own.

Beth Jasper told Jeb what would happen next. Like a cat losing its balance, she moved forward as Ryan snapped the arm he had locked behind Calvin. He roared in agony, holding his injured limb as Ryan's boot came high over his head to smash his face.

Jeb stilled.

Surely Rachett will disallow this?

Beth moved behind Ryan, like a shimmer of water on a sheet of glass. She executed a spinning kick that knocked the standing man on his ass. Beth bounced away in avoidance, her fists riding beside her jaw, fear swimming in her eyes.

Calm in its economical movements, her body belied the windows to her soul.

Rachett stepped away as medics pulled the moaning and shocked Calvin away.

He would heal.

But that's not the fucking point, is it?

Ryan lacked integrity—a critical component of the militia that comprised the Reflective.

Ryan stood, his eyes nailing Beth. Her timely intervention had screwed the order.

They circled each other cautiously.

Jeb knew Jasper had no friends within the trainees circle. However, she'd moved almost compulsively to help Calvin.

While every other recruit had observed another being cut down unfairly, Jasper had acted.

And she would pay.

Principle, this will not end well.

Jeb's guts churned. He wasn't easily affected by fights and blood, but as they said on Sector Three: this was wrong on a hundred different levels.

Jasper backed up, neatly outside of Ryan's long reach, which was easily twice her own. She appeared to be following her training, relying on a drumbeat that was part of every Reflective's internal clock.

It wasn't enough, though. Ryan caught Jasper before she had a chance to block his assault. He nailed her gut in a sucker punch then landed a subsequent fist into her jaw.

Beth was already moving evasively, thank Principle, or she would have been out and at his mercy.

Ryan showed no mercy.

Jasper fell in a spinning backward arc, landing with her palms splayed behind her to arrest her fall. Blood from her cut lip splattered the mat.

Ryan stalked toward her, hatred leaking from his every pore. Their final match played out in a sick parody. Unforgiving eyes watched Jasper from every corner of the mat.

Rachett's tense voice rumbled from a distance, "Get the fuck up, Jasper."

Jeb's felt his face tighten into a scowl, though Rachett had been just as tough when Jeb was a recruit.

Jasper swung her head back and forth as though clearing it.

Blood from the blow she'd taken fell like scarlet rain.

Ryan smiled, his hands curling into abusive fists of presumed victory. He spoke quietly so only Jasper heard, though Jeb leaned forward to try to catch his words, as did everyone else.

The roar of the crowd made it impossible.

"This ends here, Jasper."

A cruel smile overtook his face. "The Reflective doesn't have room for mongrel females."

Jeb's eyes sharpened on her utter stillness.

Her form began to waver, shimmering on top of the bloody mat.

Jeb squinted at her, thinking maybe his eyes were playing tricks on him.

The noise of the crowd was disorientating.

Ryan flicked the switchblade as smoothly as he'd been trained to do. Training blades were all ceramic.

Jasper wore the scars to attest to that, but reflective blades could still be had on the black market for the right price.

Looks like Ryan paid.

Jeb watched the shining metal, his innate ability instantly online around a reflection, and his talent hummed with want. His eyes met Kennet's, and all eyes went to Rachett, wondering what he would do to Ryan for producing an illegal weapon.

The blade's mirrored surface shimmered in the low lights that bathed the interior of the coliseum.

Holy fuck.

Jeb began to push through the people. The situation was going to get ugly.

No, check that—gruesome.

Ryan planned to murder Beth Jasper; maybe he always had.

Jeb could let an inductee take licks, abuse, and unfairness. But one Reflective would not kill another on his watch.

Why, for the love of the Principle, has Rachett not interfered?

"Hey!" a man protested as Jeb pushed him aside.

Then he saw Jeb's uniform and silently moved, as did everyone else in his path.

The crowd parted like the Earth's fabled Red Sea parting; Reflectives had that effect.

Jeb grabbed the ropes around the perimeter, hesitating as Rachett bellowed too late, "No blades!"

His voice carried a note of high-keening fear.

Jeb swung to face his Commander.

He had never seen or heard fear from Rachett. When all inequalities of the fight had been dismissed—Ryan's size against Beth and her gender—he'd finally taken notice when an illegal weapon was produced.

It was beyond bizarre. None of it made sense.

Jeb saw the whites of Jasper's eyes. The inky tail of her braid was wet with her blood. Ryan's blade swung so close to her face that its breeze lifted wisps of her hair. She crab-walked backward in an awkward scuttle of escape.

Ryan braced himself as his commander screamed for Ryan to stop, but he ignored the directive.

Rachett stepped forward too late to stop his best inductee from gutting another recruit as a justified elimination tactic and grabbed Ryan's arm.

But the knife was gone.

It was already singing through the air in an expert trajectory aimed at Beth.

The blade spun in the combustible silence of the coliseum as the crowd held a collective breath.

Jeb strode toward Jasper, but she seemed unaware as her dark eyes tracked the knife.

Jeb's eyes hadn't lied. One moment, she was solid. The next, she became opaque.

Then she was gone.

Jeb had seen many jumps, but never a female's—and never into something so small. The crowd watched as a glittering rope of iridescent white, like a pearl with a rainbow wash, slammed into the blade.

Jasper's body disappeared then reappeared in the thin reflective ribbon of the jump as it collided with the metal, as she'd meant to.

When the knife landed in the mat, its tip sank deep into the soft surface with a twang.

The silence was deafening.

Beth Jasper had vanished. Only her blood remained as grim testimony to her presence moments before.

Rachett fisted Ryan's tunic, jerking him close.

"You dumb fuck," he began with the quiet menace he was known for. "All you had to accomplish was keeping weapons out of it. You could have pummeled her into the mat in a fair spar."

His eyes pegged Ryan's in blatant disgust.

"Now"—his flat eyes locked with Ryan's—"she's jumped. She *won* because you couldn't contain your shit."

Jeb's eyes connected with Kennet, who was across the ring from where he stood, and the other man was just as stunned. Jeb glanced at the blade embedded in the mat and shook his head in disbelief.

"There's no way!" one of the Reflective recruits said quietly. "That's a six-inch surface. She's a half-breed… nobody can jump that." He scoffed.

But somebody had. Beth Jasper, female, half-breed… had just shown her hand.

It looked like aces high.

The crowd began to disperse, their eyes roving for the missing Reflective female who had just made history.

There would be no jeering in her future, only jealousy.

Rachett reiterated what they'd always known, though a few had chosen to ignore.

"The Principle chooses who it will. There is no logic. That's why when we have an opponent. We do not underestimate their skills. Let this be a lesson to all who fight," Rachett expounded, spinning in a slow, deliberate circle, his eyes falling on the inductee recruits, the Reflectives, and the lesser audience who remained.

"Be ready," he finished, landing a final, leaden glance on Ryan before he stalked out of the coliseum. Guards moved up beside Ryan. His infraction would land him on Sector One, for certain. No Reflective wished to jump there.

This was an epic clusterfuck if there has ever been one. Jeb groaned.

As the recruits filtered out, Ryan's defiant gaze challenged all who dared look his way as he was cuffed with non-reflective cuffs. One of the guards jerked the blade out of the mat, giving Ryan narrow eyes.

Jeb's gaze squared off with Ryan until he dropped his gaze and the guards escorted him out.

Jeb stared after Ryan's back. He ran a frustrated hand through his cropped hair.

He knew what this disturbing mess meant for him. Jeb would be tasked with locating Jasper. His primary task was retrieval. He was meant to be reassigned momentarily.

However, it seemed that it would take longer than a moment.

The crowd thinned, and Jeb stared at the drying blood on the mat, the comments of those around him the same.

Awe mixed with fear was a bad combination. It could be a recipe for many things. When Beth returned, what reception would she find waiting?

He knew the people would forget Ryan's transgressions against her. All they would remember was her jump.

He would never forget it.

Jeb lifted his head at a small noise. Daphne, a beautiful Reflective, came toward him, her hips swaying so he would notice. And he did.

But even as her lush body moved toward him like water finding a crack in a stone, his mind was on another female, the newest member of The Cause: Beth Jasper, a jumper without compare—and his new partner.

2

Beth rolled out of her self-imposed tunnel of fire and ice without finesse or regard to safety.

Her reaction wasn't too different from that of brave soldiers cornered at the edge of a cliff. As the enemy closes in, do they stay and get slaughtered? Or do they jump, hoping to live and fight another day?

Beth had jumped.

She'd leapt at a spinning blade that made her nauseated to track. She'd known what the landing would be.

However, she'd been at the theoretical cliff as Ryan's knife beared down, not a soul to stand in her defense.

Beth exited the tunnel like an infant during a birth gone wrong.

She hurtled out of the sucking chasm that quantified the pathway that only Reflectives could travel and tried to loosen her body, remembering Rachett's words:

"Behave like a drunk imbecile when you land— every piece of you loosen," he'd said, and Beth remembered the truth in his pale eyes. "Remember, the Principle guards drunks and small children."

There'd been good-natured laughs all around—but not at this moment.

Beth knew she would land without forethought.

I'll heal.

Her body naturally tensed for landing, and she knew to resist that instinct.

Pain lanced her as she was purged from the end of the pathway. And Beth fell. Hard.

The crushing impact stole her breath.

She lay on a pebbly surface of rough stone, watching cumulus clouds form deep ripples in the blue sky as her lungs begged for oxygen.

The temperature was sultry. Her fingertips burned against the surface of the stone.

Her chest opened to the insufferable heat and Beth took great whooping gulps of oven-like air.

"Mommy, mommy," a youngling called out.

Oh no, Beth thought, experimentally moving her toes, *witnesses.*

A loud roaring filled Beth's ears, and she tried to move to find its source, but she could not force her body to cooperate.

Two forms blocked the fluffy white clouds, their shadows cooling her. The little one had long blonde hair, too much brown to be truly light. In one hand, she fisted a bear, and the thumb of her other hand was in her mouth.

"Why is the lady in the middle of the road?"

Good question. Beth tried to move and moaned through a hiss of pain. *Back's broken.* Her situation was almost as bad as Ryan trying to have her meet the Maker.

A woman, too young to be the child's mother, leaned forward. "Are you okay?"

No, I've fractured some vertebrae, and I'm on the wrong damn planet, but otherwise, things are just great. Beth did a mental eye roll and began to review their diction.

All sector language had been hammered into her from the time she was five cycles.

English, twenty-first century, Sector Three—Earth.

"Yeah," Beth croaked in English through her teeth.

The planet was a Hades of a lot different than its simulations. Beth hadn't jumped, except for brief explorations, and had never encountered other beings other than when she'd traveled when she was five.

That had not gone well.

The little girl cocked her head and gave Beth a strange look.

Better work on my accent.

The woman moved out of her line of vision and the roaring gnashing gears became unbearable.

What in the inferno is that?

Beth screamed in pain when she tried to move herself, vulnerable and laid out Principle knew where.

"Shhh." The little girl touched her arm with sticky hands. "Mimi be right back."

Boots crunched closer, and Beth tensed.

She could do nothing, but it was difficult to not act the warrior even as injured as she was.

A male of considerable size moved in front of her and Beth assessed him. *Six feet, two hundred pounds.* He moved with a languid peace, and she knew instantly that he could handle himself in a moderate engagement.

All Reflectives assessed. It was part of who they were.

Beth was pleased by the knowledge that he would not last in a match with her, though he had her by nine inches and ninety pounds.

He stooped; his light brown eyes were kind.

"Well, little lady, looks like someone's dumped ya here."

He spit a stream of brown liquid to the side.

Clever male. Beth's lips curled.

Then he touched her, and she shouted, "Do not!"

She panted, her hands gripping his shoulders. "Move me," she finished.

He smiled.

"You're not staying in the road, girl." His eyebrows shot up to a fine bristle of dark-blond hair circling his head like a golden down. Beth tried to shift and cried out through her clenched lips.

"No, no…girl. Hold your horses."

Beth searched around for animals. Seeing none, she turned back to him.

"Literal little thing, ain't ya?"

Another brown stream followed the first, and Beth wrinkled her nose. *Vile.*

"Jeremy…we can't just leave her here."

With her eyes, Beth followed the woman named Mimi.

Beth scanned her vitals. A light film of sweat dewed her forehead, and she wrung slick hands over and over in a nervous roll of reaction with a swamped pulse as if she had a bird trapped at the hollow of her throat.

Beth's eyes went to the small one, and she gave her a tired smile. The male—*Jer-e-may…? Jeremy*—had slipped his hands underneath Beth's back.

His eyes widened.

"She's full of blood, Mimi…"

The young woman came forward, her eyes searching Beth's body carefully, and too late, Beth understood what Mimi was looking at.

Her sparring uniform was still whole, spattered with blood and bearing an emblem that was as foreign as she was in this world.

"Let's take her to the hospital," Jeremy determined, and Beth stiffened as he lifted her.

Three's could never study her body. They would find things they shouldn't.

Beth screamed as agony tore through her.

That was when Merrick made his entrance, and all Hades broke loose.

JEB

Jeb folded his arms across his chest mummy style and felt the final twist when he would be expunged. Then he flung his arms wide at the last moment, moving his legs as though he were walking in midair.

Soon enough, his feet would meet something solid.

He hit the ground, his shins singing with the impact. Jeb was grateful it wasn't a slope but a manmade material. He could have gone ass over tea kettle if he'd landed on a hill.

He had.

Jeb ran at a full-out sprint to shake off the momentum of the jump, then slowed to a jog, then a walk.

He shook out his palms, restoring the feeling in his extremities. He knew from experience it would be a full minute before he was fully rejuvenated.

He stopped, closing his eyes.

Reflectives' hearing was the finest of any being, save vampires.

Jeb heard Jasper scream, and his head snapped in that direction.

He did not slow upon seeing the three humans that hailed from Sector Three.

He gauged the century to the decade from their clothing. Then he determined the year when the male who posed the greatest threat spoke.

"What the hell is this?" The male rose, cradling Jasper, whose face appeared more pale than usual.

Jeb let his sensors run from his body like tendrils, feeling her injuries. She was badly hurt from the fall: L-1 and 3 were fractured. Jasper's foot twitched, but her legs remained immobile.

Her dark cautious eyes found him.

"Merrick," she rasped.

Jeb mentally revised his superficial diagnosis. Her vocals were compromised, and he determined through greater psychic exploration that C-2 was damaged, as well. He exhaled loudly.

"Jasper," he greeted.

He executed his internal exam of the male who held his yet-to-be-assigned partner, and Merrick found him wanting.

Jeb dismissed him to assess the females. One— Caucasian, early twenties, five feet six, one hundred thirty pounds—held the hands of a youngling, perhaps four years of age.

He dismissed them as well.

Threats processed and noted, Jeb crossed his arms, folding them over his awful, classic twenty-first-century garb of stiff denim that made his balls feel like prisoners in a greenhouse and thieved his mobility.

However, they were the clothes of...Jeb looked down at his locator fashioned of mercury: 2030.

He had been to Sector Three many times. He wrinkled his nose as he detected the levels of pollution exceeding those he was accustomed to.

"This is my wife. I'll take her to..." Jeb considered his vocabulary carefully. "To seek medical treatment."

He smiled, pushing it into his eyes. Humans liked that. It settled them like colts about to run. They hadn't seen his landing, so his lies should work.

The male's brows dropped over his eyes like a brick.

"I don't know who the hell you really are, but your ass just dropped out of the sky, and whatever claim you have on this young woman is null and void, Jack."

Jack?

"Is he an alien?" the youngling asked, with wide, distrusting eyes.

Fuck.

Beth grimaced. "Smooth, Merrick, way to blend in."

Jeb scowled at her, stalking toward the male, who did not back down.

Does he not know that Jeb Merrick is a warrior of The Cause? Of course not. However, it was imperative only that Jeb know.

The Code ran through his mind, a blend of language from thirteen worlds, policed by only one.

The Reflectives will advance nothing, protect all, exploit the evil for what it is and defend The Cause without exception.

"Yes, I know it looks a little out of the ordinary."

The youngling popped a thumb into her mouth.

It was not going well. He would have to extract moments from these humans' brains. He gave a disgusted sigh; extraction was his least favorite task. It was akin to mental rape, or the thrall the vamps were known for.

Jeb calculated the distance at ten meters.

"Jasper, I need the distance."

The male glanced down at Beth, and she extracted a small silver sphere that glinted in the late sun of the day like captured silver.

Jasper held up the marble, and Jeb narrowed his vision on the warped and glossy pewter finish.

He could do a jump with something that small from his distance.

Heat washed through his body as Jeb pushed his being toward the sphere.

He could see his pale gray eye reflected even at that distance.

The concentration to jump took seconds.

Jeb thought only of the sphere. When nothing but the shape was in his mind, he spun out toward it. His body snapped like a rubber band and flashed to Jasper in a heartbeat.

Suddenly, Jeb was nose to nose with the male.

"Give me the woman," Jeb commanded, his mental dominance sliding into the male before him.

His arms went loose, and Beth began to slide out of his grasp.

Jeb caught Jasper easily as the male, slack jawed, awaited new orders.

Jasper bit her lip to keep from crying out, and Jeb tucked her arm under his own. He looked at the people who stared at him. His gaze shifted to the youngling; nothing could be done with her.

The younglings' resistance because of their age was renown.

He worked on the man and woman until they believed they had pulled over from fatigue and that his appearance was no more than a bad dream.

The youngling was different.

He sent the young one's protectors away and dropped to his haunches easily, though Jasper lay like a dead weight within his hold.

"Don't...hurt her," Jasper whispered in their native tongue, gritting her teeth against her pain.

Her eyes fluttered as she fought fatigue. She was badly injured and her body was trying to heal itself through rest.

"I am not a savage."

"I have heard stories," she replied in Latin.

Jeb was disgusted that Jasper would think him capable of harming a youngling.

He focused on the girl, but Jasper's comment rung inside his skull unpleasantly.

"Little one," he began, switching to English. "Who do you think we are?"

The little girl looked carefully at Jasper.

Then her eyes moved to Jeb, and she looked unafraid.

"Angels," she replied with the logic of a four-year-old.

Jeb went through his mental inventory, looking for the meaning, and though they were not the perfect heavenly creatures the girl thought they were, it was a safe identifier.

Jeb smiled at her.

"That's right," he lied smoothly as he cupped his large hand over the back of her head.

"Thank you for your watch care after my partner."

She nodded, though she thought the angel spoke oddly.

The lovely people blinked away like falling stars in the middle of a little-traveled road, while her relatives sat like corpses in the cab of Uncle Jeremy's truck.

She stared until twilight descended and her adult relatives finally awoke as though they'd just had a deep sleep.

"*Principle,* that was close," Jasper whispered.

She flicked her eyes to Jeb's and added, "I think you hurt me worse on the return."

"Your grateful attitude blows me away."

"I hate Earth vernacular."

"Tough, get used to it."

Jeb sat beside her, his mind on that hot Reflective he'd had to leave behind instead of giving her what she clearly needed.

Basically, he hadn't gotten his rocks off because he'd had to chase Jasper down like a skipper. Jeb understood he wasn't being entirely fair. If Jasper hadn't leapt, she would've been killed. Still, his fun had been curtailed, and it made him exceedingly grumpy.

He plowed his fingers through his tousled hair and expelled a frustrated breath, leaning back in the chair near her bedside.

"Please, I'm hungry," Jasper said, her upturned lips telling Jeb that she was pleased by his temporary slave status.

Jeb glared at her as he spooned another mouthful of the gelatin into her full lips, now marred only by a shallow cut and a yellowing bruise. Days of healing had taken only hours.

Her back would be fully mended by the morrow.

A glob of the green goo sat on one plump lip, and he scooped it off and stuffed it into her mouth.

Not that it would keep that sharp tongue at bay.

"What of Rachett?" Beth asked. She gnawed thoughtfully at her bottom lip in between bites, giving away her emotions.

Jeb busied himself with stirring the green translucent grub. It jiggled obscenely as he loaded another spoonful.

Jasper put her palm up to ward off another bite, and he noted how small—and strong—her hands were.

Jeb dipped his eyes to the bowl then set it down. "He attends to Ryan."

Jasper put her face in her hands.

Go ahead, cry, weak female, Jeb thought uncharitably, his old prejudices vying for position.

But she simply swiped at her face, raw with healing wounds.

"Attends to…or disciplines?" she asked, a defiant hook to her chin.

He grinned despite himself.

Beth Jasper obviously knew the tenor of their commander. "A little of both, I imagine."

Jasper did not smile; she appeared serious, and Jeb found his smile fading as he looked into her delicate face.

Her eyes were as hard as his own.

"Ryan will retaliate."

Jeb nodded. "If he was smart…he would not. It was a clear victory. But he will not be pleased to have been bested by a female."

"It is not that I am female," Jasper commented.

Her brown eyes laid hold on his gray ones, and he cocked an eyebrow, folding his arms over his chest.

"Then what is it, for I know you die on the vine to tell me."

Jasper rolled her large eyes in her head. "It is that I am *better*."

Jeb inclined his head, conceding the obvious. "As a jumper." He stood, throwing out his hands. "I have not seen the like."

Suddenly, Jeb whirled around. Overcome with curiosity, he gripped the ceramic bars on the hospital bed. His movement caused the thin snaking plastic tube that bit her flesh with a needle to sway like an undulating snake.

Jasper smiled. "And only Rachett truly knew what I was capable of." Her hands toyed with the many threads of the unraveling border of the wool blanket that covered her.

"Why? It is a rare gift, to jump into something that small. Why would you not spread the proof of that talent far and wide?" Jeb asked, twirling in a neat circle in the middle of the room.

Jasper met his eyes, and Jeb saw something there that caused him to stop moving.

"Because," Jasper whispered, "that was not small."

Jeb felt the air still in his lungs as he moved nearer to her bed. "Look at me, Jasper."

Her gaze rose, unwavering and dark, full of secrets.

"The six-inch blade in motion…*that* is not small?"

Jasper shook her head.

Jeb pulled a chair across the floor, and it shrieked in protest as it scraped the floor. He twirled it around and sat in it backward. "Tell me."

The air left her lungs, and she whispered the truth for the first time since their Commander had discovered what she was capable of, since that day when she had leapt into the locator sphere.

"Mist," she answered.

Jeb put a fist over his mouth to stifle a noise.

They were in such trouble. Not he…but a partner that could jump through mist particles? His eyes couldn't even track something so small because of their sheer diminutive size. It did not bode well.

She leapt by intuition. Somehow, she knew it reflected and could jump into the body of the mist? *Unheard of.*

And she was female besides.

Who is Beth Jasper, and what is her purpose?

She looked at him with guarded hope, and the look he returned was everything he felt—dislike.

3

BETH

Beth's face fell. Merrick might have been her new partner, but he was definitely not friendly. He treated her like a child he'd had to rescue and feed.

If Beth could have been an independent, she would have chosen to do so straightaway. However, that wasn't the way of the Reflective. They were partnered for a reason. And though she had not officially been advanced from her inductee status to full Reflective, she suspected Commander Rachett would see it through.

He was a tough man shaped by experience, but he was fair.

That was why Beth was surprised that he hadn't anticipated her jump when confronted by Ryan's contraband weapon. *The prick.*

Beth stubbornly adjusted herself in the bed. *I'll be damned if I ask Merrick.* He was all but whistling from boredom.

"You can go. I'm fine," Beth said, smoothing her palms down the itchy blanket.

Jeb let the front legs of his chair slam down, and it caused Beth to jump. "Nope…you're the new part of our little team, and I have to suck it up…kind of like a bad marriage."

"You know, I guess you're having some residual from being at Three?"

Merrick shrugged his broad shoulders.

"It takes time to come down from the foreign high." He winked and Beth felt a tension leave her that she didn't know she held. Merrick could be okay when he wanted to be.

"Where…have you…"

"I like Sector Thirteen best," Merrick replied casually, his eyes flicking to hers then away.

"Not Earth?"

Merrick shook his head, leaning back in the chair again.

It tilted dangerously, his muscular weight causing it to creak as he laced his hands behind his head and regarded her thoughtfully.

"No, Earth's a pain in my ass. They have great language—colorful." He gave a short laugh. "But they take a shit where they live. And the pollution, the crime…and

I think we have a tech storm brewing that we'll have to address before too long. Actually, I know it."

Beth held a secret desire to visit all the planets.

She looked at her clenched hands. Her greatest desire was *not* to police the planets they held steward over but to explore them.

She kept it to herself, along with the fact that she'd just dumped herself on Earth by random accident. That hadn't been a visit; it'd been a catastrophe.

She owed her five years of service to the Reflective, and then she was free to explore and find the one who was destined for her—a promised soul mate.

That is, if Beth survived her service.

The nature of the Reflective duties were always the issue. With a death rate of one in two, there was no guarantee that a Reflective would live long enough to claim the prize of his or her other half.

Still, the proverbial carrot dangled before them.

Beth raised her chin and leveled her stare at Merrick. He was not a chatty male. His words, like his actions, were economical.

He came from a family of pureblood Reflectives, and the old feelings of isolation kicked in. Beth did not look Reflective, she was female...and she was small even for her gender.

But Rachett had seen that essential spark within her and included her in the training.

She asked him, "Earth? We will be assigned there?"

He nodded. "Yes, it's only a matter of time. The handwriting's on the wall."

He'd used an interesting idiom that heralded from the Earth people's Bible, a relic of prophesy. Their Bible was not unlike Papilio scrolls that spoke of the Principle. *An intersecting bit of beliefs,* she supposed.

"Why thirteen?" she asked, wondering why that planet held his interest most.

"I can't manipulate the Band."

"Ah…" Beth instantly remembered her training of that world. A primitive people had been saved by a futuristic, but interfering, group from Three. *Interesting domiciles on that planet*, she remembered.

"So the challenge then?"

Merrick grunted in enigmatic response, taking a piece of candy out of his pocket. He threw it into his mouth, then jawed it around.

Without warning, the door burst open.

Merrick jumped from mid-lean, tossing the chair out of the way.

Lance Ryan entered, slapping the door against the wall.

Beth slithered out of the bed, lightly touching her toes on the cold tile of the hospital floor.

She scanned the room for anything to use as a weapon or possible escape.

Damn, her weapons were hung neatly from a new uniform at the back of a chair in the corner.

Of course they were.

Who needs weapons when there is an armed Reflective at the door? Beth narrowed her eyes. The guard had been bought and paid for by Ryan, obviously.

Beth's gaze bored into Merrick's muscular back, and her heart stuttered. Merrick would never go against Ryan.

They were most likely in cahoots. That was probably why Merrick had been so cavalier, feeding her and taking care of his injured partner as they were required to do in the event of mishap.

She was doomed.

Maybe not.

She took a deep breath, contemplating the unthinkable. Beth's eyes roamed the four corners of the room, trying to locate anything reflective.

But the hospital had been scrubbed of anything that could refract.

"Well, hi ya, Ryan," Merrick greeted him like an old friend, still in full Earth dialect.

Ryan frowned.

"Get out of the way, Merrick."

Beth backed up, moving toward the window, glancing outside.

She was at the metaphorical cliff again. She wasn't healed fully from the last jump. Her injuries would certainly be worse if she jumped again.

So few held Beth in any regard that it might have been her only free pass that Merrick had been sent to collect her.

No one would come a second time. Her jump would leave her trapped in a foreign sector void of her people, unable to travel decisively without locators.

Jumping was dangerous without a focus sphere.

She could end up anywhere…or any time.

Beth shuddered. But she supposed that fate was better than death.

"Nope, can't do that, you colossal fuckup."

Beth turned around, her mouth agape.

Did I just hear Merrick right? She had, judging by the expression on Lance Ryan's smug face.

That awareness in Ryan's expression was beginning to leak away.

And Merrick's delivery had been the most comedic of all. He'd spoken as if he were commenting on the weather and had found it fine.

"Let me pass, Merrick. No one wants her to live."

Beth's eyes met his over Merrick's shoulder. "You'd be doing the world a favor if you took a coffee break right now. Just let it happen."

Merrick planted his feet, his arms loose at his sides, and regarded Ryan like a bug. Beth had moved into his peripheral vision. She'd also caught sight of an outside streetlamp through the window.

Its glass solar panels shone like a black mirror.

Ryan somehow knows, knows I ready myself. My desperation is plain to whoever searches for it.

Her body bore the scars of his physical bullying. Her mind held them, as well.

Heat climbs, searing her insides, Beth's heartbeat is a whoosh of blood in her ears.

Ryan's eyes snagged on Beth, then with a roar, he surged forward.

Merrick pivoted on his right foot. Already focused on her mark, Beth saw them as only a pinpoint in her vision.

The shining ebony at the crown of the lamp beckoned.

Then she heard the crack of bone against bone, and blood arced up, hitting the ceiling with such force that it rained back down on the men.

The sound stopped everything—her focus, her jump.

Beth stood frozen as Merrick went toe-to-toe with Ryan.

JEB

Honorless fuck.

Jeb was disgusted the guard at Jasper's door had let Ryan through. He was even further disgusted that she'd considered jumping without having sufficient time to heal. Being a sensitive Reflective, he could sense jumping readiness.

During the battle in the coliseum, he had sensed Beth's jump before anyone else had. He possessed her signature now.

Ryan charged, and something in Beth's expression gave her away. It would be the first thing he would teach her as her partner: a blank face.

Beth didn't have one. A shadow of her every feeling clouded her face. She was, as the people of Sector-Three Earth were fond of saying, an open book.

Ryan was a dirty fighter—no surprise there—who thought to take hold of Jeb and unbalance him.

Ryan latched onto Jeb's wrist and attempted a foot sweep.

Jeb countered, twisting his wrist viciously in the opposite direction of the hold, breaking it instantly as he grabbed Ryan's forearm. He stepped into the fight, not away.

As he jerked Ryan into the circle of reach, he swung his fist into Ryan's jaw.

Always engage, never retreat.

The Reflective motto, he thought with sour pleasure as Ryan moved with him, an apt dance partner in their mutual violence.

Ryan head butted Jeb in a deft, hard move with perfect timing.

It rang Jeb's bell, but his skull was hard, and he spun his cocked fist, driving it a second time the short distance from his hip to Ryan's jaw.

And like perfectly cracked glass, his jaw rocketed back, spraying blood onto the ceiling as his teeth speared his own tongue.

Jeb popped his flattened palms into Ryan's chest as though he wanted to launch him into the wall or stop his heart.

Ryan slammed into the wall, his head smacking the surface

Jeb stalked toward Ryan, his fists like meaty hammers of punishment.

Barely breathing, Ryan slid down the wall, his eyes at half-mast.

"Are we done here, Ryan?" Merrick asked.

Ryan gave the smallest nod possible, his mouth a yawning horror of blood and gore.

Merrick turned to check on Jasper.

The sun's final rays backlit her, bathing her in red light like a watercolor of blood. It ran down her arms, accentuating her delicate build, and instead of looking sinister, it did the opposite.

She seemed terribly fragile.

"Merrick!" Beth screamed.

He dropped down and spun.

Ryan was above him, a small dagger in one hand, coated with blood.

His own blood.

His fingers found the wound and came away slick.

Merrick saw red.

"You fucking pussy," he hissed.

Ryan smiled through a mouthful of his own blood and spit it to the side, where it splattered like dumped paint on the pure-white tiles.

"I'm a pussy that just fucked you."

"Not yet," Merrick said.

Fuck it, I'll heal on the way. He'd kept his gift a secret, though Ryan would be enlightened forevermore.

As light as a feather, a smooth rectangle of paper-thin mercury-coated ceramic slipped out of his specially made pocket in Merrick's pants. He tossed, and it landed on top of their mixed blood on the floor.

It provided a single destination jump.

Ryan's expression showed true fear as Merrick punched the blade from the younger man's hand. It hit the floor with a jarring clatter of metal against ceramic.

Ryan reacted as all instinctual Reflectives would have—he ground his fist into Merrick's knife wound.

But Merrick was already on point.

His eyes held on the flat surface of the locator even as he winced in pain.

He grabbed Ryan's collar, fisting the material tightly.

They jumped—only one did so willingly.

Merrick could hear Jasper calling his name down the tunnel the Reflectives traveled.

Jeb had found himself a dandy of a slope, his fist still attached to Ryan, where it continued its brutal hold.

Jeb went ripping down an embankment of sharp prairie grass that sliced and poked as they mowed through it, finally landing on their backs at the bottom.

He'd thought of Thirteen—and that's where they'd landed.

Merrick was, of course, in perfect health, having healed completely during the jump. The glory in that was Ryan was yet unaware of Jeb's mended state of affairs.

Merrick jumped to his feet and immediately kicked Ryan in the ribs.

"I swear to Principle I will leave you in this place if you do not retire your vendetta against Beth Jasper."

Ryan spit more blood into the pasture grass that speared his back. "What...you want the half-breed?"

Jeb said nothing. *Fool.*

Ryan looked up at him.

"She is assigned to me, and she is injured. I can't help who I get partnered with any better than you can. I will not stand by and let you kill another Reflective because of your jealousy."

"I am not jealous of that mongrel," Ryan growled, coming to his hands and knees.

"I suffered through her inclusion for the past fifteen years," he offered as a lame excuse.

"No." Jeb gazed at the worthless Ryan. "I'm sure the reverse of that is true."

"Earth lover." Ryan spat at his feet.

Jeb rolled his eyes, pegging his hands on his hips. "Yes, I do enjoy Earth. Your point?"

"My point is she could be anything...she is not fully Papilion. Does that not bother you?"

"I am not looking to breed her but to partner her."

"That is all females are good for."

This is useless. Ryan was a lost cause, but Jeb could teach him caution. He did not wish to look over his shoulder for the next five years while partnered with Jasper.

Ryan stood, wisely keeping a respectable distance from Merrick.

"Where the hell are we?" His eyes narrowed on Jeb. "Where did you bring me?" He whipped his head around, taking in the faraway opaque dome-shaped structures.

A great forest stood to the north of their position.

"Sector Thirteen," Jeb replied coolly.

Ryan's face paled. Jeb imagined that took some doing. He grinned.

"This is the most dangerous sector you dick."

Jeb shook his head. "Not the *most* dangerous." No one traveled to One by choice—that was a death wish.

Jeb noted that he was not the only Reflective who had picked up the local Earth dialect with some precision.

Ryan lowered his voice as though anyone could hear them in the middle of the wilderness of this world.

A whisper of cloth against wheat made Merrick turn. *How wrong I was.*

Things instantly went from teaching a lesson to survival, as was often the way of a jump.

A group of men of various sizes, ages, and bearing circled Merrick and Ryan, just out of striking range.

"Who the hell are they?" Ryan asked, suddenly less combative toward Merrick than he'd been moments before.

"The Fragment," Jeb answered, sliding his remaining dagger out of the weapons pocket of his trousers.

Made of ceramic, it was designed to survive a jump, as metal could not survive Reflective journeys.

The cold porcelain was smooth, with a specially arced tip. It was serrated on only one side.

One of the men in the group called out, "Join us or die."

Ryan said, "I don't know this dialect. I have only used the high language of Thirteen."

"Just another reason why Jasper should remain."

"Fuck me—why?" Ryan asked, one eye on the group, which was closing in, and the other on Merrick.

"She is fluent in all sectors."

Jeb moved forward, hoping to injure enough men so that he could escape. They did not want to find themselves buried within the knot of the Fragment.

They took no prisoners.

BETH

Rachett tore into the hospital room, and Beth nearly climbed out of her skin.

The air still rippled with residual disturbance from Merrick's jump.

"Where is Ryan?" Rachett barked.

Beth took a deep breath. "He jumped with Merrick."

Rachett's jaw moved back and forth. "No…Merrick would not take a jump with Ryan."

"I don't think it was voluntary."

They looked at each other.

Rachett seemed to notice Beth was in a hospital gown, flashing her backside to the window behind her.

"The residual still remains," she said quickly, throwing her palm toward the shimmering air pocket between them.

Rachett studied the area, locked onto something and drove his palm through it in a slicing gesture that ended in his cupped fingers bringing the air back to his nose.

He waved that little bit he'd collected back and forth in front of his face.

"What signature?" Beth asked, moving to stand in front of him, her eyes on his hands as he smelled the air.

His face fell into grim lines. "Sector Thirteen."

Rachett turned to Beth. "You're so damn hot to jump, jump that."

Beth took a step back. "But...I'm a female. I don't have clearance for that sector."

Everyone understood how treacherous that sector was. It had a terrible shortage of females, an estimated one to every fifteen males.

She would be delivering herself into the lion's den.

"Afraid?" Rachett taunted.

Beth stared at him. "I've never been afraid a day in my life."

Anxiety is not fear.

"That's my girl. Now"—he touched her shoulder so briefly that Beth thought she imagined it—"get Ryan back. We have somewhere he needs to go."

Beth paused then hit the affirmative decisively. "Yes, sir."

He laid the universal locator on the hospital bed. Its sheen reflected the spattered blood on the ceiling. Rachett's eyes followed hers.

When they lowered to meet hers again, he made no comment.

Rachett never asked once if she was well enough to jump...or if she *wanted* to.

Beth was Reflective, and that was answer enough.

ACKNOWLEDGMENTS

I published **The Druid** and **Death Series** in 2011 with the encouragement of my husband, and continued because of you, my Reader. Your faithfulness through comments, suggestions, spreading the word and ultimately purchasing my work with your hard-earned money gave me the incentive, means and inspiration to continue.

There are no words that are sufficiently adequate to express my thankfulness for your support. But know this: TDS novellas continued past HARVEST only because of you.

I truly feel connected to my readers. It is obvious to me, but I'll say the words anyway for clarity: a written work is just words on pages if they are not read by my readers. As I write this I get a lump in my throat; your enjoyment of my work affects me that deeply.

You guys are the greatest, each and every one of ya-
Marata (Tamara) xo

Special Thanks:
You, my reader.
Hubs, who is my biggest fan.
Cameren, without who, there would be no books.

ABOUT THE AUTHOR

Tamara Rose Blodgett: happily married mother of four sons. Dark fiction writer. Reader. Dreamer. Home restoration slave. Tie dye zealot. Coffee addict. Bead Slut. Digs music.

She is also the *New York Times* Bestselling author of *A Terrible Love,* written under the pen name, **Marata Eros,** and over ninety-five other titles, to include the #1 international bestselling erotic Interracial/African-American **TOKEN** serial and her #1 Amazon bestselling Dark Fantasy novel, *Death Whispers.* Tamara writes a variety of dark fiction in the genres of erotica, fantasy, horror, romance, sci-fi and suspense. She lives in the midwest with her family and pair of disrespectful dogs.

Connect with Tamara:
www.tamararoseblodgett.com